In Default
Of Heirs Male

by

Jann Rowland

One Good Sonnet Publishing
Publishers of Fine Romance
and Fantasy Fiction

By Jann Rowland

Published by One Good Sonnet Publishing:

PRIDE AND PREJUDICE VARIATIONS

In Default of Heirs Male
Prisoner of Longbourn
Bonds of Friendship
Quitting the Sphere
Upstart Pretensions
Scandalous Falsehoods
Love and Libertine
A Tacit Engagement
Her Indomitable Resolve
Mrs. Bennet's Favorite Daughter

This is a work of fiction based on the works of Jane Austen. All the characters and events portrayed in this novel are products of Jane Austen's original novel or the authors' imaginations.

IN DEFAULT OF HEIRS MALE

ISBN: 1-989212-54-9
ISBN-13: 978-1-989212-54-7

To my family who have, as always, shown
their unconditional love and encouragement.

PROLOGUE

$\mathcal{A}$ ll was quiet at Longbourn.

It was a situation rare in Elizabeth's experience, as her beloved father had so often observed. A house containing five young women, two of whom were among the silliest in all England, could never be a place so silent as a grave. This did not even consider the mother of these young women, a woman who was no stranger to noise herself. And yet, Elizabeth might have been alone in the house, for she could hear nothing from beyond the door.

Idly tracing the wood grain of her father's dark cherry desk, Elizabeth's eyes fell on the last book they had been reading together, lying in the corner of its surface. Paradise Lost had been a particular favorite of them both, and they had debated its contents more than once over the years since her father had taught her to read, to think critically, and question what she learned. Feeling the familiar throbbing well up in her heart, Elizabeth gathered the book, cradling it to her breast, and put it back into its place on the shelf.

With a sigh, Elizabeth leaned back in the chair and considered how she had come to this moment. The closest of Mr. Bennet's daughters to the man himself, Elizabeth had grown to adulthood certain of her father's love. Such childish notions of the eternal nature of life aside, her father had still seemed like such a solid, dependable part of her life, one she had often taken for granted. More the fool was she, it seemed.

Of course, it had been Elizabeth who found him when the unthinkable happened. The only one of her sisters welcome in her father's room, it had long been her custom to join him in the morning for a cup of tea and, perhaps, a discussion of whatever literature they were reading at the moment. That her beloved father had expired in the night had not crossed Elizabeth's mind, even when she entered the room to the peculiar sight of her father slumped over his desk, his head on his arms, seeming to sleep in a peaceful, though awkward position. Elizabeth had shaken her head at her father's dedication to the written word and stepped forward to wake him from his slumber, tempt him with the small pot of tea she carried.

"Oh, Papa!" murmured Elizabeth as the memory, accompanied by a fresh wave of grief, enveloped her, threatening to undo her composure. "Whatever shall we do without you?"

That was the question. As her mother had lamented many times over the years, the estate was not to be theirs after the death of her father. Longbourn was entailed to the male line, the heir being a man none of them had ever met, one whose father Mr. Bennet had decried as a man he could not respect, to whom he had not spoken in many years. All they would have to their names was their mother's four thousand pounds, the interest of which would be entirely insufficient for the support of six women. Elizabeth was not certain what they would do. Perhaps they would separate from each other to live in their uncles' homes. Their status would suffer if it did not evaporate altogether.

Already Elizabeth was contemplating the possibility of going into service. Becoming a servant, to look after another woman's children, was not a future Elizabeth had ever wished to contemplate. The practicalities of the situation, however, dictated she must consider it, for the burden their uncles would accept with their support must be lessened. Jane, her elder sister, was considering the same, which broke Elizabeth's heart. A woman as beautiful as Jane should be married, make some young man happy, and provide him with children as beautiful and temperate as she. And now it appeared it would never be.

As Elizabeth reached up to wipe a tear from the corner of her eye, the sound of a knock on the door interrupted her reverie. It opened at once—the master of the demesne would nevermore call out his permission to enter again—and her Uncle Gardiner entered the room, followed by Jane, Mary, and Uncle Phillips. A smile, one strained as she knew they all were, lit up his face upon seeing Elizabeth.

"I know not why we searched for you, Lizzy," said her uncle, not unkindly. "I should have known you would be here."

"You have hardly left this room since you discovered Papa, Lizzy," said Jane, joining Elizabeth and brushing the back of her hand against her cheek. Elizabeth leaned into her sister's touch, eager for the comfort it brought.

"That is an exaggeration," said Elizabeth, managing a smile for her sister. "But I feel . . . closer to Papa in this room."

"It is understandable," said Uncle Gardiner. "I wish circumstances did not require you to leave it, Lizzy."

"If wishes were horses, beggars would ride," replied Elizabeth. "We all know we must leave. That does not make it any easier."

"No, I dare say it does not," said Uncle Gardiner.

Elizabeth motioned her relations to the chairs in the room. "Then let us speak of the practicalities. Something informs me that we must complete this discussion before Mr. Collins arrives."

"I suspect you are correct," murmured her uncle. Mr. Gardiner paused and said: "As you know, there is little enough available for your support. Your father did make some provision for you all before his death, but I am certain you all understand you will not live in the style to which you are accustomed."

"Of course not," murmured three voices. Elizabeth, however, was interested to hear her uncle say as much, for as far as she was aware, her father had saved nothing, left them nothing other than his wife's dowry. It was one of his failings, much as Elizabeth had loved the man, that he cared little for the estate and did not rouse himself to do much beyond what was required.

"I see you are curious, Lizzy," said Uncle Gardiner, noting her surprise. "As it happens, my brother contacted me when Lydia was about five years of age and asked my advice for certain investments he planned to pursue. It seemed he realized there was little chance of siring a son. The amount he transferred to me was not so much as he might have wanted, for it seems my sister has little head for economizing."

They all shared knowing smiles, more resembling grimaces, for Mrs. Bennet was infamous in the family for demanding the best dresses and fabrics for her daughters, an effort to make them more appealing to gentlemen. It was silly, in Elizabeth's opinion, for more of that money might have gone toward the future.

"How much did Papa set aside?" asked Jane.

"Through investments and interest and the principal your father injected," said Mr. Gardiner, "the amount has grown to almost three thousand pounds. Added to your mother's fortune, the amount will be about eight thousand."

"That is more than I expected," said Elizabeth.

"Indeed. Your father kept it from your mother, knowing she would not see the benefit of it, and I cannot disagree with him. Regardless, the interest on the entire amount will still be less than three hundred pounds per year."

"But a fraction of Longbourn's annual income," murmured Elizabeth.

"That is true," said her uncle. "With that amount, you can provide food on the table and perhaps pay for a maid."

"What of our home?" asked Elizabeth.

"Phillips and I are searching for a home for you in or near the neighborhood," said Uncle Gardiner. "We have deemed it best that you all stay together for the moment, though that might change in the future. Until your mourning ends, there is little reason to separate you. For your place of residence and a manservant, I have pledged myself, and Phillips will assist."

"Thank you, Uncles," said Elizabeth, giving them a watery smile. "The ability to stay together for a time is a priceless gift. We cannot thank you enough."

The two men smiled and murmured their pleasure. "I am sorry we cannot do more. We are not wealthy men, as you know. My business is prosperous at present, and in time I hope it will expand enough that such considerations as the support of you and your mother will be of no consequence. If your father had passed five years from now, I might have been in a position to do more."

"It is enough, Uncle," said Jane, Mary and Elizabeth nodding with her.

"Then let us consider other matters," said Uncle Phillips. "There is the question of your father's will."

"Does he have any specific bequests?"

Uncle Phillips shook his head. "Your father, as you know, has no living siblings, and no near relations other than Mr. Collins, who will receive the estate. The bequests consist of a few odds and ends, items not attached to the property. The books will be split between Elizabeth and Mary, which we will transport to your new residence. There is a piece of jewelry from his mother that Mr. Bennet wished Jane to have, and a few items for Kitty and Lydia. Other than that, there is very little that is not tied to Longbourn."

"One matter of some interest, however, is Mr. Bennet's wish that Lizzy manages Longbourn until such time as Mr. Collins arrives to claim his inheritance."

"Papa wished for me to manage the estate?" asked Elizabeth, shocked at the suggestion.

"Who else could it be?" said Jane. "I do not have the head for it, Mama, Kitty, and Lydia do not have the temperament, and while Mary would acquit herself well, she is younger and does not command as much respect from the tenants."

Mary nodded her agreement to Jane's assessment while her uncles looked on, diverted at Elizabeth's protests. It made sense, Elizabeth supposed, but it seemed a moot point.

"That is all good and well, but Mr. Collins is to come today. There seems little enough to do as he will soon take charge of the estate."

"Mr. Collins will be here today," said Mr. Gardiner, "but he will not take control of the estate. By all accounts, he has recently accepted a clerical living in Kent, and must resign his position and set his affairs in order."

"It is the accepted custom," added Uncle Phillips, "that a man inheriting an estate allows the widow time to grieve in her home before she must leave. I believe you can expect to live in Longbourn until at least your mother's deep mourning has ended."

"But now that Mr. Collins is to own Longbourn," said Uncle Gardiner, "you must remember that all proceeds from the estate are his unless he specifies otherwise. Thus, while your immediate needs, such as food, repairs, the servants' wages, and the like will be covered, new dresses or other excessive expenditures will not be allowed."

"As we are in mourning," said Elizabeth, "I hardly think dresses will be necessary."

"Of course," said Mr. Gardiner. "Then you will accept this duty?"

"It seems I have little choice," said Elizabeth.

"There is always a choice, Lizzy," said her uncle. "Sometimes the choices are not what we might wish, but that does not take away your right to choose."

"Then I accept," said Elizabeth. "I shall manage Longbourn until Mr. Collins claims his inheritance."

As if on cue, there was a knock on the door, and when Mr. Gardiner called out permission to enter, Mrs. Hill, the housekeeper, entered.

"Mr. Collins has come, Mr. Gardiner."

"Thank you, Mrs. Hill," said Mr. Gardiner.

The new master of the estate stepped into the room and regarded them all, allowing Elizabeth to inspect him. First impressions suggested that Mr. Collins was not a remarkable specimen. The man was tall and spindly, an almost gaunt look about him. His hair, which bore the shape of a hat recently removed, was dark and lank, thinning at the top. His eyes held an almost shifty look, his countenance pale, his cheeks sunken, and his clerical collar encircled his neck, giving the impression of choking him. Then the man opened his mouth, and within a few words, Elizabeth knew she had taken his measure.

"My dear cousins," said he in a voice high and nasally, "it grieves me to come before you in such circumstances, for the death of your beloved father must still weigh upon your delicate sensibilities. How I mourn for you in your acute suffering, for no one understands the sorrow afflicting you more than I, having lost my sire several years ago myself. Though I must offer my sincerest apologies for taking your beloved home from you, it is the way our world works. Please know that I will do my utmost to ensure your distress is not increased as I take control of this estate."

"Thank you, Mr. Collins," said Mr. Gardiner, ever diplomatic, even as Elizabeth could see his surprise and disdain for the parson. "Allow me to provide introductions, so we may discuss the particulars."

Mr. Collins gave him a beatific smile, yet when the introductions were offered, he seemed little interested in them, impatient for something else. Then Mr. Gardiner invited him to sit, which he did even as he eyed Elizabeth as she sat behind the desk, a question in his gaze. Elizabeth ignored him—she had no need to explain and no intention of moving.

"As you know," began Mr. Phillips, "the estate is now yours to do with as you wish. My Brother Bennet has kept an inventory of the items attached to the estate. There are a few more I need to confirm, after which I will send the list to you for your records."

"Thank you, Mr. Phillips. That will be acceptable."

"Then the final matter we must discuss," said Mr. Gardiner, "is the timing of your control over the estate."

"Oh, that must be as soon as possible," said the parson, heedless of the consternation he provoked. "As my beneficent patroness has informed me, I must take control over my inheritance as soon as may be, for only by my oversight can I be certain it is whole and solvent."

"Are you questioning the integrity of my sister and her daughters?"

asked Mr. Gardiner, his tone deceptively mild. To anyone who knew him, his calm voice hid a rising perturbation of spirit.

"I suggest nothing," said Mr. Collins, waving his hand as if to dispel some offensive odor. "But a man of business must understand that I must protect my inheritance. I am to be a gentleman; it is only right that I claim my birthright as soon as may be."

"What you forget," said Uncle Gardiner, "is the steps you must take to order your life before you are at liberty to make your claim, and the time afforded the grieving widow to mourn her loss. The accepted custom is to wait until she has entered half mourning."

"A further reason," added Uncle Phillips when Mr. Collins seemed about to protest, "is to ensure there is no other heir of my brother's body to inherit the estate."

Mr. Collins peered at Mr. Phillips, his homely visage screwed up in what Elizabeth could only call suspicion. "It was my understanding my cousin's wife birthed only daughters."

"That is true," said Mr. Phillips. "The mourning period, in addition to what we have discussed, also serves to ensure that a landowner's widow is not with child."

"From what I understand, there is no trouble there." Mr. Collins favored them all with an airy wave. "She is a woman with five full-grown daughters. Surely she must be past childbearing age."

"She is not yet forty," said Uncle Gardiner, his patience waning. "It is not common, but not unheard of for a woman to conceive at her age. The possibility is remote, but not nonexistent."

"But I cannot wait six months!" exclaimed Mr. Collins, aghast at what he was hearing. "How shall I live in that time?"

"Have you already resigned your living?" asked Mr. Gardiner.

"I have not," said Mr. Collins with a frown. "Her excellent ladyship advised that I refrain from doing so yet, and she needs time to interview potential replacements."

"Then your patroness has some knowledge of these matters. I urge you to consult with her to clarify, Mr. Collins."

"I shall. But six months . . ."

"It may be possible to move them earlier," said Uncle Gardiner. "But you cannot simply evict them without due consideration, sir. We must have time to make the arrangements. Furthermore, the Bennets are highly regarded in the neighborhood; their friends would not look with favor if you were to expel them from the only home they have ever known the moment their father passed."

"Yes," said Mr. Collins, his tone patronizing, "we should not wish to offend them."

Mr. Gardiner bristled at the man's tone, but he controlled his temper. "We appreciate your willingness to assist, Mr. Collins. You may be assured that we will search for a new home for them with all speed."

"Very well," said Mr. Collins.

A commotion arose outside the door, drawing their attention, and Elizabeth exchanged a look with her uncles. A moment later, there was another knock on the door, revealing Mr. Jones, the local apothecary, when Mr. Gardiner called permission to enter the room.

"I beg your pardon," said the man with a bow, "but knowing what I do of the situation, I have news I believe I must disseminate to you at once."

"Of course, Mr. Jones," said Elizabeth, inviting him into the room. "This is the local apothecary; we called him this morning when my mother felt ill."

After Elizabeth had introduced Mr. Gardiner and Mr. Collins to Mr. Jones's acquaintance, the man proceeded to the business that had drawn him hither.

"I have seen Mrs. Bennet this morning and prescribed a draught to help calm her nerves." The man paused and gave them a wry grin. "As you know, she has often experienced nervous complaints, and now as she is under great stress, it has become worse."

"Trust me, Mr. Jones," said Mr. Gardiner, exchanging a wry look with his brother, "I am intimately acquainted with my sister's nerves."

"Indeed," said Mr. Jones. "Some of Mrs. Bennet's other complaints led me to speak in more depth to her. After investigating the matter, I believe I have made a most astonishing discovery, for it is my professional opinion that she is with child."

For a moment silence descended on the room, such that Elizabeth could hear the gardener trimming the lawn outside the window. Then a strident burst of voices erupted, punctuated by Mr. Collins's disbelief.

"But that is impossible!"

"It is quite possible, I assure you, Mr. Collins." Mr. Jones regarded the parson, his enjoyment plain to see. "Might I assume you understand how such things happen?"

"Of course, I know!" spat the parson. "But how could Mrs. Bennet be with child at her age?"

"As I informed you before, my sister is nine and thirty," said Mr. Gardiner. "At the risk of repeating myself, while conceiving at that age is not common, it is not impossible either."

Mr. Collins peered at Mr. Gardiner, suspicion written on his brow. "Given our earlier conversation, one cannot help but be suspicious. And how can I be certain that the child is Mr. Bennet's?"

"Are you impugning my sister's honor?"

"O-Of course not!" blustered the parson.

"Are you certain, Mr. Jones?" asked Uncle Phillips to diffuse the tension.

"As certain as I can be," replied the apothecary. Though he was not directly involved in this matter, even he regarded Mr. Collins, displaying a hint of distaste in the set of his mouth. "All the signs are there. It is not certain beyond any doubt until she feels the quickening and increases. But I have been an apothecary long enough to know the signs."

"Very well," said Mr. Gardiner. "Thank you for informing us."

Mr. Jones took his words as the dismissal they were and went away, though not before directing another severe look at Mr. Collins. The parson ignored him, however, making his case as soon as the door closed.

"This matters not. I have already inherited Longbourn—it cannot be undone. If you persist in pushing this farce, I shall insist on my cousin's wife and daughters' removal as soon as may be."

"You may insist all you like, Collins," said Uncle Phillips. "The law is clear. There is now a question of ownership of the estate, and only the birth of Mrs. Bennet's child can resolve it. As Mr. Bennet's is the clear senior line under the terms of the entail, his child will inherit if Mrs. Bennet births a boy."

"But that is impossible!" exclaimed Mr. Collins yet again.

"It is not impossible," said Mr. Phillips. "If you doubt my word, I invite you to seek counsel with any other man of the law. They will not disagree with my assessment."

Mr. Collins regarded Uncle Phillips as if he suspected him of ulterior motives. When Mr. Phillips did not respond, the parson huffed his annoyance.

"I shall. What if she is not with child? From what I understand, it is not assured until certain signs make themselves known."

"As I stated before," said Mr. Phillips, his tone a little dry, "that is one reason for the wait before you assert control over your inheritance. By the end of her six-month mourning period, it will be clear whether she is with child. If she is not, then you will come into your inheritance. If she is, then you must wait until the child is born for the question to be resolved."

"Then there is little to do but wait," said Mr. Gardiner, his intent on being rid of the parson at once clear to Elizabeth. "Phillips, as Mr. Bennet's solicitor, I trust you will take on the responsibility for informing Mr. Collins of any news regarding the estate's disposition."

"I will. I shall send you monthly reports of Mrs. Bennet's condition, including the quickening if it occurs. You will understand, I presume, that I cannot send you the detailed list of the estate's effects given this development. If Mrs. Bennet's child is another girl, I shall send the list to you at that time and make arrangements for the control of the estate to pass to you."

"I shall expect to receive your communication," said Mr. Collins, his tone reverting to the superiority he had displayed when he entered the room. "I shall also investigate your claims for myself."

"Of course," was Mr. Phillips's complacent reply. "There is one more thing you must understand, Collins. Under the original terms of the entail, it ends with the next generation to inherit the estate."

Mr. Collins peered at Mr. Phillips. "This I understand. What of it?"

"Simply this: should Mrs. Bennet birth a boy, the child will inherit, and entail will end. You will no longer be part of the line of inheritance of the estate."

"B-But that is not possible!"

Smiling at the parson's inability to find another exclamation he might use, Mr. Phillips shook his head. "It is quite possible, I am afraid. The terms of the entail were specified to last for five generations, and you—or Mrs. Bennet's son—will be the fifth. Once the fifth master takes possession, the entail ends. Future heirs will be determined by the new master alone, or, if he deems it necessary, by the institution of a new entail. If Mrs. Bennet should have a son and that son decide to enact another entail, you would not be a possible heir, as you are not of his issue."

"And what if the child dies in infancy? I shall still inherit. The child obviously cannot determine an heir for himself, being but an infant."

"Yes, that is true." Elizabeth had the distinct sense that Mr. Phillips was enjoying himself. "In cases such as these, it is not the ability of a child to see to his affairs that is important in the law, but the fact that the law has been met. The only limiting factor is the child's age. The law does not consider him as having completed the terms of the entail until he becomes of age and comes into his inheritance.

"But while he is a minor, the estate is in the hands of the one designated to see to his interests until he reaches the age of one and twenty. In this instance, that responsibility devolves to Elizabeth, for all matters concerning the estate, and to Gardiner and me for consideration of all legal, financial, and guardianship matters."

At the mention of her name, Mr. Collins shot a look at Elizabeth. It caused a shiver to roll up her spine, though Elizabeth could not determine why that was.

"Thus," continued Mr. Phillips, "the entail is still in force until he reaches the age of one and twenty, and you maintain your position as heir until that time. When he is one and twenty, the terms of the entail are fulfilled and it ends, and he may designate whomever he wishes as his heir. Of course, if Mrs. Bennet births another daughter, this whole point is moot."

"That is ridiculous," exclaimed the parson, "and evidence of your machinations. The matter of Mrs. Bennet's supposed gravidity only came to light this morning."

"As a solicitor," said Mr. Phillips, his tone now frigid, "it is my duty to consider all such matters, Mr. Collins. A solicitor friend of mine encountered this exact situation several years ago, and knowing of the entail, I advised Bennet accordingly. The clause in question has been part of his will since before his fifth daughter was born."

Mr. Collins seemed to believe there was some grand conspiracy, for he regarded them all with suspicion. That he did not speak was a matter of some relief, for Elizabeth had grown fatigued with the man's manners. It was not surprising he would be distressed to learn that he was denied his inheritance a moment before he received it. His inability to control his responses and his open hostility and suspicion, however, were not endearing him to anyone in the room, and his protests of ill-use were nothing more than the bleating of a sheep.

"As I informed you before," continued Mr. Phillips, "if you doubt anything I have said, I invite you to seek legal counsel. No one will contradict what I have told you. The best you can do is return to your parish in Kent and await the final resolution of the question of inheritance. I shall keep you informed, as I pledged."

The parson rose and fixed them all with a sneer. "Very well, then. You may expect a letter from my solicitor once I have spoken with him. Let there be nothing underhanded about our dealings, for I will not hesitate to seek redress with the law should you attempt to defraud me."

Then, without excusing himself, giving all the appearance of high dudgeon, Mr. Collins stalked from the room. Those remaining exchanged looks after he was gone, some of amusement, some of annoyance, while Elizabeth felt little but contempt for the man just departed.

"Perhaps I am the only one," said Mary, "but I found Mr. Collins to be a . . . curious sort of clergyman."

"He is a fool," was Mr. Gardiner's more blunt assessment.

"I think we can expect trouble from him," added Uncle Phillips.

"This changes matters completely," said Mr. Gardiner, acknowledging his brother's point. "Given what you said about the details of the law, the estate remains in the Bennet family's control pending the birth of my sister's child. The incomes of the estate will still be available to you."

"As we will be in mourning," said Elizabeth with a nod for her uncle, "there is little need to spend more than we ought. Perhaps we can put more money aside against the possibility of being required to leave after we collect the next rents."

"That would be wise," agreed Mr. Gardiner. Then he turned to his brother. "It would also be advisable to search for a new place of residence while we wait for the birth of Maggie's child. Should it prove to be another girl, Mr. Collins will demand to receive his inheritance at once."

"I concur."

"Then I think we are agreed." Uncle Gardiner turned back to Elizabeth and fixed her with a smile. "It seems you may manage the estate longer than you had ever expected, Lizzy."

"I will do what I can to increase our fortunes," said Elizabeth. "With any luck, the harvest this year will be a good one."

"Let us all hope so." Mr. Gardiner rose and addressed them all. "Then I suppose we must visit your mother and inform her of these transactions. Margaret's immediate fears will be put to rest by this development."

"But I imagine that relief will be short-lived," said Elizabeth.

Mr. Gardiner laughed. "Yes. I imagine you are correct."

CHAPTER I

*Y*oung ladies with nothing to occupy themselves become fractious, with arguments breaking out where there should be harmony. So the residents of Longbourn found themselves through no fault of their own.

Amusement, however, was on the horizon, for that night they were to attend an assembly, their first since their father's passing. It had been three long months of seclusion, three months of wearing clothes that the youngest sisters complained did not flatter their appearances. But while some members of the family were anticipating their freedom, there was one who was still subject to the mores of society.

"There is no need to be so joyful; it is nothing more than an assembly, after all."

Elizabeth could not help but share a look with her elder sister, for their mother had been making such comments all day. If Elizabeth recalled correctly, she had been saying the same since they discovered the assembly would take place after the expiration of the girls' deep mourning. For the occasion, Elizabeth had allowed for the purchase of new dresses, gowns that would adhere to the conventions of half mourning but provide a treat for her long-suffering sisters."

"On the contrary, Mama," said Lydia, ever heedless, "it is an excellent day. These past months of captivity are now over! I cannot wait until we go!"

Mrs. Bennet gave her youngest daughter a sour look and swept from the room. At least, she attempted to look dignified, which was becoming difficult, given her ever-increasing midsection.

"Perhaps it would be better to offer Mama understanding," suggested Jane, her look as harsh as could be expected from Jane. "It has been as hard for her as it has been for us, and Mama must endure it three more months."

"And longer," observed Elizabeth. "For the child is due to arrive at about the same time Mama's deep mourning is to end. It will be several months before she can rejoin society."

"I am not insensible to Mama's suffering," said Lydia, though her light tone and bouncy step as she flounced about the room belied her statement. "But I am simply so happy that we are to have amusement again. I have been so fatigued with this business of mourning!"

"And Maria tells us a company of militia is to be quartered in Meryton this winter!" added Kitty, her excitement a match for her sister's. "How merry we shall be!"

"We deserve it," said Lydia. "After all we have suffered, it is time we had a bit of entertainment."

"A bit of amusement you will have, Lydia," said Elizabeth, fixing her sister with a level look. "But you must remember decorum; on that, Jane and I will insist."

"Oh, do not be such a spoilsport, Elizabeth! We are to have fun again!"

"I have no thought of denying you," said Elizabeth. "But I will have you remember we are still in half mourning, and our neighbors will expect us to behave as if we are."

"Jane!" whined Lydia, looking at her mildest sister. "You are the eldest. Tell Lizzy to stop!"

"I shall not, Lydia, for I agree with her. Do you wish to invite the censure of our neighbors? Papa had the respect of these people and he provided for our needs all our lives; it would not do to show anything other than the proper reverence for him."

"Well, when you put it that way," muttered Lydia.

"Indeed, we do," said Elizabeth, exchanging a grin with Jane.

"But that does not prevent us from dancing," said Lydia, brightening. "I shall do as you ask, Lizzy, for I do not wish you to write to Uncle Gardiner. Kitty and I shall behave."

"Thank you, girls," said Elizabeth with a smile for them both.

"Now, we should all prepare, for we must depart soon."

Chattering and bickering about who would best suit a length of ribbon Lydia held in her hand, the two girls left the room, leaving their two eldest sisters. A moment later, Mary replaced them, her severe expression speaking to her feelings about her younger sisters.

"It will be a miracle if Lydia does not embarrass us tonight."

"If she does," replied Elizabeth, "she knows the consequences. I do not relish the necessity of bearing tales, but I shall write to our uncle if I must."

"Lydia knows this and will not jeopardize her newfound freedom," said Jane, ever the optimist.

"It is not freedom, Jane," said Elizabeth. "We are still a house in mourning and will be for the next nine months, even if our own mourning will be over in three. Furthermore, you know what Uncle Gardiner said—Lydia is not out, regardless of how much she insists she is. In this, I am happy for our uncle's resolve, for at fifteen Lydia is too young to be out."

"I was out at fifteen," said Jane.

"You were too young too, Jane," said Mary. "I remember well your apprehension before your first event."

"It is also pertinent to recall the difference between you and Lydia, Jane," added Elizabeth. "Lydia is an immature fifteen-year-old; you were the opposite."

Jane sighed and offered a smile. "I am not insensible to these things, Lizzy. And I cannot but agree with you—uncle was correct to restrict Lydia and Kitty's participation in society. At the same time, I think we need to be cognizant of Lydia's feelings."

"I do not disagree, dear sister," said Elizabeth, affection for her angelic elder sister overflowing.

The smile ran away from Jane's face and she regarded Elizabeth with an atypical seriousness of manner. "You sent Mr. Collins's letter to Uncle Phillips?"

"His most recent letter," said Elizabeth with a sigh, thinking about the major source of aggravation the Bennets had endured since their father passed away.

"I did," confirmed Elizabeth. "When last this happened, our uncle promised me he would send a strongly worded letter to Mr. Collins, instructing him to desist or face a defamation suit."

"As well he should," said Mary, her usual primness showing in her voice and expression of disapproval. "Given his behavior, I cannot but think that Mr. Collins is the worst clergyman in all England. What sort of man accuses a grieving woman of consorting with other men and conspiring to defraud him?"

"A stupid one," said Elizabeth. "One who is afraid of losing the inheritance he believed was his."

Harsh though Elizabeth's statement had been, neither Jane nor Mary could refute it. Since the summer, Mr. Collins had continued to bombard them with letters, demanding to know the state of affairs, the latest news of their mother's health, and information about the operation of the estate he had no right to hear. So abusive had he become on more than one occasion their uncles had warned him against bothering them again amid implied legal action.

"The worst part of Mr. Collins is he directs his letters to you, Lizzy," said Mary. "What sort of coward is he that he will not deal with our uncles?"

"The very worst sort," replied Elizabeth. "Uncle Phillips informed me that he would openly threaten Mr. Collins with legal action this time. I hope that will induce him to desist."

"It seems a hopeless business to me," replied Mary.

Elizabeth could not refute her sister's opinion, and she did not attempt it. Thus far, the parson had shown little interest in moderating his words or his accusations; Elizabeth had no notion he would see sense now.

"What do we do if he comes to Longbourn?" asked Jane.

"We have John to protect us," said Elizabeth of their long-time footman. "And Theodore, the new footman Uncle Gardiner sent to us, appears capable. Mr. Whitmore will also act to protect us. There should be no difficulty withstanding Mr. Collins."

The sisters agreed and dropped the subject. Mr. Bennet had not used a steward, citing the estate's size and the lack of sufficient income to allow the expenditure. The sad fact, however, was that if anyone required a steward, it was Mr. Bennet, for he could rarely bother to see to his property. Mr. Whitmore was technically Mr. Gardiner's employee, for their uncle had insisted on taking the expense on himself. Should Mr. Collins inherit, it was possible he would dismiss the steward at once, and Mr. Whitmore had taken the position with that understanding. As the man was yet young, he had accepted the condition in exchange for the early prosperity he would realize as the steward of an estate, no matter how small. Thus far, Mr. Whitmore had proved capable, and Elizabeth thought it likely he would have little trouble finding a new position if required.

"I do not trust Mr. Collins," said Jane, an astonishing statement from a woman who never had a poor word for anyone.

"Nor do I, Jane," replied Elizabeth.

"Then let us hope he will not disturb us here at Longbourn," said Mary.

It was a boon to have such sisters as these. Elizabeth had taken to the management of the estate with little trouble, and she made all the important decisions, sometimes with the approval of her uncles and always with the steward's participation. Her eldest sisters, however, were intimately involved, offering their voices and supporting her in everything she did. Longbourn was not a large estate and its management was not the complicated endeavor she knew many of the great properties were. At the same time, for a young woman who had not been raised with such responsibilities in mind, the encouragement of her sisters meant everything.

"Well?" said Elizabeth, turning back to the task at hand. "As we have informed Lydia, we had best be ready to depart on time. If we are late, we are certain to suffer complaints such as we have never heard."

With a laugh, they agreed, and they returned to their rooms to busy themselves with a few final preparations.

The way their neighbors greeted the Bennet sisters, one might have been excused for thinking they had been away for some time. In a sense, Elizabeth supposed it was true they had been absent. Most of those people, however, had visited Longbourn during the three months of their mourning, so their isolation had not been as complete as their welcome would suggest. More than once, Elizabeth heard condolences expressed amid welcoming statements of their happiness to see the Bennets' return. Several asked after their mother too, which Elizabeth and her sisters answered with as much diplomacy as they could. Only one objectionable comment was made within Elizabeth's hearing.

"Well, it is fortunate that your mother has one last chance to bear an heir of the estate. I shudder to think what will happen should she fail this time."

Objectionable though the comment was, Elizabeth decided there was no reason to snap back at Mrs. Goulding, who had long been a woman as thoughtless as Elizabeth's mother. Thus, she summoned a banal reply and excused herself soon after. Finding Charlotte, Elizabeth passed the rest of the time waiting for the dance to start in pleasant conversation.

"How are you all, Lizzy?" asked Charlotte after they had been speaking for some time. As Charlotte had visited more times than everyone else in the community combined, she knew their status better than any other. "Please do not give me the platitudes you have offered to everyone else in attendance tonight. I wish to know your true feelings."

Affection for her dearest friend welled up within Elizabeth and she pressed Charlotte's hands. "You are such an excellent friend, Charlotte, I can hardly fathom how we would have managed without your constant support. It has been difficult—this I will own. But we are all well, even if Mama chafes at her restrictions and complains about being great with child."

"Mrs. Bennet appeared well the last time I saw her."

Elizabeth sighed and gave her friend a wry smile. "Yes, she is better than she might let on. For the rest of us, we are waiting and praying Mama bears a son, as much for her peace of mind as for our future security."

Fixing her with a commiserating smile, Charlotte murmured: "I can imagine how it would be a burden on your mind."

"It is. But all we can do is hope and pray. Whatever God wills, we shall bear it however we can."

"That is for the best."

Eager to change the subject, Elizabeth queried: "Now, what news of the new arrivals in the community?"

With a laugh, Charlotte said: "And you suppose I possess all their intimate details?"

"You are the daughter of Sir William Lucas, are you not?"

The ladies laughed together. "You know my father very well, indeed. There are two estates let out, you understand."

"So I have heard," acknowledged Elizabeth. "The new residents of Pulvis Lodge may add to our society, but those at Netherfield Park are on the tongues of everyone."

"That they are. The latter has been empty for much longer than the former, after all. And I understand that our new neighbors of Pulvis Lodge were delayed, while those at Netherfield are already in the neighborhood."

At that moment, the noise of conversation died around them, and they turned to look at the entrance, noting the arrival of a group of newcomers. Among them were a pair of gentlemen, both tall, one dark, one light, and both handsome, while two women, one dainty, the other willowy, and both pretty. There was no sign of the veritable army of gentlemen the gossip had suggested were about to descend upon them.

"It appears, Lizzy," said Charlotte, as conversation once more rose about them, "that you are about to learn of them, for they have arrived."

"It appears they have, Charlotte. I anticipate making their acquaintance."

The curse of a man ill at ease in society with which he was not familiar weighed heavily on Fitzwilliam Darcy that evening.

In truth, he had little of which to complain. The people in the assembly hall that evening were perhaps not the finest, or the most cultured, but that was a point in their favor. Rarely had Darcy attended an event in London among the supposed cream of society and not seen objectionable behavior. His residence at Netherfield Park was among the dearest of friends and his sister, who had declined to attend that evening, her disposition even more reticent than his own. No, everything was well in his world, and for that Darcy was grateful.

But he simply could not find comfort in a room full of people with whom he was unacquainted. Their concerns little interested him, he found difficulty in knowing what to say or how to speak, and the rumors of his wealth and consequence, which had circulated from the moment he entered the room, could do nothing other than render him ill at ease. His companions' situations ensured some of the attention was diverted from him, but that did not assuage his discomfort to any great degree.

It was fortunate he was among those of such cheery dispositions, for he might have stalked on the sides of the floor all evening if he had not. But they would not allow it, meaning he danced with each of the female members of his party and they introduced him to other ladies, with whom he stood up for a set. Dancing was not Darcy's favorite activity, but he thought he acquitted himself well that evening, better than he had at many a ball in London.

One family, in particular, caught his attention that evening, a family of five young women, if such a thing was to be believed. The youngest could not have been more than sixteen, and was a little boisterous, to say the least, while the eldest was tall and beautiful, and perhaps two and twenty. She also, he noted, caught the eye of his companion, who danced with her and watched her for many long minutes after.

It was not, perhaps, strange that there should be so many young ladies in a family, as such was not unknown. It was more that the gentlemen of the neighborhood appeared to treat them with the utmost in care. Whereas they were all pretty enough to have danced every set, though gentlemen were scarcer than the ladies, Darcy observed several of them sitting out occasionally. Then the mode of their dress, muted colors and modest styles, informed Darcy they were in half mourning, and Darcy wondered who they had lost. Perhaps their mother, as Darcy had not seen an older woman attending them. They did not seem to suffer from the loss, for the eldest two women appeared to play the parts of mother hens to perfection. Then Darcy chanced to overhear a conversation which further piqued his interest.

"Miss Elizabeth," said the portly gentleman who had greeted them and introduced them around the room that evening. "Perhaps an assembly is not the best place to speak of such things, but I should like to ask you what you mean to do about the fence between Lucas Lodge and Longbourn. Several sections are rotting beyond repair and must be replaced."

"Perhaps we should inspect it together?" asked Miss Elizabeth, a petite young lady with mahogany hair, impossibly long eyelashes, and the most beautiful eyes Darcy had ever seen. "I should be happy to meet you there with Mr. Whitmore at any time convenient."

"The day after tomorrow?" Sir William favored her with a bright smile and added: "I know I shall endure Charlotte's scolding if I interrupt your gathering tomorrow."

Miss Elizabeth laughed, a beautiful sound. "No, we cannot interrupt or delay our discussion the night after an assembly. The day after tomorrow would be acceptable."

"Very well," said Sir William, beaming. The man paused and considered for a moment, and then he ventured: "You know I esteemed your father very much, but there were times when inducing him to action was difficult. I appreciate your diligence, for your father, though he had many fine qualities, was not inclined to concern himself much for the estate."

The smile Miss Elizabeth directed at Sir William was a mixture of exasperation, amusement, and sadness. "That he was not, Sir William. I hope we shall have the opportunity to discuss such things many more times in the future."

"Let us all hope so," said the kindly man. "Give your mother our best wishes and our prayers for her."

"I shall."

The conversation left Darcy with a clearer picture of the situation, though there were still pieces missing from the puzzle. The Bennets' father had passed away, and as the estate appeared to be managed by his daughter, Darcy thought her mother did not have the head for estate management. Many did not, so Darcy did not think poorly of the woman on such scanty evidence. It also meant they did not have a brother—at least, not a brother of age to attend assemblies or manage an estate. What the rest of the exchange portended, Darcy could not say. The opportunity to learn the rest of the story came later that evening when he chanced to speak with her.

"My father passed away a little over three months ago, Mr. Darcy," said Miss Elizabeth when Darcy made some slight observation of her mourning attire.

"You have my condolences, Miss Elizabeth. My father passed five years ago, and my mother about seven before that. As I was yet a boy when my mother passed, the pain has dulled with time, but my father's loss is still fresh in my mind."

The smile with which Miss Elizabeth favored him carried equal parts sadness and wistfulness. "I cannot imagine the pain will ever recede, though I suppose it must over time. While I can recall my father's character, his voice, and many other things about him, the immediacy of his loss has turned more melancholy in nature."

"You were close to him?"

"He often called me the son he never had. As I was the most like him of all my sisters, he was closest to me."

"Then you have inherited the estate?"

Miss Elizabeth shook her head. "The estate is entailed, Mr. Darcy."

Confused, Darcy regarded her. Seeing his uncertainty, Miss Elizabeth explained: "After my father passed, my mother was found to be with child."

"Ah, then the ownership of the estate is uncertain." Darcy ignored the other implications of her statement to focus on the salient point.

"It is. Should there be another girl, the entail will force us to give way in favor of my father's heir, a distant cousin we have met but once. The man is not an impressive specimen and has already accused us many times of conspiring to defraud him."

"That is strange," said Darcy with a frown. "No one should make such claims unless they have proof of wrongdoing. There is no way to be certain, of course, but when a woman falls with child, it is presumed to belong to her husband unless irrefutable evidence can be obtained to prove otherwise. Such evidence is almost impossible to acquire."

"Especially since Mr. Collins had never met us until after my father's passing and still has never received an introduction to my mother."

The name tickled at Darcy's memory, but a moment's thought brought no clarity. "That is strange, indeed. But you are managing the estate until the birth of your sibling?"

"I am the only one of my sisters who has any aptitude for such things, Mr. Darcy," was her simple reply. "My father specified it in his will, though even had he remained silent, I believe it would have fallen to me."

"If it is as you say, I cannot imagine you are incorrect. From what I understand, your father has a competent steward—the assistance of such a man is invaluable."

"That it is, though I must correct you," said Miss Elizabeth. "My father never had a steward. The man occupying the position was hired at my uncle's insistence. He serves both as steward and protects us, for we are a house of women, albeit two of our number are of age."

"Yes, that is prudent, indeed." Darcy paused and considered how he might broach his question. "I hope your uncle investigated this man and found him to be trustworthy? Many an unscrupulous man has caused substantial damage to unsuspecting landowners."

Miss Elizabeth smiled, indicating she was not angry with his presumption. "My uncle is a careful man, Mr. Darcy. His investigations, as I understand, were no less than exhaustive."

"I am happy to hear it, Miss Elizabeth." Darcy turned and noted the set had ended and another was forming. "Shall we dance, Miss Elizabeth? I suspect it will be just the thing to turn you from your melancholy thoughts."

"Thank you, Mr. Darcy," said she. "I should love to."

CHAPTER II

$\mathcal{A}$s Sir William had mentioned the previous evening, the consternation would have been great, indeed, had the Longbourn and Lucas Lodge ladies been required to miss their gathering the morning after the assembly. It had been a firm tradition for such gatherings to occur since Jane, the eldest Bennet daughter, began attending events in the neighborhood.

Whereas in the past such a meeting might have included Lady Lucas, that morning only Charlotte and her sister, Maria, made their way down the driveway to Longbourn's door. Elizabeth suspected this was because Lady Lucas's primary conversation partner, Mrs. Bennet, was in ill humor of late, and a morning spent in conversation after a night when she had been denied amusement with her daughters would render her waspish and prone to complaint. Mrs. Bennet did not seem to notice the lack, for her grievances flowed freely, her primary audience's absence notwithstanding.

"It seems it was a successful evening," said Mrs. Bennet at length after the well of her grievances ran dry.

"You might have heard of it had you waited for us to return last night," observed Lydia. As the closest to her mother in character, Lydia had returned home, impatient to inform Mrs. Bennet of her doings the previous evening, and she had not been at all happy to learn her mother had retired before they had arrived at home.

"Was there any reason for me to wait for you?" asked Mrs. Bennet, more than a hint of petulance in her voice.

A warning glance from Elizabeth prevented Lydia from responding. After a moment's thought, Lydia seemed to realize there was no reason to provoke their mother's further claims of ill-use. Thus, she shrugged, and the conversation continued.

"Lizzy and Jane appeared to be most favored," observed Charlotte, showing a grin to the two eldest Bennets. "Jane danced twice with the man leasing Netherfield, and Elizabeth was one of the few with whom the other stood up, and further she conversed with him for some time."

"I did enjoy his company," said Jane, while at the same time Elizabeth protested: "Mr. Darcy was just being kind. He asked after my family and the events that led to my stewardship over the estate at present."

"It is unladylike to behave like a man and run the estate," declared Mrs. Bennet. "How do you suppose you will ever marry if you insist on continuing in this fashion?"

"It is not unusual for a woman to manage an estate, Mama," said Elizabeth, repeating a well-worn refrain between them. "There are many ladies who are widowed or have inherited their properties. I do nothing more than any of them."

"Mrs. Clancy near Stevenage does the same," said Jane to support Elizabeth, earning her a grateful smile.

Mrs. Bennet harrumphed and turned her attention to another grievance. "And what of your tightening of the purse strings? Just because the duty of watching over the estate belongs to you does not mean you control everything."

The fact that Elizabeth had been given control of the family budget was a matter Mrs. Bennet well knew, for her uncles had supported her in this. All her sisters knew Elizabeth had slashed the budget hoping to put as much money as possible away against the prospect circumstances would force them to leave Longbourn, and while Kitty and especially Lydia complained at times, they all understood the reason for it. Mrs. Bennet, however, was not in the habit of seeing reason when she thought herself ill-used.

"Mama," said Elizabeth, praying for the patience to appease her mother one more time, "you are still in deep mourning, and my sisters and I emerged into half mourning only a matter of days ago. There was little reason for purchases these past three months and every reason to economize, as you well know."

Mrs. Bennet eyed Elizabeth, her manner unwilling to be placated. Then she huffed again and said: "Yes, well perhaps that is true. But you should know, Lizzy, that when I come out of deep mourning, I shall not put up with this miserly behavior from my own daughter. The Bennets have had a presence in Meryton society for many years, and we shall not shirk from our duty as a family."

"Should we remain in possession of Longbourn, Mama," said Elizabeth, "you may be assured we shall uphold our position in society as we ever have."

Elizabeth's pique provoked her response when she should have thought better, for the reminder of their possible removal hit Mrs. Bennet like a bludgeon. For a wonder she did not wail or lash out or any of the other behaviors her daughter might have expected. Instead, she swallowed thickly and turned an imperious glare on them all.

"It would behoove you, girls, to ensure these gentlemen fall in love with you and offer marriage. Given my history bearing children, it is more than likely this child is another girl, meaning Mr. Collins shall throw us into the hedgerows to starve as soon as she arrives. Do not fail, for our circumstances will be desperate if you do."

With those ominous words, Mrs. Bennet rose and exited the room, her loud cries for Hill to attend her echoing back down the stairs. For a moment, those left behind could only stare at each other in bemusement.

"Has Mama always been this . . . fatalistic?" asked Lydia after a moment.

"Lydia, you should not speak of Mama in that way," admonished Jane.

"No, you should not," said Elizabeth, interested to once again see the flash of improvement from her sister when Lydia blanched and shook her head in apology. Such things had arisen occasionally after their father's death, though Lydia still had much growing to do. "But at times, yes she has."

"One beaten down by life and suffering multiple disappointments inevitably expects calamity," observed Charlotte. "I should not call any of you disappointments or question your worthiness. But for a woman who has long lived in fear of poverty after your father's passing, it is not surprising she would feel this way."

"No, it is not," said Elizabeth with a smile at her friend. "But it also does no good to dwell on it, and Mama would be better served to regulate the expression of her feelings."

"Yes, Lizzy. This I understand."

"Enough of this dreary talk!" exclaimed Lydia. "If that is all we shall discuss, I may as well trim my bonnet."

"What of last night?" asked Charlotte, grasping onto Lydia's words. "What were your impressions of our new neighbors?"

"It is difficult to say," said Elizabeth. "After only a single night in company with them, it is impossible to know much of their characters. Mr. Darcy was an erudite man, but I did not speak to his friend. The ladies were pleasant, though one was reticent and the other lively."

"Which could be said of you and Jane," said Charlotte.

"For myself, I did not like the younger much," said Lydia, her superior sniff making her next words all that much more ridiculous. "She seemed to be everything proud and disagreeable."

"I did not find her so at all," said Jane. "And if she is, well, I can only say that she has reason to be so, considering her position in society."

"All the position in society does not give one the right to look down one's nose upon everyone else."

"If she did so, I would agree with you, Lydia," said Elizabeth. "I only exchanged a few words with her, and I observed no hint of improper pride."

"Of more importance, in my opinion," said Charlotte, "was the performance of our two new bachelors toward the eldest Bennets. Do either of you care to share your impressions of their attentions to you?"

"Oh, yes!" exclaimed Maria, clapping her hands together in her glee. "Do share, Jane, Lizzy. Are you both now madly in love with your gentlemen?"

Elizabeth and Jane shared a look. Charlotte was a master of teasing, but Maria's inclination led her to more serious reflections, for every glance of admiration must be a declaration of love to her romantic heart. Kitty and Lydia were little better.

"One night in company, a dance, and a few words spoken with civility do not lead to a lifelong devotion, Maria."

When the girl seemed disappointed, Elizabeth laughed and fixed her with an affectionate smile. "As I said before, Maria, Mr. Darcy seems to be an estimable gentleman, indeed. Other famous romances have had worse beginnings, I suppose, though I cannot oblige you and declare my everlasting love for Mr. Darcy at this moment."

"But what of Jane?" asked Charlotte, turning her fire on Elizabeth's sister. "Jane shared two dances with her beau. Is that not tantamount to an engagement?"

Accustomed as she was to Charlotte's ways, Jane was not embarrassed. "He is an excellent man, but I agree with Lizzy. Should he carry on charmingly I can imagine it will not be difficult to come to esteem him very much. It is still too early for such regard, however, so there is nothing more at present to report."

"Then we shall watch it unfold with great enthusiasm and anticipation," replied Charlotte.

Whether anything would come of it, Elizabeth could not say. The thought had occurred to her it would be easier for them all if one of their number could entice a man to propose, for they would not need to fear the birth of another girl. But Elizabeth would not compromise her principles, and she knew Jane would not either. Should either man make them love him, the choice would be easy. If not, the situation still demanded they make what they could of this brief season where Mr. Collins's hand was checked.

The rents had been collected and in December they would have another opportunity to collect them, should the child remain unborn. The cost of living on the estate meant that what they had accumulated would be depleted. But Elizabeth was determined to save as much as she could. If the child was a boy, they could take stock then.

Netherfield Park was a good estate. Darcy had seen that much within moments of touring the grounds, seeing the house which, though not one of the great houses, was spacious and solid, a house to make its owner proud. What it was not was in a location that was as desirable as some.

To be clear, the location was not poor. The land on which the estate stood was, for all Darcy could see, fertile, its fields productive, and they would become more so when the hand of a master was applied with the diligence occasioned by residence, rather than a distant master who did not seem to care. Its four-and-twenty-mile distance from London was also a boon, for it was quite convenient if one enjoyed the scene and society of the city.

The neighborhood in which it sat was adequate, and nothing Darcy had not seen before. The inhabitants seemed to be good people, though their manners were not fashionable. Then again, much of what seemed to constitute fashionable manners offended Darcy, so that was not a strike against the neighborhood. It was to those who considered themselves fashionable that the neighborhood would lack, for there would not have been enough sophistication for them. It was fortunate, then, that no one in residence at the estate cared for such things, though they were all descended from the same noble line; had they espoused such feelings most would have thought nothing of it.

"Well, Darcy?" asked his cousin the morning after the assembly in Meryton. "Having had your first taste of society here, does this place still meet with your approval?"

"I might ask you the same, Cousin," replied Darcy, turning a bit of Fitzwilliam's teasing back on him. "After all, I am not the son of an earl."

Fitzwilliam laughed. "Perhaps I am. At present, however, I am merely the brother of one, and naught but Mr. Fitzwilliam."

"I can hardly believe we are even here, to own the truth," said Charity, Fitzwilliam's youngest sister. "The speed with which you resigned your commission caused us all surprise, especially after mother begged you for years to leave your dangerous life behind."

Sobering a little, Fitzwilliam nodded. "I will own that the sudden and unexpected inheritance provoked me to action. Were Mother still here to know of my resignation, I am certain she would be grateful for it. I had tired of soldiering and wished for a sedate life, with a home and a wife to keep me company. Even though the French are inept with their weapons, one might find luck if given enough opportunities."

It was a well-worn jest, and its delivery, more with an absence of mind and a touch of melancholy than with Fitzwilliam's usual joviality than his wont, spoke to the seriousness of his thoughts. Though Darcy's parents had passed on twelve and five years before, his uncle, the old earl, had departed life a short time after Darcy's father, and their mother a scant two years before. Their grief was thus more immediate than his own.

"It is interesting that the only one of the previous generation still with us is my mother," said Anne de Bourgh, who had hitherto remained silent. "As she is the most difficult, we might have wished her gone before any of the others!"

"Anne, that is hardly a proper way of speaking of your mother," chided Darcy.

"Perhaps it is not," said Anne, her manner completely unrepentant. "But I will wager more than one of you have had the same thought."

"Aye, we have at that!" exclaimed Fitzwilliam.

"We seem to have strayed from the original intent of this discussion," said the final member of their party, Darcy's sister Georgiana. "I wish to know what happened at the assembly last night, and you are not obliging me." She turned to Charity and addressed her, though her eyes slid back to Darcy. "Did William dance with anyone other than you and Anne, or did he remain by the dance floor all night?"

"You have a healthy interest in my dance partners, Georgiana," interjected Darcy before Charity could speak. "By my account, you have never attended an assembly with me; is your understanding of my behavior anything more than conjecture?"

"She has had enough accounts of it to know, Darcy," said Fitzwilliam.

"In fact," said Charity, taking control of the conversation, "your brother acquitted himself rather well. It would not be correct to accuse him of overly frivolous behavior, but I dare say he stood up with at least three or four local ladies during the evening."

"And with both of the eldest Bennet sisters," said Anne, "whom I heard described more than once as the jewels of the county."

"Those accounts are nothing less than the truth," averred Fitzwilliam. "Miss Bennet is a lovely woman, and Miss Elizabeth is a sparkling gem of the first order."

"I have already noted your opinion, Brother," said Charity. "By my account, you stood up with Miss Bennet twice, which is an uncommon show of favor for a first meeting."

"Perhaps we shall hear wedding bells before long," added Anne with a stifled giggle.

"If I should choose Miss Bennet," said Fitzwilliam, "I have not the slightest doubt of her worthiness to receive a proposal from any man. But as you know, Annie, it is still early for any such declaration."

"And the timing is incorrect," said Darcy. The rest of the company looked to him for clarification, which Darcy readily offered. "They are newly into half mourning. I cannot imagine Miss Bennet is ready to hear a proposal from the first prancing dandy to waltz into town."

"I shall have you know I did not waltz into town," sniffed Fitzwilliam with a credible imitation of the affected lisp of an aforementioned dandy. Then he winked and added: "I do not even know how to waltz. We proper British do not succumb to such lascivious pastimes, so the French had best keep it to themselves."

There was a smattering of giggles from the ladies, but Anne turned her attention again to Darcy. "I noted their attire and heard something of their recent bereavement. Might I assume it was their mother who passed away?"

"If you did, you would make the same mistake I made," replied Darcy. Darcy then informed them of what he had heard from Miss Elizabeth the previous evening, including his observations of what the family now faced. It was clear after he shared what he knew that it touched the hearts of his companions, who were already disposed to approve of the Bennet ladies based on what they had already experienced in their company.

"That is an interesting tale, Cousin," said Charity when he fell silent. "While I will own I spoke little with Miss Elizabeth, she seemed to me to be an active, worthy sort of woman. It was evident that she is much more suited to such responsibility than her eldest sister."

"Miss Bennet is not deficient," said Fitzwilliam, fixing his sister with a frown.

"Nor did I say she was," was Charity's unperturbed reply. "There is no stain of dishonor in not having the aptitude for estate management, Anthony. Miss Bennet has strengths aplenty, the extent of which I am certain we have not even begun to scratch the surface."

"Given my discussion with her," said Darcy, "I am impressed with how she has upheld her duties. Miss Elizabeth said little on the subject, but I suspect her father was not a man much given to such minutia as managing an estate often requires. It is difficult, as I did not know the man, but I believe his daughter outstrips him in this matter."

"And yet, if the coming child is not a boy, she will have no further opportunity to prove her mettle," said Anne.

"Aye, that is the rub," said Fitzwilliam, while everyone nodded their agreement.

Entails were not something with which Darcy had much experience, as his family had always eschewed them; the Darcys instilled enough duty in their scions that such considerations as breaking up the estates for multiple daughters was not something that they would ever consider. Of course, many entails were also instituted to protect an estate against the ruinous actions of a profligate master. But that was also a situation of which the Darcys had been particularly conscious. More than one heir had been disinherited because the master at the time had not been completely certain of his eldest son's character.

For the women of a small estate such as Longbourn, having no heir to inherit the estate was a situation to be feared. The vagaries of the world in which they lived were such that it was far from a guarantee that any heirs born would live to adulthood and protect a mother and any unmarried sisters. Living on an entailed estate was not a matter to be treated lightly.

Of the situation in which the Bennets found themselves, Darcy could infer from what Miss Elizabeth said the previous evening that they would not have much to support themselves should they need to leave. That showed an astonishing level of dereliction of her father's stewardship of the land. If they had several years, perhaps they could save a tidy sum. With the birth fast approaching, however, Darcy knew the previous quarter-day had been the only means of augmenting their finances.

"I believe," said Charity, pulling Darcy from his thoughts, "I would like to know the Bennets better, especially the eldest. There is something intrinsically estimable about them."

"Acquaintance will necessarily include the younger girls," said Fitzwilliam with a grin. "They are not the equal of their sisters and may corrupt our dear Georgiana if we encourage a closer acquaintance."

"The other girls," said Anne, fixing Fitzwilliam with a look that suggested he best be silent, "are young and immature. I, for one, believe Georgiana could do with a little of their liveliness."

"And they may benefit from her calmer demeanor," said Charity.

Fitzwilliam laughed and put his hands forward in a gesture of surrender. "It was a jest, and nothing more. While I suspect they might have been less restrained if last evening had not been their first sally into society after their father's death, they in no way offended me."

"Young girls released from a long period of being shackled have behaved worse in the past," observed Darcy. "After three months in deep mourning, they must have chafed from their restrictions. Given that, their restraint was admirable."

"And likely the work of their wiser elder sisters," said Fitzwilliam. When they all regarded him, he again laughed and protested: "It does not do them any less credit, but you must own it is likely their sisters informed them of the consequences of misbehavior."

"Which makes me wonder after their guardian," said Charity. "Did Miss Elizabeth say anything of a relation tasked with seeing to their interests?"

"She said nothing to me. But their mother is still living, and the eldest is of age, so there should be little trouble in that respect."

"Then shall we visit them?" asked Anne.

"Perhaps we shall," said Fitzwilliam. "I, for one, have no objection."

"Then let us go tomorrow," said Georgiana, clapping her hands. "These accounts have rendered me eager to make their acquaintance!"

That decided, they drifted out into their sundry activities, Fitzwilliam and Darcy taking themselves to the billiards room. As Fitzwilliam was racking the balls, he turned to Darcy.

"Did Anne mention her mother wrote again threatening to visit us here?"

Darcy grimaced. His aunt, as they had so irreverently observed, was a tiresome woman at times. "Presumably to help us along?"

"You know her too well, Darcy," replied Fitzwilliam with a guffaw, gesturing to the table. "As you are aware, the only reason Lady Catherine allowed Anne to accompany us was that she thought time alone would provoke you to propose."

"Anne and I have no desire to marry," said Darcy, his tone more abrupt than he intended.

"And you suppose I do not already know this?" Fitzwilliam shook his head and laughed while Darcy broke. "Just remember, Lady Catherine would not appreciate your display last night. Any woman who dances with you must have her eye on the vacant position as mistress of Pemberley."

"Lady Catherine will not make a scene, Fitzwilliam," said Darcy. "She has more self-possession than that."

"You had best hope so. Otherwise, scenes agreeable to none of us might ensue."

CHAPTER III

*O*f the many tasks with which a landowner must concern himself, Elizabeth knew her father had detested the keeping of Longbourn's ledgers the most. The state of the books attested to this deficiency without the possibility for error.

When Elizabeth had first looked at the ledgers after her father's passing, she had been appalled by the messy entries, often incomplete, the haphazard way he had done the sums. She thought he hurried through them whenever he focused on them at all, for there were many errors, and much of what he had written was nigh incomprehensible.

Much of Elizabeth's activities in the first few weeks of her stewardship over the estate had concentrated on accounts, revising, fixing what she could, and trying to develop a new system that would make more sense and be easier to read. When her uncle had hired Mr. Whitmore, he had shown her a method of bookkeeping he had seen used at an estate at which he had been employed before. Introducing this system had proven its worth, easing Elizabeth's concerns and rendering it easier to locate an entry than the mess her father had left her.

The longer Elizabeth had managed Longbourn, the more she realized her father had not been a good steward of the property.

Perhaps it was fair to say that his lackadaisical style and revulsion for the work involved were the real culprits, but Elizabeth also knew he had not possessed any true talent for it; diligence would have made up for some of that. Elizabeth had loved him, esteemed him as the father who had educated and loved her. At the same time, she was not blind to his faults, and now understood he had not done as he ought, particularly with the threat of the entail hanging over their heads.

A knock on the door interrupted her thoughts, and she gratefully put them to the side, not wishing to dwell on the faults of a beloved parent. When she called permission to enter, the door opened, revealing Mr. Whitmore, the estate's young steward, who entered with a bow and left the door ajar as was proper.

"Good morning, Miss Bennet," said he. "I hope this is a good time to discuss a few matters of the estate?"

"Of course, Mr. Whitmore," said Elizabeth with a smile gesturing to a chair. "I have just finished with the books for this morning and am quite at my leisure."

The man nodded at the mention of the books. "I hope the new system is meeting your approval."

"It is. Had my father adopted it many years ago, he may not have had as much aversion for the work."

Again, a nod was Mr. Whitmore's response. Though he had never said as much, Elizabeth was convinced her steward disapproved of Mr. Bennet's neglect; Elizabeth did herself, to own the truth. Had her father hired a man even half as competent at managing the estate on his behalf, their looming penury would not be nearly so grave as it was.

Mr. Whitmore was yet a young man, not thirty years of age, but it was clear he had studied under men of knowledge, for he was competent and eager to put his stamp on the affairs of the property. They discussed their plans for the coming spring, alternative methods of eking every bit of prosperity of the land they could coax from it, though he always deferred to her for the final decision. Would that she knew the estate would still be in their possession after the birth of her sibling!

"Thank you, Mr. Whitmore," said Elizabeth when their discussion ended. "As always, I appreciate your insight and guidance. I do not know what I would do without you."

The young man eyed her and in a voice laced with sincerity said: "You would have done as you must, Miss Bennet. Your instincts are good and your understanding astonishing for one who was not raised to be the proprietor of an estate. What you lack in ready knowledge, you more than make up for in your desire to learn and your intelligence."

It was not the first time he had praised her thus, bringing a rosy hue to her cheeks. "Thank you for that bit of flattery, sir, for it is much appreciated." Elizabeth sighed. "Now we can only hope we will be in a position to put these measures in place. That will only happen, as you know, if my mother births a boy."

Mr. Whitmore gave her a kindly smile. "Hope for the best, Miss Bennet. After five successive daughters are the chances not excellent that your mother will produce a son?"

Elizabeth laughed and shook her head. "I am not certain it works that way. I should think the chances the child will be a girl are as great as it will be a boy, notwithstanding my four sisters and I."

"Aye, in that you are correct," replied Mr. Whitmore. "But it is best to cling to hope, is it not?"

"Yes, that is very much like my philosophy. I prefer to laugh, for there is much in the world to make one cry and laughing is so much more agreeable."

"Then by that standard, hope is far superior to despair."

"Without a doubt, sir. I shall be guided by you."

After exchanging a few more words, Mr. Whitmore departed, announcing his intention to inspect a tenant cottage to the north of the estate, leaving Elizabeth to her thoughts. A few moments later, another arrived to interrupt her solitude.

"Lizzy?" came Jane's voice through the cracked door.

Elizabeth looked up and smiled at her dearest sister. "Jane. Has Mama begun complaining of her situation again?"

It should not be supposed that Jane was not also fatigued with their mother's behavior, even as she possessed the most patient temperament of all the sisters. The severe look she directed at Elizabeth in response to her jest set Elizabeth to chuckling.

"You need not say it, Jane, for I know what you will say before you say it. And you are correct. Mama tries my patience, but I suppose we must all endure it with whatever fortitude we possess."

Mollified, Jane nodded. "In fact, I came to inform you that the Netherfield party has arrived for a morning visit."

Curious, Elizabeth regarded her sister with surprise. "That is remarkably civil of them, as we have only made their acquaintance last night." Elizabeth paused and grinned, adding: "Then again, perhaps it is not such a surprise, given the impression the eldest Bennet daughter made upon Colonel Fitzwilliam last night."

Jane turned a stern look of warning on Elizabeth. "Do not say such things, Lizzy! I should not wish to scare the gentleman away."

"Then you confess you like him very well."

"What is not to like?" asked Jane, a rhetorical aspect to her question. "Yes, I find I like Colonel Fitzwilliam very well, indeed. But I would remind you, Lizzy, that I have yet been in his company but once, and the sons of earls do not look to young ladies of my station with any interest out of the common way."

"I will agree with you about the first, Jane," said Elizabeth, rising and coming around the desk to put her hands on Jane's shoulders. "As to the second, we must wait and see. While I will own my acquaintance with Colonel Fitzwilliam is as brief as yours, I suspect he is not a man to pay much attention to societal position beyond that which every gentleman must consider."

Jane colored and said: "Perhaps you are correct, Lizzy. But I would not wish to raise my hopes too soon and without reason."

"In that, you are correct. Promise me, Jane, that you will give the gentleman a chance. Based on his interest from last night, I suspect there may be something there."

"I shall give the gentleman every opportunity, Lizzy."

"Excellent!"

"And what of you? Shall Mr. Darcy be the man who teaches you what it is to love?"

Jane unleashed her playful side so infrequently that Elizabeth was surprised when she did; now was one of those times. Noticing her sister's surprise and sudden annoyance, Jane giggled, though she soon stifled it, showing Elizabeth a demure front.

"Perhaps you should leave the teasing to me, Jane," said Elizabeth. "I am the expert, after all."

"You did speak to him for some time last night."

Elizabeth sighed. "Yes, and I found him agreeable and intelligent. There was nothing, however, that indicated any interest out of the common way. Furthermore, I do not have time at present to entertain any thought of a gentleman paying me any attention. The estate must take precedence, and I am focused on its improvement."

"Lizzy," said Jane, her voice slightly chiding, "in three months we may not even be in possession of the estate any longer. Should you not grasp any opportunity for happiness while it exists? These are the best years of your life, Lizzy, where you are young and vibrant. Do not waste them."

"If Mr. Darcy is a man to pay attention to a young woman of little dowry who manages an estate, I cannot imagine he would regard her any differently if she made her home in another place."

"No, I do not suppose he is," agreed Jane. "But as you and Charlotte have informed me many times, a man needs a little encouragement if his regard is to blossom beyond faint interest."

"That is true, Jane," said Elizabeth, embracing her sister. "Come then. Let us go and give Colonel Fitzwilliam a bit of a push. I dare say he will be unable to resist you within a seven day if we show him your qualities."

While Jane blushed, Elizabeth urged her sister from the room, ignoring the censorious look Jane shot toward her as she acquiesced. When they entered the sitting-room, it was to the sight of their guests, though their positions were not precisely comfortable. Lady Charity Fitzwilliam was seated with another young lady Elizabeth had never met near Elizabeth's youngest sisters, and as she might have expected, there was little in common between them, rendering their conversation stilted. Anne de Bourgh sat close to their mother, who appeared to be regaling her with tales of her troubles, while Colonel Fitzwilliam and Mr. Darcy appeared ill at ease. That was to be expected, she supposed, for they were the only gentlemen at Longbourn. The sight of Elizabeth entering the room with Jane, however, was enough to prompt their countenances to lighten.

"Miss Bennet, Miss Elizabeth," said Lady Charity, rising and drawing her young companion with her. Elizabeth did not misunderstand the action seemed calculated to relieve her from Kitty and Lydia's company. "It is good to see you returned. I had thought Miss Bennet meant to take the opportunity to absent herself from my reprobate of a brother."

"Perhaps she simply meant to escape from my miscreant sister," rejoined Colonel Fitzwilliam, his expression all laughter.

"Perhaps we should simply introduce my sister and dispense with the jests," said Mr. Darcy, standing at the same time.

Taking control of the situation, he did just that, presenting his sister, a Miss Georgiana Darcy, to Elizabeth's acquaintance. Elizabeth took in the girl's measure, noting how she stated her pleasure in a quiet voice, displaying her reticence to all. Within moments, Miss Darcy resumed her seat by Kitty and Lydia, to Elizabeth's surprise, while Mr. Darcy and Lady Charity sat next to Elizabeth herself. The colonel, who appeared disinclined to cede her company to anyone else, commandeered Jane's attention. It was no surprise when the conversation between Elizabeth and her companions consisted of accounts of their families, as those newly acquainted must be curious about such things.

"The Darcys are a small family at present," said Mr. Darcy, referencing himself and his sister. "We lost my mother twelve years ago and my father in the last five. My father was an only child, so we have no relations on his side nearer than a great uncle, a great aunt, and their families. With them, we are not at all close."

"Ah, but our family makes up for that lack," chimed in Colonel Fitzwilliam from where he was speaking with Jane. "As you have the close society of the family of an earl, what need have you to be close to those who are not even your equal in consequence?"

"Anthony!" scolded Lady Charity. "With such comments as this, our new friends will consider us insufferably proud!"

"Perhaps we should introduce them to Rachel. Then they will understand the true meaning of pride."

Laughing, Colonel Fitzwilliam turned his attention back on Jane, leaving Lady Charity shaking her head. "I hope you do not mistake his jests for earnest opinion, Miss Elizabeth. We Fitzwilliams are, in general, not a proud bunch, though Rachel, my sister, can claim the largest share of the affliction."

"Not at all," replied Elizabeth with a smile. "His jesting tone was marked." Then Elizabeth turned an arched brow on Mr. Darcy. "Is your cousin's assertion at least the truth?"

"We have long been intimate with our cousins," acknowledged Mr. Darcy. "We are also close to the de Bourghs of Kent, my Cousin Anne de Bourgh's family, though that family consists of only Anne and her mother." Mr. Darcy paused, shot a glance at his cousin who was still listening to Elizabeth's mother, her demeanor an exercise in patience. "Of course, anyone who has met Anne's mother will not soon forget her."

Elizabeth could not help the laugh that slipped from her mouth as she said: "But Miss de Bourgh is perfectly unassuming!"

Mr. Darcy and Lady Charity shared a look and a laugh, though it was Lady Charity who essayed to respond. "If you met her, you would understand. Lady Catherine is a force unto herself, for she is a woman of firm opinions and she does not suffer fools easily."

"No, she employs them," said Mr. Darcy.

This was too much for Lady Charity as she burst into laughter, drawing the attention of the rest of the room. To Elizabeth's mortification, her mother spoke up, entirely misconstruing what had taken place.

"Oh, Lizzy, I hope you are not carrying on in your impertinent way!"

"Not at all, madam," said Mr. Darcy, though to Elizabeth his expression was unreadable. "It was my jest that prompted my cousin's laughter."

"If anyone has the reputation for impertinence," added Miss de Bourgh, "it would be Charity. I doubt Miss Elizabeth could match her in that respect."

"And I own it without disguise," said Lady Charity.

Then she turned back to Mr. Darcy and fixed him with amusement. "That was not kind at all, Darcy."

"Maybe it was not. But can you dispute it?"

Lady Charity shook her head and turned back to Elizabeth. "As my cousin has so inelegantly stated, my aunt has a penchant for employing those who will not dare question her and will do anything she instructs them to do. Whether they are all fools, I cannot say."

"They are not all fools," drawled Mr. Darcy. "But she has a higher concentration of them at Rosings than anywhere else in the land."

Something about the name Rosings pricked Elizabeth's memory, but she could not remember where she heard the name. A moment later, she shook it off as irrelevant and focused again on her new friends.

"Then it is a small family, but a diverse one too."

"It is," said Lady Charity. "Of course, this does not encompass all those in society who are connected to us either by marriages, friendships, alliances, or whatever else. There are enough of those that we cannot go to an event in London without wading hip-deep in them."

"There are far more than I would wish," muttered Mr. Darcy, "and with most of them I could dispense."

The gentleman noted Elizabeth's look and colored. "I apologize, Miss Elizabeth, but I am not a man who is comfortable in society, and I cannot withstand poor behavior. It has always seemed to me that most of those who aspire to high society claim it only by virtue of their wealth or descent, and not through their behavior."

"Though I have little experience in London," said Elizabeth, "I have heard enough to agree with you. My late father, in particular, despised London and the pretension of those who inhabit it."

"I believe I would have gotten on famously with your father," murmured Mr. Darcy.

"What of you, Miss Elizabeth?" asked Lady Charity. "Have you relations aplenty hiding in the shadows?"

"We have few near relations," said Elizabeth with a laugh. "My mother has a brother in London and a sister in Meryton, an importer and the wife of the town's solicitor. On my father's side there is no one nearer than a cousin several times removed, the heir of the estate, should my mother give birth to another girl."

"Have you ever met this heir?" asked Lady Charity, curiosity coloring her tone.

"Once," said Elizabeth, "days after my father's passing. Mr. Collins came to Longbourn from Kent, where he is a parson. We found him disobliging and difficult to endure, and since he went away, he has continued to bombard us with letters accusing us of attempting to defraud him from his inheritance."

A queer look came over Mr. Darcy's face. "Your cousin is Mr. Collins? A parson in Kent? Do you know the name of his parish?"

"It is Hunsford, I believe," said Elizabeth, mystified as to his meaning.

"Well, this is surprising," said Mr. Darcy, exchanging a look with his cousin. Then he looked across the room and said: "Anne, might we borrow your company for a moment?"

Miss de Bourgh appeared eager to separate herself from Mrs. Bennet by this time, and Mary stepped into the breach, sitting with her mother and allowing her retreat. Mrs. Bennet watched, her manner, suggesting a hint of offense at Miss de Bourgh's abandonment. It was fortunate Mary spoke to her, for Elizabeth thought her mother was about to say something impolitic.

"Anne, is your mother's new parson a Mr. Collins?" asked Mr. Darcy when Miss de Bourgh joined them.

"He is," said Miss de Bourgh, her nose wrinkling in distaste. "He is an odder specimen than those with whom my mother usually surrounds herself."

Elizabeth released a surprised giggle, and Lady Charity ventured: "I told you, Miss Elizabeth."

"What does Mr. Collins have to do with Miss Elizabeth?" asked Miss de Bourgh, clearly curious.

"It seems Mr. Collins is Miss Elizabeth's cousin," said Mr. Darcy, "and heir to Longbourn. At least he is heir at present, though I suppose if your mother births a son, his position as heir will not change."

"No," replied Elizabeth. "His consternation concerning the property is that the entailment is to last only one more generation.

Should I have a brother and he grow to the age where he may inherit the estate, the entail will end."

"And this Mr. Collins has likely expected for many years now that he would inherit," said Mr. Darcy.

"Lydia is fifteen. I suspect my parents lost all hope of an heir nigh to a decade ago."

Miss de Bourgh regarded Elizabeth with gravity for a moment before she offered: "I have heard it said that Mr. Collins considers himself ill-used. It is my understanding that he has complained to my mother of it whenever he is in her company, though I avoid him for obvious reasons."

Diverted as she was by Miss de Bourgh's assertion, Elizabeth focused on the man's tales of betrayal. "Mr. Collins has not been treated unfairly, regardless of what he says. We had no notion my mother was with child until after my father's passing. The delay in Mr. Collins assuming his inheritance is nothing less than lawful."

"It was not my intention to suggest I suspect you of misbehavior, Miss Elizabeth," said Miss de Bourgh, reaching out and touching Elizabeth's hand. "Mr. Collins's claims have always struck me as the petulance of a child. What you have told me makes sense."

"There is little of sense in Mr. Collins," muttered Elizabeth.

"And now you understand my comment about my aunt finding fools with whom to surround herself," said Mr. Darcy. "Charity may laugh, but Mr. Collins is the latest in a long line of similar characters."

Mr. Darcy's words necessitated an explanation to Miss de Bourgh, who had not been present for the exchange, and provoked her to the same mirth displayed by Lady Charity. "It is very true! My mother is an intelligent woman herself, but she does like being infallible so much that she will suffer no one to question her!"

Again, they descended to mirth, this time joined by Colonel Fitzwilliam, who had been listening to their conversation. "I believe he arrived in Kent sometime after our visit in the spring, Darcy, so you would not have made his acquaintance."

"You have?" asked Mr. Darcy.

"Yes, I have," replied Colonel Fitzwilliam. "I passed through Kent this summer on business for the regiment and stayed a night in Rosings. You may consider old Chambers to be a ridiculous sort of specimen, but he is nothing compared to Mr. Collins."

"Then we have a previously unknown connection between us," said Mr. Darcy, turning back to Elizabeth with a smile. "Whether the connection is a good one I cannot say, for you do not appreciate Mr.

Collins, and we avoid my Aunt Catherine whenever we can."

Lady Charity and Colonel Fitzwilliam laughed at Mr. Darcy's characterization of their relation, while Miss de Bourgh swatted at him and exclaimed: "That is not a kind thing to say about my mother!"

"Do you dispute it?" asked Mr. Darcy, unperturbed by her displeasure.

"Well, perhaps not," said Miss de Bourgh after making a show of thinking on it. "But it is still unkind."

"I assure you, Miss de Bourgh," said Elizabeth, "I shall reserve judgment until I make your mother's acquaintance."

It occurred to Elizabeth after she said it that they may perceive her comment to be presumptuous, but her companions said nothing, their lively conversation continuing apace. The rest of the visit passed in this pleasant manner, and when the Netherfield party arose to depart, it was with expressions of regret and wishes to meet again soon. It also included a surprising request.

"Thank you, Miss Bennet, Miss Elizabeth, for your ready welcome and interesting conversation," said Lady Charity. "If I may, shall we not dispense with formalities between us? I should be happy to have you call me by my Christian name if you will afford me the same privilege."

Elizabeth was uncertain if referring to the daughter of an earl without the honorific before her name was proper, but Lady Charity asked with such earnestness she did not think they could refuse.

"Thank you, we would be honored," said Elizabeth for her sisters. "If we slip and use your title occasionally, you must forgive us."

Charity laughed and pressed Elizabeth's hands. "It is nothing more than a courtesy. For my true friends, I prefer to act like friends rather than adhere to stuffy rules of propriety."

It was Mrs. Bennet who summed up the thoughts of all after their visitors were gone. "What excellent people they are. I might never have expected it from those of their positions in society."

"I cannot agree more, Mama," said Elizabeth.

CHAPTER IV

Everyone in the neighborhood understood that Sir William Lucas was fond of society. Since his ascension to the ranks of the landed, the gentleman's parties had gained the status of infamy, both for the frequency with which he held them, but also for the sheer number of those invited to attend. As the Bennet family had been in mourning the past three months, it had been some time since they had experienced one. That was about to change, it seemed.

"My father's soiree is set for Thursday," said Charlotte when she visited that morning to inform them of it. "As you have all been absent for some time, I hope you will attend."

Sharing a glance with Jane—and not missing her mother listening close with obvious displeasure—Elizabeth turned back to their friend. "Of course, we shall attend, Charlotte. Your father's parties are always so interesting. We have missed them."

"Yes, we have missed them," said their mother, her tone sour. "And I shall continue to miss them, for I must still don black and waste away at Longbourn while you all make marry at Sir William's party."

"Oh, Mama," said Jane, standing and moving to her mother's side. "But you have an important duty, that of bearing the next heir of Longbourn. Even if you were not still in mourning for Papa, you would not wish to risk your health and that of the child."

"Why should I care?" grumbled Mrs. Bennet. "It is another girl child—I am certain of it!" Mrs. Bennet moaned and said: "Mr. Collins shall turn us out of Longbourn before your sister is even an hour old!"

"There, there, Mama," said Jane, taking her mother's hand and patting it to calm her. "I am certain you are worrying for nothing. You should consider boy's names, for I am certain your child will be the long-awaited heir."

Mrs. Bennet eyed her eldest, clearly not of a mind to give up her complaints. But Jane had a way with their mother, possessing a touch for soothing her none of her sisters could emulate. Within moments she had calmed Mrs. Bennet and induced her to speak quietly, or as quietly as Mrs. Bennet could ever speak. Grateful to her sister for her patience and ability to manage their mother, Elizabeth turned back to Charlotte.

"I see your mother still chafes under her restrictions," observed Charlotte.

"You have no idea," was Lydia's impatient response. "Mama is trying all our patience, for she persists in asserting we shall soon lose our home. It is most annoying!"

Elizabeth regarded her youngest sister, wondering at her. Lydia had always been the most like their mother, Mrs. Bennet her closest supporter, their heads often together in some matter or another. Elizabeth might have expected Lydia to return the favor. Then again, perhaps it was that likeness of character which made her unable to tolerate her mother's ill humors.

"Perhaps you should attempt to see matters from your mother's perspective," said Charlotte, her mild tone belying her reproof. "If your mother is cynical after so many disappointments, you can hardly blame her for it."

"I suppose," said Lydia, though most grudgingly. "I only wish Mama would be more like Lizzy. She never allows herself to be dispirited. Mama should take her likeness and try to remember all the good in our lives."

"I could not have said it better myself," said Charlotte, turning a grin on Elizabeth.

For her part, Elizabeth could not help but feel a little flattered. She had not known that Lydia felt that way about her, for the girl was eager to ignore her advice and prevent Elizabeth from ruining her fun, as she termed it.

"There are a few matters that will interest you about my father's party," said Charlotte, turning her attention back to the reason for her visit.

"Are there?" asked Lydia. "In my experience, they are always the same."

"Lydia," said Elizabeth, a warning note in her voice. This time the girl had gone too far. She seemed to realize it and fell silent, though she looked at Charlotte, expectation in her manner, contradicting her previous words.

"You must know of the company of militia that has arrived in the neighborhood?"

"We do," ventured Kitty. "But Lizzy and Jane have not yet let us associate with them."

"As is proper," said Charlotte, forestalling any comment Lydia was about to make; from her expression, she realized what their friend had done and desisted.

"As yet you are still in half mourning, Kitty," continued Charlotte with a kindly smile at both girls. "It would be improper for you to go running after the officers as some of the local girls do. Our neighbors would notice, and you may be subjected to the censure of those who esteemed your father.

"Regardless, tomorrow you shall make the acquaintance of the officers, for my father has issued a general invitation for their attendance."

"Oh, that is a fine thing, is it not, girls!" exclaimed Mrs. Bennet, who it seemed had been listening to their conversation. "You shall finally make their acquaintance. Why, I remember well when Colonel Brady's regiment wintered in Meryton when I was a girl! What fine fellows, what excellent, gentlemanly manners! I cannot but imagine these men will be the same!"

"Making their acquaintance is, of course, permitted," said Elizabeth, before her youngest sisters could break out into celebration at their good fortune. "But remember, girls, that we must observe decorum."

"You *are* determined to ruin our fun, Lizzy," grumbled Lydia. When Elizabeth directed a pointed look at her sister, she desisted. "We shall, of course, behave ourselves."

"Excellent!" said Elizabeth with a nod.

"What can you tell us of them?" asked Kitty, speaking with less exuberance than Elizabeth might have expected, regardless of her reproach.

"For that, you must speak to Maria," said Charlotte. "Of course, without you to accompany her, my father has restricted Maria's access to the officers, so she does not know as much of them as she might wish."

"But surely you can tell us something," said Lydia, appearing quite put out.

"I can," said Charlotte. "As I have no experience with soldiers, I have little with which to compare them. They seem like a pleasant lot to my eyes. There are handsome men among them, as well as those who are not so pleasing to look upon. There are tall and short, burly and diminutive, open and reticent, and friendly and standoffish men among them, I dare say."

Lydia regarded Charlotte, a faint hint of displeasure in her air. "With that, you have told us nothing. We might have inferred as much ourselves."

"As I noted," said Charlotte, unperturbed with Lydia's discontent, "I have not given them nearly as much notice as others. For the particulars, I believe you must wait to ask them yourselves."

"You said you have other matters that will interest us?" asked Elizabeth, having heard enough talk of the officers.

"Only one other, actually," replied Charlotte. "The other party new to the neighborhood has finally arrived. My father paid a visit to them and invited them to attend the evening, and they have accepted."

"The elusive Mr. Bingley and his party," said Elizabeth, understanding her friend's reference at once. "Were they not to have arrived in time for the assembly?"

"Or so they led us to believe," replied Charlotte. "Mr. Bingley arrived to take possession of the estate, and after a few days, he returned to London to escort his family here. Why they were delayed I cannot say, but they are here now. My father reports Mr. Bingley is eager to join society."

"That is good to hear," said Elizabeth. "As we have no one in residence to visit newcomers, we must rely on your good information, Charlotte. Can you tell us something of Mr. Bingley and his family?"

"Of his family, I know little," replied Charlotte, "save that he has two sisters, one of whom is married to a gentleman from the northern coast of Norfolk. Of Mr. Bingley himself, I know only a little more, for Papa, as you must understand, does not bring details of interest to a woman. Whether he is handsome or ill-favored, civil or cross, kind or surly I cannot say. Papa, however, informed us he thought Mr. Bingley enthusiastic, so I suppose I must grant him a good and open character."

"Until he proves otherwise," agreed Elizabeth. "On that day, we may abuse him as above his company, a man of pride and arrogance. Now, however, he must be everything agreeable."

"Oh, Lizzy," said Jane with a fond shake of her head. "How you do carry on! I am certain this Mr. Bingley must be everything amiable."

"I hope so, Jane," replied Elizabeth. "Avoiding the assembly as it seems he did, does not speak well of his general civility."

"There is no word of why he was not present, Lizzy," reminded Charlotte. "It is possible business in London delayed him."

"Yes, it is possible. I shall not convict the gentleman without learning more of him, but something of the matter speaks to other reasons for his unexpected absence."

Jane, Elizabeth knew, would continue to believe there were some extenuating circumstances, and Elizabeth could not dispute this. Elizabeth did not suspect the man of any incivility regardless of her words. How he and his party could be as agreeable as the Netherfield party, she could not imagine, though she kept this observation for herself.

"Thank you for this intelligence," said Elizabeth, turning back to Charlotte. "We are, of course, happy to attend and make the acquaintance of our new neighbors of Pulvis Lodge."

"And we are eager to have you return," said Charlotte, fixing Elizabeth with an eager smile. "It is unfortunate you will not play for us, for I wish to hear your performance again."

"And yours too, of course, Mary," added Charlotte with a smile at Elizabeth's younger sister.

"For my part, I shall not repine the loss," said Elizabeth, shaking her head at her friend's continued eagerness to induce Elizabeth to display whatever talents she possessed. "Finally, I have a reason to refuse your entreaties to perform."

"There is nothing specifically improper about playing for a company when you are still in half mourning," chided Charlotte.

"It is questionable enough that I have no compunction at all about refusing," returned Elizabeth.

Charlotte grinned and put her hands out in surrender. "Do not concern yourself, Lizzy, for I know better than to insist."

"Good," was Elizabeth's relieved reply.

The rest of the time Charlotte remained they spoke of inconsequential matters, those things of interest to friends of longstanding. When Charlotte rose to depart, she did so with smiles for all the Bennets, and a few words for Mrs. Bennet herself who, though still feeling peevish about her restraints, appreciated Charlotte's attention. Then Elizabeth led her friend from the room, intending to see her to the door.

"Lizzy," said Charlotte when they stepped out onto the stoop, "how *are* you truly? I hope you are not working yourself to exhaustion now that Longbourn is under your control."

"I am well, Charlotte," said Elizabeth, warmed by her friend's interest. "There is no need to concern yourself for me. The harvest is in and there is little to do on the estate, though I do still visit the tenants occasionally. I shall not overwork myself—you have my promise."

"That is good," replied Charlotte. "If you require any assistance at all, you know you may call on my father." Charlotte paused and grinned, saying: "Papa is not the most knowledgeable, not having been raised as a gentleman, but he has been the master of Lucas Lodge long enough that he can assist if required."

"Thank you, Charlotte," said Elizabeth. "But for the present, all is well. Mr. Whitmore has proven a godsend, for he handles everything that requires a man's touch. Why Papa did not employ a steward, I shall never know, for it would have allowed him to while away the hours in his room without neglecting the estate."

Charlotte peered at her for a moment, seeming to hear what Elizabeth had not said. "You are hard on your father, I think."

With a sigh, Elizabeth shot her friend a rueful smile. "No, I am not. I always knew my father was not the most diligent master, which was unfortunate. Papa would, indeed, have benefited from a steward, and I dare say the expense would have been more than made up in the extra income the estate generated."

"I cannot but imagine you are correct," said Charlotte. Her friend grasped her hand and squeezed once before excusing herself. "Thursday, then. I am quite anticipating it, my friend."

As Charlotte walked away from Longbourn down the drive toward her home in the distance, Elizabeth watched her go, reflecting that she was awaiting it as much as her friend. The Bennets had spent enough time at home. It would be a relief to once again be active in the neighborhood.

That very moment, a discussion was taking place at the aforementioned Pulvis Lodge. Miss Elizabeth's Bennet's concern for the characters of the residents at that estate was not misplaced, though her thought of Mr. Bingley's character being suspect was. Charles Bingley was a good man, one comfortable with any society and an eager to please attitude. His sister, unfortunately, was not cut from the same cloth, and she was in the habit of making her displeasure known when it was aroused.

"I cannot imagine why you would have accepted this invitation, Charles," declared she, fixing her brother with a stare of utmost disapproval.

"And I cannot understand why you believe I would demur."

The stare turned to a glare, indicating his sister's anger. As it was a state with which he was not unfamiliar and seemed to be more and more a part of her character as time passed, Bingley was unaffected by her show of severity.

"Because, Charles," said she, as if it were the most obvious thing in the world, "I am utterly certain there is no one in this neighborhood who is worth knowing. Why should we give them consequence when they are unworthy?"

"I am well acquainted with your opinion, Caroline," replied Bingley. "After you delayed our departure from London in a bid to prevent us from attending the assembly, your opinion has been clear to us all."

"Then, if you agree with me, why did you accept?"

"Your thoughts are laced with fallacy, Caroline. I do *not* agree with you. I do take issue with your stratagems, however. As I am now master of Pulvis Lodge for the moment, it is incumbent upon me to make a good impression on our neighbors. What they must think of me, after I accepted the invitation to the assembly and did not return in time, I cannot say, though I suspect it is not good."

"You should take my philosophy," said Caroline. "These people have no fashion, no sophistication, no consequence whatsoever. It will be a punishment to associate with them."

"It seems you have taken their likeness without the possibility for error, Caroline," said Hurst, the sardonic note in his voice typical, though perhaps a little more severe than was his wont. "You must tell me how you do it, for by my calculation, you have not made the acquaintance of even a single resident of this neighborhood, and yet you know them all intimately." Hurst turned a lazy eye on Bingley. "Are you certain your sister does not practice the occult arts? I know of no other way she would have gained this knowledge."

"I have no need of meeting them!" snapped Caroline. "Residents of neighborhoods such as this are all the same. Truly, Brother, I have no notion of why you have signed a lease in such an insignificant speck of a neighborhood as this. Why did you not search for an estate in a neighborhood peopled with those of more consequence? You know we must associate with those of the highest echelons of society if we are to ascend to their level."

Bingley shared a glance with his brother by marriage and refrained from shaking his head as he wished; Hurst had no such compunction.

"I accepted the lease on this estate," said Bingley for what seemed like the hundredth time, "because it was a good opportunity for me to learn and very near town, which as I recall, was one of *your* requirements. We were fortunate to get it on such excellent terms."

"As for the neighborhood, *dear Caroline*," said Hurst, his contempt for her equal to his sister's for him, "it is incumbent upon anyone who means to live in a neighborhood to have good relations with those around them. There is nothing worse than living next to a family with whom you cannot meet and associate with civility."

"*If* they were of any consequence, I might agree with you," said Caroline. "But they are not. We would do well to pack our trunks and return to London at once, for there is nothing for us here."

"Nothing except experience learning how to manage an estate," said Bingley, feeling fatigued with her continued harping. "And taking our first steps to become accepted as gentlefolk in our own right."

"Had you made any useful acquaintance at university, we would not be required to fend for ourselves. A patron of consequence would smooth our way in society."

"You appear to think such patrons line the boulevard of every street in London, Caroline," said Hurst.

"And I did make some useful acquaintances, Caroline," said Bingley. "But I understand, as it seems you do not, that most of society considers us to be *nouveau riche*. Purchasing an estate now will perhaps make my grandchildren acceptable. They will always regard me as being tainted by the stench of trade."

Caroline's nostrils flared at the reminder of the truth of their status, but before she could speak, Hurst interjected.

"It would be best if you remained silent, Caroline."

The proud young woman stared at her brother by marriage, neither giving an inch. At least Caroline was sensible enough to hold her tongue for the moment.

"These people will not prove so reprehensible as you believe. They are not so far below me in consequence that I may turn up my nose at them and act as if I am a lord. You, the daughter of a tradesman, decrying them as unsuitable is laughable."

"Oh, yes," said Caroline, contempt dripping from her tone. "And you are the height of sophistication in your own right. To those who frequent the bottoms of their cups by mid-day, you must be akin to a duke."

"Be silent, Caroline!" spat Hurst, now infuriated. "If you will recall, I am the only one of this company who is gentle by birth, so you had best remember your place!"

"Louisa could have done so much better than you!" Caroline returned venom for venom.

"I married Hurst because we have affection for each other, Caroline," said Louisa, who had heretofore remained silent. "As our brother reminded you, we cannot expect to marry into the highest of society. I have not forgotten that fact."

Caroline opened her mouth to retort, but Hurst stepped in before she could. "That is enough, Caroline. Your brother is the head of your family, and you will obey him."

"Thank you, Hurst," said Bingley, not wishing to allow his brother to endure the brunt of the argument. "I have accepted the invitation, and we shall attend. I shall not further insult our hosts by reneging on my promise. And before you suggest you will not attend, let me inform you now that you *will*. Do not test me in this, Sister, for you will not like the response."

With a sniff, Caroline rose and quit the room in high dudgeon, lightening the atmosphere with her welcome departure. Bingley sank back into the cushions of the sofa, massaging his temples. Unfortunately, Caroline-induced headaches were a common occurrence, for his sister could make a rain squall appear out of a bright summer day.

"Where did our parents go wrong?" asked Bingley plaintively of his elder sister. "Father never coveted such status as Caroline, and she was too young when Mother died, even if our mother had been inclined to impart such nonsense. Father was content knowing that I would purchase an estate. He did not wish me to marry a duke's daughter!"

"Caroline has always been that way, Charles," said Louisa. "I cannot say from where she learned this ability to look down her nose at all and sundry, but she has long had it, regardless."

"Well do I know it," replied Bingley. "She is becoming ever more ungovernable the closer we come to becoming landed, and her education at that seminary to which father sent her does her no good."

"Friendship with such ladies as Lady Diane Montrose do not a position in society make," said Hurst. "I am not of the first circles, as you know, and yet I have heard of the woman. Anyone of any sense at all despises her and all with whom she consorts."

"And yet Caroline loses no opportunity to drop her name."

Hurst shook his head and fixed Bingley with a stern look. "You are a good man, Bingley, and I am proud to call you my brother, regardless of your background. The one area in which you lack is your ability to control your sister. I shall not tolerate her stupidity any longer."

"Nor should you," replied Bingley.

"Then we understand each other. But know this, Bingley: if you do not take your sister in hand, I shall. Someone must inform her of her own insignificance. It would be best if it were you, but I shall not allow her to treat us in such an infamous manner."

"I shall do my best, Hurst," said Bingley.

Hurst nodded and rose, beckoned to his wife, and left the room, leaving Bingley alone with his thoughts. A sister such as Caroline could drive a man to drink. Bingley felt the need for a brandy at that moment, for of late, any interaction with his sister was certain to leave a foul taste in his mouth.

CHAPTER V

athering at Lucas Lodge was much the same as most events of local society. By now, being twenty years of age and having joined society—at her mother's insistence—at the age of fifteen, Elizabeth could predict how such evenings would progress. There would be flirting, of course, made worse by the company of militia in their midst, and there would be other conversations aplenty, most of which did not interest Elizabeth much. At least Charlotte would not require her to play, for that was another common occurrence at these events, particularly at Lucas Lodge where Charlotte often insisted on her performance.

The problem was, Elizabeth knew, the lack of interesting people in attendance; or perhaps it was the lack of new people to liven the events a little. The men were prone to speaking in droning voices of their estate concerns, the lack of eligible—or wealthy, Elizabeth interpreted—women nearby, and sundry concerns common to gentlemen. Now that Elizabeth shared some concerns of estate management, she could see how those topics might be of interest, but most of those men who managed their estates had no interest in debating such subjects with a mere woman. As for the women, the matrons would gossip and titter about this incident or that event, the young ladies would bemoan the lack of eligible—which Elizabeth interpreted to mean interested—men, speak of their latest bonnet or dress, and giggle at anything and everything.

For perhaps the first time in many months, even before her father's passing, Elizabeth looked forward to the evening, for there would be new faces aplenty. Most interesting was, of course, the Netherfield party, as they had become particular friends to those at Longbourn. The militia company now in the neighborhood, however, would also provide a greater circle of those with whom to converse, not that Elizabeth expected much of them, regardless of Kitty and Lydia's fevered imaginations of how dashing and handsome the officers would be.

In that last respect, Elizabeth was correct. If there was one word to describe the officers, that word would be "green." The Lieutenants, in particular, appeared to be young men, lacking life experience, and she found they had little to say of interest, though her youngest sisters were soon hanging off their every word. Of the older officers, there were a few who were interesting, and Colonel Forster appeared to be a good man, but as a whole, Elizabeth found she could cheerfully dispense with the officers' company altogether.

It was to be expected, then, that Elizabeth's perception of the evening changed once the first of the new residents in the neighborhood appeared. Charlotte, though an excellent friend, was engaged in assisting her mother as the hostess, and thus was not available to speak to Elizabeth. Elizabeth had no notion of why the Netherfield party was late that evening, but she was relieved when they finally arrived.

"Anne, Lady Charity," said Elizabeth as her friends approached her upon entering the room. "I had despaired of your arrival."

"And we were wild for your company," said Lady Charity. Then she fixed Elizabeth with a stern glare and added: "But I thought we had reached the point of referring to each other by our given names."

Elizabeth colored and looked down. "It is not every day we even meet the daughter of an earl in Meryton, let alone have her request to dispense with formality."

"Well," said Lady Charity, "if you do not wish to anger this daughter of an earl, you had best drop this 'lady' nonsense before I become displeased."

"There is that pride and arrogance Elizabeth might have expected," said Anne, laughing behind her hand.

"Only when a woman I consider a friend refuses to treat me as one," said Charity with a wink at Elizabeth.

"Very well," said Elizabeth with a smile. "But should one of my neighbors remark concerning my impertinence in addressing you so familiarly, I shall leave the explanation to you."

"Oh, they would never dare question the daughter of an earl, so I believe you will be quite safe."

Anne and Charity exchanged a look, then both looked at Elizabeth, and none could hold their laughter any longer. Elizabeth had the presence of mind to check her mirth to avoid appearing ill-mannered, but they still drew looks from around the room. Most of those watching them, Elizabeth thought, were interested to see her in such good spirits after the last months. But there were a few who looked on with envy.

"I declare," said Charity after their laughter had run its course, "if anyone overheard us, I must now be the most insufferably haughty woman who has ever graced this neighborhood!"

"On the contrary," said Elizabeth, "I should say any damage to your reputation is now repaired since you have deigned to laugh with one of the local ladies."

"Ah, that is well then." Charity grasped Elizabeth's hands and said: "I truly do enjoy your company, Elizabeth. It has been some time since I met a lady anywhere close to your position in society who would dare speak to me in such a familiar way. I hope we shall become the best of friends, for I feel we are already on our way."

"And I feel the same," said Anne. The woman grinned and added: "Though my character is not so open as both of yours, I feel capable of anything when I am in your company."

"As long as you wish me for a friend, I am willing."

"Then of what shall we speak?"

They ended spending some time together, their conversation animated as if they had been friends for months instead of days. Elizabeth had not much experience with those of higher society, but if they were all as Anne and Charity, her father's words of contempt for society would have been proven false. Mr. Darcy, Elizabeth noted, had been waylaid by Sir William, who kept him nearby longer than he could ever wish. Though Colonel Fitzwilliam had been with him for a few moments, he took himself to Jane's side and remained there for a long time after. Elizabeth was not the only one to notice his position.

"Have you ever seen Anthony pay so much attention to a woman, Charity?" asked Anne.

"Not at all," replied Charity. "In fact, Anthony has been accused of frivolous behavior to many ladies."

This account would have alarmed Elizabeth, had it not been for Charity's fond smile in her brother's direction. "He is eager to be pleased by all he meets?"

Charity smiled and shook her head. "While I have seen many who can be accused of that, Anthony possesses such happy manners that he is incapable of refraining from his attentions to all and sundry." Charity paused and glanced at her cousin. "Quite unlike Darcy, to be certain, who is often so taciturn that he gives offense without trying."

"But Mr. Darcy has been nothing but civil since he came here!" protested Elizabeth.

"Yes, he has been open and engaging to an astonishing degree," agreed Anne. "He must not feel threatened here, for that is the surest way to induce him to incivility."

While Elizabeth acknowledged her friends knew their cousin better than she, she had a difficult time imagining Mr. Darcy as giving offense wherever he went. But it would be best to change the subject.

"And what of Georgiana?" asked she. The girl was near Kitty and Lydia, who were in close conference with Maria Lucas, and if she was not speaking as much as they, it appeared she was following along closely.

"Georgiana is only shy," said Anne. "My mother intimidates her so much she becomes as quiet as a mouse! I think your sisters are good for her, for I cannot call them timid by any stretch."

"That is quite true," said Elizabeth.

Then her eyes found Colonel Fitzwilliam and Jane again, and she considered the situation for some moments. Elizabeth could not accuse the colonel of improper behavior. Then again, if he continued in this manner, Elizabeth knew rumors would begin.

"Perhaps it is yet early to consider such things," said Elizabeth, speaking carefully to avoid giving offense, "but Colonel Fitzwilliam is paying Jane almost exclusive attention."

"Aye, he is at that," said Charity. "I like Jane very well. Should he pay his addresses to her, I should be happy to welcome her as a sister."

"And I as a cousin," said Anne.

Elizabeth regarded them with some surprise; neither overlooked her reaction.

"Do you disagree, Elizabeth?" asked Charity, fixing her with a sly look. "Is even the son of an earl unworthy of your angelic sister?"

"Not at all!" protested Elizabeth. "I believe Jane welcomes his presence, though I am certain no thought of . . . anything deeper has yet crossed her mind. Jane, you see, has a natural modesty which leads her to demur and undervalue her appeal. I dare say I am aware of a gentleman's interest in her long before she is herself."

Anne and Charity both laughed at this portrayal of Jane. "Yes, I can imagine that of Jane. Modesty is a trait to be prized in a woman, for there are far too many who are assured of their charms and many more who overestimate what they possess."

"And yet," said Elizabeth, turning the conversation back to her original thoughts, "I am uncertain what should happen if Colonel Fitzwilliam were to turn his attention on her with an eye toward more than friendship." At Charity's questioning look, Elizabeth added: "We are gentlefolk, but we are in no way prominent. Should we retain possession of the estate, I hope to augment my sisters' dowries, but they shall not be vast fortunes. And of connections, we have none of any consequence."

"Do you perhaps refer to the reaction of our family to Anthony's choice?" asked Anne.

"If he should make such a choice," replied Elizabeth.

The two women shared a glance, but it was Charity who spoke. "Of that, you should not concern yourself, Elizabeth. Anthony is his own man and is accustomed to doing as he wishes. It is true he was not independent for many years until he inherited a fortune from a distant relation, but he defied my parents for many years, insisting he wished to make his own way in the world. As you are aware, he made his way in the army, though Father wished him to take a safer path."

"Then your father will not protest?" asked Elizabeth.

"My father passed on five years ago," said Charity gently. "My mother three years after that."

"I apologize for speaking so," said Elizabeth, worried she had offended.

"Not at all," said Charity, to Anne's agreeing nod. "You could have had no way to know of my father's passing, as we have never raised the subject."

"Truly, do not concern yourself, Elizabeth," said Anne. "Your bereavement is much more recent than Charity's or mine."

"Your father has also passed on?"

"More than fifteen years ago. My father left this life preceding even Lady Anne Darcy."

"And my brother will not protest," said Charity. "James is a good man, even as he is Father's eldest and now holds the earldom. He has a great sense of his position in society, yet he is not an arrogant man. James and Anthony have always been close; should Anthony decide he wishes to make your sister an offer, I have no doubt James will be the first to congratulate and wish my brother joy."

"That is well then." Elizabeth paused and gave her companions a rueful smile. "I would not have you think I am boasting, but I think Jane is worthy of any man. I shall expect nothing from Colonel Fitzwilliam, but I hope he sees what an excellent woman she is."

"He already has, Elizabeth," said Charity. "He could hardly have missed it."

There was a bit of a commotion at the door and four people stepped into the room, led by the housekeeper. Elizabeth and her companions were a little too far away from the door to hear the housekeeper announce them, but it was obvious this was the long-awaited Bingley party.

"It seems the Bingleys have finally made an appearance."

Charity glanced at her, curious. "Bingley? Anne, did Darcy not have an acquaintance by that name?"

"A slight acquaintance, as I recall," said Anne. "The Bingley name is not unknown in town, but I have never met them. Some speak of them, and not all their words are flattering."

Eyes widened in recognition, Charity said: "Yes, I remember now. I believe, Elizabeth, the coming spectacle should satisfy even your sense of the absurd."

Elizabeth glanced at her friend askance, but Charity offered nothing further. Thus, Elizabeth turned her attention to the newcomers.

At that moment, Caroline Bingley wished to be anywhere else in the world. There were few things she could abide less than a company of provincial nobodies, and this society was full to the brim of them. Less than a minute in the room informed Caroline there was no one of any consequence in the room, no one with whom she could speak without it becoming the severest punishment.

Not for the first time, Caroline cursed her brother for bringing them to this backward neighborhood, peopled with those Caroline could not tolerate. How he could have found the most uncouth location in the kingdom, she could not understand, but he had outdone himself.

"You had best wipe that sneer off your face, Caroline."

Angry, Caroline glared at her drunkard of a brother, noting his stern glare which was rendered less than effective by his ample paunch and pudgy face. How she detested him! Would that Louisa had made a better marriage than the one she agreed to with this poor excuse for a gentleman! Had she done her duty, Caroline would have found it easier to capture a husband of the highest circles.

"Your brother needs to have the goodwill of these people," continued Hurst when she did not speak. "The way you are looking at them all, no one can fail to understand your feelings."

"I am well aware of how to present myself before others," snapped Caroline.

"Then I suggest you put this vaunted knowledge to use," rejoined Hurst. "Do not ruin this for him, Caroline. I do not suppose Bingley will settle here, but he has the estate for the next twelvemonth; you will make it difficult for him to be accepted if you insist on looking down on all and sundry."

With a sniff, Caroline looked away, eager to end this conversation with the objectionable man. For a few moments, Caroline looked about the room, trying to find an out of the way corner in which she could hide, and failing that, the most unobjectionable person in attendance with whom she could tolerate a few moments of conversation.

That was when she noted her brother approaching a tall man and exclaiming something akin to surprise. As he spoke, Caroline frowned and gazed at the gentleman, noting his erect bearing, his finely tailored suit, and his handsome countenance. Then she noticed near to him was another man even taller, fair of hair and face whereas the first man was dark. Beside him was a young woman a step above the rest of them, though she still appeared provincial and unsophisticated.

And then Caroline knew that somehow, her prayers had been answered, for these two men, though she could not know why they were there of all places, were not country bumpkins like the rest. Perhaps there was someone here worth knowing after all.

"Darcy?" asked Bingley, shocked at meeting an acquaintance in this of all places.

"Bingley," was Darcy's even reply, the man's inscrutable countenance betraying nothing. "I am surprised, for I did not think to see you here."

"Nor did I think to see you," replied Bingley, gaining his bearings. "I have recently taken the lease at Pulvis Lodge." Bingley paused and gave his acquaintance a shrug. "Perhaps I mentioned I wished to purchase an estate, for it was a particular wish of my father that I raise the family to the ranks of the landed."

"Yes, I believe I remember you mentioning such a thing."

Darcy paused, seeming to consider him, possibly wondering why it had taken Bingley so long to take the step. For Bingley's part, he felt a hint of embarrassment steal over him, for he had often heard it said he was too unserious. His father's admonitions, however, remained with him, and while perhaps he had delayed, Bingley was now determined to do his father proud.

"Then I hope you find success," said Darcy at length, eschewing whatever other thoughts passed through his mind.

"Excuse me," said Bingley, "but I am curious as to your presence. Your home is in Derbyshire, as I recall."

"It is," confirmed Darcy. "Lately, my cousin, Colonel Fitzwilliam, received an inheritance from a relation. He resigned his commission and now seeks to purchase an estate himself. We are currently staying at Netherfield Park."

"Ah," said Bingley, nodding his understanding. "I had heard there was another estate to lease in the neighborhood, but by the time I inquired after it, another had already taken the lease."

After that the conversation became stilted. Darcy was a man of society, one sought after in London, well-known to those of a certain level. Bingley had made his acquaintance in university; Darcy had been attending his last year when Bingley began his first. For a time, Bingley had thought a friendship might spring up between them, but nothing ever came of it. Bingley had not seen Darcy since a chance encounter two seasons before.

At length, Darcy excused himself and Sir William Lucas took his place, introducing Bingley to the principal people in the room. Hurst and Louisa came along, Hurst appearing bored and looking for the refreshment table and Louisa with a sense of ennui hanging about her. Caroline was her usual self, though Bingley noted her regarding him with intense interest. The only people in the room to whom Sir William did not introduce them were Colonel Fitzwilliam and a trio of ladies who appeared higher in society than the rest of the room. Bingley understood at once—these people, by precedence, would need to initiate any acquaintances with the Bingleys and Hursts.

After a time, Caroline cornered him, her face alight with an intensity which only shone when she was scheming to better her position in society. Had Bingley been a less genial man, he might have forestalled her with a sharp comment, taking himself to another part of the room. He was still rather annoyed with her, not only for delaying their arrival at Pulvis Lodge but also for her stratagem that evening, ensuring they were, in her words, "fashionably late." Caroline's bloated sense of self-worth did not allow her to see that unknown as they were, being late would be an insult rather than fashionable.

"Charles," bleated she, her tone harsh and demanding, causing a pounding behind Bingley's eyes with only one word. "I saw you speaking to that tall gentleman. Are you acquainted with him?"

Bingley had no desire to unleash Caroline on Darcy, given his aloof manner and lack of interest in speaking. There was little he could do to put her off, however, so he essayed to respond in a manner which would cool her fervor.

"Yes, Caroline, though it is a slight acquaintance."

Eyes blazing, Caroline tapped her foot with impatience, then demanding: "Well, who is he? And who are those others with him? They appear to be very high in society, though I cannot imagine how such people would be here, of all places."

Nearby, a woman of about middle age—one of the ladies to whom they had been introduced, though Bingley could not remember her name—huffed and glared, then took herself to another part of the room. It was all Bingley could do not to groan. Clearly, she had overheard Caroline's imperious words and would now share them with the rest of the room.

"Keep your voice down, Caroline!" hissed Bingley. "Do you wish to turn the entire room against us?"

"I care nothing for these people," spat she, though she had the sense to keep her voice low.

"I do," replied Bingley, giving her a quelling glare. "If you do not mean to treat my neighbors with kindness, I should send you to our family in the north."

Caroline huffed again and said: "Who are these people, Charles?"

Defeated, Bingley sighed. "Darcy possesses an estate in Derbyshire, Caroline, an exceptional property, from what I understand. The other man is Colonel Fitzwilliam, though I am not acquainted with him. It is my understanding he is the brother of James Fitzwilliam, the Earl of Matlock."

Caroline goggled at him. "The brother of an earl is in the room?"

"I believe so. As for the ladies, I am not acquainted with them, though I suspect they are all related. The youngest I believe, based on the resemblance, is Darcy's sister. Who the other two ladies are I cannot conjecture, though I know Colonel Fitzwilliam has at least two sisters. Whether they are sisters or other relations, I cannot say."

A most unpleasant gleam shone in Caroline's eyes, one he had seen before; it spoke of avarice, zeal to place herself in the upper echelons of society, determination to suffer nothing to stand in her way. If it would not create a spectacle, Bingley might have grasped her arm and escorted her from the room, taken her back to Pulvis Lodge, and locked her in her chambers until he could make her see sense.

"You must introduce me," said she, determination in her eager demand.

"No, Caroline, I shall not." When she tried to protest, Bingley spoke again. "You know it is not done. As they are the higher in society, it is their prerogative to determine whether they wish to know us—not the reverse. I do not know if you could see it, but Darcy only tolerates my acquaintance. Do not presume to suppose they wish to know you. They are good people, so I suspect they will request an introduction at some time or another, but they must make the first move.

"Now come, there are many others in the room who are worthy of knowing."

Guiding Caroline, he put her in Louisa's care, hopeful she would not embarrass them all that evening. It was, perhaps, a vain hope, but Bingley thought his sister was not so gone from an understanding of how society worked to do anything foolish. If nothing else, her social ambitions would keep her in check. Besides, there were other, more pleasant subjects on which to think. There were good people here, and Bingley intended to come to know them better.

Unfortunately for Bingley's peace of mind, his sister was not as prudent as he might have wished. Elizabeth could not know his thoughts, but she knew her own. Witness as she was to Mr. Darcy's brief words with Mr. Bingley, she wondered about the connection between them. It was fortunate for Elizabeth's sense of curiosity that the gentleman himself joined them a few moments earlier and explained it.

"So you would not call him a friend?" asked Charity when Mr. Darcy had made his explanations.

"Our acquaintance is too slight," said Mr. Darcy. "Bingley is possessed of a happy disposition, but I have always thought him frivolous."

"It is interesting to hear that," said Charity, "given you number among your closest friends my brother."

Mr. Darcy chuckled and shook his head. "Your brother is pleasant to all he meets, but I should not call him frivolous. His years in the army put that charge to rest."

"Perhaps. But he often gives that impression."

Thereafter the friends drifted apart, though they came back together often. Elizabeth, though she enjoyed their company, was pleased they made an effort to be known to others in the room, for it showed their excellent natures to all. Of more immediate concern, she did not wish to gain the reputation of wishing to keep their company to herself.

It did not escape Elizabeth's attention when Miss Bingley took her brother aside, her manner demanding and eager. The glances she directed, not only at Mr. Darcy and Colonel Fitzwilliam but at their three relations, spoke to her eagerness to know them. This was a woman who gave all the appearance of a social climber, one her new friends would find difficult to endure. Elizabeth shook her head and put Miss Bingley from her mind.

Endeavor to avoid Miss Bingley she did, but the woman soon intruded on her notice. After speaking with her brother, Miss Bingley stood with her sister for some time, but while the elder attempted to be agreeable to the company, the younger said no more than two words to anyone, and soon gossip was winging through the room concerning something disparaging she had said about the neighborhood. Elizabeth shook her head—while she was willing to allow the woman her opinion, to state it where another might hear was crass. That she had said it where Mrs. Long, an eager gossip, could overhear was unfortunate.

Later, Elizabeth came together again with Anne and Charity, this time in Georgiana's company. The ladies stood and talked for some time, and as Elizabeth gave her friends her attention, she also noted Miss Bingley watching them, eagerness and avidity in her countenance in equal measure. Then determination seemed to settle over her and she left her sister's side, approaching Elizabeth herself. It was unfortunate, Elizabeth reflected, that Sir William had introduced them, for she could see Miss Bingley's purpose the moment she moved and would have preferred not to speak to her.

"Miss Eliza Bennet," said she when she came close. "How interesting this event has been tonight. Do you live nearby?"

"Longbourn is the next estate to the west, Miss Bingley," said Elizabeth. "We have long been friends with the Lucas family."

"That is fortunate for you," replied the woman, her glances in the other ladies' direction revealing she wished to speak to them but could not as she had not yet been introduced. "I believe I have heard something of Longbourn. Is it a large estate?"

"As large as any in the neighborhood, other than Netherfield Park.

It has been in my family for generations."

"I see." Miss Bingley paused and appeared to be thinking of how to approach the introduction she meant to provoke. "And you have five sisters?"

"I do not," replied Elizabeth, by now amused with this woman's attempts at making small talk. "At present, I have four sisters, and one more sibling due to arrive in the next two or three months."

That seemed to catch the woman by surprise. "Your mother is with child. At her age?"

"Yes, though it seems to me, you can have no more than an imprecise notion of my mother's age. We are anticipating the addition of the newest member of our family eagerly."

The woman did not appear to know what to say to that. Her eyes darted between Elizabeth, Charity, and Anne for a few moments, but Elizabeth, who was now well acquainted with them, understood from their posture and veiled amusement they were enjoying the show and would not request an introduction that evening.

Miss Bingley attempted to make small talk some few more moments before she appeared to become frustrated and excused herself. Returning to her sister's side, she stood there for the rest of the evening, her glares at Elizabeth suggesting she thought her to blame. Elizabeth shook her head and turned back to her friends.

"She was . . . eager, was she not?" ventured Georgiana, who joined them as Miss Bingley left.

"Aye, that she was," said Anne.

Charity huffed with annoyance. "Even after so brief an exposure, I believe I can say that Miss Caroline Bingley is among the foremost fortune hunters in England. Did you not see how she wished for an introduction? Had she attained one, I have little doubt she would have attempted to push Elizabeth away in favor of ingratiating herself with us."

"That is why I did not ask for an introduction," said Anne. "I suppose at some point it will be unavoidable."

"Indeed, it will," said Charity. "Our silence bordered on rudeness as it was. But I will not have her pushing my dear friend aside."

"You need not concern yourself for me, Charity," said Elizabeth. "I can handle Miss Bingley."

"Yes, Elizabeth," said Charity, fondness coloring her voice. "But you should not have to endure her. For tonight, at least, I hope you have that reprieve."

Charity was correct; for the rest of the evening, Miss Bingley did not approach them. Elizabeth could not help but think she would be a disobliging neighbor. It was unfortunate, for Mr. Bingley appeared to be everything gentlemanly and civil.

CHAPTER VI

M atters of the estate beckoned the following morning, prompting Elizabeth from the house in the company of Mr. Whitmore. Longbourn was not a large estate, the number of tenants few, and as such, they tended to take great care to ensure whatever tenants they had were happy. Or that had been Elizabeth's policy since she had been old enough to understand the importance of tenants to a well-run estate. Her father, though he had always done what was necessary to ensure everything was maintained, took little thought for their happiness, allowing Elizabeth and Jane to take over those responsibilities. Mrs. Bennet, unfortunately, had not been reared a gentlewoman and had little interest in such issues.

Such behavior was, in part, the reason for the issue they must address today. As her father had paid little attention to the estate, the tenants had grown accustomed to fending for themselves, and it had led to some friction between them. In particular, on the northeastern edge of the estate, lived a troublesome man who had been there longer than any other tenant, his lease inherited from his father, who had inherited it from his. It was fortunate, to Elizabeth's way of thinking, the man had no children and would not hold the land much longer, for he was difficult and fractious. Elizabeth had considered relieving him of the land he farmed and moving him to a pensioner's cottage. It might be necessary to do it sooner rather than later.

"How do you wish to approach Mr. Bates, Miss Bennet?"

Pulled from her thoughts, Elizabeth turned to Mr. Whitmore, who rode beside her. "Directness is the key with Mr. Bates. It is unfortunate my father did not concern himself much with the tenants, for Mr. Bates now has the impression he can do as he will."

Mr. Whitmore considered her words. "Do you wish me to take on the burden of speaking with him?"

Elizabeth considered it for a moment. "No, I think it best I deal with him, for he must become accustomed to me as the mistress of the estate. If you present a firm demeanor, inform him by your posture that you will enforce my decisions, I hope that will be enough to prompt him to back down."

"So I must keep my own counsel and look menacing?"

Laughing at his words, Elizabeth nodded. "Yes, that may be for the best. If you were taller and more imposing, it would be better. But I suppose we must make do with what we have."

"If you wish for taller and more imposing . . ."

Elizabeth followed Mr. Whitmore's pointed hand to where two gentlemen were riding just on the other side of the border with Netherfield, where the path intersected with one leading onto the adjacent property. When Mr. Darcy waved at her, Elizabeth returned the gesture and urged her horse forward, pulling close to the gentlemen after a few moments.

"Miss Bennet," said Colonel Fitzwilliam, showing her an irrepressible grin. "How are you this fine day?"

"Very well, Colonel Fitzwilliam," said Elizabeth, acknowledging Mr. Darcy's quieter greeting at the same time. "I will own I had no notion of seeing you here this morning."

"There was a problem on the estate this morning," said Colonel Fitzwilliam. "The tenant in question informed us there is a man on Longbourn's lands in the habit of driving his cattle wherever he likes without concern for the other man's lands."

Elizabeth groaned and shook her head. "It appears we are on the same mission, gentlemen, though I had no notion Mr. Bates was encroaching on Netherfield's lands too. Usually, he is content with bedeviling his fellow tenants of Longbourn."

The gentlemen shared a glance. "This man, he has often been a problem?"

"Since long before I can remember," said Elizabeth.

"Then perhaps we should join you, Miss Elizabeth. Not only would it be a good opportunity for my cousin to gain experience, but it sounds like the support might be required."

Elizabeth laughed and nodded. "Mr. Whitmore and I were just speaking of how it would be useful if he were taller and more imposing. You gentlemen may fill that role admirably."

"Then that is what we shall do!" exclaimed Colonel Fitzwilliam with a grin. "I have extensive experience, I assure you, for I served many years in the army."

"We shall put your skills to good use."

Turning, the foursome made their way down the path on Longbourn's side of the fence, heading steadily north. As they rode, Elizabeth looked about with a hint of melancholy welling up within her. This was a path she traveled when she had been a girl, unacquainted with the cares of estate management. If one followed it long enough, it led to Oakham Mount, a prominence two miles from Longbourn, a place she had visited when feeling particularly energetic or wished for utter solitude. A pang of longing for those carefree times entered her heart, though she shook off the feeling at once, knowing she could not afford it.

"Are you acquainted with dealing with this man, Miss Bennet?" asked Mr. Darcy, drawing Elizabeth from her thoughts. "Have you determined a way of approaching him?"

"Mr. Bates is a man without a family of his own," said Elizabeth, "thus I have had little congress with him. This is the first time I will be speaking with him since Longbourn's management fell to me.

"As for how to approach him, I had nothing more in mind than to speak to him and admonish him to respect the tenants surrounding him, Mr. Whitmore providing firm support." Elizabeth paused and considered her previous thoughts, venturing: "I had thought it may be best to persuade him to retire and set him up in a pensioner's cottage, for he is not a young man."

"That may be for the best," said Mr. Darcy. "How do you suppose he would take such a suggestion?"

Elizabeth shrugged. "Likely with the same displeasure he displays when confronted by anything not to his liking. He may very well think he will remain long after we mere mortals are gone."

With a chuckle, Mr. Darcy shook his head. "Then Fitzwilliam and I shall provide that stern support you require, but we shall leave the possibility of pensioning him to you to discuss with him at another time."

With a grateful nod, Elizabeth turned her attention to Mr. Bates's house, rapidly approaching in the distance. As October was nearing its midpoint, most of the harvest was already in, leaving the tenants to prepare for next year's planting. The winter, Elizabeth knew, would involve storing seeds, repairing tools and making certain everything was in order, inspecting fences and cottages, all tasks that could determine a family's comfort and solvency in the future. Mr. Bates was the same as any other, though he had no one else for whom to provide. That he kept only a tiny plot and was responsible for the herd of cattle he managed meant his tasks would be slightly different, though the principle was the same.

Much as Elizabeth might have expected, they found him seated near the front door of his cottage, a collection of tools scattered about. The man looked up as they approached and scowled, spitting on the ground as he rose to greet them. He was a stocky man, broad of shoulder, and barrel-chested, his hair steel gray, his face weathered and beaten, like a wall torn down by the elements after years of exposure. An old scar decorated the left side of his face, from ear to chin, giving him a sinister look. Elizabeth did not know, but were she to guess, she thought he was about five and fifty years of age, the work he did on the farm both benefiting his fitness level and beating him down by its hard nature. When she had been a girl, Elizabeth had been afraid of him; as an adult, she was feeling nothing but vexation at his continued fractious ways. From a large barn beyond, Elizabeth could hear the lowing of the cattle, several of which wandered a large paddock in front of the building.

"Miss Bennet," rumbled the man, his voice low and gravely. "I suppose Johnson complained about me cattle again?"

"Mr. Bates," said Elizabeth, dismounting and facing the man. "I am certain you know Mr. Whitmore, Longbourn's steward. These gentlemen are Colonel Fitzwilliam and Mr. Darcy, both of Netherfield Park."

The man eyed the two gentlemen, a hint of respect in his manner, likely from the fact that both were physically tall and intimidating men. Underneath the respect, however, Elizabeth sensed an annoyance, likely because he understood what their presence meant.

"I suppose you are here to protest too," grumbled Mr. Bates. She thought he might spit again, but he seemed to understand they would not appreciate it and refrained.

"There has been some mention of the herd straying from where they should graze," said Elizabeth, keeping her tone even. "Yes, Mr.

Johnson has said there was some damage to his fields, though he noted the harvest was already in. As for Netherfield's lands, there seems to have been some problem there too."

The man grunted. "There is a section of fence knocked loose. The cattle escaped through it before I knew. Had a devil of a time corralling them."

"A section of fence is loose?" asked Colonel Fitzwilliam. "Darcy and I inspected the fences after we came and there were no issues we could find."

"Then it happened since you looked," snapped Mr. Bates. "Or maybe you didn't inspect it well enough."

Mr. Darcy exchanged a look with his cousin, but both seemed to decide it was better to remain silent for the moment. Seeming to feel his victory, Mr. Bates turned back to Elizabeth.

"Please, Mr. Bates, keep the cattle where they belong. This time the fields were empty, but should they escape before the harvest is in, they may affect the profitability of the estate."

"They don't cause no trouble," complained the man. "I have lived on this estate all me life and had no trouble. Your father never took issue with me management of the herd."

"That is because my father could not be bothered to deal with matters such as this," snapped Elizabeth. "This is not negotiable, Mr. Bates. I have the management of Longbourn for the moment, and I intend to see it become more profitable. Please keep the cattle under control, and there will be no problems."

Mr. Bates's eyes narrowed, and his stance became more belligerent, but before he could speak, Mr. Darcy stepped forward. "You are a tenant; she is the mistress of the estate. You would do well to do as she has asked you, for if you do not, Miss Bennet has the power to ensure you must leave this farm."

"I have a lease!"

"And she can revoke it if need be," said Mr. Darcy, his tone implacable. "I also possess an estate, Mr. Bates, and I understand how these things are done. Tenants who cannot get along with their neighbors affect the entire estate. The days when Mr. Bennet would ignore your antics are over—Miss Bennet is more active in the stewardship of her family's lands. I suggest you behave yourself."

"From what I hear," sneered the man, "if Mrs. Bennet don't produce a son, they won't possess nothing."

"Until then," said Darcy, "she is your mistress. It would be the work of a moment to have another family replace you by the spring."

Mr. Bates watched Mr. Darcy, sizing him up, unless Elizabeth missed her guess. At length, he grunted and turned away.

"There's no need for threats. I will watch the herd."

"Excellent, Mr. Bates," said Elizabeth. "Longbourn appreciates your efforts in this matter. Is there anything else you require?"

"Nothing," was the man's terse answer. "I have all I need."

"Then we shall not detain you any longer."

Elizabeth nodded to the man, who did not deign to respond, and turned to mount her horse. Darcy and Fitzwilliam followed suit, and soon they were guiding their horses back toward the south.

"It seems I must thank you, gentlemen," said Elizabeth when they had attained enough distance from Mr. Bates that he would not hear them. "If not for your support, I suspect it would have been much more difficult to gain his agreement."

"It is no trouble, Miss Bennet," said Colonel Fitzwilliam. "The matter concerns me, after all."

"When dealing with men such as Mr. Bates," added Mr. Darcy, "it is best to be unyielding. I suspect the man would pounce at any sign of hesitation or lack of resolve."

"That is what I thought," agreed Elizabeth. "I shall remember that for the future."

Mr. Darcy regarded her for a moment, considering, and when he spoke, it was concerning a subject Elizabeth might have preferred not to address.

"What he said of your father—did he allow Mr. Bates to have his way?"

Sighing, Elizabeth fixed the gentleman with a rueful gaze. "My father had many sterling qualities, Mr. Darcy. Unfortunately, one of those qualities was not an affinity for the management of his lands. My father loved nothing more than his bookroom, where he could retreat from the concerns of six women, for he felt quite outnumbered by his wife and daughters. Rarely did he stir himself to deal with estate matters above that required to keep the enterprise solvent."

"If you will pardon my saying it, Miss Bennet," said Colonel Fitzwilliam, "that was rather short-sighted on his part."

"Well do I know it, Colonel Fitzwilliam," replied Elizabeth. "But my father's heir is the son of a man to whom he had not spoken for many years, and as his family would not inherit the property, he did not do as he ought on the estate. Though he knew intellectually his diligence would improve our position when we were forced to give way for his cousin, in practice, it was a matter he did not like to consider, so he ignored it. I loved my father. But I was not blind to his faults."

The two gentlemen nodded in response to her quiet declaration, but they made no further comment. Elizabeth fancied she knew what they were thinking, and she could not disagree with their opinions. At this late date, however, there was little reason to belabor the past. Hopefully, they would have many more years at Longbourn in which Elizabeth could work to mitigate the effects of her father's neglect.

When it came time to part, Elizabeth farewelled the gentlemen, thanking them for their support that morning. As well-bred men often did, they demurred, declaring she had handled the matter better than they might have expected.

"I am impressed, Miss Bennet," said Mr. Darcy. "There are many men of my acquaintance who would not have handled the manner half so well as you did."

"Thank you, Mr. Darcy," said Elizabeth. "I do only as I must, for it is my hope I shall have a brother to inherit the estate someday. It is a duty I accept willingly."

"It is clear Mr. Bennet chose the best sister for the task," said Colonel Fitzwilliam. "Should you require us to intimidate Mr. Bates again, please do not hesitate to call on us."

Laughing, Elizabeth agreed and farewelled them. Soon, she could no longer see them in the foliage. They were, she reflected, fortunate to have such excellent people in residence at Netherfield. Elizabeth hoped they would stay for some time, for she had become attached to them.

"What do you think, Darcy?"

Startled from his thoughts, Darcy turned to his cousin, wondering what he was speaking about. Fitzwilliam, noting his contemplative state, grinned and nodded. "I see you are considering the impressive Miss Elizabeth Bennet. She is remarkable, do you not agree? I cannot think of half a dozen young women of her age who would respond to the responsibility of caring for an estate in such circumstances with the aplomb of a woman twice her age."

"I think Miss Elizabeth is as competent a woman as I have ever met," said Darcy. "None of her sisters would have fared half so well as she has."

"In that you are correct. Miss Bennet is an excellent woman, but her strengths do not lie in such activities."

Interested in what his cousin was saying, Darcy turned his full attention to him. "Do I detect a hint of admiration for Miss Bennet?"

"More than a hint, Darcy," said Fitzwilliam. "She possesses depths the likes of which I have not even begun to comprehend."

"It is interesting to hear you speak of her in such terms, Fitzwilliam. By my account, you have known her for a matter of days and been in her company only a handful of times."

"That is true," agreed Fitzwilliam. "At present, I have no notion of anything beyond initial regard. But every time I meet her, I become more aware of her appeal."

Darcy nodded. Careful consideration of the woman was nothing less than he would have expected of his cousin. What he did not expect was his cousin's next words.

"What of you and Miss Elizabeth?"

Looking at him blankly, Darcy queried: "What do you mean?"

"I am as acquainted with you as any man in the world, Darcy. While others might see nothing of your admiration of her, it seems to me that she has impressed you, which is tantamount to a declaration of interest by others."

"I have already agreed she impresses me," said Darcy. "But I find myself in the same situation as you are; the Bennets have not been known to us long, so I cannot say anything at this time."

"That is true enough," said Fitzwilliam. "But I hope you will not allow your fastidious nature to come between you and seeing Miss Elizabeth's qualities. Unless, of course, you finally mean to give in to Lady Catherine's demands and marry Anne. If that is your plan, you could scarcely have chosen a better manner to pursue her. The benefits of having Anne here while Lady Catherine is at Rosings cannot be underestimated."

Darcy laughed and shook his head. "No, Fitzwilliam. As you know, Anne and I have no desire to marry. She has my undying affection as my cousin, but I do not wish her for a wife."

"Then your path is clear if you determine Miss Elizabeth to be the woman you wish to pursue. Only take care not to delay, for I suspect it will not be long before other men become aware of her fine qualities."

Then Fitzwilliam spurred his mount forward, whistling a jaunty tune as he rode. Darcy followed him more sedately, his mind on their conversation. Though he had said nothing to his cousin, Darcy was well aware of the fine qualities of Miss Elizabeth Bennet, and he had noticed a stirring of interest in his heart. Admiration was still premature, but an awareness of her was unmistakable. Darcy was not a proud man, did not consider himself above his company. Should he determine he wished to pursue Miss Elizabeth Bennet, then only she could prevent him.

"Charles, I believe I should like to pay a visit to Netherfield Park today."

Startled from his thoughts, Bingley looked up at his sister, noting Caroline had finally appeared after staying in her room most of the morning. She was dressed in her usual attire, a gown that was heavy and made of shiny fabrics, something beyond what he usually saw in a day dress, even if the woman intended to pay calls on acquaintances. She was devoid of a headdress that day, though feathers were a prominent part of her wardrobe, often brought out for balls or parties. They were also a singularly unattractive accessory, in Bingley's opinion, though Caroline's use of them made it apparent she did not agree.

"That is not possible, Caroline," said Bingley, knowing saying so would provoke an argument with his sister.

"Of course, it is," said his sister.

"How so, Caroline?" asked Bingley. "Unless my memory is deficient, I am the only one of this company who is acquainted with Darcy, and as yet I have not been introduced to his relations. Colonel Fitzwilliam is leasing Netherfield—not Darcy. And even if it were Darcy's estate, it would be improper for anyone other than me to pay a call."

"It is not improper," said Caroline. "I am aware of the customs of people such as Mr. Darcy and his kin, and I understand they would consider an overture from us to be a mark of our desire to give them their due."

Bingley watched her; she seemed to have decided that demands would not work and had tried honey instead of vinegar, for her tone was all saccharine, though laced with steel. It was pathetic, Bingley thought, for she was so accustomed to having her way that she did not consider any possibility of failure. It was unfortunate for her, but Bingley had no intention of allowing her to have her way in this matter.

"Yes, it is improper, Caroline, and you may as well stop trying to wheedle me to change my mind. As I noted before, I have never called Darcy a friend, as he always kept himself aloof. At present he tolerates me, and as I am hopeful for more, I shall not antagonize him by intruding where I am not wanted when he and his relations have not yet signaled they wish to further the acquaintance."

Caroline huffed and threw herself into a chair. "I do not know why you are being so mutinous about his, Charles. Mr. Darcy and his family reside in the same neighborhood; I am certain they do not mean to ignore us for as long as we are both living here."

"Perhaps they do not," agreed Bingley. "But propriety dictates we wait for them to make their wishes known. Thus, we shall not go to Netherfield today or any day until that happens."

"Very well," snapped Caroline.

She rose and with a swish of her skirts, she exited the room, relieving those remaining of her presence. Bingley, who had difficulty tolerating her of late, suppressed a sigh of relief.

"I agree with you, Charles," said Louisa, rising and smiling at him. "But Caroline will be impossible if I do not settle her, so I shall go to her now."

With that, Louisa departed, leaving Bingley in Hurst's company.

"I know not what has caused your mirth," said Bingley after enduring Hurst's grin for several minutes.

"My amusement is not for you," replied Hurst, "it is for your sister. I have never seen a woman of any level of society so blind to her position in it. Caroline is quick to point out the faults in others, but she seems blind to her behavior. In her mind, the slight matter of a lack of acquaintance will not prevent those at Netherfield from welcoming her with open arms."

"It has always been thus," replied Bingley. "Even as a child, she would misbehave with every expectation of our parents ignoring it."

"What a truly ridiculous woman she is," said Hurst, chuckling under his breath. "I am happy to see you meeting her excesses with firmness. When I informed you of the possible ruination she may be on your position in society, I was not jesting. Firm control of her behavior now will yield dividends later."

"Well do I know it," said Bingley. "If only she was not so difficult to endure."

"The more you control her, the easier she will be to tolerate." Hurst paused and considered him. "What do you plan to do for the season?"

Bingley grimaced. "Caroline will no doubt consider it unnecessary, as long as Colonel Fitzwilliam and Darcy are in the neighborhood. Even now, I suspect she is plotting how she will become wife to one of them."

The snort with which Hurst responded was ample evidence of his opinion on the subject. "That is a fool's wager, Bingley. As is her desire to wed one of them. I doubt either will give her a second glance that she does not provoke by showing them how absurd she is. She is not getting younger, Bingley. This season you should make it clear she must find a husband. And she must know she cannot reject an eligible suitor."

"If one can be found."

Hurst nodded agreeably. "If she reins in her behavior a little, she will fit in with the other social climbers. Her dowry is enough to attract some interest."

"I agree," said Bingley. "But I suggest we wait to make this clear to her. With her schemes for our neighbors running through her head, I doubt she would listen at present."

"Very well," said Hurst. "I shall leave the details to you."

CHAPTER VII

"*J*ane, has it seemed to you that Mr. Bingley has been paying you an inordinate amount of attention of late?"

As was her custom, Jane protested, saying: "I have noticed no appreciable difference in his manners, Lizzy."

"Oh?" asked Elizabeth, arching an eyebrow at her sister. "Then he did not stand with you for almost an hour at the Gouldings' last night? It seems to me you draw him as a moth to the flame every time we are together in company."

Jane blushed. "I am certain Mr. Bingley means nothing by it, Lizzy."

"I would not be so certain," replied Elizabeth. "He can see Colonel Fitzwilliam's actions toward you, and yet he persists. That must tell you something, I think."

"The colonel is an amiable man," said Jane. "But he has made no declaration."

"Yes, I know," replied Elizabeth. "If he does not, I shall be very much surprised."

Jane ducked her head and refused to speak on the subject again, leaving Elizabeth alone to her speculation. In the matter of Colonel Fitzwilliam, it was obvious that Jane had an admirer, and while Elizabeth could not determine how serious his interest was, it appeared promising. To induce Jane to confess to her knowledge of it was difficult, to say the least, for she was among the most modest of ladies Elizabeth had ever met.

As for Mr. Bingley, the previous days had testified to his interest, in Elizabeth's view. There had been extensive meetings between the Netherfield party and Longbourn, and not as much between either of those estates and Pulvis Lodge. Whenever they were in company together, however, Elizabeth could detect more than a hint of partiality on Mr. Bingley's side. Not that it would do Mr. Bingley any good — Jane's affections were firmly fixed on Colonel Fitzwilliam at the moment, and Elizabeth doubted it would change. To Elizabeth, Colonel Fitzwilliam was the more serious gentleman, and he possessed one benefit Mr. Bingley did not — he was not cursed with a harpy for a sister.

"I know something of Bingley," said Mr. Darcy when Elizabeth asked his opinion. "The Bingley family is respectable in the north, from what I understand, and have found much success in trade. Bingley has inherited a fortune from his father, along with the wish that his son purchase an estate and join the ranks of the landed. It seems Bingley is making good on his promise to his father, as his current residence at Pulvis Lodge will attest."

"That is very well for Mr. Bingley, I am sure," said Elizabeth. "But this account puts Miss Bingley's behavior in a new light altogether. Given the airs she gives herself, one might have thought she is the daughter of a duke. And yet she is naught but the daughter of a tradesman."

Mr. Darcy appeared amused by Elizabeth's declaration. "Do you suppose she is less estimable because of that fact?"

"I do not," replied Elizabeth, shaking her head with annoyance. "But I do take offense when someone who is, in fact, lower in society than my sisters and I, acts as if we are vastly inferior."

"Yes, I can see how that would be offensive." Mr. Darcy paused and chuckled. "I have been acquainted with Bingley since university, though our association never strengthened to friendship. Bingley always seemed a little too frivolous for my taste, which is why we never became closer. But while I have never met his sister before, we have all heard of her in London, for her antics have become the stuff of legend."

"Then you cannot be happy that circumstance has led to your introduction to her," said Elizabeth, grinning at the gentleman. "Now that you cannot escape the acquaintance, I suspect she has firmly set her sights upon you and your cousin."

"That is a shame, indeed," said Mr. Darcy, though his manner suggested complaisance. "But do not despair. I have been avoiding such huntresses all my adult life, and Fitzwilliam is not deficient in the art."

"You consider it an art?" asked Elizabeth, amused at his words.

"In many respects, it is."

"Oh, we do not like Miss Bingley much at all," said Charity another time when the subject of the woman came up. Charity, being rather more outspoken than Elizabeth was herself, could always be counted on to say exactly what she was thinking. "Mr. Bingley is a gentlemanly man, but his sister is a drawback to his interest in any woman of any quality."

"Mr. Darcy alluded to her reputation in town," said Elizabeth.

Charity huffed, her disgust clear to see. "And given her continued behavior, it is clear she cannot see how others disdain her. Yes, Elizabeth, Miss Bingley is infamous in town, and she associates with those who, though some have standing, are little better than she in essentials. Few in London possess such notoriety with so little prominence to their name. She truly is a curious creature!"

At the same time Mr. Bingley showed unabashed interest in Jane, it was clear Miss Bingley was quite intent upon catching one of the gentlemen for her husband, and it did not seem to matter whom she snared in her web. Whenever they were together, if she was not disparaging the locals, Miss Bingley accosted whichever gentlemen was the closer. While Elizabeth could see their disinclination for her company, Miss Bingley was single-minded, assured that one could not help fall to her charms. Charms, Elizabeth thought was a strong word for her qualities, for they were nothing more than an acid tongue, an overly obsequious manner which provoked her to agree with anything either gentleman said, and an insincere manner. Elizabeth might have been happy never to have made Miss Bingley's acquaintance.

One day, in particular, displayed this state of affairs between the families and led to an incident that firmed every member of the Bennet family's opinion of Miss Bingley. It was one of those fair days that often made October pleasant, though the signs of the coming winter were unmistakable. Having completed some estate business that morning with Mr. Whitmore in attendance, Elizabeth was soon at liberty to join her family in the sitting-room, which was when they received visitors that were becoming a fixture at Longbourn of late.

"Good morning, Mrs. Bennet," said Colonel Fitzwilliam as he led his family into the room. "Please forgive us for intruding upon you this morning, for it seems certain members of our company cannot do without you."

While Mrs. Bennet had by now become accustomed to seeing the scions of an earl in her sitting-room, she was a little nonplused by his greeting. Colonel Fitzwilliam, with the laughter that was such a part of his character, smiled at the matron and paid her his exclusive attention for a few moments.

"And how are you this fine day, Mrs. Bennet? Happy and hopeful for the future, I hope."

This turned out to be a mistake, for Mrs. Bennet took his question as an opportunity to regale him with the frustration of her current situation. The colonel proved his good temper by sitting for some time listening to her, until Mrs. Bennet, seeming to remember this gentleman was paying her eldest daughter the most exquisite of attention, started and peered at him.

"Thank you for listening to my complaints, Colonel Fitzwilliam," said she after a moment of regarding him. "But I suspect there is another with whom you would rather visit."

"Nothing of the sort!" said the colonel. "This conversation has been fascinating, Mrs. Bennet."

Though he spoke of his willingness to listen to her, Colonel Fitzwilliam lost no time in escaping to Jane's side, much to the amusement of those looking on. Elizabeth, who had by this time become firm friends with Charity and Anne, stifled her laughter, as did her two friends.

"Your mother is a gem, Elizabeth," said Charity in a low tone. "Why, I declare she would make a most interesting mother-in-law."

"And Fitzwilliam seems to have no compunction toward offering her that position," added Anne.

As the ladies descended into their mirth, Elizabeth reflected how welcome it was to meet these ladies, devoid of pretension and pride, who would not condemn Jane as a fortune hunter for even daring to entertain the attention of a man of Colonel Fitzwilliam's position in society.

"And Georgiana finds your youngest sisters agreeable, it seems," said Charity.

That much was true, and everyone in the company had noticed it. At present, the three girls were sitting together, with Mary nearby, giggling at something one of them had said. Elizabeth, who found Georgiana an agreeable young girl, appeared to have dragged

Elizabeth's sisters closer to her behavior than the reverse, which was a relief for Elizabeth. Not only were her sisters benefiting from the association, but Georgiana was an excellent young woman, and she did not think Mr. Darcy would have been pleased to see Lydia's brash fearlessness creep into her behavior.

"I think she appreciates having friends her own age," said Anne.

The ladies shared a look, and when they noted Elizabeth's curiosity, they hastened to explain.

"Georgiana is the youngest member of our extended family by several years." Charity fixed a look on her young relation. "I am the next youngest, and I am one and twenty. Couple that with a reticent character, tending toward shyness, and it will not surprise you that she often has trouble putting herself forward."

"She does not have many other friends?" asked Elizabeth.

"A few, from what I understand," said Anne. "Acquaintances from school she has, but few close friends. Since she left school and has prepared for her coming out, even those acquaintances have distanced themselves. I, for one, think it is very good your sisters have become such good friends."

"The trick," said Charity, "is to ensure they can continue to associate. I have no notion if my brother means to purchase Netherfield, but absent that, keeping these friendships would continue to help her gain confidence."

The ladies exchanged a significant look, and Elizabeth was certain they were speaking of the current state of affairs between Colonel Fitzwilliam and Jane. As it was not a subject she could approach without sounding gauche or avaricious, Elizabeth allowed it to pass and changed the subject.

The one constant of their association in Longbourn's sitting-room that morning was the position of the aforementioned couple, who appeared content to remain in each other's company. Mrs. Bennet watched them, eager to witness their continuing interaction, and Elizabeth, who knew her mother well, was aware of Mrs. Bennet's present thought, consisting of dreams of a summer wedding, the finest celebration Meryton had ever seen. It was fortunate she was circumspect enough to avoid saying anything, which was a welcome change from her usual behavior. It would not be long before Mrs. Bennet would need to withdraw from these morning visits, for it would be improper for a woman so close to her confinement to be seen by those visiting. That would make her behavior ever more fractious, but there was little choice.

It was when the visitors had shifted a little, leaving Elizabeth in conversation with Mr. Darcy that Mrs. Hill led a new group of callers into the sitting-room. It was Mr. Bingley and his family.

"Mrs. Bennet," said the man, bowing and grinning in his irrepressible manner, "how good it is to see you today. How do you do?"

While the gentleman spoke to Mrs. Bennet, Elizabeth, who was watching, witnessed as the Hursts and Miss Bingley entered the room. Thus, she could see the exact moment when Miss Bingley's countenance changed from annoyance to calculation, seeing the visitors already there.

"I presume you saw what I did?" asked Mr. Darcy softly from her side.

"That Miss Bingley was unhappy to be here until she saw you and your family?" At Mr. Darcy's amused nod, Elizabeth confirmed it. "I suspect Mr. Bingley insisted on the visit and would not accept his sister's refusal. Longbourn cannot be acceptable if you are not here."

"She may as well put such notions of us aside," said Mr. Darcy, giving the woman a severe look. "As for my family, we care little for her brand of insolence."

As they were speaking, Miss Bingley was surveying the room. Georgiana, who was sitting with Mary discussing music, drew a long look, but it seemed the woman did not consider it worth it to dislodge Mary to ply her trade with Mr. Darcy's sister. Kitty and Lydia, she dismissed without a second glance, though Charity and Anne were in attendance with them. For a moment, Elizabeth thought she might approach Colonel Fitzwilliam and Jane, but her brother preceded her there. That left Mr. Darcy and Elizabeth herself. With a look of determination, the woman approached them.

"Mr. Darcy," said she, a brief gaze raking over Elizabeth, "how surprised I am to see you here today. I should not have thought to find you in a location such as this."

Elizabeth, instantly offended by the woman's insinuation, responded before Mr. Darcy could. "Is that so? Your brother has leased Pulvis Lodge, has he not?"

While Miss Bingley directed a withering glare at Elizabeth, a warning to be silent, she allowed Elizabeth's observation to be true.

"Then I must wonder at your meaning, Miss Bingley. Longbourn's income is superior to Pulvis Lodge's by five hundred pounds per annum, and the manor house is much larger. And I have it on good authority that the attics in that venerable house are absolutely dreadful."

While her authority on this matter was none other than her mother, whose information was suspect at best, Elizabeth could not resist further tweaking Miss Bingley's nose. "There is also the matter, of course, that Pulvis Lodge is only leased, while my family has held Longbourn for more than two centuries."

Then not allowing the woman to respond further, Elizabeth turned to Mr. Darcy. "Have you visited Pulvis Lodge yet, Mr. Darcy? Perhaps you could lend Mr. Bingley some of your experience."

"I have not yet had that pleasure," said Mr. Darcy, his tone informing Elizabeth he would postpone the pleasure indefinitely because of the objectionable company living there. "Should Bingley ask, I should be happy to assist, of course, but I have not yet. As a woman managing your family's estate, you know that after the harvest there is little to accomplish on your lands."

"That is true," agreed Elizabeth, "but as you know, there is plenty of planning to do."

"It is my understanding," said Miss Bingley, cross at being ignored, spearing Elizabeth for her insults, "that you are only managing the land based on the possibility of your mother producing an heir. Given her history, I suspect that eventuality is unlikely."

Elizabeth glanced at Mr. Darcy and could not help but laugh. "It seems I have had this conversation before, Miss Bingley. Perhaps the workings of such mathematics are not your forte; should a woman give birth to twenty daughters, there is still an equal chance the next will be a son."

The glare Miss Bingley fixed on Elizabeth for that bit of impertinence could have curdled milk. "Those are interesting observations, Miss Elizabeth. If your expectations do not come to fruition and the lack of an heir forces you from your home when your sibling is born, I shall remember you in my prayers, for your reduced standing will be pitiable, indeed."

"I have no expectations, Miss Bingley," said Elizabeth, certain Miss Bingley had no experience in prayer. "I do not know the sex of my sibling, and I shall accept whatever comes. But I would have you remember that even if we find ourselves in 'reduced circumstances,' as you say, we will always be the daughters of a gentleman."

"Which is what matters," said Mr. Darcy, neatly cutting off what Elizabeth thought would have been an impressive outburst. "For my part and that of my family, our friendship will not alter whether you inhabit Longbourn or live in a cottage. You will always be acceptable to us."

Elizabeth was grateful for the gentleman's words, even as Miss Bingley appeared shocked he would speak so. Her next words were no more palatable to Elizabeth than her previous had been.

"That displays your liberality, Mr. Darcy. Charity to those less fortunate is always to be lauded."

"Did someone say my name?"

Elizabeth noted the approach of her friend and grinned at her, even as Charity winked where Elizabeth could not see. Miss Bingley turned to this new prey and welcomed her with flattering words and insincere blandishments. The way she glanced at Elizabeth suggested she considered her an interloper—notwithstanding the woman's position in the Bennet home—and wished for her to withdraw. Charity saw it too if her wink in Elizabeth's direction was any indication.

"What a wonderful welcome, Miss Bingley," said Charity. "If I did not know better, I might have thought you were mistress of this estate, rather than a visitor."

"Oh, no, your ladyship," simpered Miss Bingley, completely misunderstanding the irony in Charity's voice. "My ambitions are much higher than an estate such as Longbourn."

"An estate such as Pulvis Lodge," said Elizabeth sotto voce.

Again, a harsh glare was Miss Bingley's response. "Pulvis Lodge is nothing more than a stop along the way. Charles would never purchase such an insignificant estate as Pulvis Lodge, for the location is atrocious, and it is not nearly large enough. There is a much more illustrious property in our future."

"Perhaps Mr. Bingley should purchase Pemberley," said Elizabeth, turning to Mr. Darcy. "I understand it is an estate without peer."

"I apologize for upsetting your dynastic ambitions, Miss Elizabeth," said Mr. Darcy, his tone tinged with laughter, "but Pemberley is not for sale."

"Perhaps the neighborhood in which you live would be possible?" interjected Miss Bingley. "Surely there must be other acceptable estates near your home."

"There are," said Mr. Darcy, prompting a slow smile from the supercilious woman. "But there are none that I know of for sale."

"What of the neighborhood in which your brother's estate lies, Charity?" asked Elizabeth. "Living near an earl must be acceptable, I should think."

"I shall ask him," said Charity, her eyes sparkling in her mirth. "Perhaps he could recommend something for Mr. Bingley."

"Miss Eliza," said Miss Bingley, her affronted tone drawing their attention to her annoyance, "I am amazed at the effrontery you show to your guests, who are among the highest of society. As a woman raised in a gentleman's house, I would have thought you would have known the proper mode of address. As she is the daughter of an earl, you must address her as 'Lady Charity,' lest you offend her."

"That is true, Miss Bingley," said Elizabeth, "unless she has given permission to dispense with such titles."

Miss Bingley's manner became ever more severe, and she looked down her nose, risen to an impressive angle. "I am certain you must have misunderstood."

"Actually, Miss Bingley," said Charity, by now all amusement gone, "you are incorrect. I had not known Elizabeth for three days when I knew I wanted her for a friend. Friends do not stand on such ceremony, and as I despise such pretension, I hastened to ask her not to cling to formality."

It was clear Miss Bingley did not understand how Charity could espouse such esteem for Elizabeth. It was also no surprise that she completely misinterpreted Charity's meaning.

"That is good of you, to be certain. It is wonderful to be among such friends, is it not? I have never been so happy to make new acquaintances in my life!"

No one could miss the hope in Miss Bingley's tone that Charity would afford her the same privilege as Elizabeth. Charity regarded her for several moments, considering her, and while Miss Bingley was confident in the beginning, her nervousness rose the longer Charity remained silent.

"Making new acquaintances is always welcome," said Charity. "However, it is what you do with those people, how you treat them that is most important. There are some of my level of society who will look down on everyone they meet. But I hope I am not one of them."

"Nor I," said Mr. Darcy in a quiet tone.

"Elizabeth," said Charity warmly, approaching her and grasping her hands. "As always, your hospitality has been second to none. I hope we will see you at Netherfield tomorrow?"

"I believe we should be happy to return your visit," said Elizabeth.

"Excellent! I cannot wait. For now, however, I believe our time here has elapsed and we must depart."

With those words, Charity gathered the rest of the Netherfield party, and with warm regards for the Bennets—their felicitations for the Bingleys were more muted—they left the estate, leaving the

Bennets with the Bingleys. Turning to Miss Bingley, Elizabeth wondered if she would say something after Charity's statement, but true to her character, Miss Bingley huffed and went to her brother, insisting that they depart.

"We have been here for but fifteen minutes, Caroline," said Mr. Bingley, pleased to have Jane's company to himself. "When the half-hour has elapsed, we shall depart."

Miss Bingley appeared ready to protest, but seeing her brother's determination, she desisted. Instead, she sat on a sofa near to Mrs. Bennet, and pouted—there was no other word to describe it. The position was an unfortunate one, for while Elizabeth was distracted, something passed between them. When Elizabeth fixed her attention on them again, she could see that Mrs. Bennet was furious and Miss Bingley faintly triumphant. Unfortunately for Miss Bingley, her brother overheard the exchange, appearing as furious as Mrs. Bennet.

"Mrs. Bennet," said Mr. Bingley, spearing his sister with a quelling look, "I thank you for your hospitality today. At the same time, I apologize for my sister's words. I do not think she meant them in the way they sounded, and you can rest assured I will speak to her about her behavior."

Miss Bingley appeared startled her brother would speak of her in such a fashion, but the combined force of Mr. Bingley's stare joined with Mr. Hurst's informed her it would be best to keep silent. While it was clear Mrs. Bennet was still offended by whatever had passed between them, she was magnanimous, turning her attention to Mr. Bingley.

"Thank you, sir. Perhaps it would be best if your sister learned to choose her words with care, for misunderstanding can damage relations, especially between those newly acquainted."

Perhaps Mrs. Bennet was not so generous in her response as Elizabeth thought when she first spoke, though it was less than she might have thought her mother would say.

"I cannot agree more, Mrs. Bennet. The welcome we have received in the neighborhood has been warmly offered; I would have nothing come between us.

"Now, it seems we must depart. Again, I thank you for your hospitality and hope we may deepen our acquaintance some other time."

Mrs. Bennet nodded her head, a regal gesture which seemed to vex Miss Bingley further. Then the Bingleys made their farewells and departed the room, Mr. Bingley's longing looks at Jane informing them all he was leaving under duress. At length, they left the Bennet ladies to their devices.

"What did Miss Bingley say to you?" asked Lydia, voicing the question each of the sisters had foremost in their minds.

Mrs. Bennet sniffed with disdain, showing her ability to hold a grudge. "When Mr. Darcy left, she sat nearby and I could hear her muttering under her breath, criticizing our home. I asked her to clarify her statements, she abused me for being in company in my condition. Furthermore, she insinuated the parentage of my child is suspect and questioned my character for allowing myself to fall with child at my 'advanced age.'"

Elizabeth exchanged a look with Jane, even as Lydia exclaimed: "What an odious creature she is! What kind of woman comes into another's house and speaks with such disdain to those living there?"

"A woman such as Miss Bingley," said Elizabeth with a shake of her head. "She is so intent upon climbing society's ladder that she cannot see the repulsive way she behaves to others."

"Miss Bingley is not that bad," said Jane, though her countenance was troubled.

"In this instance, I must disagree with you, Jane," said Elizabeth, her mother nodding vigorously in agreement. "Miss Bingley is not a pleasant woman. She cares for nothing other than her selfish ambitions and will do whatever it takes to realize them."

"I mean to have nothing further to do with the woman," said Mrs. Bennet. "Her brother is an amiable man, so I shall endure her for his sake. But any further comments such as those she made to me shall see her evicted from Longbourn."

"You need not bear such incivility," said Elizabeth, sitting by her mother and smiling at her. "You have been an excellent mistress of the estate, Mama, and no one can control when they fall with child. Do not give her words a moment's consideration."

"Thank you, Lizzy," said Mrs. Bennet, her countenance softening. "You have all brought me the greatest pride. I only hope this last gift from your father will bring us security. How I hope for a son!"

"We all do, Mama," said Mary, the other girls gathering close. "But whatever will be will be. And remember," added she with a sly look at Jane, "with Colonel Fitzwilliam paying such handsome attention to Jane, I suspect our futures are secure, regardless."

"What a wonderful thing! I knew you could not be so beautiful for nothing, Jane! He is an excellent man."

Elizabeth could not but agree with her mother. The entire family was as estimable as any Elizabeth had ever met. They were blessed to have made their acquaintance.

Chapter VIII

Charles Bingley seethed the entire distance of their return to Pulvis Lodge. Having heard everything that Caroline had said to Mrs. Bennet, it appalled him that a sister of his, even one he knew possessed an unfortunate character, could speak so to a woman in whose home they were visiting. It was fortunate Caroline seemed to realize his anger—and that of Hurst, though Hurst did not know the full measure of her disgusting behavior—for if she had spoken, Bingley might have called for the carriage to halt and thrown her from it. The desire to see the last of her raged in his breast; to be free of Caroline would be akin to the release from prison!

When Pulvis Lodge came into sight through the trees, Bingley steeled himself for the confrontation to come. A genial man, Bingley abhorred contention of any kind, especially within his own family. Of late, however, Caroline's behavior had become so abhorrent that his dislike for her was causing his patience to dissolve with distressing frequency. The worst was that she was pushing him to this man of little patience and constant anger. Bingley did not like it in the least!

The carriage rolled to a halt and Bingley allowed Hurst and Louisa to alight first before descending and turning to hand Caroline down. He did this for a specific reason, as he knew Caroline would attempt to avoid the reprimand that had hovered on the tip of his tongue since they left Longbourn. His knowledge of his sister was not mistaken, for she attempted to pull her hand from his, the moment she was on the ground.

"I shall retire to my room, Charles, for I am fatigued."

"No, you will not!" spat Bingley. "You will accompany me to the sitting-room, for I wish to speak to you at once."

Not waiting for her to reply, Bingley grasped her arm and directed her into the house, ignoring her squawk of protest. Louisa regarded them with a worried look, while Hurst was watching him, satisfaction in his gaze. They made their way through the house and to the small sitting-room Pulvis Lodge boasted, and as soon as they attained the room, Bingley led her in, motioning for Hurst to close the door behind them.

"Why did you speak to Mrs. Bennet in such a repellant manner, Caroline?" barked Bingley as soon as he was assured of their privacy from the servants.

"I know not of what you speak, Charles," said Caroline, her glare suggesting she was considering what she must do to regain control.

"'If you even know the father of that child you bear,'" spat Bingley. "Is that not what you said to her?"

Hurst's countenance became stony and Louisa gasped. "Caroline, you did not!"

"I assure you, she did," said Bingley. By now he could hear in his own voice a quality akin to the snarl of a rabid dog. He was so angry he could not bring himself to care. "And that was after she suggested to Mrs. Bennet that her condition rendered her unfit to remain in the sitting-room and telling her that allowing herself to become with child at her age showed a distinct lack of judgment."

"Oh, Caroline," said Louisa, shaking her head. "How could you have made such stupid comments?"

"She could make it because she is completely lacking in basic decency and cares for nothing more than her own selfish desires."

"I care about fulfilling our father's wishes," rejoined Caroline, her anger rising to match Bingley's. "Why do the opinions of these people concern us at all? They can be of no aid to us in society."

"People, Caroline," said Bingley, by now shaking with rage, "are not simply steppingstones to your ambitions. Our father would not have wanted us to insult those about us and look upon them with meanness, even if he wished us to ascend to the heights of society. We cannot forget such worthy traits as decency, civility, kindness, and charity, or we risk losing our humanity."

Caroline rolled her eyes. "These people are below us by every measure, Charles. Perhaps I should not have spoken as I did, but there is no reason to concern ourselves for their opinion."

"You are rather conceited for the daughter of a tradesman, are you not?"

Gasping, Caroline regarded him with shock before her countenance purpled in anger. Though she might have spoken, Bingley did not mean to listen to her again.

"To say that the Miss Bennets are below us is nothing less than a delusion on your part. Are they not the daughters of a gentleman?"

"If you can call the late Mr. Bennet a gentleman," snapped Caroline.

"Be silent, you insolent harpy!"

Hurst's entrance into the argument allowed Bingley to catch his breath and calm his breathing. Had it proceeded much longer, Bingley might have lost his temper and slapped his sister. Caroline gasped at Hurst's words, but he did not allow continued vitriol.

"To speak of the dead in such terms is appalling," continued Hurst. "By every definition, Mr. Bennet was a gentleman, for he owned land and had tenants who farmed it for him. That is the very essence of being of the gentleman class. Furthermore, it displays a shocking ignorance for you to blame a woman for being with child when you well know no one has any control over such things. If you were not a woman full-grown, I would put you over my knee."

"I am contemplating that very thing," said Bingley, his dark glare at his sister never dimming. "Moreover, my dear Caroline, you should remember that the Darcys and Fitzwilliams will likely learn of what you said to Mrs. Bennet today, and their opinion of us will worsen as a result."

"As if Mr. Darcy will care what I say to such a woman." Caroline sniffed her disdain.

"Sometimes I wonder if you go through the world determined to delude yourself," commented Hurst. "The Darcys and Fitzwilliams have, by all accounts, become close to the Bennets since they have been here. If you think they will not concern themselves for your rudeness, you are sadly mistaken. Did Lady Charity not deny you the privilege of dispensing with her title?"

There was little for Caroline to say to that, though Bingley had no knowledge of the event. Hurst nodded grimly at her blush, his glare as disgusted as Bingley had ever seen.

"If you think Darcy is interested in you at all, you are deceiving yourself, Caroline."

"You simply want to prevent me from realizing my ambitions," spat she in a burst of defiance. "You cannot stand the thought that I will be higher than you in society."

"If you think I care a jot for standing, you are blinder than I thought," said Bingley. "I do not wish to speak of this further. But know this, Caroline."

Bingley stepped close and looked down on his sister, not caring his greater size could be taken for intimidation. "Should you ever speak in such a way to anyone of our acquaintance again I shall cut you off. Your dowry is enough to see to your support if necessary. I shall not endure a woman who continually embarrasses me with behavior that would make a duchess blush."

With those words, Bingley turned on his heel and stalked from the room, unwilling to listen to her abuse. Out the door he strode, barking for his horse to be saddled at once, pacing the yard as he waited. When his mount was ready, Bingley kicked his heels to its flanks and galloped away, hoping to work his anger off through exertion. By the time he reined in his mount, it was blowing hard and Bingley was feeling the effects of a headache.

The worst part was that Bingley had developed an interest in Miss Jane Bennet. With Caroline behaving worse than a queen, Bingley wondered if Miss Bennet would ever see him as anything other than the brother to a rude woman. And Fitzwilliam was already paying her overt attention and had been since he had arrived in the neighborhood. Bingley was already behind in the race, and Caroline was making it worse.

Bingley bowed his head, allowing his horse to wander as he would, its heaving sides gradually calming. The truth of the matter was that he was likely too late to woo the beautiful Miss Bennet. Had he been here first, he could imagine he would be the one paying her the most exquisite attention, regardless of what Caroline thought on the matter. She was a jewel of the first order, a woman worth all the rubies in the world. Curse Caroline for her ways, for making them late to the neighborhood, and delivering Miss Bennet on a plate to Fitzwilliam!

Perhaps it was foolish, but Bingley would not give up. He may not be the catch that Fitzwilliam was, but he knew he was a good man and possessed an excellent fortune. Riches or societal position, he thought, would not draw Miss Bennet's interest, for she was as excellent a woman as had ever lived. Surely his chances must be as good as his rival's.

* * *

"I have been thinking. Perhaps we should have a ball to thank those of the neighborhood for their welcome."

Fitzwilliam looked on his companions, watching the ladies, wondering what they would think. Anne, he knew, had little experience in planning such events, as her mother preferred the comforts of Rosings to town and rarely entertained such frivolity. Charity, however, had some training before their mother had passed; between them, Fitzwilliam thought they could plan a creditable event. And Georgiana could do with the experience herself.

"There are some among us for whom attending a ball would be a punishment rather than a pleasure." Charity turned her laughing countenance on Darcy. "Or perhaps Darcy should retire early that night? Then he would not need to endure an activity he detests so much."

"Nothing could be further from the truth," said Darcy. "While I will own dancing is not my favorite activity, I have no objection to attending a ball."

"It seems the company in this neighborhood is bringing out the civility in our cousin," said Anne, showing her mirth. "Or perhaps it is the company of one lady in particular?"

Fitzwilliam guffawed. "Darcy has been in Miss Elizabeth's company much of late."

"Not as much as you have been with Miss Bennet."

"I believe he has you there, Brother," said Charity.

"And I own it without disguise. Miss Bennet is a rare woman, combining beauty, sweetness, and the most even temper of any woman I have ever met."

"Those are words of admiration."

Fitzwilliam returned Darcy's interested look. "Again, I own it without disguise."

"I have met few better ladies than she," said Charity. "Should you decide you wish to bestow your attention on her, I would welcome her as a sister."

"That is yet premature, Charity," said Fitzwilliam, though he smiled at her to show his appreciation. "Now, what of the ball?"

Charity and Anne shared a glance, Anne shrugged, and Charity turned back to him. "If you wish to hold a ball, I believe we can manage it." Charity then smiled at Georgiana. "Perhaps you would like to assist us?"

Shy as she was, Georgiana hesitated, her confidence lacking. Then she nodded, however, drawing a smile of approval from her cousin.

"Then we are decided." Charity turned back to her brother. "When were you thinking of holding this event?"

"Will two weeks be sufficient to prepare?" asked Fitzwilliam.

Charity considered his question. "Mother would often plan a ball for months in advance. Then again, we are in the country, rather than the bosom of society, and our neighbors will expect less. The only issue I can see is whether we can contract musicians in so short a time."

"As it is October," said Fitzwilliam, "I should think we can find some for the right price."

"Then wait to announce it until we have confirmation. If we cannot find someone within the next week, we should postpone."

"That is acceptable," said Fitzwilliam.

With that, the ladies huddled together and began to plan. Darcy regarded him, speculation alive in his gaze, but he did not speak, which was agreeable to Fitzwilliam at present. It was obvious what Darcy would say if he should speak about Miss Bennet. If he asked, Fitzwilliam did not think he could respond with any surety, for he still did not know his own heart. What he was certain of, however, was that Miss Bennet was an excellent woman. Even if Fitzwilliam was not already in love with her, a man could do far worse than Miss Jane Bennet for a wife.

The very day after the Fitzwilliam and Bingley visit to Longbourn, the arrival of a letter threw the estate into chaos. Postmarked from Kent, Elizabeth knew as soon as she read the address on the front it came from Mr. Collins. It was unfortunate that her mother saw the letter before Elizabeth could hide it from her.

"A letter from Mr. Collins!" Mrs. Bennet's exclamation was nearly a shriek. "What does that odious man have to say? Is he intent upon throwing us from our home to starve in the hedgerows?"

The situation went from poor to worse from that point, for Mrs. Bennet was certain they were all to be evicted as soon as may be, and no one could say anything to calm her. It finally took Elizabeth confronting her with the reality of their situation.

"Mama! This is not healthy for the child. You must settle yourself, or you risk harm to yourself and your son!"

The reference to the child being a boy was deliberate, for Elizabeth thought it would help her mother to understand how she could hurt her child. With so much depending on a successful birth to see if the child could inherit, settling their mother was imperative. Wide-eyed, she peered back at Elizabeth, and for a moment she thought her mother would break out into sobs yet again.

"Perhaps I should go to my room," said Mrs. Bennet, the edge of hysteria still in her voice.

"That would be for the best, Mama," said Jane, stepping forward to deal with their mother. "Allow Lizzy to handle Mr. Collins, Mama. If we require our uncles' support, Lizzy can involve them."

"You will do so?" asked Mrs. Bennet in a voice drained of strength.

"Yes, Mother, I shall. When I know what Mr. Collins is about, I shall inform you."

"Very well," said Mrs. Bennet, reaching for Jane's hand.

With the aid of Mrs. Hill and Jane, she rose to her feet, allowing them to escort her from the room. Elizabeth breathed a sigh of relief when her mother departed, an action echoed by her sisters.

"I wish Mama would not carry on so," said Mary with a shake of her head.

"Especially when we do not even know what the letter says," added Kitty.

Though she would have preferred anything other than to read the words of her father's loathsome cousin, Elizabeth supposed there was no point in delaying. Thus, she broke the seal to the missive and opened it. As she suspected, there was nothing contained therein she would wish to read, and within moments she was furious as the stupid man.

"What is it, Lizzy?" asked Lydia, worry coloring her voice.

For a moment, Elizabeth thought of keeping it silent. The array of faces about her, however, demanding or pleading, convinced her to share it. With a sigh, Elizabeth relented.

"This is the worst letter I have received from Mr. Collins. In it, he renews his claims of our intention to defraud him and demands we leave Longbourn at once. He claims he will come next week to evict us if we do not remove ourselves voluntarily."

"We are to lose our home?" asked Kitty in a small voice.

"Do not be silly, Kitty," said Lydia. "Mr. Collins cannot expel us from Longbourn. Regardless of whatever he thinks, we have done nothing wrong."

"Lydia is right, Kitty," said Elizabeth. "By the law, Mr. Collins has no claim on Longbourn until it is proven there is no other heir, and that will not happen until Mama's child is born."

"But we cannot ignore his letter either," said Mary.

"No, we cannot." Elizabeth rose and fixed her sisters with a look that demanded obedience. "Do not tell Mama of this. If she asks, you must tell her that all is well."

"I do not wish to lie to Mama," said Mary with a frown.

"Do you wish her to have another attack of her nerves?" asked Lydia, her tone pointed.

"Lydia is correct," said Elizabeth. "Mama must know nothing more of Mr. Collins's nonsense. The healthy delivery of her child might depend on it.

"Additionally, Mary, please have a word with Mrs. Hill. Inform her that any letters from Mr. Collins are to be brought to me directly without Mother's knowledge. If Hill cannot find me, she should put it in the study or give it to Jane or one of you. We must protect Mama's health."

While none of her sisters wished to deceive their mother, they saw the sense in Elizabeth's words and agreed, albeit in a subdued manner. Truth be told, Elizabeth did not wish to tell her mother falsehoods either, but she did not think there was any choice.

"I shall have Nelly saddled and ride to Meryton at once to consult with Uncle Phillips."

Mary gave Elizabeth an odd look. "You usually walk to Meryton, Lizzy."

"Trust me, Mary, I shall require Nelly's dependable temperament to go to Meryton without venting my frustration with Mr. Collins. In such situations as this, I prefer to walk off my anger, which will do no good in this situation."

"Very well, Lizzy. If I can manage a moment with Jane away from Mama, I shall inform her what we have decided."

With a nod, Elizabeth departed the room, giving instructions to see to the saddling of the horse. Then she went to her room and changed to her riding habit, taking care to avoid thinking of Mr. Collins so she would not lash out at the poor maid who assisted her. In a short time, Elizabeth was ready to depart, which she did with a final word to Mr. Whitmore concerning the estate.

Of Elizabeth's thoughts during the brief ride to her uncle's house, there was little to say. Equal parts seething at the ignorance of her father's cousin and determination to ensure they put him in his place raced through her mind. When she rode into the small town it was with some surprise the journey had passed so quickly. As her uncle lived on the far end of the town, Elizabeth made her way thither, greeting a few acquaintances as she rode, avoiding the hails of several who wished her to stop and speak with them.

It was fortunate that she found her uncle in his office working on some documents, for had she found him busy with a client she did not think she could have waited with any patience. Furthermore, it was vital that her aunt did not learn of what had happened, for she had a way of riling her sister to an ever-greater frenzy.

"Lizzy!" said her uncle, his tone suggesting he realized at once this was not a social call. "What brings you here today?"

"This," said Elizabeth, holding the letter for her uncle.

At once her uncle noted the postmark and scowled. This was not the first time she had come to his office with a letter from Mr. Collins in her hands. And yet, this time was different, for Mr. Collins had never made such overt threats as this before. Elizabeth did not think her uncle had read two sentences before he shot to his feet and paced the room, still holding and reading the letter, muttering imprecations under his breath as he did.

"It is difficult to understand how Mr. Collins can be related to your father," said he at length when he had read the missive through. "For all his faults, your father was an intellectual man. Mr. Collins is nothing less than an imbecile. How he can fathom that making such threats as this will gain him what he desires is beyond my comprehension."

Taking his seat again, Uncle Phillips peered at Elizabeth and gestured at the letter which he had thrown onto the desk in a fit of pique. "Do not respond, Elizabeth. This is not a matter for you to concern yourself. I shall consult with Gardiner and draft a response to him, and this time I think I shall threaten legal action if he should persist."

"Do you think it will cause him to desist?" asked Elizabeth.

Uncle Phillips grimaced. "Perhaps it will not, but it may prompt him to hesitate. If I am not mistaken, your mother should be due to give birth in the second week of December?"

"As near as the apothecary could determine," said Elizabeth.

"We must only induce him to keep his silence until then," said her uncle with a nod. "One way or another, this will be resolved then. I hope you will not blame me, Lizzy, if I express my hope that your mother births a son not only for your future security but also to deny that worthless cretin your father called cousin the estate. I cannot imagine Longbourn would do well under his stewardship."

Elizabeth chuckled and shook her head. "No, I cannot imagine it would. I have two further concerns." Mr. Phillips motioned for her to continue, which Elizabeth did, saying: "First, Mama's reaction to this letter was entirely predictable. To prevent further attacks of her nerves, Mrs. Hill is to bring any letters from Mr. Collins to me directly, so she does not learn of them. Should you receive anything, please do not speak of it in my mother's presence."

Having grimaced at the mention of his sister's nerves, Uncle Phillips nodded. "That would be for the best. Collins has never written to me directly, which tells you something of his character. I shall keep whatever I can from Leticia, for she will not make matters any better."

Elizabeth smiled and nodded gratefully. "The second concern is this threat of Mr. Collins to come to Longbourn. Do you suppose he will follow through and attempt to confront us?"

"If he does," said Mr. Phillips shortly, "you should call the constable. Mr. Collins has no business at the estate. You have John, Mr. Whitmore, the new footman, and the stable hands, so you will be well enough protected. Treat him as a trespasser if he dares to go to Longbourn. If you have him thrown into prison, perhaps he will think twice about continuing to badger you."

"I shall do so," said Elizabeth, appreciating her uncle's advice, amused it mirrored her own opinion. They spoke of the matter of Mr. Collins for a few more moments, after which her uncle asked after her mother. When he was satisfied that Mrs. Bennet had settled, he excused himself, informing her he would travel to London the following day to consult with Mr. Gardiner. Elizabeth offered him the Bennet carriage, which he gratefully accepted, and then she let herself from the room.

The journey back to Longbourn she accomplished with an absence of mind. This latest evidence of Mr. Collins's senselessness was disquieting, and Elizabeth wondered if it might be better to ensure the girls stayed close to home. Still in half mourning, they did not go out as often as they might have liked, but when they did go out, they took no precautions, as the Bennet sisters had been walking between Meryton and Longbourn as long as Elizabeth could remember. She would discuss the matter with Jane and Mary to obtain their opinions.

As she rode through Meryton, Elizabeth noted a group of officers speaking with several young ladies of the neighborhood. Elizabeth waved as she rode past, but did not stop to speak with them, for she had no desire to be delayed. There was an unfamiliar man in their midst, a tall, handsome fellow, one who seemed to understand the effect of his good looks, if the way he showed his smile to the young ladies was any indication.

Knowing she would make his acquaintance eventually, Elizabeth pressed on. Longbourn beckoned.

CHAPTER IX

Word of Mr. Phillips's intention to go to London, consult with Mr. Gardiner, and then threaten Mr. Collins, gave some relief to Mrs. Bennet's nerves. While Mrs. Bennet understood that the Bennets' continued residence at Longbourn depended on the sex of her child, her fears led her to imagine calamities that could befall them, regardless of how many times they had emphasized that point with her. Still, they all preferred a calm Mrs. Bennet to a fretful one, and Elizabeth made certain to inform her mother of their doings so she would be easy.

"That is well," said Mrs. Bennet when Elizabeth brought the news to her. "I knew my brothers would manage it. That Mr. Collins is as odious a man as has ever lived. Your father's stories of his father are nothing compared to the man himself."

"Yes, Mama," said Elizabeth, reflecting that her mother was not incorrect. "I dare say Mr. Collins is not a good man, regardless of that clerical collar he wears."

Mrs. Bennet sniffed her disdain. "I shall remain in my room today, Lizzy, and possibly tomorrow as well, for all this ruckus has made my head very ill, indeed."

"That is for the best, Mama. Sleep well."

It was fortunate, Elizabeth decided after the fact, that her mother had determined to keep to her room. The time was swiftly approaching that her condition would require her to withdraw from the sitting-room regardless, so it was better she become accustomed to it.

The next day, Longbourn received the visit of several officers of the militia, those adventurous fellows resplendent in their red coats and white trousers, much to the delight of her youngest sisters. Upon seeing the callers, Elizabeth glanced at Jane, noting her sister was as troubled as she felt. It was possible to argue that such a visit by a group of men to a house containing only women was unwise, though not precisely improper. As Jane was already two and twenty and of age, Elizabeth decided they could allow the visit to proceed. But she determined to speak to the ranking officer and remind him of their situation; if she worded it properly, they may refrain from repeating the gesture.

"Miss Bennet, Miss Elizabeth," said Lieutenant Denny, speaking for the company, "how agreeable it is to see you. It seems the welcome at Longbourn is not exaggerated, for we are pleased to be here."

The statement was silly, Elizabeth thought, for what did the welcome at Longbourn, which had yet to be offered, have to do with Denny's pleasure? He was a good sort, however, so Elizabeth and Jane essayed to welcome them to their home, calling for refreshments. Their youngest sisters, of course, displayed their eagerness to mingle with the officers, while Mary looked on with a severe expression of reproach, though at whom Elizabeth could not be certain.

"And moreover," continued Denny, "There is a recent addition to our number who has informed me of a desire to become acquainted with you all."

That was when Elizabeth noted the man she had seen while riding through Meryton the previous day. Now that Elizabeth could see the man closer, she noted his tall and erect bearing, the handsome countenance displaying an expression at once genial and eager. When he spoke, he was revealed to have a voice deep, yet melodious.

"Mr. George Wickham," said Denny, introducing him to the ladies. "Wickham, these are the Bennet sisters: Miss Jane Bennet and her sisters Miss Elizabeth, Miss Mary, Miss Catherine, and Miss Lydia."

The gentleman bowed and spoke of his pleasure, though when he rose, Elizabeth noted he cast a searching glance at both Jane and Elizabeth herself. Unable to fathom the meaning of it, Elizabeth returned his scrutiny, watching him pleasantly, but indicating no further interest.

"Thank you for your welcome," said Mr. Wickham after greeting them all by name. "I have only arrived yesterday, and yet I can already say I have never received such hospitality as I have here."

The greetings completed, the company sat down to visit, Kitty and Lydia corralling the attention of Lieutenants Denny and Sanderson, while another pair approached Jane and Mary. It was to Elizabeth herself that Mr. Wickham directed his attention, and Elizabeth could not determine whether she should feel flattered or confused.

"Miss Elizabeth," greeted he again with another bow. "Please let me say again how lovely it is to make your acquaintance. My fellow officers had much to say of Longbourn and its mistress in particular. I am pleased to report the praise was not at all overstated."

"The officers spoke of me?" asked Elizabeth, fixing the man with a skeptical look. "I cannot imagine what they could have to say. I have not been in company much with them; Kitty and Lydia are far more at liberty to speak to your fellows."

"They spoke of you all, of course," said Mr. Wickham.

Elizabeth nodded, though she thought she detected a hint of attempted deflection from the man. "The regiment's arrival coincided with our transition to half mourning. We lost our father this previous spring, you understand."

"Yes, I do," replied Mr. Wickham, his voice gentle. "And I offer my condolences. My father has been gone these five years. It is not long enough that I do not remember the melancholy of those months after I lost him."

"Thank you," said Elizabeth. Wishing to change the subject, she said: "It must be agreeable for the colonel to have a new officer. I understand that lieutenancy has been vacant for some time."

"Indeed. And as I needed occupation, the recent meeting with my friend Denny was serendipitous. I had planned . . ." Mr. Wickham paused and seemed to reconsider, saying: "But you do not wish to hear of my past, I am certain. Let us simply say that were it not for the cruelest of fate—and the actions of a man of my past who is without conscience—I would never have been in London to meet with Denny and come to the colonel's attention. I was, you see, to be a parson."

"That is interesting, Mr. Wickham, for the life of a parson is quite different to the life of an officer."

"That it is," agreed a complaisant Mr. Wickham. "While I dearly would have loved to accept the high calling, it was not to be. It is fortunate, I believe, that I possess the happy ability to adapt myself to other means of supporting myself. There are some lives to which I would be entirely unsuited, to be certain, but the life of an officer suits me as well as that of a parson."

Elizabeth was not quite certain what to make of the man's assertion, so she offered a noncommittal response. This did not seem to deter him, for he continued to speak without hesitation.

"I understand you have assumed control over the estate with your father's unfortunate passing. While you must remember that my fellow officers are not experts in the matter, I have some familiarity with estate management, and from what I can see, you have done a marvelous bit of work in a short time."

"The hiring of a good steward assisted," replied Elizabeth. "Estate management is not difficult, especially with a property as small as Longbourn."

"And yet you have taken to it with aplomb worthy of one who has many years of experience." Mr. Wickham paused, seeming in thought, and ventured: "It is strange, though, for I would have thought your father would have left the estate to your elder sister."

"Jane is an excellent woman," said Elizabeth, "yet Papa believed I was better suited to manage the family legacy."

"And an excellent choice he made!" was Mr. Wickham's expansive response. "I cannot imagine your sister would have done better. What a pleasant sight this is, for you and your sisters are so welcoming and amiable. I have never been in such a situation as this!"

From there the man continued to speak, controlling the conversation while Elizabeth listened and wondered. Mr. Wickham, she thought, was a charmer, wielding his smile with the same devastating effect a swordmaster would wield a favored blade. Before long, she had the impression the use of blandishments in his conversation was a habit of longstanding, for he flattered and flirted and made love to her with the skill of a virtuoso.

What Elizabeth could not determine was what the man was about. Militia officers, Elizabeth knew, came from the ranks of the lower gentry, their rank determined by the value of the land they or their father held. In Mr. Wickham's case, Elizabeth knew he possessed no land and was thus an exception, one often used as there was a scarcity of lieutenants. Most militia officers would pay attention to a woman with an eye toward her position in society and the amount of her fortune. For a man in Mr. Wickham's position, that need must be doubly important, for the man did not even have enough to support himself let alone a wife.

At length, the time of the visit passed, and the officers rose to leave. The grins with which Mr. Wickham's fellows regarded them did not escape her attention, though again she could not understand why that should be so. The sisters escorted them from the house, and as they did so, Elizabeth chanced to find herself near Mr. Denny; while he was not the senior officer present, he was the man to whom she was the most closely acquainted, and as there was no one higher than a lieutenant, she decided he would do to receive the important communication.

"Thank you for coming today, sir," said she, hoping her smile would disarm him. "But please remember that we are a house still in half mourning—my mother is still in first mourning—and we cannot receive visitors often. That we are all young women with no father also makes frequent visits inadvisable at best."

The officer regarded her and said: "I apologize if you believe we overstepped."

"Not at all, Mr. Denny," said Elizabeth, fixing him with a smile. "Having company is agreeable to be certain, and we are pleased to make Mr. Wickham's acquaintance. I only ask you to be sensitive to our particular needs."

The man grinned, though Elizabeth could not see what she had said to provoke such a response. "I will ensure we do so, Miss Elizabeth. Thank you again for your hospitality."

The officers soon departed, though Mr. Wickham could not leave without bowing low over her hand. As they disappeared down the drive, her sisters turned to her, and the youngest could not suppress the desire to tease.

"Lizzy has an admirer," said Lydia in a singsong voice.

"And so handsome too," added Kitty. "I wonder if we shall hear wedding bells before long."

"Not between Mr. Wickham and me," said Elizabeth, shooting them a look.

"But why not, Lizzy?" asked Kitty. "Mr. Wickham is ever so handsome."

"And utterly penniless. He informed me himself he was to become a parson, but he could not do so because of some problem. His residence in the regiment is new, his only means of support. We may lose our home within a month; does that sound like the recipe for a successful marriage, when we are each lacking the funds to support ourselves?"

"Should you truly love him, I am certain that would be no impediment." Lydia's airy reply reminded Elizabeth just what silliness her sisters could dream up.

"All the affection in the world cannot make up for an inability to provide for oneself," said Elizabeth, aware her tone had become somewhat chiding. "Mr. Wickham has no means of supporting more than himself and I have no fortune. That will not make a successful marriage.

"Moreover, you should remember that I met Mr. Wickham today. Though he oozes charm, I suspect it comes to him as easily as a duck takes to water. My heart is in no danger from the likes of Mr. Wickham."

Lydia shrugged as if it did not signify, and the Bennet sisters returned to the house.

As the days passed, the sisters noticed that Mrs. Bennet became ever more waspish. Her temper was so unsteady that the littlest thing could set her to bemoaning fate or delivering a stinging reprimand, the recipient of which could easily be an inconsiderate daughter or a sluggish servant. Soon, she confined herself to her rooms, the bulk of her care falling to Jane and Mrs. Hill. Noting this, Elizabeth promoted Sarah, their longest-serving maid, to assist with Mrs. Hill's usual duties, knowing the poor woman could not wait on her mistress at all hours of the day and night and complete the tasks associated with her position.

"Was Mama like this when confined with Kitty and Lydia?" asked Elizabeth of Jane one morning when her elder sister had sought solace in the dining room away from her demanding mother. "I have tried to remember, but as I am only five years older than Lydia, I cannot."

"I cannot say for Kitty," said Jane, "but I remember Mama being difficult before Lydia was born. Aunt Gardiner said in her last letter that for some women, being with child is a most uncomfortable time."

"And it seems Mama is cursed with every affliction suffered by women over the centuries," said Elizabeth.

Jane sighed and agreed. "She complains of pains in her back and head, the inability to move about as she would like, and the frustration of how long it is taking."

"And many other things besides," said Elizabeth. "Does she believe it is taking longer with this child? What a silly notion!"

"I believe she is uncomfortable," said Jane.

"And she is determined to make us all as uncomfortable as she."

It was not possible for Jane to refute this, for they all suspected it was the truth. Jane soon excused herself to return to her mother's room, leaving Elizabeth alone with her thoughts. Mary assisted whenever she could, but Kitty and Lydia, with their boisterous behavior, were kept away as often as possible, for their antics seemed to irritate their mother's nerves to a higher state. Elizabeth, when she could not avoid it, attended her mother, explaining some doings of the estate, or informed her of the news. She always went away quickly, for Elizabeth had no ability to calm her, no touch akin to Jane's.

Of Mr. Collins there was no further word; for the moment, her uncles' threats seemed to have done the trick. Mr. Phillips reported to Elizabeth some of what they had included in their letter, and Elizabeth found herself impressed. Surely their strongly-worded demands would have caused a man of much more mettle than William Collins to desist. Either way, the man did not write, which suited Elizabeth well.

In those days Elizabeth thought they might almost go distracted if not for the Netherfield party and her dearest friend Charlotte. As the Bennet sisters were still in half mourning and the situation at Longbourn did not allow them to leave for frequent visits, their newest neighbors visited Longbourn often, almost daily, offering the sisters a respite from their mother's ill-humors, and Charlotte came almost as often. It seemed the only time Mrs. Bennet was quiet, for she did not wish to frighten Colonel Fitzwilliam away with her loud cries.

"Oh, do not concern yourself, Elizabeth," said Charity one morning when Elizabeth made a jesting comment on the subject. "Anthony is not that faint of heart that he would run to the hills at the first sound of your mother's complaints."

"No, Charity," said Elizabeth. "I do not suppose he would."

"Perhaps we should come every day," said Anne. "We do not hear so much as a peep when we are here; if we stay all day, your mother would be much more sanguine."

Elizabeth laughed. "I cannot say if it is sanguinity, but the respite is welcome, nonetheless."

It was fortunate, to Elizabeth's mind, that the Bingleys stayed away. Mr. Bingley had shown interest in Jane and had Colonel Fitzwilliam not already impressed her as a man suited to her beloved eldest sister, Elizabeth might have welcomed him. But the disadvantage attached to his situation of having a vicious shrew for a sister rendered him less attractive as a suitor, to say nothing of Jane's obvious preference for Colonel Fitzwilliam. The Netherfield ladies, however, were not nearly so fortunate.

"Miss Bingley and Mrs. Hurst have visited us several times these past days," observed Charity when the subject of the Bingleys came up.

"Mrs. Hurst is not objectionable," added Anne, "though I will note we have little in common with her. But Miss Bingley is a woman impossible to endure. She simpers and preens and congratulates herself with every other breath, an obvious attempt to impress us. Her behavior their first visit was so objectionable that William and Anthony now absent themselves at the first hint of her coming."

It was so apt a portrayal of Miss Bingley that Elizabeth could only shake her head. Given her behavior the last time she had come to Longbourn, no Bennet sister wished her to visit again.

"I . . ." Georgiana paused, uncertain of herself until a smile from her elder cousins prompted her to speak again. "Perhaps I misunderstand her, but she has made several comments of late that make me believe she wishes me to marry her brother."

"I had wondered when you would recognize what she was saying, Georgiana," said Charity, grinning at her younger cousin.

"But I am naught but sixteen years of age!" protested Georgiana.

"Do you think that would prevent her?" asked Anne.

"And it makes perfect sense from Miss Bingley's perspective," said Elizabeth. "Marrying you would give Mr. Bingley and his family the connections to pass themselves off with credit in society."

"It would also bring her closer to her ambitions," said Charity, laughter in her voice. "If you marry her brother, she draws a step closer to marrying your brother or mine."

"That is a rather enormous leap of logic," said Elizabeth, stifling her laughter.

"One marriage often begets another, does it not?" said Charity.

"Perhaps such thinking might be understandable," said Anne, "if her brother were Darcy or Fitzwilliam's friend. But Darcy only watches him and hides behind his mask of indifference, and Fitzwilliam seems to be impatient with him."

"But why does she not fix on you or Anne as her brother's future bride?" asked Georgiana.

"Perhaps because she knows she cannot direct us," said Charity.

"I rather think it is because she believes she can rule Georgiana as she wishes," said Anne. "Any such attempt to rule you or me will gain her nothing more than a stinging set down."

"Which she might get anyway," said Charity. "There are few who deserve it more than Miss Bingley, I think."

Georgiana soon left their company to sit with Mary, and Jane joined them, reporting that their mother was quiet, though perhaps not as comfortable as she might have wished. As the gentlemen had not come that day—the ladies mentioned some matter of estate business—they settled into a comfortable visit with their new friends.

As for Mr. Bingley, Elizabeth could not think about the gentleman without some perturbation of spirit. He had, she thought, the qualities to be an exceptional man. Yet, his sister was a detriment attached to his situation that could not be ignored. Had he shown a tendency to defer to her, Elizabeth might have been ready to break the connection altogether. The way he had apologized and taken his sister from Longbourn the last time they had been there, however, spoke to his understanding of her character and brought her some hope he would reform her or do what was necessary to ensure she did not embarrass him.

Later that day after their friends left, Elizabeth retired to her father's study to accomplish a bit of work on the estate ledgers. Even almost five months after her father's death, Elizabeth could not help thinking of the room as her father's demesne, for she had associated it as such from her earliest memories. There were still times when she entered, expecting to see him behind his desk, expecting to hear his greeting as he looked up from his book and fixed her, his favorite daughter, with a wide smile. The knowledge of the way he had avoided his responsibilities was nothing compared to how much she had loved him.

Elizabeth had not been in this attitude for long when a knock on the door surprised her. When she called out permission to enter, Jane slipped into the room and approached the desk, an expression of uncharacteristic seriousness in her mien.

"Is there a problem with mama, Jane?" asked Elizabeth.

"No, Lizzy. Mrs. Hill tells me Mama is sleeping. I thought I would use the time before she wakes to speak to you."

"Oh?" asked Elizabeth, intrigued by her sister's statement. "Do you have something particular to say?"

Jane hesitated, and Elizabeth thought she sensed a hint of abnormal diffidence in her manner. "I have observed," said she at length, "that you have done much for the estate; much more, in fact, than our father ever did."

Sighing, Elizabeth leaned back in her chair and gazed down at her hands folded in her lap. "Do not suppose I am attempting to criticize, Jane, but these past months have taught me that Papa did not do as he ought. I understand his unwillingness to improve an estate he thought would not prosper his family, but it was such a shortsighted stance that I can scarce comprehend it."

"It was," agreed Jane. "You know Papa was never happy doing estate work, and when he did not like something, he ignored it until he had no alternative."

"Well do I know it." Elizabeth paused and sighed. "Yet, if he had paid more attention to the estate and tried to raise the profits, had he attempted to control Mama and economize for our future support, we would not be facing the uncertainty we are now. There is not much money, even after Mr. Whitmore collected the rents, and we shall depend on Uncle Gardiner if Mama's child is not a son. Had Papa worked to improve the production of the estate, it would have been possible to save more than he did, which would have improved our position."

Jane nodded. "This I understand, Lizzy. But even so, there is little you can do to alter our fortunes in such a short season. Should Mama birth a boy, our futures will be assured."

"As long as he stays healthy," interjected Elizabeth.

"Yes. What I am trying to say, Lizzy, is that you are often in this room—too often, in my opinion. You are a young woman and should have the concerns of a young woman. Dusty tomes and estate matters cannot rule your life to the exclusion of all other concerns."

"If a son arrives," said Elizabeth, feeling obstinacy well up within her, "I must be ready to implement the changes Mr. Whitmore and I discussed. I wish to improve our position, Jane, to add to the dowries my sisters possess and make them more attractive to potential suitors. Mr. Gardiner has pledged to assist in whatever way he can."

"That is commendable, Lizzy, and we all thank you for it. But I have two questions: what of your dowry and what of your need to live, not just care for Longbourn?"

"As for the first," said Elizabeth, "I do not think I shall wed anytime soon. Let us take care of you and Mary first, after which I can give thought to myself and the younger girls. As for the second, I do not think I am doing too much."

Jane sighed. "We all appreciate your efforts, Elizabeth, but we think you sometimes lose yourself to the management of the property. When we were girls, we were carefree and hopeful for the future. I know we are adults now and have the cares of adults. But I would see a hint of that carefree attitude in you again, for I fear it is being suppressed in the minutia of your ambitions for Longbourn."

"Thank you for your concern, Jane," said Elizabeth. She rose, made her way around the desk, and sat in the chair next to her sister's, laying her head on her shoulder. "I do not wish to become a slave to duty. It is my hope we will have a brother soon, though he will not inherit the estate for many years. With that, however, we can relax a little."

"I hope so, Lizzy." Jane turned away a little, and Elizabeth pulled her head off her shoulder. "Shall we perhaps go for a short walk? It has been some time since you last walked; I am certain you must miss it."

The carefree laugh with which Elizabeth responded was an old friend, one she thought she had missed now that Jane's words had opened her eyes. "I will have you know I range long and far when I walk for pleasure. Shall you keep up with me?"

"I shall do so if I must."

"Then let us go, Jane. The outside world beckons us."

It was more than an hour before they returned. Mrs. Bennet was calling for Jane, and the study called for Elizabeth, for there were a few matters that required her attention. The sisters separated to handle their sundry tasks, and Elizabeth felt lighter because of her sister's actions. Hope filled her, such hope as she had not known since she had been a girl.

CHAPTER X

"What is that you have there?"

Fitzwilliam's gesture to the paper held in his hand prompted Darcy to look up from the letter he was perusing. "A note from Bingley."

"That is unusual," said Fitzwilliam. "You are not well acquainted with him. What does he want?"

"He begs my opinion with some problem of his estate." Darcy paused and grinned at his cousin. "It seems I am forever at the beck and call of those who claim little experience and wish to induce me into managing their estates for them."

"And here I thought I would maintain the secrecy of my plan for a little longer," jested Fitzwilliam. "You have already found me out!"

Darcy chuckled along with his cousin. "If I were not here, I am certain you would do well enough on your own."

"As would Bingley, I presume," said Fitzwilliam to Darcy's nod. "What do you mean to do?"

"There is no difficulty in offering my help," replied Darcy. "Though I would not appreciate being called upon day and night to handle every little detail, Bingley has not done that, though he knows I inherited some years ago."

Fitzwilliam nodded, distracted. "What do you think of him?"

"Other than the utter disaster of a sister?" Grinning, Fitzwilliam motioned him to continue. "Bingley is a good enough fellow, I suppose, but he has always seemed a little . . . thoughtless to me. His current situation managing an estate is a point in his favor, so perhaps he is outgrowing his tendency to treat the future as a lark."

"He is a jolly fellow. Did you know he reprimanded his sister the day they came to Longbourn while they were there?"

With a grimace, Darcy nodded his head. "Miss Elizabeth would not say much on the subject, but she said enough. How Miss Bingley would think it is acceptable to treat anyone with such contempt is beyond me. Even if she had the largest dowry and was the most beautiful woman in all the land, I could not bear to live with such a woman for five minutes, let alone a lifetime."

"It is often said the true measure of a person is revealed in the way they treat those beneath them. Or perhaps, in Miss Bingley's case, those she thinks are beneath her."

"She is delusional if she believes a handsome dowry raises her to the heights of society," said Darcy.

"Of course, she is. The Miss Bennets are high above her in every way that matters, regardless of the poor state of their fortunes. But Miss Bingley will not see that."

Fitzwilliam paused and eyed him with interest. "So, you mean to go, I presume?"

"I have no hesitation of offering my assistance." Darcy grinned at his cousin. "Bingley informs me his sisters mean to visit Netherfield again this morning." Fitzwilliam's look skyward told Darcy his opinion of Miss Bingley's obstinacy. "As he has given me the time of their intended departure, if we leave some time before that and make ourselves scarce in Meryton until they pass by, we can miss them altogether."

The laugh with which Fitzwilliam responded echoed what Darcy was feeling. "Bingley seems to be far more erudite a gentleman than I might have thought, for he understands our feelings for his sister."

"And gives me some hope for his character," replied Darcy. "Most men in his position would do whatever they could to forward a match with one of us."

"Most men would personally see their sisters to our bedchambers to compromise us, particularly given the lady's character and Bingley's obvious desire to be rid of her."

"True, Cousin."

"Then let us depart thirty minutes before we expect Miss Bingley to leave Pulvis Lodge. If we can avoid her, I shall be very well pleased."

As they had designed, they did not meet the Bingley carriage between Netherfield and Meryton. In the town, they spent some moments perusing the shops, Fitzwilliam making a purchase in the town's small general store. Then, when they judged it likely that the carriage had already passed through the town, they mounted their horses again and took the correct road, arriving at the estate soon after.

Pulvis Lodge, Darcy noted, was similar in size to Longbourn, but the similarities ended there. The house was an older building, a more sprawling complex of a house, one that had been added to several times over the years. The drive was not so well maintained as Longbourn's, the grounds were less extensive, and there was no village near its entrance. Yet, it appeared sound and maintained such that the house would provide comfort, if not luxury to its inhabitants.

"Darcy," said Bingley as he greeted them, extending his hand. "Thank you for coming. The matter is, I believe, not a difficult one, yet I am afraid of making a mistake which might be costly."

"It is no trouble, Bingley," said Darcy. "Shall we?"

The issue at hand was the cottage of a tenant near the manor, a structure, though sound, that had been inundated with water during a recent rain, and the tenant had asked for the Bingley's support. The culprit was, Darcy noted quickly, an inadequate drainage system that had not diverted water from the house as it was supposed to, coupled with a recently collapsed bank on a nearby stream. Darcy pointed out the defects to both his companions, helping them understand how the problem could be ameliorated with a little labor. Then when he explained the matter to the tenant, the man appeared relieved, promising to gather some neighbors together to assist, Bingley agreeing to take on the expense of the alterations.

"Thank you again," said Bingley as they rode away, his tone relieved and anxious to relay his gratitude. "I had some notion of what had to be done, but the problem with the stream had quite missed my notice. The measures of which I was thinking would have helped, but by next spring the problem likely would have returned."

"It is no trouble, Bingley," said Darcy, eager to reassure his acquaintance. "Estate management is, the same as anything else, equal parts hard work, experience, and a determination to confront problems when they occur. The first and third you have, while you can only develop the second by being engaged in your estate. I would be much more concerned if you were a man who preferred to procrastinate, for minor problems tend to become significant problems if they are left unattended."

"There is a bit of sage advice in that statement, I think," said Fitzwilliam with his typical levity.

Darcy's companions laughed at Fitzwilliam's jest, Darcy looking on diverted at how they seemed to get on. Bingley and Fitzwilliam, he decided, were not dissimilar characters. Where they differed was that Bingley, when Darcy knew him at Cambridge, did not seem to have a more serious side, while Darcy's cousin knew when to refrain from jesting and concentrate on the task at hand. It was possible that this venture into estate management was providing valuable life experience to Bingley, though it was equally possible his troubles with his sister had forced him to mature. Darcy almost felt he could like this Bingley.

"Shall you join me at Pulvis Lodge for a drink?" asked Bingley. "By my calculation, Caroline should not be returning for some time yet, which should allow you to make your escape unmolested before she comes."

Darcy agreed for the cousins, seeing Fitzwilliam had no real disliking for the scheme, but then he turned an interested look on his acquaintance. "I must own to some surprise, Bingley. I am much more accustomed to men with unmarried sisters and daughters eager to push them toward me rather than helping me avoid them."

The grimace with which Bingley responded spoke to his feelings on the subject. "While I will own the thought of ceding Caroline's protection to another man fills me with eagerness, I can readily see that you do not favor her. I have no desire to push her on a man who does not want her, even if it would make my life easier if she was no longer living in my home."

Again, Darcy exchanged a glance with his cousin, for Bingley's reply had impressed him. "My cousin and I thank you, Bingley. Many men would not care if I favored a daughter or sister with whom they were intent upon dispensing."

Bingley shrugged and changed the subject. In this agreeable manner, they traveled the short distance to the house where Bingley invited them inside and showed them to the small study near the manor's entrance. There they met with Mr. Hurst, who appeared to be more energetic than Darcy might have expected. When they ensconced themselves in the study, Hurst observed his brother by marriage.

"Was Darcy's advice to your liking, Bingley?"

"It was excellent, Hurst. I apologize if you feel slighted with my determination to ask him, for I expect you might have told me the same."

Darcy wondered if he should be affronted, that Bingley had somehow brought him here to ingratiate himself on Darcy's notice. The situation, however, seemed more than that, for Bingley turned to Darcy and regarded him, an apology in his mien.

"I believe I did well to call on Darcy, for beyond the obvious deficiencies, he discovered a problem with the stream bank."

"Is that so?" asked Hurst, turning an appraising look on Darcy. "It seems my indolence has caught up to me, for it never occurred to me to check such a thing."

"It was not difficult to notice," said Darcy with a shrug. "I have learned to watch for other contributing factors to a problem. There is no great secret to it."

"Knowing that much is half the battle," observed Hurst. "Having the experience to spot such flaws the other half."

"Do you own your estate?" asked Fitzwilliam with interest.

Hurst grimaced and shook his head. "My father is yet among the living, Colonel, and a more irascible man would be difficult to find. Though I have some experience, most of what I require I will gain when he finally shuffles off this mortal coil and ceases to bedevil me."

"The way you speak of your father still amazes me, Hurst," said Bingley, shaking his head in disbelief. "I would give much to have my father with me even now."

"As would I," said Darcy quietly.

"Because your fathers were good and amiable men, while mine is impossible." Hurst turned back to Darcy and Fitzwilliam. "My father married late and is thus quite elderly now. While I cannot say he is a bad man, he is difficult. I dare say he hastened my mother's demise with his ways, though she was many years younger. I can understand cherished ties to a beloved parent, even if I have never been close to my father. Though I do not wish ill on him, I do await the day when I become my own master."

It was not an unusual sentiment, Darcy reflected. There were several men of his acquaintance who had voiced the same within his hearing, usually accompanied by a shrug or a look of disbelief when Darcy spoke of his ties with his own father. Their relationship had been close, regardless of what a certain libertine with whom Darcy no longer associated said on the subject. Even now five years after his passing, there were times when Darcy's wish for his father's presence was akin to a physical ache.

From there, the discussion wound along other pathways, becoming more desultory in nature, until Darcy, deciding they had best be on their way, looked to Fitzwilliam and signaled their need to depart when his cousin agreed. It was unfortunate, but not unsurprising when they learned they would not make their escape as completely as they hoped the moment they left the room.

"Mr. Darcy!" exclaimed Miss Bingley when she espied them. "I had no notion of your presence here today. And you too, Colonel Fitzwilliam."

"Your brother asked for our opinion with a matter of the estate, Miss Bingley," said Darcy, not quite successful in hiding his distaste for this woman. While everyone else likely noted it, Miss Bingley appeared blind.

"And a better pair of mentors Charles could not find if he searched the length and breadth of England!"

Fitzwilliam, grinning at the woman's overdone flattery, said: "For my part, I thank you, Miss Bingley, though I will note I am as new to estate management as your brother. Darcy, here, is the old hand at it."

The glare Darcy directed at his cousin did nothing to wipe the grin off his face. Miss Bingley only simpered at him.

"You are far too modest I am certain, Colonel Fitzwilliam. Now that you are here, shall you not stay for dinner? We may dispatch a note to your excellent relations so they can join us too."

"Thank you, Miss Bingley," interjected Darcy, unwilling to allow her to continue to flatter them. "But I believe Fitzwilliam and I must return to Netherfield."

"But—"

The clearing of Hurst's throat cut short whatever argument she intended to make. The woman did not hide the glare she directed at her sister's husband, but she did not make an issue of it.

"That is unfortunate, Mr. Darcy. Then I shall send our card around for another night. I am certain I speak for our entire family that we are eager to have you for dinner."

"Again, you have our thanks, Miss Bingley," said Fitzwilliam, now as eager as Darcy to depart. "We shall wait with breathless anticipation."

With alacrity, the cousins made their farewells, exiting through the doors with Bingley and Hurst in tow. Miss Bingley, Darcy noted, saw nothing of the insincerity in Fitzwilliam's tone, for the woman fairly preened at the supposed eagerness to be in her company. Darcy could think of several barnyard animals with whom he would prefer to dine rather than Miss Bingley.

Before long, they were in the saddle and cantering down the drive to the road beyond. Soon after, Darcy became aware of his cousin's sniggering.

"Well, Cousin?" asked he. "Which of us do you suppose she will try to entrap first?"

Darcy could not withhold the mirth he felt at his cousin's jest. "Oh, you without a doubt! Why, you are the son of an earl, while I am naught but a gentleman, after all. As you possess the means to purchase your own estate, I cannot imagine Miss Bingley would pass up the status of being a close relation to an earl for a simple gentleman."

"But you are much wealthier," was Fitzwilliam's agreeable reply. "My wealth is a pittance next to yours and Pemberley is a powerful lure." Fitzwilliam laughed and added: "If Miss Bingley ever saw Pemberley, I suspect she would move into your bedchambers at once and ignore the insignificant fact that she had not even had the benefit of a wedding!"

It was all too apropos an observation. But Darcy was not about to cede defeat. "Being in a position to tell her cronies that she is the sister of the Earl of Matlock is far more valuable than wealth."

"Wealth trumps all other concerns with her, Darcy. And she could still say she is married to the scion of an earl."

Laughing, Darcy had to own his cousin had a point. "And your paying attention to Miss Bennet must be a point against you."

"Can you imagine she would care about that for even a moment?" asked Fitzwilliam, his tone incredulous. "I am certain Miss Bingley feels capable of triumphing over a country nobody such as Miss Bennet. And if she must, she may push the upstart out of the way and take her place."

"Though we jest, you know she is capable of all this and more."

"Without a doubt." Fitzwilliam paused and considered the woman of whom they were speaking so irreverently. "Let us simply be grateful we do not live in the same house. If we did, we would need to keep the keys on our persons at all times and lock the door of whatever room in which we were alone. The threat of a compromise would always hover over us."

"Too true," said Darcy.

With those words, they left the subject of the woman behind. Darcy did not wish to speak of her, and his cousin had another woman about whom it would be much more pleasant to think. For that matter, considering Miss Elizabeth was far more pleasant than Miss Bingley could ever be.

When the inquisition came, Elizabeth found herself surprised by it, though she supposed she should not have been. Jane was, after all, the focus of the attention of a man of considerable standing in society. What surprised her more was what their friends had to say about her relationship with the other gentleman of the party.

"What a pleasant time this is," said Charity, sitting with Jane and Elizabeth in Longbourn's sitting-room. On this occasion, Kitty and Lydia had gone into Meryton for a time, complete with a stern warning of what would happen if reports reached their ears of their misbehavior in the town. As Mary had taken Jane's place in sitting with their mother so Jane could be present, it was only they two with Charity and Anne; Georgiana had remained at Netherfield with her companion for some lessons.

"Much more pleasant than our last visitors." Anne paused and shook her head. "Miss Bingley was not best pleased to learn that Darcy and Anthony had been at Pulvis Lodge while she was visiting us, and even less when they declined her invitation to dinner."

"We are fortunate they have not visited Longbourn since the last time they came," said Elizabeth.

"You have not seen them?" asked Charity.

"Once, at another function," replied Jane.

"As we do not go out much, our exposure to them has been limited."

"And yet, I suppose Mr. Bingley was by Jane's side as much as he could manage?"

The arch manner in which she spoke suggested amusement, but Elizabeth was certain there was a hard undertone in Charity's words. Yet Jane could not refute an obvious truth.

"Mr. Bingley was . . . quite attentive."

The ladies regarded Jane, trying to understand her feelings on the matter if Elizabeth was any judge. When Jane was not more forthcoming, Charity raised the subject directly.

"And how do you feel about Mr. Bingley, Jane?"

"He is an amiable man," said Jane. Elizabeth knew her sister would not dissemble, though she could be counted on to speak of another in the best possible terms. "I enjoy his company, but I do not ask for it."

"I hope you do not find our questions officious," said Anne, the more diplomatic of the two.

"Not at all, Anne." Jane shared a bright smile with their guests. "I am not blind to your cousin's preference for me. You will forgive me if I say that I prefer his company in equal measure, but I assure you that I have no expectations of him. I am content to wait for him to state his intentions and will have nothing with which to reproach him if he refrains."

The two ladies regarded her for a moment, wide grins on their faces. "If Darcy were to hear what you are saying, I am certain he would fall over from his shock. It is his cherished belief that every woman of society is hunting for a wealthy husband and will stop at nothing to obtain one."

"But surely he does not suspect such a thing of me!" protested Jane.

"No, Jane, I do not think he does," said Charity with a pat of Jane's hand. "But you must understand that Darcy is a wealthy and prominent man, one who has been master of his property from a young age. Many ladies of high society are exactly as he suspects, and that colors his view of the rest."

"And is Colonel Fitzwilliam afflicted by this same brand of cynicism?" asked Elizabeth. When Charity looked at her, Elizabeth chuckled and added: "Not that I would blame him, of course."

"No, I cannot imagine you would," replied Charity. "My brother is well aware of the machinations of many young ladies of society, but his more open and jovial character protects him to a certain extent from such cynicism."

"If you are trying to understand my feelings," interjected Jane into the conversation, "please know that I like your brother a great deal. But I cannot say what he feels about me. Thus, I take care of my feelings and do not wish to hope without reason. Should he give me that reason, I shall allow myself to dream."

"I do not know my brother's mind," said Charity. "At the same time, I can tell you that he likes you very well. One would have to be blind to miss it."

"What of you, Elizabeth?" asked Anne. "You are often in Darcy's company. Do you like him as well as Jane likes Anthony?"

Surprised that her friend would suggest such a thing, Elizabeth was quick to shake her head. "Mr. Darcy is an agreeable man, but I have no hopes in that quarter. The gentleman does not give the appearance of a man who admires a woman, and at present, with my duties to Longbourn, I cannot give thought to such matters."

"Remember, Darcy is not as open as my brother. For him, I suspect his seeking your company establishes his regard for you as no less than a fact."

Elizabeth eyed them with skepticism, but she decided it did not signify. "He is an excellent man, as you well know. At present, however, I suspect there is nothing of admiration in his manner. He seems to be fascinated that I can manage the estate without significant errors, and that draws his attention."

Charity and Anne looked at each other and burst into laughter. "What a picture you paint of my cousin!" exclaimed Charity. "By this account, Darcy is a dreadful misogynist!"

"And he has seen my mother manage my estate for many years," said Anne. "Mother is adept, so it cannot surprise Darcy to meet another woman who possesses similar talents."

"You simply want Darcy married to another so your mother will stop harping on her cradle arrangement story."

"Cradle arrangement?" echoed Elizabeth confused.

Anne looked skyward, her exasperation marked. "Mama has been saying as long as I can remember that she and her sister—Darcy's mother—agreed when we were both children that we should wed."

"But that is not true!" exclaimed Charity. "Your mother did not begin to speak of the matter until after Lady Anne's passing, and more particularly, after Robert Darcy's death."

"Perhaps she did not speak of it to the rest of the family," said Anne, her manner a little prim, "but she spoke of it to me constantly. What you all received with surprise after Robert Darcy died, I had heard from my earliest childhood."

"Then you are not engaged to him?" asked Elizabeth, interested in their account.

"Darcy has declined to offer for me," replied Anne. "And I would not accept him if he did. We say little to Mother on the subject, knowing the strife that would arise if we informed her of our opinions. But we have been determined for several years now that we will not bow to her wishes."

"Your mother sounds like a forceful lady," observed Elizabeth.

"You have no idea," was Anne's wry reply.

"Then shall she join you at some point? I feel a great curiosity to meet her and take her likeness for myself."

"You should take care in wishing for such things, Elizabeth," said Charity. "If you do not, they may come true."

"Surely she cannot be so very stern!" exclaimed Jane.

"My mother is not in the habit of being gainsaid," said Anne. "You should hope that my cousin proposes to you before you meet her so he can present your marriage as a fait accompli. If he does not, there is no telling what she will say in opposition. Lady Catherine de Bourgh is a woman who prefers to keep the distinction of rank in mind at all times!"

Together they laughed and by common consent changed the subject. That they approved of her dearest sister was a relief to Elizabeth, for she knew many of their station would not. Now that they had gained some measure of understanding of Jane's feelings, they appeared more confident on the subject.

As for Elizabeth's situation with Mr. Darcy, she could not imagine that any such interest existed, so she could allow the matter to rest with tolerable ease. When she wished for a husband, Elizabeth knew well that a man such as Mr. Darcy would be an excellent partner. But she could not see any interest from the gentleman's side, so there was nothing to consider.

CHAPTER XI

*P*ersistence, it seemed, was a trait that Mr. William Collins possessed in abundance, though Elizabeth wondered at a man who continued to write a house full of women rather than the men who were tasked with speaking for them. It seemed to suggest a man who was a coward and a bully, one who would attempt to get his way by preying on those he perceived were weaker than he. Given Elizabeth's opinion, the contents of his letter were not at all palatable for any young woman of sense.

"You have received another letter from Mr. Collins?" asked Jane when she entered the study that morning.

"I have, little though I might wish it," replied Elizabeth, throwing the letter down on the desk with disgust. "It occurs to me to wonder if Mr. Collins is simply silly or malevolent, for there is something entirely wrong with him."

"What does he have to say?" asked Jane.

"Nothing we might wish to hear. First, he opens by 'suggesting' he come to Longbourn to visit us for a time."

Jane frowned. "But that would be improper."

"And it astounds me that a supposed man of the cloth would not see it," replied Elizabeth. "Either that or he ignores it in favor of satisfying his selfish desires. Then once he is finished spouting that bit of nonsense, Mr. Collins offers to marry one of us so he can 'provide us with a home' when he inherits."

The contemplative look which came over Jane's face surprised Elizabeth, though she supposed she should have expected it, given what she knew of her sister. "Perhaps that is for the best, Lizzy. Should I marry Mr. Collins, there would be no question of our support, regardless of Mama's child."

"Jane!" cried Elizabeth. "You cannot possibly suggest that you sacrifice yourself for our sake."

"It should be my responsibility," was Jane's mild reply. "As I am the eldest, the task of lifting our fortunes should fall to me."

"And what of Colonel Fitzwilliam? Do you think he will be so calm when you 'lift our fortunes' by marrying a man without sense or honor?"

"I do not think Mr. Collins without honor, Lizzy," said Jane.

"If that is all you concern yourself about what I asked, I could not be more surprised, Jane. It seemed to me you were enjoying the colonel's attentions to you."

With a sigh, Jane sat back and acknowledged Elizabeth's point. "I do like Colonel Fitzwilliam very much, Lizzy. At present, I will not say I am in love with him. But I am painfully aware of how much I could love him if I allowed myself to do so."

"Then let us have no more talk of sacrificing yourself to Mr. Collins for our sake." Elizabeth glared at her sister until Jane agreed, though she did not do so without pausing first. "Good. Whatever else we face in life, Jane, we cannot compromise our integrity. Better we should be in reduced circumstances than to throw away our dignity for the security of a man of suspect character."

It appeared to Elizabeth that her sister was relieved, though Jane made little outward reaction. Jane could be stubborn when she felt she was in the right, so her easy capitulation was welcome. Elizabeth would not see her dearest sister married to a fool if there was anything she could do about it.

"Then what will you do, Lizzy?" asked Jane.

"What have I done every other time Mr. Collins has importuned us?" said Elizabeth, shaking her head with disdain and turning her attention back to the letter on the desk. "I shall engage our uncles to respond to him. Uncle Gardiner will instruct me to call the constable should Mr. Collins show himself here regardless of his warning. That is a direction I will have no hesitation in following."

Again, Jane appeared to hesitate. "Is it not wiser to attempt to keep Mr. Collins's good opinion?"

"I do not believe we have Mr. Collins's good opinion even now," replied Elizabeth. "There is something . . . I do not know, to be honest. But something is strange about Mr. Collins and his insistence on his ownership of Longbourn. I cannot quite make the man out."

"It is not surprising, Lizzy," replied Jane. "Given he was assured he would inherit the estate until Mama's condition came to light, you can hardly blame him for his displeasure at the possibility of being pushed to the side."

"No, I do not speak of that, Jane. It is, as you say, unsurprising he would be unhappy given the circumstances. But there is something strange about him, nonetheless, something I cannot quite understand."

"Do you suppose he is capable of unchristian or improper behavior?"

"I cannot say for certain of what I believe him capable," said Elizabeth. "But we have evidence enough of his silliness for me to be wary of him. I shall not relax my guard where Mr. Collins is concerned."

A knock on the door interrupted their conversation, Sarah entering the room when Elizabeth called permission. The woman appeared a little hesitant as if she did not wish to speak. Then she plucked up her courage and spoke.

"Miss Bennet, Miss Elizabeth, visitors have come to Longbourn."

"Oh?" asked Elizabeth with a frown. Visitors had been scarce since their father's passing, and other than the recent visits of the Netherfield party—of which they had had one that morning—the only other visitors they had other than Charlotte had been . . .

"The officers of the militia," said Sarah.

Exchanging a look, Elizabeth turned back to the maid. "Can I assume the officers are in the sitting-room with my sisters?"

"Yes, Miss," said Sarah. "Misses Kitty and Lydia were eager to see them, and Miss Mary is keeping watch on them."

"As we might have expected," said Elizabeth with a laugh. "Very well, we shall go there directly."

When Sarah curtseyed and departed, Elizabeth turned an expressive look on her sister.

"Did you not speak to Lieutenant Denny about visiting us often?"

"It appears to have done little, as you can see," said Elizabeth. "By my count, this is the fourth time they have visited since Mr. Wickham joined the regiment."

"Do you suggest Mr. Wickham is the instigator?" asked Jane with a frown.

"If it is not he, I do not know who it is. The timing suggests a correlation, and with the man so intent on charming me, this constant imposing upon us is more than a little suspicious, would you not agree?"

It was difficult for Jane to confess such things, Elizabeth knew. Here, however, Elizabeth knew her arguments were sound.

"What do you mean to do?"

Elizabeth considered the question. "It appears I was in error when I spoke to Mr. Denny. Perhaps I should make it clear to Mr. Wickham himself that we do not wish for his presence."

"Yes, perhaps that would be best."

"Miss Elizabeth!" greeted Mr. Wickham as soon as they entered the room, his pleasure upon seeing her evident, though some niggling thought wormed its way through Elizabeth's consciousness that there was something off about his enthusiasm. "How wonderful it is to see you. I would very much appreciate your company if you will oblige me."

Had Elizabeth not suspected the man's motives, she might have missed the grins sported by his companions. Yet uncertain why Mr. Wickham might have focused his attention on her though she was, the behavior of these officers was beginning to perturb her. Thus, she decided she was not about to endure it any longer.

"Of course, Mr. Wickham," said she out loud. "I am at your disposal."

It seemed to Elizabeth as they spoke that Mr. Wickham was supremely confident as if he were getting exactly what he wished. Was his motive simple seduction? That was possible, for there were many rakes in the world who interested themselves in the affairs of young ladies for no more reason than instant physical gratification and the ability to boast of his prowess to all his friends. That it may be for her person, Elizabeth discarded without another thought. Men such as Mr. Wickham did not throw their affections at a young woman when they could not even hope to support themselves.

For a moment, Elizabeth toyed with the notion that he might think he could gain control of Longbourn by marrying her. But that did not seem right either, for the truth of the situation was not a secret in Meryton. Even if Mr. Wickham succeeded in his apparent desire, the estate would pass to her brother when he came of age, if they were not all required to leave within the next month if their mother gave them a sister.

Regardless of what the gentlemen meant by his attentions Elizabeth was not interested in him. Mr. Wickham was a man, as Elizabeth had thought more than once, who oozed charm, one who wielded it like a mace. To a young woman who had nothing but a handsome countenance in her head, he would likely prove irresistible. But Elizabeth thought the application of his charm was more than a little heavy-handed, and she had met many more handsome men than he.

The image of Mr. Darcy rose in her mind, filling Elizabeth with contentment. It did not escape her notice that Mr. Wickham seemed to take this as encouragement, for he redoubled his efforts to charm her. Elizabeth ignored this, murmuring a response when she thought it likely he expected one, yet her thoughts were more fixed on the gentleman from the north. Mr. Darcy, she decided, was a man whose affection any woman would be fortunate to receive.

When the time came for the officers to depart, Elizabeth rose with her sisters to see them to the door. In a scene reminiscent of the previous occasion in which she spoke with Mr. Denny, Elizabeth decided it was time to acquaint him with the particulars of the situation.

"It seems to me, Mr. Wickham," said Elizabeth, hanging back, prompting the officer to remain with her, "that you have come frequently of late."

Mr. Wickham smiled, seeming to believe her purpose was to thank or welcome him, rather than warn him away. "The neighborhood is a welcoming one, Miss Elizabeth, but no other house can compare with Longbourn."

"I thank you for that bit of flattery, sir," replied Elizabeth. Mr. Wickham started a little at the word "flattery," though his countenance did not break. "It appears that I must remind you, however, that we are still a house in mourning, and frequent visits are not proper."

"You are in half mourning, as I understood," said the lieutenant.

"That is true, Mr. Wickham," said Elizabeth. "But my mother is still in deep mourning."

"And yet we have not seen your mother."

It was a crack, a slight one to be sure, but one Elizabeth could not miss, considering the scrutiny with which she regarded the officer. "My mother has kept to her room of late, Mr. Wickham."

"I see," said the officer.

"Regardless, as we are a family of young women, I would ask you to respect that. While we do not refuse visitors entrance into the house, four times in the past week is excessive. Please respect our need for privacy."

"Of course," said Mr. Wickham with a low bow. "I should never presume to bring discomfort to you, Miss Elizabeth."

They made their way to the entrance where the others awaited them, and Elizabeth did not misunderstand the grins the other men were giving Mr. Wickham. Elizabeth did not concern herself for their assumptions, for they would discover the truth of the matter soon enough. If Mr. Wickham did not make up some other story for why they went to Longbourn less.

"You stayed in Mr. Wickham's company for some moments, Lizzy," said Lydia, giving her a coy look when the officers had departed.

"To warn him that the officers presumed much by coming so often."

Surprised as she was by Elizabeth's clipped tone, Lydia understood the implications at once and was not pleased by them. As such, Elizabeth spoke to forestall her coming outburst.

"It is not proper, Lydia. This you must acknowledge."

"No, it is not," interjected Mary, her tone all primness. "These officers should know better than to visit a house containing naught but women so often."

That Lydia did not appreciate what Mary was saying was no surprise. That she decided it was best not to argue the matter was a relief.

"Then I suppose it must be so since you already spoke to them," grumbled Lydia.

"I have," said Elizabeth. "And I hope they will amend their conduct. I have no wish to deny them entrance, though Jane and I will if we must."

Jane nodded, putting an end to any argument Lydia thought to make. The sisters entered the house again, and this time Elizabeth hoped Mr. Wickham had understood the point and would exercise greater circumspection in the future.

Netherfield Park was the recipient of a long-feared yet expected visitor only a few days before the ball. That she arrived in the middle of their ball preparations was a fortunate happenstance.

Darcy and Fitzwilliam rarely concerned themselves with their planning, for as their relations informed them amid laughing jests, their assistance was neither welcome nor helpful. Yet, as the ball was rapidly approaching, they were often called in to assist with tasks that required their greater height and strength.

"Can the servants not manage this?" asked Fitzwilliam when the ladies demanded their presence, his wide grin informing them he was teasing.

"The servants have their own tasks to complete," was Charity's prim reply. "Remember, Brother, that you asked us to plan this event for you. It is only fair that you assist in its execution."

"Yes, Fitzwilliam," jibed Darcy. "Do pay more attention."

"Yes, Mr. Darcy," was Fitzwilliam's irreverent reply.

They were ensconced in the ballroom for some moments when the sound of a cane striking the tiles reached their ears. It was only a moment before the dread countenance of Lady Catherine de Bourgh appeared through the door, regarding them all with her usual interest and intensity.

"Mother!" said Anne, rising to greet her mother. "We had no word of your coming."

"Of course, you did not, Anne," said Lady Catherine, though regarding her daughter with a softness she reserved for her. "For I did not inform you."

"You are welcome, of course," said Fitzwilliam, though Darcy knew his cousin's opinion of his aunt's presence mirrored his own.

"How are you finding this first foray into the world of a landed gentleman, Fitzwilliam?" asked Lady Catherine as she moved into the room. "Is it everything you thought it would be?"

"I am not unfamiliar with the life, Aunt," said Fitzwilliam with a shrug. "It is far more pastoral than the experiences of a soldier, and after years of such a life I am not unhappy to transition to a new purpose."

"As you should be, Nephew," said Lady Catherine with a nod. "Had your mother lived to see you give up your commission, she would have been well pleased. You know how much she worried about you."

Fitzwilliam nodded but did not reply.

"I shall have a room prepared for you to occupy, Aunt," said Charity.

"A good hostess has such rooms available for unexpected guests," replied Lady Catherine, her tone sharp.

Charity, far from being offended, grinned and said: "I did not say it was unavailable, Aunt. Only that it needed to be prepared for an occupant."

"Very well," said their aunt. She peered at them all critically. "It appears you are preparing for an event of some sort."

"I have decided to host a ball," said Fitzwilliam. "It is only proper to thank our neighbors for their ready welcome of us to the area."

"That is prudent, indeed. I should be happy to offer my expertise, for as you know, I am capable of planning for all such activities."

Five younger members of the family hid smiles or looked carefully blank at their aunt. Lady Catherine, they all knew, was fond of declaring her abilities or claiming she would be the best at any activity had she only learned, and in this instance, it had been many years since she had had any involvement in any sort of ball.

"Your advice is, of course, always welcome," said Charity. The only one in the room who did not understand the overt diplomacy in Charity's tone was Lady Catherine herself.

The lady nodded at her young niece and turned her attention on Darcy. "What of you, Darcy? You have said nothing since I entered the room."

"I am well, Aunt," replied Darcy, deciding to say anything further would be a mistake.

"Yes, it appears to be so." Lady Catherine paused and peered at him. "You, of all people, cannot be at a loss to explain my coming, Darcy. While I gave you this opportunity to be in Anne's company these months, I expected you to act. And yet, I still have heard nothing of an engagement."

Darcy thought it was to his credit that he did not groan; only his expectation that Lady Catherine would broach this subject before she left the room allowed him to refrain. It was still a powerful urge to shake his head in exasperation for Lady Catherine's single-minded focus on the subject.

"Shall you advise us, Mother?" asked Anne, a blatant attempt to distract her. "Perhaps we should see you to a room where you can refresh yourself before you give us your opinion on our arrangements."

Darcy might not have expected it, but it seemed, given Lady Catherine's sharp look at her daughter, that she noticed Anne's purpose in speaking. It was even more surprising that she did not insist on further pressing her wishes.

"I shall, of course, assist, but there is another matter which draws me here."

"Another matter?" asked Fitzwilliam, speaking for them all. "That is a surprise, Aunt, for I cannot imagine what business you might have in Hertfordshire."

"It is not something that affects me to any great extent," said Lady Catherine, confusing them all. "Rather, it is a concern of my parson."

"Mr. Collins?" asked Anne, suspicion coming over her countenance. Darcy was feeling the same suspicion, though he supposed it should not surprise him that any lackey of Lady Catherine's would share every detail of his life with her.

"Yes," replied Lady Catherine, though she appeared distracted. "He is the heir to an estate near these parts. It seems there is some problem with the family releasing his inheritance, and as I am to be here for a time, I thought to investigate and determine if he is being defrauded."

"Longbourn." Darcy knew he must take command of the situation, for Lady Catherine would respect his opinion in this matter more than any of his cousins.

"Yes, that is the name," said Lady Catherine, eyeing Darcy with a certain curiosity. "Are you familiar with the place?"

"I am, Aunt, and though it pains me to inform you of this, Mr. Collins has misrepresented the situation."

The frown Lady Catherine showed him informed Darcy of her inability to imagine such a thing. "Misrepresented the situation? How so?"

"That I cannot say, Lady Catherine," replied Darcy. For a moment, he considered asking her of what Mr. Collins's accusations consisted, but he decided it would be better to inform his aunt of the true state of the dispute. "What I can tell you is what has happened and why Mr. Collins has not come into his inheritance."

"And how can you know?" asked Lady Catherine, her frown deepening.

"Because it is obvious," replied Darcy. "Though the previous master has, indeed, passed, and the estate is entailed, Mr. Bennet's wife is now with child."

"Thus, the question of ownership is unresolved," said Lady Catherine, understanding Darcy's meaning at once. The lady scowled, though Darcy could see her pique was not for him. "Mr. Collins neglected to mention this. He only stated the family refused to leave the estate and make way for him, and when I asked why he did not appeal to the law, he muttered something of the Bennets' uncles threatening him."

Lady Catherine grimaced, and she directed an apologetic look at him. "While Mr. Collins fills his role adequately, the man is not of a towering intellect, and more than once I have detected a petulant inability to believe he can be in error."

Hiding a smile from his aunt, Darcy noted his relations doing the same. It was diverting to hear Lady Catherine de Bourgh leveling that particular charge at another.

Then Lady Catherine directed a suspicious look at Darcy and said: "Is it certain the child is Mr. Bennet's?"

"Lady Catherine, you know it is the greatest of vulgarity to question the lady's morality," said Fitzwilliam. "It is my understanding that she was three months gone when Mr. Bennet passed. It is not as if she conspired to become with child after her husband passed, and at her age, such an eventuality would be unlikely to succeed."

"No, I suppose you are correct," replied Lady Catherine. The lady was silent, considering the matter for a moment before coming to a resolution. "What you say makes sense, but I believe I should like to investigate for myself. Ball preparations may wait for another time, for I should go thither as soon as I refresh myself from my journey."

That was a terrible idea, Darcy thought, and the looks of consternation on the faces of his relations informed him that he was not the only one.

"It would be best to refrain, Mother," said Anne quickly before her mother could depart.

"Why that should be I do not know," replied Lady Catherine. "In this instance, frankness would serve, I should think, though I should not present it as if I am interfering in their affairs."

"And that is exactly how they would take it," replied Darcy, injecting a firmness into his voice that he knew from experience his aunt would recognize. "The situation demands more subtlety than to inquire directly of them. The ball is scheduled for two days hence. Would it not be better to observe the Bennets and come to your own conclusions?"

"And Mrs. Bennet is already confined to her rooms," added Charity. "It would hardly be proper to confront the poor woman when she is in the midst of her confinement."

Lady Catherine regarded them, and Darcy thought she would insist on making her way to Longbourn. It was surprising when she nodded, slowly at first, then with greater determination.

"Yes, I suppose you are correct. These Bennets are to attend the ball you say?"

"The daughters are in half mourning, so their attendance is

acceptable," said Fitzwilliam. "The mother, of course, will not attend, as she has withdrawn from society. But you can tell much from the behavior of the woman's daughters."

"Very well," said Lady Catherine. "Then I shall wait to make their acquaintances when they come to Netherfield in two days. For now, I should like to refresh myself in my rooms. I believe you mentioned something of ball preparations."

"As we informed you," said Charity, in her voice a note of relief Darcy knew they all felt, "we are happy to have your involvement. Let me call Mrs. Nichols to show you to your room."

A moment later the housekeeper arrived and escorted Lady Catherine from the room, leaving a group of bemused relations behind. Darcy exchanged a look with Fitzwilliam and was not surprised when his cousin burst into laughter.

"That was close, was it not?" asked he of no one in particular.

"We shall keep her attention on the ball," said Anne. "Thus diverted, she will forget about her determination to go to Longbourn and content herself with waiting to make their acquaintance."

"I hope you are correct, Anne," said Darcy, shaking his head. "Lady Catherine possesses the ability to embarrass us all if she holds to her purpose."

It was a fact that all knew, and Darcy could see from the looks of determination that they all meant to ensure it did not happen. For Darcy, he made a mental note to ensure Fitzwilliam had a rope on hand, for it might be needed if Lady Catherine took it into her head again to do as she had originally thought.

CHAPTER XII

*H*uman folly, it seemed, took many forms. One of the most detestable in Darcy's opinion was that which led one to suppose they were better than others. Such weakness could take many characteristics, and Darcy no more approved of it in those who were, by society's measure, more deserving of espousing such opinions. Where two such specimens came together, it was unsurprising that sparks flew between them.

"Does it seem to you our aunt has been . . . softer, perhaps, since her arrival?"

Darcy considered the question his cousin posed, watching the woman as she discussed some facet of the coming ball's preparations with the ladies. "If you mean she has not badgered me to come to the point or Anne to practice her wiles on me, then I suppose I must agree with you."

It was the truth and a matter of some surprise to Darcy. Having witnessed his aunt's behavior and her overwhelming desire for an understanding between them, Darcy might have thought his aunt would promote it without cessation upon joining them in Hertfordshire. Whatever the reason, Lady Catherine had not so much as spoken of it since her comments when she had first entered the estate.

"That is part of it, I suppose," replied Fitzwilliam. "But there is something more about her I do not understand. I cannot put my finger on it. She seems quieter, perhaps, almost civil, though there have been many times I have been reluctant to ascribe such adjectives to her."

"Lady Catherine is not uncivil," chided Darcy. "She simply understands what she wants and is not afraid to voice those wishes."

"Oh, aye, without end if she does not get her way. Irascibility is her old friend."

Lady Catherine's quick temper was a facet of the woman's character they were to experience in abundance, even as she did not direct it at them. Another provoked it, a woman more eager to proclaim her superiority than their aunt had ever been. No one at Netherfield wished for this woman's company; that she did not recognize it herself was a testament to Miss Bingley's ability to see whatever she wished.

When the lady and her sister entered the morning before the ball, when a morning visit was akin to an imposition, Darcy noted her entrance, head held high, as if she were a queen entering her throne room. Lady Catherine noted her demeanor at once, her gaze fixed on Miss Bingley as a hawk gazes on its prey before swooping down for the kill. At once Darcy knew that Miss Bingley's likely behavior coupled with Lady Catherine's inability to tolerate those she considered unworthy giving herself airs was a recipe for acrimony. To her credit, Mrs. Hurst appeared hesitant, as if uncertain of their welcome, and noted Lady Catherine's narrow look at once.

"Lady Charity, dear Miss Darcy, Miss de Bourgh!" exclaimed Miss Bingley as if they were all the closest of friends. "How lovely it is to see you today!"

The only one feeling such ecstasy was Miss Bingley, for the ladies greeted her with civility and nothing more. That she had greeted them with more formal monikers was a boon, for Lady Catherine would not have tolerated familiarity. And it resulted from the ladies informing her more than once that they preferred formality.

"Miss Bingley," said Charity, speaking as the mistress of the estate. "How do you do today?"

"Tolerable, Lady Charity. How happy we are to be in your company, for there is no one in this neighborhood who is of your quality."

The conversation continued with such transparent blandishments thereafter, and while Miss Bingley did not approach requesting an introduction to Lady Catherine, it was clear from her looks that she wished to know the lady. For her part, Lady Catherine did nothing more than watch her, weighing her with her eyes, her pinched look informing all but the woman in question that she did not like what she was seeing. At length, it appeared Lady Catherine had taken the measure of Miss Bingley and spoke up.

"Charity, it seems you have made friends here in Hertfordshire."

"Do you suppose we have lived in this society for two months without making new acquaintances?" What went unsaid was Charity's distaste at the word "friend."

"No, I would not expect it of you," said Lady Catherine, missing Charity's irony in her response. "Would you do me the honor of an introduction?"

"Of course, Aunt," said Charity, as Miss Bingley brightened at the mode of address Charity used.

The introductions were completed, and Lady Catherine regarded their guests, frank appraisal in her gaze. "Well, you seem to be pretty sort of girls," said Lady Catherine at length, "though your dress appears rather heavy for a morning visit, Miss Bingley. I do not believe I know the name 'Bingley.' Where are you from?"

Miss Bingley started at the comment concerning her dress, but she was not at all opposed to replying. "We are from York, Lady Catherine. My brother is currently leasing an estate near to Meryton, though we expect he will purchase anon."

It seemed Lady Catherine heard more than Miss Bingley may have wished to say. "York, you say. Then do you suppose your brother will purchase here? I might have thought you would prefer to settle closer to your home."

"Oh, I have no notion Charles would purchase in so unsuitable a neighborhood as this. In fact, I suspect the north will be his eventual destination, though perhaps a little further south of York might be preferable."

The woman's glance at Darcy and Fitzwilliam when she said this left no one in doubt of her meaning, least of all Lady Catherine. "It is not unusual that you would prefer the north, Miss Bingley, for many do. I am curious of one thing, however—in what way do you consider this neighborhood unsuitable?"

"There is nothing of interest here," was Miss Bingley's cutting denunciation, given without hesitation. "No one of fashion lives here, the denizens can claim to be gentlemen by only the loosest definition of the word. I believe we should all prefer a more refined society, people who are more polished than the savages we find here."

"Is that so?" Lady Catherine's eyes swung to Darcy. "Do you agree with Miss Bingley's assessment, Darcy? Are the people here so unsuitable?"

"Far be it for me to disagree with the esteemed Miss Bingley," replied Darcy, noting the look in Miss Bingley's eyes, part shock he would not immediately support her and part a plea that he do so. "But I find these people no different from those in any other neighborhood. No one here is of high society and country manners are common but they are good people and lack the superciliousness one so often finds in the city."

"Perhaps you were not paying attention because you are fascinated with the Bennets, but the society here is nothing less than medieval. It astonishes me you pay so much attention to them, for I never would have expected the scions of an earl to give so much consequence to those so clearly below them."

Miss Bingley's tone was all saccharine, but of more concern to Darcy was the way Lady Catherine appeared to receive this news of their closeness with the Bennets, which was more than they had informed her. A long look at Miss Bingley told Darcy she had planned it that way, a curiosity, for if she did not know their history in trade made the Bingleys less acceptable than the Bennets, she was less intelligent than he might have thought.

"All men of high society must deal with those of lower stations, whether they will or no, Miss Bingley." Darcy gazed at her, believing his look was stony, but not able to summon the ability to care. "An earl has neighbors and others who live in the local neighborhood with whom he must interact. Near my home, at Pemberley, many are of a lower consequence in society, most of whom are excellent people. I do not look down on them because of their humbler origins, nor do I think it right to do so."

"Here, here, Darcy!" added Fitzwilliam. "My father would have agreed with you, and I have personal knowledge that my brother does. Perhaps we should leave this objectionable subject for others more palatable."

"Yes," said Lady Catherine, still eyeing Miss Bingley. "Let us speak of other matters."

While it was clear their arguments had confused Miss Bingley, to say nothing of her annoyance they had not agreed with her at once, she moved to other subjects. Unfortunately, her choice of topic was no more agreeable to the company than the previous.

"What a fortunate situation it is for us all that you will host a ball! Not only will the locals receive a little sophistication which will do them no ill, but such an event must be exquisite. Have you completed the arrangements yet?

"Of course, you have!" exclaimed Miss Bingley, answering her own question. "I am certain you have had everything in hand for days now. And what an event it shall be! It can be nothing the people of this district can have seen before."

Even when praising her present company, it seemed Miss Bingley could not refrain from insulting their neighbors. Charity, who accepted the burden of responding, gave Miss Bingley a faint smile and said: "There are a few more details, but I am confident they will be done in no time."

Miss Bingley could hardly misunderstand Charity's reference to the imposition of their visit that morning, but the woman ignored it. Mrs. Hurst's heightened countenance suggested she understood the reference very well.

"Then I hope you are ready to do your duty," said Miss Bingley, turning to her attention to Darcy and Fitzwilliam. "As we missed the assembly last month, I have never seen you dance, but I must assume you are all adept at the art. As I have been educated in all these courtly manners, I stand ready to accept your civility and help impart some society to these people."

This blatant attempt to induce one of them to ask for her first dances was a bridge too far for Lady Catherine. "Miss Bingley," said she, and if Miss Bingley's sudden consternation was any sign, she understood the lady's imperious tone very well, "I would recommend you refrain from reaching too high. When Icarus flew too close to the sun, he was burned and fell into the sea. You would not wish for the same experience."

"I have no notion of your meaning, Lady Catherine," said Miss Bingley. It was plain to them all she was dissembling.

"Then let me speak plainly," said the lady, much to the mixed amusement and exasperation of all her family. "Given what you have told me, you are not even gentlefolk, as your brother does not own his estate. Your dress informs me you have some wealth as does your pretension, which leads me to suppose you are the scions of a wealthy tradesman, intent upon ascending to the gentry. While that is not contemptible itself, pretending a higher position in society than you possess to give yourself airs most certainly is.

"Let me state without the possibility of misunderstanding that you should not look to either of my nephews to improve your lot." Lady Catherine was, by now, glaring at Miss Bingley, her dislike clear to them all. "Not only is Darcy engaged to Anne, and thus not available for you, but Fitzwilliam is the son of an earl and destined for a more appropriate match. Please discontinue this objectionable behavior."

It was clear to Darcy that Miss Bingley was on the edge of making a mistake from which she would suffer more of a set down than she already had. It was fortunate for then all that Mrs. Hurst cleared her throat, prompting her sister to silence, and spoke for them both.

"Thank you all for your hospitality, especially as it is the day before the event you are to host. I believe we should depart now and allow you to complete your preparations."

"Thank you, Mrs. Hurst, Miss Bingley," said Charity, rising to take the opportunity to be rid of them. "We shall welcome seeing you tomorrow, and your brother and husband, of course."

With no other choice, Miss Bingley rose with her sister and departed, clear though it was to anyone with any wit that she was unhappy. When she was gone, Darcy wondered if there was a buzzing in her ear, for the conversation revolved entirely around what a disobliging, insolent girl she was.

"I have seen her like many times," said Lady Catherine with a superior sniff, one which resembled Miss Bingley's closely, though neither would have appreciated the comparison. "Women such as she are leeches, for they mean to ascend society's ladder and entrap gentlemen to improve their position by any means necessary. She means to have one of you for a husband, so you had best take great care."

"That, Lady Catherine, we apprehended within minutes of making her acquaintance."

Lady Catherine gave then a look of approval. "I would not injure you by supposing you are incapable of fending off such ladies. But one can never be too careful."

As the lady continued to drone on, Fitzwilliam leaned close and spoke to Darcy in a whisper. "As soon as I can, I mean to slip away. Please keep Lady Catherine occupied."

Darcy regarded his cousin with some interest. "You have an errand, do you?"

"A most particular errand, one I hope will lead to great future happiness."

With a nod, Darcy did not ask for further clarification. No such was necessary, for he was certain he knew what his cousin was about.

*   *   *

At Longbourn, Mrs. Bennet's complaints had increased in inverse proportion to the proximity of her time to give birth. There was little that escaped her ability to complain, for the room was too hot or cold, the maids slow to respond, her back ached and her head pounded, or her midsection was too distended to allow her to move properly. As it was difficult to endure her mother's complaints, Elizabeth spent little time in her company. Mrs. Wainwright, the local midwife, spoke to Elizabeth and Jane the day before the ball.

"It is common for women to have such complaints in the days before giving birth. For some women, there is less discomfort. As I assisted your mother in her lying in with both your youngest sisters, I can inform you this time is little different from those two occasions."

Elizabeth shared a look with Jane. "That is good to hear, Mrs. Wainwright. I had worried there was something wrong."

Mrs. Wainwright sighed. "As you know, birthing children is a time fraught with danger for we women, for we can never be certain when something will go wrong. I have seen far too many perish in the attempt. Having said that, I see nothing of particular concern in your mother, though I will note that she is much older than her last lying in. That brings me some concern, but nothing out of the common way."

"Thank you for your reassurance," said Elizabeth.

The woman instructed them to call her at the first sign their mother was entering childbirth and departed, promising to return in two days to look in on her again. As Mr. Jones was also standing by to offer his expertise, they had done all they could. They could do nothing more than trust in God and allow nature to take its course.

The rest of the day passed as many others before them. The youngest Bennets were immersed in their planning for the following evening, amid complaints that they could not wait for the time of their departure to come. Elizabeth took some time to complete a few minor tasks herself, while Jane and Mary took turns sitting with their mother, inducing her to whatever calmness they could.

There were two events of note that day, one concerning Jane, and the other Elizabeth. While one was welcome, however, the other was most decidedly not. Elizabeth had been in the study, having completed what she set out to do, and took one of her father's treasured books from the shelf to read, an old favorite they had perused together more than once. When the knock sounded on the door, Sarah stepped into the room.

"Excuse me, mum," said she, seeming uncertain, "but there is an officer of the militia here to see you."

"A single officer?" asked Elizabeth.

"Yes, Miss Elizabeth. He requested a moment of your time at the front stoop, as I told him it was not proper he should enter by himself."

Certain who it was, and uncertain of what he meant by it, Elizabeth nodded. "Is John available? Or Mr. Whitmore?"

"Mr. Whitmore rode out onto the estate some time ago, but I can have John summoned."

"Good. Please do so at once."

Elizabeth waited for the footman to appear, feeling a perverse sort of pleasure in forcing the officer in question to cool his heels, while wondering what the devil Mr. Wickham meant by coming to Longbourn alone. When the footman arrived, Elizabeth nodded to him.

"Mr. Wickham has come to see me, John. Please provide chaperonage and ensure he behaves himself."

Cocking his head to the side, John regarded her askance. "Do you think he means harm?"

"No, I do not suppose so," replied Elizabeth. "But I do not understand him, and that makes me wary."

"Of course, Miss Elizabeth," said John.

The footman led the way to the vestibule, and stepped aside, allowing Elizabeth to pass him through the door. The man then took up station just inside where he could watch them yet remain unobtrusive. Elizabeth, who had known John for years, knew he possessed greater strength than his slender frame would suggest, and felt safe in the knowledge he could move with great speed when required.

Mr. Wickham, Elizabeth noted, was leaning against a column, his manner all ease, as if Elizabeth had not just required him to wait for five minutes alone. She thought he did not miss the presence of the footman, but he made no comment and gave no signal it bothered him. At the sight of her, a wide smile came over his countenance.

"Miss Elizabeth," said he with a courtly bow. "How lovely it is to see you today. Might I say how utterly enchanting you are?"

It was one of the many times Elizabeth had caught a hint of overdone flattery in this man. While Elizabeth would not accuse him of falsehood, for she thought he found her attractive, she was dressed in a simple day dress, her face likely pale from a morning secluded in the study. Flattery, it seemed, spilled from this man's lips with little effort or conscious thought. It was a part of his character, one it seemed he had cultivated, for he was not a sycophant.

"Mr. Wickham," said Elizabeth, a distant greeting to avoid encouraging him. "I am surprised to see you here."

"And I apologize for my sudden appearance," said the gentleman, all smug confidence. "I hope it does not follow that surprise leads to displeasure. It would be hard, indeed, to have a woman such as you refuse to welcome my presence."

To this, Elizabeth decided it was better to make no comment. "Then what may I do for you, sir? It was with me you wished to speak?"

"Straight to the point," said Mr. Wickham. "Very well. I came because I wished to solicit your hand for the first sets to the ball at Netherfield Park."

"You wish for my first sets," echoed Elizabeth, uncertain what he was about. "Why?"

"Is it not obvious?" asked Mr. Wickham. "Because you intrigue me, and I wish to come to know you better."

"But the first set is an unmistakable sign of favor."

"And not one I am unwilling to make."

Smooth though his reply was, it did little more than exasperate Elizabeth. Not knowing why he had fixed his attention on her, Elizabeth could not help but wonder what he meant by it.

"Perhaps I do not wish to acknowledge or legitimize such favor," ventured Elizabeth.

"You certainly know how to destroy a gentleman's confidence," said Mr. Wickham, his downcast countenance no more than a front, she was certain. "I might go away, drown my sorrows in a bottle, forever mourn my failure to provoke your good opinion."

"Come, Mr. Wickham. You and I both know that any such regard is imaginary. We have only been acquainted for a matter of ten days."

"Then what better way to know each other better than to dance at a ball?"

Elizabeth's patience with the gentleman was nearing exhaustion, rendering her unable to further endure his flattery. She did not know why he insisted on showing her this favor, but a dance was nothing more than a dance. Perhaps she could disabuse him of any interest on her part during that dance.

"Very well, Mr. Wickham. Those dances are yours. Now, if you will excuse me, I must return to the house."

"Of course," said Mr. Wickham, giving her another bow. "I shall not keep you, for I also must return to my duties. Please give my regard to your excellent family."

Elizabeth watched him stride away, relieved at his going, but feeling the pressing need to remove all pretense of interest on her part from his mind. Considering how she might do so, Elizabeth returned to the study, her book forgotten in her introspection.

The second event was much more palatable, consisting as it did of another solicitation for the first dances. As Colonel Fitzwilliam was now high in Jane's esteem, she accepted with pleasure.

"That is curious, indeed!" said Lydia as the four sisters gathered outside the door with Colonel Fitzwilliam, who had come to Longbourn not long before. Mary was sitting with their mother. "For a gentleman also requested Lizzy's first sets!"

"Is that so, Miss Elizabeth?" asked Colonel Fitzwilliam, turning an expression of appraisal upon her.

It seemed to Elizabeth that the colonel saw or suspected something though she knew not what. In the end, he did not speak further, contenting himself with other subjects. He did not stay long, but when he went away, it was with a clear affection for Jane that left none of them in doubt. The rest of the day, Jane was the target of her sisters' gentle teasing.

"I must hand it to you, Wickham," said Denny, shaking his head. "Your ability to woo a young lady is unparalleled, as this most recent example shows. I wish you the best in your endeavors."

Wickham accepted his friend's praise as it was nothing more than his due. And it was, he reflected, for he had wooed young ladies of more difficulty than Miss Elizabeth Bennet. It was only a matter of time, he thought, before he had her eating out of the palm of his hand. That she had possession of an estate and a pleasing figure was to Wickham's benefit, for while he would bed a woman for pecuniary advantage, it was so much better when the woman was comely.

What Wickham would never inform his friend was that Miss Elizabeth was not so firmly under his thrall as he might have wished. There was, he sensed, a reluctance to engage with him, something Wickham had often noted in more observant and intelligent women. Not that he was in doubt of his eventual success—in fact, Wickham had every confidence he would succeed. Perhaps he would sell the estate off once it became his possession. That would gain him a fortune in ready funds to feed his habits. Miss Elizabeth and her family could then be shunted to a cottage and forgotten.

"Contemplating the coming delights already, are you?"

"There is much to contemplate; would you not agree?"

"Without a doubt," said Denny with a lusty sigh. "The Bennet sisters are all pretty, and if Miss Elizabeth is less enamored with us than her younger sisters, the air of mystery about her makes her the greater conquest."

"Without a doubt," said Wickham. Pausing, Wickham fixed his friend with a pleasant look. "Do you know anything of the family at Netherfield? I would not wish to impose where I am not acquainted with them."

"A little only," replied Denny. "The proprietor seems an excellent man, and his family is equally welcoming. They do not consort with us much, but they are no less estimable because of it. And they have issued a general invitation to us all. Besides," said Denny with a wink and a grin, "I have heard it said that the ladies staying at the estate have fine dowries themselves. Perhaps I shall try my hand with them."

"And I wish you the best of luck," said Wickham with a laugh.

In truth, Wickham had paused when he had heard the name "Fitzwilliam" upon arriving, for it was a name with which he was familiar. But further thought convinced him that these people must not be the ones with whom he was acquainted, though they might have been related in some manner. The earl, Wickham knew, had passed some years ago, and his son, while not a supercilious man, would have no reason to lease an estate in Hertfordshire of all places, and would be called by his title besides. His brother was a man to fear, but the last Wickham had heard, Fitzwilliam had been a colonel in the dragoons, and was likely off somewhere fighting the French.

Thus assured there would be no difficulty in attending the ball, Wickham allowed himself to anticipate it and the delights that would come after. Perhaps he would follow Denny's example and acquaint himself with these ladies of whom he spoke. If their dowries were as substantial as Denny intimated, Wickham could turn his attention to one of them. And if they did not fall under his spell, he could always return to Miss Elizabeth. A bird in hand is worth two in a bush some said. But Wickham had always preferred to focus his attention on the greatest available prize. The trick was to determine which was the most valuable. His instincts had never steered him wrong before.

CHAPTER XIII

$\mathcal{M}$ eeting Lady Catherine de Bough at the ball at Netherfield was nothing less than a shock. Having heard mention of the lady from Mr. Collins, and further colorful accounts from their new neighbors, Elizabeth was uncertain what to expect when Anne introduced her mother, even as she noticed Lady Catherine's steady look at her which presaged nothing good.

"Do not concern yourself for my aunt, Elizabeth," whispered Charity when Elizabeth left the lady and her daughter and made their way to the end of the line where Colonel Fitzwilliam and his sister greeted her. "It seems she came to Hertfordshire with some inaccurate observations shared by the detestable Mr. Collins. But Darcy set her to rights and now she is more curious than anything else."

Elizabeth directed a glance back at the gentleman where he stood at the other end of the line greeting the estate's guests. "Then I shall thank him for his intervention." Turning her gaze back on Charity, Elizabeth quirked an eyebrow. "Shall I escape her ladyship's interrogation?"

"Oh, no, Elizabeth," replied Charity, her smirk completely inappropriate to the situation, or so Elizabeth thought. "I suspect Lady Catherine will wish to know every minute detail of you and your family, and likely how you manage Longbourn too."

By Charity's side, Colonel Fitzwilliam chortled, exclaiming: "Of that, you can have no doubt. You should expect it almost as soon as her duties in the receiving line are complete."

"It may even be before," said Charity. "Lady Catherine agreed to stand with us, but she argued that as she's unknown here, there was little point. This way, we will introduce her to everyone who attends."

"That is fortunate for everyone in the neighborhood," said Elizabeth, her wryness provoking mirth in her companions. "When Lady Catherine approaches me, I shall do my best to refrain from running back to Longbourn, screaming the entire distance."

Again, they could not restrain their mirth, and Elizabeth excused herself, for she did not wish to slow the line. She and her sisters made their way to the ballroom, the youngest exclaiming over what they saw. Elizabeth looked about with interest, noting the tasteful yet understated arrangements, the large, chalked diagram on the floor, and the candles situated in out of the way locations where they would not drip on the revelers. Charity and Anne had done wonders, for Elizabeth did not think she had ever seen anything so fine.

After the fact, Elizabeth determined to congratulate Charity, for she was correct about her aunt's eagerness to speak to Elizabeth. There was still a steady flow of people entering the ballroom when Lady Catherine appeared in their midst, her eyes fixed on Elizabeth from the moment she appeared.

"Miss Elizabeth Bennet," said Lady Catherine. "It must come as no surprise to learn that I have heard much of you."

"From Mr. Collins, I assume," said Elizabeth.

"Indeed," was the lady's answer. "After I arrived, I heard much more from my relations, though I will own I struggle to give credit to everything they said. Perhaps you will oblige me and speak a few moments?"

It was *not* a request, no matter how Lady Catherine had phrased it. Eager to avoid a scene and wishing to be done with the inquiry, Elizabeth assented.

"The first thing I wish to know is the question of my parson's insistence of your unwillingness to leave Longbourn. It may not surprise you to learn that he told me nothing of your mother's condition; I learned that from my family."

"No, I am not surprised," said Elizabeth, wishing yet again they were free of the odious Mr. Collins. "Given this, I wonder if he counted on your support to assist him. He has been most insistent since my father passed away."

"It is not only to you he has been insistent," replied Lady Catherine. "While I might have agreed to assist when I had only his testimony, you should know I now have nothing to say on the matter." Lady Catherine's mien softened, and she asked: "When is your mother's time?"

"Soon, your ladyship. Our apothecary estimated the second week of December."

The lady nodded. "If you require another pair of hands when the time comes, please send for me. I should be happy to stay with your mother. You and your sisters, as unmarried women, have no place in the birthing room."

"Thank you, Lady Catherine," said Elizabeth, surprised by the lady's civility. "My mother's sister lives in Meryton and will surely attend. If my mother should wish it, we would welcome you."

The lady nodded. "Then let us speak of your estate. I understand you have been managing it since your father's passing?"

"Yes, Lady Catherine," said Elizabeth.

"I have managed my estate since my husband's death nearly fifteen years ago, so I have much experience. How are your tenants getting on?"

The ensuing discussion could not have consumed more than five minutes. Yet to Elizabeth it seemed to take years, for Lady Catherine proved to possess the knowledge she claimed and drew every facet of Elizabeth's management from her with effortless efficiency. It was almost ruthless, Elizabeth decided. While the lady dispensed advice as easily as she took a breath, she also appeared impressed with the measures Elizabeth had taken. At length, she nodded and fixed a look on Elizabeth that appeared approving.

"You are yet still young, Miss Bennet, but you have learned much in a short period it appears. The actions you have taken have fulfilled your duty, such that should Mr. Collins ultimately inherit, he will have no reason to find fault. I shall not venture an opinion on the subject, for I can see why you wish to retain control and sympathize with Mr. Collins at the same time."

"There is nothing any of us can do on the matter, Lady Catherine," said Elizabeth. "Whatever will be, we shall accept it with as much grace as we can manage."

"An excellent attitude, Miss Elizabeth," replied Lady Catherine, nodding with approval. "I believe I shall stay at Netherfield for some time. Should the opportunity arise, I hope we may continue our acquaintance."

"I hope so too." Elizabeth surprised herself by meaning what she said.

Soon thereafter, Lady Catherine departed, citing a need to assist her nieces in their duties. Elizabeth looked about when she was alone, noting that the Bingleys had arrived. Jane was speaking to Mr. Bingley, who looked crestfallen—no doubt he had learned that Jane was to dance the first with Colonel Fitzwilliam. Georgiana was standing with Kitty and Lydia, speaking with animation, while Mary looked on. To the side, Miss Bingley was waiting by the side of the door like a bird of prey waiting for a fat, juicy rabbit to appear below her, the Hursts standing nearby. Then the final few guests entered with Colonel Fitzwilliam and Mr. Darcy, and the sign was given for the dance to begin. Elizabeth felt relief steal over her; for whatever reason, Mr. Wickham had not come.

Some sixth sense informed Wickham that it might be best to avoid greeting the family upon arriving at Netherfield. While he still considered it impossible that the Fitzwilliam who was master of the estate could be related to the Fitzwilliams with whom he was acquainted, if they were, meeting them in the vestibule and being denied entrance would not look good to his fellow officers. If Wickham were already within, they could do nothing if they did not wish to make a scene.

Thus, he arrived with a few final stragglers among the officers and made his way into the estate. The entrance was bare of greeters, and Wickham nodded in satisfaction. The music for the first set was already beginning as he stepped into the ballroom, and after he took a quick glance around, he did not see anyone he knew. There was a young woman present, who appeared to be the mistress, given her activities, but though she was pretty, Wickham filed the knowledge away for later, instead eager to pay his addresses to Miss Elizabeth at once.

It was the work of a moment to find her, for she was standing near the door, looking at the dancers. With a grin, one predatory, or so he had been told, Wickham stepped forward, put himself within Miss Elizabeth's sight, and bowed low.

"I hope you did not suppose I would renege on our agreement to dance."

"Mr. Wickham," said she, showing a decided detachment at his coming. "I will own I had wondered."

"A delay arose, and I could only arrive just now. Shall we?"

The woman looked at his arm as if she wished to refuse, but soon took it and allowed him to guide her to where the other dancers were forming. Wickham was unconcerned about her lukewarm reception. He had no doubt he would charm her, much the same as he had all the others. For the present, he allowed himself to appreciate her appearance, which was quite fine, and imagine the delights to come.

It was times like these that Lady Catherine could be a trial on Darcy's patience. Not that Darcy had ever attended a ball with her—Darcy did not know that Lady Catherine had attended a ball in the past fifteen years, so settled at Rosings she had been. On the present occasion, it could not be supposed she would allow the opportunity to push Darcy closer together with Anne to pass.

"Darcy," said the lady as the music was beginning. "You must stand up with Anne for the first set."

"I apologize, Lady Catherine," said Darcy, giving her ladyship a quick bow. "But I never dance the first."

"You may make an exception for your future wife, Darcy."

Anne, standing nearby as she was, overheard the exchange and shot Darcy a grin where her mother could not see. At that moment, salvation presented itself in the person of a young man of the neighborhood—Darcy did not know the man—who stepped up to Anne and asked her to dance. Lady Catherine, Darcy noted, stepped forward, an objection poised on the tip of her tongue, which went unsaid when the man escorted Anne to the dance floor.

"Why did you not say something to him?" hissed Lady Catherine. "Now you have lost the opportunity to make a statement before the neighborhood!"

"It was a statement I do not wish to make, as you know." Darcy noted her pursed lips and the lines on her forehead, a sure sign of an impending explosion. "Besides, you know the convention; had Anne refused to stand up with the man, she would have lost the ability to dance for the rest of the evening."

"That would not be a loss," muttered Lady Catherine. "You know how delicate Anne is. She will damage her health if she carries on like this all night."

It was with considerable displeasure that Darcy turned his focus to his aunt, for he had about had enough of her silliness. "Lady Catherine, I would have you remember a few important points. First, I am not engaged to Anne. We have both informed you many times we do not wish or intend to marry, and yet you continue in this delusion. Please desist. Also, Anne has been in excellent health these past months. She is not robust, but she is hearty and has not suffered from even the smallest ague. Do not hold her back from living her life, for she is of age. If you persist, you will only create resentment."

"This is not over, Darcy!" hissed Lady Catherine. "I will not stand for you failing in your duty in such a way."

"It is over for tonight, at least," rejoined Darcy. "Do you wish to create a spectacle in front of all these people?"

Lady Catherine's eyes narrowed, and Darcy thought she might speak to declaim all interest in what their guests might think. To forestall her, Darcy spoke up again. "I know you have harbored this fantasy for many years, Lady Catherine, but it is time to allow it to rest. You may not like it, but you will respect our wishes."

"We shall see," said Lady Catherine, and she turned and stalked away.

From where she was passing him in the line, Anne shot him a diverted yet commiserating smile. Darcy shook his head, content to allow the matter to rest for now. For some moments he stood watching the dancers, ignoring Miss Bingley who stood nearby, her calculating gaze on him filling him with no warm feeling for her. It was a moment later that his eyes fell on a red-coated officer, and his annoyance with Lady Catherine turned to rage at the sight of George Wickham, bold as brass, moving through the steps on the dance floor.

What could the cur be doing here? And in the uniform of an officer, no less. Those at Netherfield had had little to do with the officers and they did not visit the estate, but Darcy thought he knew most of them at least by sight, and he had never seen Wickham in Meryton before. Had he followed them here, intent on more mischief? A glance at Fitzwilliam, where he guided Miss Bennet on the other end of the dancers informed Darcy he had not noted Wickham's presence. If he had, Darcy could not imagine him speaking with Miss Bennet in such genial tones.

Then Darcy realized another would need to know of Wickham's presence. Skirting the dance floor, unwilling to allow Wickham to catch sight of him, as he did not seem to have noted Darcy there, Darcy approached his sister where she was standing and speaking with animation with the youngest three Bennet sisters. Those ladies, Darcy knew, would dance less tonight, a restriction due to their present condition of half mourning. The youngest appeared to be a little put out but enduring her disappointment as best as she was able.

"Miss Mary, Miss Kitty, Miss Lydia," said Darcy when he reached them, mustering a smile to hide his current feelings. "Might I borrow Georgiana for a moment?"

The girls chorused their agreement and Darcy led his sister away, promising to return her to them at once. Georgiana regarded him askance, clearly wondering what he was about when Darcy turned to face her.

"I do not know how, but George Wickham is here tonight."

The first sign of her distress was the paling of her features, followed by a darting look onto the dance floor. Darcy, taking pity on her, pointed him out, as the plethora of redcoats in attendance rendered him not immediately recognizable. Then a curious change came over his sister, for she regarded the man, first with shock, then with worry, and finally determination.

"He is dancing with Miss Elizabeth, Brother," said she.

Darcy, who had not paid attention to Wickham's partner, regarded him, noted it was true. The man was plying her with his ever-present charm, but Miss Elizabeth, he noted, appeared less vivacious than was her wont, for he noted more than once she gave soft answers to whatever he was saying.

"We must warn her," said Georgiana as Darcy contemplated dragging Wickham from the room and administering retribution for his crimes, the least of which was not his temerity in approaching a woman the quality of Miss Elizabeth. "She cannot know what he is."

"Yes," said Darcy with a nod. "I believe you are correct." Then he turned his full attention on his sister. "What do you wish to do? It will create a scene to have him removed."

"This does not affect me, William," said his sister with a cutting gesture. "I am in no danger from the likes of Mr. Wickham. I shall stay close to Kitty and Lydia and my other friends."

Heartened at the evidence of his sister's growing maturity, Darcy nodded and kissed her forehead. "Very well, Georgiana. I am glad he does not affect you. Do not suppose that means I shall not have a word with him."

Georgiana laughed and touched his cheek. "Just keep Anthony from damaging him *too* much. It would be a shame to stain that scarlet coat he wears."

"On the contrary," said Darcy with a malevolent grin. "I believe the color would hide any evidence. It is sad we can do nothing about his face."

Mirth overflowing, Georgiana returned to the youngest Bennets.

Within moments, Darcy could see her gesturing toward Wickham, her speech low and intense. Knowing she was warning them away, Darcy was satisfied and situated himself in a hidden location to prevent Wickham from seeing him, waiting for the sets to end. When they did, he approached his cousin at once as unobtrusively as he could.

"Wickham is here."

As Darcy might have expected, a murderous scowl came over his cousin's face. "We have seen hide nor hair of him since Ramsgate," spat his cousin, his eyes roving over the company. Darcy pointed to the man and Fitzwilliam's eyes widened. "An officer? What a laugh! I know of no man less suited to discipline, even that of the militia, than Wickham."

"Come, Cousin," said Darcy. "This is our chance to discover what trouble he intends."

Catching Wickham was the work of the moment, far easier than Darcy might have expected given the man's tendency to ingratiate himself without cessation. At the moment, he was facing a little away from them, his gaze seeming to rest on Charity. Fitzwilliam noted it, Darcy saw, for his scowl tightened further. Wickham did not seem to recognize her, and Darcy recalled he had not seen her for several years before he had last been at Pemberley.

"You had best remove your serpent's gaze from my sister, Wickham," growled Fitzwilliam as he and Darcy put themselves in front of the detestable man.

Wickham's eyes widened, his visage turning white. "F-Fitzwilliam! And Darcy! What a s-surprise it is to see you!"

"A surprise it must be," said Darcy, "since I doubt you would have dared to come here if you thought you might encounter us. What I cannot understand is how you came to wear the scarlet, and why you are here since everyone in Meryton knows Fitzwilliam is leasing Netherfield."

"*You* are leasing Netherfield?" demanded Wickham with more incredulity than tact. "What of the constant comments of your need to make your own way in the world? I did not know the army paid so much else I would consider joining the regulars."

It was a comment typical of Wickham's bravado and prompted a feral grin from Fitzwilliam. "The whys of it are not for you to inquire, Wickham. Perhaps you *should* join the regulars, for if you did some enterprising French soldier might put an end to you for us and make the world a better place."

"Since it is obvious you did not know we were here," said Darcy, interjecting as he knew this could easily degenerate to a loud confrontation, "I suppose we need not account for your daring. And I care little how you came to be an officer. But I do not care for your brand of insouciance, Wickham, and will not have you defrauding the people of this town or leaving ruined girls in your wake as is your wont."

Wickham laughed, a harsh, grating cackle, and fixed them with his usual malevolence. "That is rich, Darcy. I suppose you saw me dancing with Miss Elizabeth? You always had good taste in women, though your manner of interacting with them has ever been inept. What I do not understand is why she, a woman possessing a small estate and no lineage worth repeating, would be of interest to a conceited ass like you. Is Miss de Bourgh's estate not enough for your dynastic lusts?"

Though Fitzwilliam appeared ready to speak with his fists, the import of Wickham's words hit them both at the same time and they began laughing. Wickham, it appeared, was not amused, for the threat of violence was all on his side now.

"You should have been a court jester, Wickham," chortled Fitzwilliam, appreciating the irony of the man's misunderstanding. "For an expert marksman, you have the ability to miss the target in such a spectacular fashion that one cannot help but laugh."

"You are simply unhappy I found her first," said Wickham, his fury replaced by sulkiness.

"We have been in the neighborhood for more than a month, Wickham," said Darcy. "Trust me, we are familiar with the Bennets and their quality. What you do not comprehend is that while Miss Elizabeth manages the estate in her late father's stead, it is not her possession."

Wickham regarded them, suspicion marked in his countenance. "It will do no good, you know. I will not give up my pursuit of her based on this feeble attempt to distract me."

"If you do not believe us, speak with Miss Elizabeth yourself. The truth of the matter is that the state is entailed. Miss Elizabeth's mother is with child at present, rendering the ownership of the estate uncertain. Should the child be a boy, they will continue at Longbourn. If not, they must make way for the heir, a cousin who is, though you may not credit it, Lady Catherine's parson."

Eyes widened, Wickham looked past them at Miss Elizabeth, who stood with her younger sisters while the second sets had begun. Darcy, diverted though he was at Wickham's misunderstanding, wished to be rid of the man and spoke again to make the situation clear to him.

"Wickham," said he, drawing the libertine's attention back to him, "in the interest of avoiding a scene, I will not insist on removing you from this room. But let us ensure you understand a few facts, for if you break the strictures under which we place you, nothing will protect you from our wrath."

"I will take great relish in taking vengeance from your hide," said Fitzwilliam, cracking his knuckles to emphasize his point.

"We shall warn the merchants and your commanding officer. I would suggest you do not obtain credit, or I shall see you in Marshalsea. Georgiana is here, as are Anne and Charity, whom you were ogling when we reached you. If you approach them, it will go ill for you."

"Trust me, Darcy," muttered Wickham, "I have no intention of entangling myself in *that* business again."

"Good," said Fitzwilliam.

"Furthermore," said Darcy, "you should know that the Bennets are our particular friends."

"I might never have thought to see the great Fitzwilliam Darcy slumming in a town such as this," sneered Wickham.

"If you do not wish to have your pretty face marred, I suggest you keep your jibes to yourself." The pleasant manner with which he delivered it made Fitzwilliam's statement all the more effective. Wickham, it seemed, got the point if his paled countenance was any sign.

"You may speak with Miss Elizabeth to confirm what we told you, but it would be best if you refrained from dancing with any other lady this evening. And if you attempt to seduce any young lady of the neighborhood, it will not go well for you."

"In short," said Fitzwilliam, "behave yourself here. I cannot imagine you are capable of it, which will lead to your flight from the neighborhood before long. I care not what you do or where you go, but if you hurt any of our friends, you shall reap what you sow."

With a final imperious glare, Fitzwilliam stalked off leaving Darcy with his erstwhile friend. Already, he noted Wickham's gaze returning to Miss Elizabeth, his look considering. Darcy decided at that moment there was nothing left to say and stepped away from the man. His destination was Miss Elizabeth, for not only did he wish to show Wickham that he was friendly with her, but he had an important communication to make to her.

"I see," said Elizabeth when Mr. Darcy had finished speaking of Mr.

Wickham. Her eyes found the man, and she noted his chiseled jaw, for he obviously understood they were speaking of him. "That something was off about Mr. Wickham was unmistakable from the moment I made his acquaintance."

"Then I applaud your perspicacity, Miss Elizabeth," said Mr. Darcy. "There are many whom Wickham has deceived over the years, for he wears his manners like a well-worn cloak. The most surprising matter of this business is that Wickham thought you owned Longbourn."

The grin she returned lit up her countenance, making her appear to uncommon advantage. "I suspect he heard of my position managing the estate and leapt to a conclusion without verifying the facts. I shall take great relish in confirming the truth of the matter and abusing him for his greed."

"Then I shall leave his further chastisement to you. I have no doubt you are eminently capable of it."

The ball proceeded as such events are wont to do, and Elizabeth enjoyed herself as she ever did. Their situation prevented as much dancing as Elizabeth would normally engage in, which bothered her sisters more than it did Elizabeth herself. As Georgiana was not out and danced little, and Charlotte was often by their side keeping them company, they always had a ready occupation, which was a relief to Elizabeth and her sisters. Mr. Darcy, Elizabeth noted, danced less than he had at the assembly—his only partners were Charity, Anne, and his sister—and while she might have wondered at his lack of civility that evening, she put it down to the presence of Mr. Wickham and did not question it. It also worked to Elizabeth's benefit, for she stood with him in interesting conversation for much of the evening.

Of Mr. Wickham, Elizabeth saw much but did not speak to the man. The considering gaze she well understood, given Mr. Darcy's account of their conversation, and while Elizabeth wished to prick his insufferable vanity, she was content to know he would approach her before the end of the evening. The other truly objectionable presence, Miss Bingley, was in evidence much, but while she danced often with the men of the neighborhood, neither Mr. Darcy nor Colonel Fitzwilliam solicited her hand, and she appeared to feel the lack of their civility. In time, Miss Bingley's sour disposition and haughty attitude rendered her a disagreeable dance partner, and the men of the neighborhood ceased requesting her hand, leaving her by the side of the floor with Mr. and Mrs. Hurst, her disdainful gaze raking over them all. It was unfortunate her disposition was soon to become much worse.

"I believe the supper set is upon us, Miss Elizabeth," said Mr. Darcy when the evening had progressed. "Shall we dance it together?"

A tiny fluttering appeared in Elizabeth's heart, and she accepted, gratified to be the focus of such a man's attention. Elizabeth noted the whispers of the company when she did so, though they did not reach the crescendo Colonel Fitzwilliam's attentions to Jane had provoked. She also could not miss the anger with which Miss Bingley regarded them; Elizabeth cheerfully ignored the woman, instead focusing on the gentleman with whom she danced.

The dance passed without incident, their conversation continuing unabated. When they went into the dining room, Mr. Darcy assisted her by asking after her preferences, and they spent the hour together, near to her sisters and the other members of his family.

On a night such as this, the Bennet sisters might be counted on to provide part of the after-dinner entertainment. Charity took her place at the pianoforte when Colonel Fitzwilliam called for a song, but Anne did not play and Georgiana could not be induced to perform, so the local ladies followed suit. Mary, who wished to perform whenever possible, regarded the instrument with regret, the Bennet sisters having decided their mourning rendered it best to refrain. Then when the music ended, the diners sat for a few moments conversing before the call to return to the ballroom.

Elizabeth did not know if Mr. Darcy stepped away to allow Mr. Wickham the opportunity to approach her. But the man did so with alacrity when she was alone at the table. Mr. Darcy, she noted, hovered nearby, ready to assist at a moment's notice.

"Miss Elizabeth," began Mr. Wickham without preamble. "I trust you are well. It seems you have enjoyed this evening very much."

Regarding him for several moments, Elizabeth decided not to belabor the point. "I am accounted a social woman, Mr. Wickham, my mourning notwithstanding."

"Yes," interjected he. "I have seen you with Darcy much of the evening." The man released a harsh laugh. "That is interesting, for Darcy rarely notices a woman except to consider her imperfections. I might have thought him interested in you."

The comment aroused Elizabeth's interest but the man's sardonic tone fanned the flames of her ire, and she fixed him with an imperious glare. "Let us not trade words, Mr. Wickham, for I suspect you have approached me for a reason. In the interest of not allowing you to make any more disgusting comments about my friends, allow me to elucidate you on the subject.

"Longbourn is not mine. The estate is entailed, and my mother is with child. Should she, God willing, have a son, he will inherit the estate. If the child is a girl, we must make way in favor of my father's distant cousin who is his heir. Inducing me to marry you would gain you nothing, for you cannot sell all or part of the estate, nor is there much in our coffers to allow you to live in whatever profligate style you prefer."

"I see," said Mr. Wickham, his only answer. This proof of the man's worthlessness only infuriated Elizabeth all the more.

"Let me further state, Mr. Wickham, so there is no misunderstanding, how much you disgust me. To fix on a woman you suppose owns an estate so soon after her father's death speaks of a disregard for the feelings of others which could only exist in the most depraved of men. I had not known you for five minutes before I determined you were far too smooth to be genuine. There was never any chance of you charming me, sir, for my interest in you is nonexistent."

Mr. Wickham's lips tightened with displeasure and he seemed on the verge of making some retort. But Elizabeth had not finished with him.

"Mr. Darcy has informed me he will speak with the shopkeepers and Colonel Forster. I will further tell you I will not endure any improper behavior on your part. I will not defame your reputation with the gentlemen, but I will intervene if I hear of you paying attention to any young women of the neighborhood. Please know that Longbourn is closed to you—the housekeeper will turn you away if you dare to show your face there again."

This proved too much for Mr. Wickham, for he rose and departed with nary a word. The way he strode from the room, Elizabeth wondered if he meant to quit the estate altogether. With Mr. Darcy and Colonel Fitzwilliam in residence, men with whom he shared a mutual animosity, Elizabeth thought it best if he did. Then Mr. Darcy returned to his place beside her.

"Please allow me to inform you how masterful you were, Miss Elizabeth." Mr. Darcy's eyes were shining with approval. "I do not believe he has ever endured such a set down at the hands of a young woman he considers his prey. No doubt he will shake it off and make excuses for it, but at this moment I think you have quite befuddled him."

"Thank you for your warning, Mr. Darcy," said Elizabeth. "I shall ensure all my sisters know of Mr. Wickham's worthlessness."

"I believe you do not need to concern yourself for it. When I noted his presence, I informed Georgiana. Thereafter, I noted her speaking with your sisters and have no doubt of the subject of their discourse. I suspect your sisters will give him the short shrift if he should attempt anything with them."

Mirth flowed freely, and Elizabeth felt as comfortable as she ever had in a man's company. "Then I shall thank Georgiana when the opportunity arises. Do you suppose Mr. Wickham will leave Meryton?"

"It is possible," said Mr. Darcy. "With his usual activities denied him, he will in all likelihood find the situation intolerable. I suspect he is nearing the end of his rope in England, for he has made himself unwelcome in many places. Should he desert, matters will become difficult for him."

Elizabeth nodded, but before she could respond, a commotion arose at the door. It was John, the footman from Longbourn, who caught sight of her at once. With a hurried gait, he approached her and gave her a sloppy bow which spoke to some perturbation of spirit.

"Miss Elizabeth. You are wanted at home. Your mother's time has come."

CHAPTER XIV

❧❧⟨∞⟩❧❧

S hock did not even begin to cover what Elizabeth felt upon hearing her footman's words.

"The child is to come tonight?"

"That is what Mrs. Hill informed me," said John. "She sent Theodore to fetch your aunt to Longbourn and begs you to return home."

"Of course, I shall come," said Elizabeth. "Please find the coachman and have him prepare for an immediate departure."

John knuckled his forehead and departed the room, leaving Elizabeth looking for her sisters. There was no need to search, for they had seen the footman's arrival and converged on her, questions on their lips, such that the cacophony prompted Elizabeth to demand silence.

"Quiet, Lydia, and I shall explain," when her youngest sister persisted. When she fell silent, Elizabeth took in the questioning gazes of all her sisters and said: "Mama's time has come. Mrs. Hill has asked that I return to Longbourn."

The murmur of voices that rose about them did not escape Elizabeth's attention, and for the first time, she noticed the rest of the company, most of whom still occupied the dining-room. Mrs. Bennet was known in the neighborhood, and most of these people, Elizabeth knew, hoped she would give birth to a son.

"Your mother's confinement has begun?" came the voice of Lady Catherine. Her ladyship approached with the rest of the Netherfield family in tow, their expressions ranging from concern to anticipation.

"It has, Lady Catherine," said Elizabeth. "I must return to Longbourn at once."

"We shall all go with you, Lizzy," said Jane, her voice filled with determination. Her sisters chorused their agreement at once, even Lydia, who could not be pulled from a ball by any persuasion.

"Perhaps you should remain and return when the ball ends," said Elizabeth. "I do not suppose there is anything you can do at home."

"There is likely not," said Mary. "But I believe I speak for my sisters when I say that I shall not remain here while Mama is laboring to bring our sibling into the world."

"We shall not!" stated Kitty, Lydia nodding beside her.

Overwhelmed with affection for her sisters, Elizabeth gathered them all in close, exclaiming her love and appreciation. When the moment between them ended, Elizabeth turned and regarded her hosts.

"Please accept our apologies for our abrupt departure, but I believe we must return to Longbourn."

"Of course, you must," said Lady Catherine. "If you will, I believe there are many here who wish to receive whatever news you can impart. When you have a moment, please send word and we shall dispense it to the neighborhood. And remember that I have offered to assist. If you will allow it, I shall come tomorrow."

It was a bit of civility Elizabeth would not have expected from the lady. With a smile, she nodded and thanked her. The Bennets could not depart without receiving the good wishes of the neighborhood, and for several moments those wishing to say a word or two besieged them. Dear, dependable Charlotte, Mrs. Long's nieces, the Gouldings, and many others besides all had a few words for Elizabeth and her sisters. And Charity, Anne, and Georgiana were effusive in wishing them well, promising they would visit when the occasion permitted it. Given their departure and what was occurring at Longbourn at that very moment, Elizabeth wondered if there would be any further dancing that night.

"I wish to offer my compliments too, Miss Elizabeth," said Mr. Darcy as she turned to depart. "We shall all pray your mother and her child are safe after this ordeal."

Elizabeth appreciated that the gentleman focused on the more important concern of her family's wellbeing, rather than the sex of the child. "Thank you, Mr. Darcy. I shall pray that all is well too."

As Elizabeth gathered her sisters together, she could not help but overhear Colonel Fitzwilliam speaking to Jane. Though he spoke in a low tone, Elizabeth could hear it as if he had shouted it to the room, and it gave her hope for her sister's future.

"Do not concern yourself, Miss Bennet. Whatever happens, please know that your future is not in doubt. Focus on the health of your mother and your sibling."

With those final words ringing in her ears, Elizabeth led her sisters out of the house into the night. The time of reckoning had finally come.

Longbourn, when they arrived, was quieter than Elizabeth might have expected. A house managed by the excitable Mrs. Margaret Bennet could never be a tranquil one, and Elizabeth might have thought the servants would be in a frenzy, whipped up by their mistress's current plight.

Mrs. Hill, however, had matters well in order. The servants were quiet, going about their tasks, though the hour was late, with efficiency and purpose. There was some activity in the kitchen, though the sisters did not investigate, and the midwife and Mrs. Phillips had arrived sometime earlier.

"I suspect Mrs. Bennet was already feeling the birthing pains when you departed for Netherfield," said Mrs. Hill when Jane inquired after her mother. "In the beginning, however, these can be misunderstood. They began in earnest about an hour ago."

"Then the child will come tonight?" asked Lydia.

Directing a kind look at her, Mrs. Hill corrected her perception, saying: "These things can take time, Miss Lydia. The child may come quickly, but it may be tomorrow evening or even later when you have a sibling."

A look of horror came over Lydia's face, accompanied by a long moan from above stares. Knowing she needed to take control of the situation before her sisters became unnerved, Elizabeth addressed Mrs. Hill:

"May we see our mother for a moment?"

Mrs. Hill pursed her lips. "A birthing room is no place for a maiden. As the process is still in the early stages, I believe a brief visit would be acceptable."

There were several mutinous glares from her sisters, but Mrs. Hill spoke again to preclude them. "Please trust us. Mrs. Wainwright is an experienced midwife, and your aunt will also assist. I myself have birthed four fine sons and understand what needs to be done. We shall do our utmost to ensure your mother comes through this ordeal as quickly as possible."

"Of course, Mrs. Hill," said Jane, speaking at once to prevent any dissent. "We shall put our trust in you all."

The five sisters followed the housekeeper up the stairs and to their mother's room, the sounds of their mother's distress increasing as they went. Upon entering the room, Mrs. Wainwright shot a glance at Mrs. Hill, then seemed to understand the situation at once and subsided. Mrs. Bennet, they noted, was seated in her chair, her face pale, screwed up in an expression of pain.

"Jane, Lizzy!" exclaimed she upon seeing them.

They approached her, each reaching out to grasp a hand she extended to them. Their sisters crowded around them, exclaiming as to their pleasure to have a sibling and exhorting their mother to courage. Mrs. Bennet seemed to rally for a moment, for she fixed them all with affection she did not often display.

"What a wonderful gaggle of girls you all are!" cried she. "No mother could be more fortunate with you all than I."

"And we are fortunate to have you for a mother," averred Lydia.

Mrs. Bennet smiled at her, then grimaced as another pain shot through her. The pressure of her grip on Elizabeth's hand caused her concern, wondering if there was not something amiss. When it subsided, Mrs. Bennet returned her eyes to them and gave them an encouraging smile.

"Do not concern yourself, girls. This is no worse than it was with any of you. When it is finished, hopefully, I shall have a son to coddle and spoil!"

"Your health and that of the babe is the most important," said Mary.

"I dare say it is," said Mrs. Bennet. "But I hope very much I can finally do my duty and produce an heir for my dearly departed husband."

"Let us all hope so," interjected Mrs. Wainwright. "For now, it would be best if your daughters departed, Madam. This is no place for innocent young ladies."

"Do as she instructs, girls," said Mrs. Bennet, shooing them from the room. "I shall be well and shall have you summoned when you may greet your sibling."

Jane nodded and began chivvying her sisters from the room,

reluctant though they were to depart. The last sight Elizabeth had of her mother was with her face still screwed up in pain. Then the door closed behind them.

It could not be supposed the sisters would find much sleep that night. The hour was late—already well past midnight—and a sense of anticipation had settled on the ladies as they waited for any news. Having pity on her sisters, Jane sent for tea and some cakes to keep them occupied, but while they drank the tea, no one could do more than nibble on a cake. Kitty and Lydia spoke together in low tones, while Mary, Jane, and Elizabeth were lost in their own thoughts. Even when yawns stretched mouths wide open, her sisters refused to retire.

"It is not as if we shall find sleep anyway," said Kitty when Elizabeth suggested they find their beds. "Not with Mama's cries of pain."

The infrequent moans issuing from the upper floor had gradually changed to cries of pain. Elizabeth did not insist at that moment that her sisters retire, but as the time wore on, she noted her sisters' increasing distress. Their mother's travails were unnerving them, a sentiment with which Elizabeth could empathize.

"Kitty, Lydia," said Elizabeth after a strident cry prompted them to jump in alarm, "I believe it would be best if you retired." Turning to Mary, Elizabeth said: "Perhaps you would go with them, Mary. The guest room at the end of the hall might be for the best, as you would hear less from there."

Mary considered her suggestion for a moment and nodded, regarding her younger sisters. "Yes, perhaps that would be for the best. I shall speak to Sarah to ensure the room is in good order."

Despite the girls' protests, they were soon climbing the stairs, Sarah having confirmed the room had been cleaned recently. Elizabeth followed her sisters up the stairs, noting when they hurried past the door to their mother's room, not wishing to linger and further hear her distress. The girls disrobed in their rooms and donned their nightgowns, and soon they were all huddled in the bed, lying close to each other for comfort and support.

"I did not think they would give in," said Jane when Elizabeth rejoined her sister in the sitting-room. Jane had taken the opportunity to change into a nightgown herself, after speaking with the cook about the following day.

"Nor did I," said Elizabeth, now more comfortable in her nightgown. "I think their exhaustion played a large role in their tractability, such as it was."

Jane nodded and Elizabeth turned an interested look on her sister. "I heard what Colonel Fitzwilliam said before we left Netherfield."

A rosy hue coming over her cheeks, Jane darted a glance at Elizabeth. "It would be best not to read much into what he said, Lizzy. He was not explicit."

"He did not come out and state his intentions, Jane," chided Elizabeth, "but there was no ambiguity in his words. The question is, what do you feel for him?"

Jane sighed and leaned back on the sofa, drawing the blanket she had brought from her room about her shoulders. "I think Colonel Fitzwilliam is the best man of my acquaintance, Lizzy. Should he propose, I cannot imagine I would give him any response other than an enthusiastic acceptance. But I do not know he means to propose, so I will keep myself under good regulation."

"Yes, that is for the best," said Elizabeth. "I am happy for you, Jane, for I suspect he meant every word of what he said tonight. Should he offer his hand, you will be a fortunate woman."

"If he does, I am sure I shall." Then Jane turned an arched look on Elizabeth. "What of Mr. Darcy's attentions to you?"

"What do you mean?" asked Elizabeth, frowning at her sister's words.

Jane rolling her eyes was not a sight usually seen. "Did you not spend more time with him than any other tonight? I believe you were by his side more than you were on the dance floor!"

"Mr. Darcy is an excellent man," said Elizabeth. "However, I do not suppose I am anything other than a pleasant woman with whom to converse. He has given no indication of peculiar regard, Jane."

"As you have urged me to understand Colonel Fitzwilliam, so I give you the same advice, Lizzy. Mr. Darcy is not as open as Colonel Fitzwilliam is, so his way of making his interest known will be subtler. A man does not lavish his attention on a young woman to the exclusion of all others if he considers her nothing more than a 'pleasant woman with whom to converse.'"

"Then I suppose we shall need to wait to see what will be," said Elizabeth. "If he should make any intentions known, I shall respond with what is in my heart."

"And is there enough in your heart to accept him?" asked Jane.

"At present, I hardly know," said Elizabeth. "Given the uncertainty of our current situation—"

"Which will be speedily resolved one way or another within the next day," interjected Jane.

Elizabeth smiled and nodded. "Then given our situation, it would be prudent to accept regardless of what I feel. You and I have always determined to marry for love, but now that we might be thrown from our home with little to sustain us, the folly of that sentiment has never been so clear to me."

"And yet I would not act any differently," said Jane.

"Nor would I. Mr. Darcy is an excellent man, and I sense he feels deeply. I would not wish to marry him under false pretenses."

"No, I would not wish to do so with Colonel Fitzwilliam either. Or any other man, for that matter."

The sisters fell silent, each deep in their own thoughts, punctuated by the occasional cry from their mother. Though she was wilting by the moment, Elizabeth had no notion of seeking her room, and she thought Jane was similarly determined to remain. Sarah looked in on them sometime later, and seeing their attitudes, provided them with additional blankets and pillows.

"Mrs. Hill has sent the staff to their beds," she informed them as she took her leave. "I shall respond if summoned, but John, Theodore, and Clara have retired."

"Then please retire," said Elizabeth with a smile to the diligent girl. "Should anything occur, we shall send for you."

With a curtsey, Sarah departed, leaving Jane and Elizabeth to their vigil.

"I do not suppose I shall sleep tonight," said Elizabeth.

"Nor I," replied Jane.

Contrary to their expectations, the sisters found a few hours of precious sleep, though Elizabeth's rest was disturbed by ominous dreams which she could not remember. When they awoke the following morning, they separated to their rooms to dress, noting that while it was still early, their sisters had already arisen themselves. Breakfast was served soon after, and Elizabeth and Jane urged their sisters to eat, knowing they would have little appetite.

Of Mrs. Hill, they saw little, and Mrs. Wainwright, not at all. Mrs. Phillips, however, found the sisters in the sitting-room, where they had gathered to wait for news, and accepted their questions with a patience Elizabeth had never known the woman to possess.

"The birthing continues," she said in response to their questions. "It will take some time yet, though all appears to be proceeding as it should."

"Is Mama well?" demanded Lydia, her tone demanding reassurance.

"As well as can be expected," replied their aunt, not unkindly. "We are doing what we can, girls. Lizzy, if you do not mind, I shall rest in your room for a time, as Mrs. Wainwright wishes us to be rested should she require our presence."

"Of course, Aunt," replied Elizabeth. "Tell Mrs. Hill to retire at once."

Mrs. Phillips nodded and hesitated. "I heard something of a lady at Netherfield Park who had offered to attend your mother, Lizzy. Can you send word to her? Another pair of hands in your mother's room would be welcome."

Having forgotten of the lady's offer and her promise to send word, Elizabeth started. "Of course, I shall send word to her. The events of the night have driven it from my mind."

"Thank you, Lizzy. I shall leave you now."

There was something in Mrs. Phillips's manner which spoke to some concern she had not shared with the sisters. The occupation of writing a note to Lady Catherine, however, provided a useful distraction from her worries. Completing the letter quickly, Elizabeth dispatched it with John. Only a few moments later, Sarah entered with a letter for Elizabeth.

"It seems Lady Catherine has anticipated me," she told her sisters after perusing the letter. "The lady asks for news, though in a manner as imperious as I might have expected from such a noble lady."

The sisters' responding grins were weak, distracted as they were by the events of the day. No one had the heart to make a similar jest in response, leaving them sitting in moody silence. This was how Lady Catherine found them when she arrived at the estate an hour later.

"Miss Bennet, Miss Elizabeth," greeted the lady as she stepped into the room, reserving a smile for the youngest sisters. "Thank you for sending word to me. Charity, Georgiana, and Anne are spreading it throughout the neighborhood; I would not injure your excellent servants by supposing they are incapable of the task, but word spread by gentle families is always the best."

"Thank you, Lady Catherine," replied Elizabeth. The lady, she noted, was not dressed in costly materials, her finery of the previous evening set aside in favor of a simple day dress.

"Now, if you will show me to your mother's room, I shall assist your aunt and the midwife."

"My aunt has retired for a brief rest," said Elizabeth. "But I shall show you to Mrs. Wainwright and my mother's room."

It was on Elizabeth's mind that she might glimpse her mother when she led Lady Catherine to the room, but the lady anticipated her. "I know you wish to see her, Miss Bennet, but this is not the place for you. I shall send regular updates as to your mother's condition."

Thus dismissed, Elizabeth watched as the lady opened the door and slipped through, closing it behind her. Through the door, Elizabeth could hear the murmur of the lady's greetings, accompanied by the more strident tones of her mother. With nothing else to do, Elizabeth retreated from the hall and rejoined her sisters in the sitting-room.

True to her word, Lady Catherine sent several messages informing them of the status of the coming birth. They contained little actual information, but as word had been sparse previously, they were welcome, nonetheless. It seemed to Elizabeth that the cries of her mother became fainter over time, and she did not know whether that should be of concern. As her sisters were occupied in speaking in low tones—Mary played the pianoforte for a time—each dealing with the events occurring above stairs in their own ways, Elizabeth decided she would not further worry them with her conjectures.

The situation continued until that evening when Elizabeth thought the sisters' moods were frayed to where the slightest noise would provoke them to jump. Tempers tattered, leading to several minor spats between their youngest members, which were put to rights by their sisters with a word of admonishment or encouragement. It seemed there was little of life left in them all, for they were numb, caught between one world and the next, incapable of even the slightest action while their mother struggled to determine their fate.

When the door to the sitting-room opened, the sisters all jumped at the change, and Sarah, who entered, regarded them all with an expression akin to pity. At once, Elizabeth rose, welcoming and dreading the interruption in equal measure. Around her, her sisters all rose, fear displayed on each face as they looked to the maid for news.

"Lady Catherine has sent for you all, Miss Bennet. I believe it best that you come at once."

"What is the matter?" wailed Lydia.

"It is better you go for yourselves."

"Come, Lydia," said Jane, fixing her youngest sibling with a look of utmost affection and compassion, though tinged with trepidation. "Let us go and see our Mother."

Lydia went to Jane and clung to her, refusing to move from Jane's comforting arms. Jane allowed her to remain close, even as it proved difficult to move in such circumstances. It was somehow fitting that their mother's two favorite daughters were to lead the way into their mother's room, Elizabeth leading her other two sisters, keeping them close. Whether it was for her comfort or theirs, she could not say.

The first thing they all noticed when they entered the room was the alarming pallor of their mother's face. Her eyes drooped, heavy-lidded and weary, and what Elizabeth could see of her eyes were glassy and unfocused. Mrs. Bennet's hair was plastered against her forehead, evidence of her struggle to bring new life into the world.

Then a soft cry caught their attention, and they looked as one to Lady Catherine, who stood to the side with a swaddled bundle in her arms, a tender look such as Elizabeth might not have thought the severe woman could muster on her face. Seeing their scrutiny, Lady Catherine turned her smile onto them and presented the bundle.

"You should look to your mother. But I am certain you all wish to meet the newest member of your family. This is your brother."

With wonder, Elizabeth watched as Lady Catherine laid the babe in Jane's arms, noting for the first time the tiny fist that protruded from the blankets. The child opened his eyes, seeing nothing, yawned, and then closed them again, asleep at once.

"Mama!" exclaimed Lydia, in a voice excited, yet subdued at the same time. "You have done it! You have borne Papa's heir into the world."

The soft words caught their mother's attention, and she opened her eyes, her gaze bright, falling on the child in Jane's arms. Mrs. Bennet smiled once in contentment and regarded them all.

"What a wonderful sight this is," said she, though her words were slurred, her eyes losing focus. "My beautiful daughters, you are the jewels of the neighborhood. I am so happy I have finally done my duty and presented your father with an heir. Please give him my regards."

Confusion reigned over the girls at this declaration, but their mother's drooping eyelids prevented any further questions. With a last smile, their mother's head fell back on the pillows, her breath stilled in her chest, and her eyes closed for the final time.

CHAPTER XV

"Mama?" asked Lydia, her voice tremulous, the first of them to recover from the shock. "Mama!"

A high, keening wail startled them, and Mrs. Phillips, who had been standing to the side unnoticed, fell over her unmoving sister, sobs wracking her body. In a moment, chaos had descended over the room, as Lydia fell over her aunt and her mother, demanding that Mrs. Bennet open her eyes, while Jane tried to console her, Kitty burrowed into Elizabeth's arms, trying to find comfort while Mary stood stoically, tears rolling down her cheeks. Elizabeth had the presence of mind to summon her sister, allowing Mary to join Elizabeth and Kitty's combined embrace. With a wild look about the room, Elizabeth's eyes fell on Lady Catherine, the lady looking to the bed with regret, the small, precious bundle once again held reverently in her arms.

"Did you know?" rasped Elizabeth, trying to understand what had just happened.

Lady Catherine sighed and nodded. "I suspected, for the midwife informed us the birth had sapped your mother's strength. Whether it was because of her age or other factors of which we cannot be certain, it was a hard birth."

"I informed the lady as soon as she arrived," said Mrs. Wainwright, stepping forward from where she had been standing unnoticed at the end of the bed. "Miss Lydia's birth was easy, and I thought this one would be the same. But the babe would not come, and the toll it exacted on your mother's body proved too much for her to overcome." The woman gave them a sad smile. "This happens far too often in our world, but we have yet to understand enough of how the body works to prevent it."

Elizabeth could not respond, for her eyes were fixed on her mother's unmoving body, her sister and eldest and youngest daughters hovering over her.

Of the next hours, Elizabeth would remember but little. The numbness that settled over her left her empty, a broken vessel that could never be repaired. Her sisters were in a similar or worse state. Jane finally pried Lydia from her mother's side, Lydia, inconsolable, slipped into a merciful sleep with Kitty by her side soon after. Elizabeth felt as bone weary as she had ever been, even exceeding the days after her father's passing when she had slept ill for weeks. Jane and Mary stayed with her, the three sisters offering support to each other, none of them able to feel anything for the emptiness they felt inside.

"We are now orphans," murmured Elizabeth, speaking to herself. "Six months ago we were young women without a care in the world, and in that short space of time we have lost both our parents."

Jane's response was a choked sob, while Mary sat ramrod straight, a fatalistic acceptance etched upon her features. It was Mary who managed a response, saying: "My greatest regret is that we did not give credence to Mama's complaints when she told us of her pains. I believe that error with stay with me for the rest of my life."

"Miss Mary," said Lady Catherine, prompting them all to look up to see the woman who had just entered the room. "Please do not give such thoughts a moment's consideration."

"Mama was always complaining of her nerves," insisted Mary. "For my part, I know in my heart I did nothing more than roll my eyes and accuse her of her usual complaints of ill-use."

"Perhaps that is true," said Lady Catherine, sitting beside Mary and daring to take her hands in comfort. "In this situation, there may have been something of her usual habit. But all women experience pain in giving birth to their children, and you have no way of knowing if her pains contributed to what has happened. By Mrs. Wainwright's testimony, the early part of your mother's travails were nothing out of the ordinary. Do not blame yourself, for it is not your doing, and none of us could have known what would happen."

Mary returned Lady Catherine's gaze, belligerence in her manner, then she crumpled in on herself and collapsed against Lady Catherine, allowing the lady to move her hand on Mary's back in comforting circles. Then the lady looked up at Jane and Elizabeth, who were huddled together in mutual comfort, and spoke.

"Miss Bennet, Miss Elizabeth, though I hesitate to bring up the practicalities at such a time as this, you cannot ignore them. There are matters which require your attention, after which I would suggest you retire for the night."

Finding some well of resolve within her, and feeling Jane stiffen in her arms, Elizabeth nodded. "What must we do?"

Lady Catherine nodded with approval. "The first and most pressing matter is a wet nurse for your brother."

"I believe a woman of Meryton has recently given birth," said Jane.

"So Mrs. Wainwright informs me," said Lady Catherine. "She recommended a Mrs. Campbell in Meryton to assist. It should be no trouble for her to come and live in Longbourn's servants' quarters until your brother is weaned so she may be at hand. While she and the child will be away from her husband for a time, the money she will receive will help the family, and the distance is not great, easing the pangs of separation."

"Thank you, Lady Catherine," said Elizabeth, relieved the lady had already thought of such important subjects. "That is an excellent solution. Mrs. Hill can make the initial arrangements, and Mr. Campbell can visit his wife and child at any time. We are greatly in your debt."

Lady Catherine fixed her with a knowing smile. "It is no trouble, Miss Elizabeth. The second matter we should discuss is whether there is anyone in particular that you must inform of these events."

"My uncle in London," said Elizabeth. "Mr. Gardiner is the guardian of those of us who are still underage and has control of our finances. He is also Mama's only brother."

"Then if you will write your letter, I will see that it is sent express."

Nodding, Elizabeth went to the nearby escritoire. Jane, she knew, had written to Mr. Gardiner that morning informing him of the imminent birth, as neither had had the presence of mind to attend to it the previous evening. Elizabeth did not know if Jane had sent the letter express, even as she suspected her sister had. The thought of sending her uncle another letter so soon after the first, proclaiming his sister's demise, was repugnant, but she knew it must be done.

As Elizabeth wrote, not knowing what she said, Lady Catherine continued to speak to her sisters, her tone solicitous and at the same time exhorting. Elizabeth completed the task as quickly as she could and entrusted the letter into the lady's care. Mary excused herself, having been convinced to seek her bed, leaving the eldest sisters in the lady's care, once she had returned from seeing to the letter's disposition. Lady Catherine regarded them for several moments before she spoke again.

"Loath though I am to depart, I fear I must do so soon. Not only are you again a house in mourning, but there are matters at Netherfield to which I must attend, and several there who must be wild for news."

For the first time in the ordeal, Elizabeth noted that drying blood flecked Lady Catherine's dress. Her mother's blood. The sight choked Elizabeth up, knowing she never would hear her mother's complaints or her boasts of her daughters' beauty, Jane's certainty of catching a wealthy husband, or Lydia's liveliness.

"Of course, Lady Catherine," said Elizabeth, mustering a warm nod of thanks, though she could not quite manage a smile. "Your assistance has been invaluable. My sister and I both thank you for it."

Lady Catherine paused for a moment before she nodded. "It is no trouble. The pain must feel like it will never depart. I have lost my parents, my brother, and a sister I loved more than my own life. Having lost your father some months ago, I know you will understand my words."

"I do, and I will own you are correct," said Elizabeth, Jane nodding by her side. "The worst is how lost I feel. I must confess that I do not know what to do."

"You will do what you must, Miss Elizabeth. Now your responsibilities must be for the estate, the care of your brother, of which you will bear the primary responsibility, and your sisters, who will require comfort and guidance in this time. Do not hesitate to call on those of greater experience, for their support will be invaluable."

Elizabeth could not say what it was, but even this simple direction helped firm her resolve. Though she still felt like she was adrift on a hostile sea, those words had given her a rudder, and now she felt as if she had some hope of navigating to shore.

"Thank you, Lady Catherine." Elizabeth paused and laughed. "It seems half of my words to you are words of gratitude. But I mean them as warmly as I can say. What we might have done without your calm guiding presence is beyond my comprehension."

"I have been happy to help, Miss Elizabeth. I am not only possessed of greater life experience, but I am also separated from these events, not having the ties of affection that bind you all together. That allows me to think with a clearer head, to make decisions unaffected by sentiment.

"Now," said the lady, not unkindly, "I suggest you retire for the night. I shall not scruple to suggest it will all be better in the morning, but a night's rest will give you a clearer head, allow you to do what needs to be done with some perspective."

"Thank you, Lady Catherine," said Jane. "I believe Lizzy and I shall take your excellent advice."

The lady gave them a regal nod. "Then I would ask you one final boon. It is not proper to receive visitors at all times, but I am certain my family will be eager to reassure themselves that you are all well. Might I request leave to bring them to Longbourn tomorrow?"

"Of course," said Elizabeth. "We should be happy to receive them."

"Then we shall come during visiting hours. I suspect there will be others who come to pay their respects, and I shall ensure we do not stay long."

Having said this, the lady gave them a last few words of encouragement and departed. In Jane's company, Elizabeth retired, leaving a few instructions with Sarah for the following day's needs, knowing that Mrs. Hill had already retired herself, exhausted because of her sleepless night. Elizabeth reminded herself to thank their housekeeper in person. Perhaps some sort of token of their esteem would be appropriate, for the woman had done yeoman's work for them all.

As Elizabeth crawled into bed a little later, huddling next to Jane, she wondered if she would find sleep, so active were her thoughts. It was to her surprise that she was asleep almost as soon as her head hit the pillow, and she slept until the following morning.

When Lady Catherine returned to Netherfield, her mien was so tired and dispirited that Darcy knew at once something had happened at Longbourn. The state of her clothing did not escape his attention either. As he was the only one to witness her return, she fixed her attention on him, giving him a wan smile.

"I know you must be wild for news, Darcy, but I have not the strength to give it more than once. Please gather your sister and your cousins together, and I shall speak to them when I have changed."

The impatience that greeted his request to the rest of the family was unmistakable, even as they attempted to endure the wait until Lady Catherine returned. When she entered the room not long after, it was as if a lifetime had passed. It was strange, Darcy thought, for they had not known the family only a few short weeks ago. Now it was clear they had become near to all their hearts.

"What news, Lady Catherine?" demanded Charity, the most fretful of them all. She had, Darcy noted, become the closest of them all to Miss Bennet and Miss Elizabeth, though perhaps Fitzwilliam was becoming even closer to Miss Bennet. "Do the Bennets have a brother or a sister?"

"They have a brother," said Lady Catherine, "though in the process, they have lost their mother."

It took a moment for the import of Lady Catherine's words to penetrate their anxiety. Anne's hand flew to her mouth and Charity regarded Lady Catherine as if she had spoken Greek, while Georgiana cried out and Darcy shared a glance with Fitzwilliam. These events would likely affect his cousin more than the rest of them.

"To be clear," said Fitzwilliam, voicing the thoughts of them all, "Mrs. Bennet has passed away in childbirth, but the child survived?"

"That is correct," was the lady's succinct reply. "The child appears healthy, and the Bennets' residence at the estate is secure for the present, but the mistress has not survived to enjoy her triumph."

"How awful!" gasped Georgiana.

"We must visit them!" exclaimed Charity.

"No, Charity," said Lady Catherine, her tone infused with her usual level of command. "Now that the mistress has passed, the house is again in mourning. The Bennet sisters are exhausted and heartsick, as you might well imagine. I have sent them to bed for the night."

"But we must visit them tomorrow," said Anne, daring her mother to disagree.

"That would be acceptable," agreed Lady Catherine. "A short visit to pass condolences and assure yourselves that they are well is permissible. We cannot stay long, but I have already received their approval."

"You mentioned the child is a boy?" asked Darcy when the ladies nodded their agreement. "He is healthy?"

"As healthy a babe as I have ever seen," said Lady Catherine.

"And the task of informing Mr. Collins? Have the ladies attended to that need?"

"The Bennets' aunt was there assisting with the birth," said Lady Catherine. "Her husband is, as I understand, the Bennets' solicitor."

"Then it will be his responsibility to notify the previous heir of the new heir's birth," said Fitzwilliam.

"And Mr. Collins will not appreciate it."

Darcy might not have credited it, but he sensed an impatience in his aunt, unusual, considering she had always preferred underlings who possessed a certain docility of manner. Having never met Mr. Collins, Darcy had no direct knowledge of him, but the Bennets' and Anne's description had left him with an impression in line with what he might have expected given his knowledge of his aunt's preferences.

"It is not for Mr. Collins to approve or disapprove," said Fitzwilliam, his tone unfriendly. "Everything has proceeded following the applicable laws. Mr. Collins is to be pitied for his continued position as the heir to the estate, but he has no case to make should he wish to claim misuse."

"A fact I shall be certain to emphasize the next time I see him."

Darcy turned an interested glance on his aunt. "It seems you have become close to these ladies in a short time, Lady Catherine. I might not have expected such affinity so soon after meeting them."

"They are excellent ladies," said Lady Catherine with a shrug. "Miss Elizabeth is capable, and Miss Bennet is lovely, possessing a core of steel behind her pretty countenance. The younger girls are still inexperienced and perhaps too lively for their good, but they have exceptional examples to assist them to become young ladies of credit to their family."

"I could not have said it better, Aunt," murmured Fitzwilliam.

The rest of the day, the company largely spent in silence, all caught in their respective introspections. Darcy could well remember the deaths of both his parents, though he had been a boy when he had lost his mother. As such, he could empathize with the ladies, could imagine what they were feeling. And yet, he had lost his parents twelve years apart—to lose both parents within six months of each other must be a different cross to bear.

In that, their situation was now similar to that of Darcy's family, having lost both of their parents. The only member of the previous generation left in the Darcy, Fitzwilliam, and de Bourgh families was with them that day. Sir Lewis had been the first—not that anyone lamented his absence—then Darcy's parents, and finally the earl and countess. In that respect, the Bennets were their equals.

Later that evening, the ladies retired, leaving Darcy in Fitzwilliam's company. They made their way to Netherfield's study and ensconced themselves within for a nightcap. For some time, they sat with their glasses and their thoughts, saying nothing. At length, Darcy sighed and looked to his cousin.

"I will own to some curiosity for your intentions, Cousin. I do not know what you said to Miss Bennet last night before she departed, but your attitude was clear enough. Do you mean to offer for her?"

"Yes, Darcy," replied Fitzwilliam with an absence of mind. "While my feelings are still a little muddled, I believe I love Miss Bennet and wish to have her for a wife."

"Our aunt will not be happy."

Fitzwilliam turned to gaze at him. "Do you suppose I will concern myself with our aunt's opinion?"

"No, I do not suppose you will," said Darcy. "But it is something to consider. You would not wish an irate Lady Catherine to frighten Miss Bennet away."

The snort with which Fitzwilliam responded accurately summed up his feelings. "Perhaps you have not noticed, Darcy, but Lady Catherine appears to have warmed to the Bennets considerably."

"Which is a shock," replied Darcy. "I have never seen our irascible aunt warm to others to this degree."

"It is not so surprising," said Fitzwilliam, turning a twinkling eye on Darcy. "Lady Catherine's true weakness, outside of her affection for her family, is her affinity for those who have suffered trials in their lives. As much as she chooses servants who will not gainsay her, how many times have we seen her take in those in desperate need of succor, assist them in regaining their footing?"

"It is a most unusual trait," said Darcy. "Given how many times she goes on about how the distinction of rank must be maintained, one might think she would abuse them for creating their own problems and leave them to fend for themselves."

"I believe it may be a consequence of her experiences with Sir Lewis."

Darcy grimaced. Sir Lewis had been a disgusting man, a libertine who had cared for nothing other than his selfish desires. That he had not abused Lady Catherine or his daughter, Darcy knew to be a consequence of the threat posed by his uncle, and his father before him. Still, Lady Catherine had suffered as wife to such a man and had not shed a tear at his untimely death.

Pushing such thoughts away, Darcy refocused on his cousin and the previous subject of discussion. "You are set in your decision?"

"I believe I have made that determination," said Fitzwilliam. "With this most recent event, I cannot do so until their mourning is over. But when it is, I believe I shall approach Miss Bennet the first day I can."

Fitzwilliam then pulled himself from his introspection. "Perhaps I shall look in the north for an estate. Miss Bennet would prefer to be close to her sister, I suspect."

Caught by surprise, Darcy regarded his cousin, wondering what he was about. Then the import of what he said washed over Darcy. His first instinct was to scowl at his cousin and deny any interest in Miss Elizabeth. But he could not, for the truth of the matter was that she interested him far more than any other woman he had ever met. Was it enough to offer for her? That was yet undetermined, even as Darcy knew it would be easy to allow himself to go the rest of the way to being completely in love with her.

"As you have told me any such talk concerning Miss Bennet is premature, so it is with Miss Elizabeth. Likewise, I have no notion that she has any regard for me."

"Then it is your task to discover the strength of her regard." Fitzwilliam paused. "The only thing that concerns me is Wickham. I might expect him to run as he usually does at the first sign of trouble, but I worry that he still has some thought of harm for the Bennets."

Darcy snorted with disdain at the mention of George Wickham. "Do not worry, Fitzwilliam. The Bennet sisters all know of his character, and Wickham has nothing to gain by attempting to force Miss Elizabeth into marriage. Perhaps he might gain a small amount of funds, but not nearly enough to finance his habits. Then there was the way he fled the ballroom after Miss Elizabeth informed him exactly what she thought of him."

Turning to Darcy, interested in his account, Fitzwilliam asked after the tale. "I do not believe you have shared this with me, Cousin."

Darcy informed his cousin of what happened during dinner and Fitzwilliam, having loathed Wickham for many years, could not hold back his mirth at the thought of a woman delivering such a blow to his vanity.

"That Miss Elizabeth is a treasure, is she not?" Fitzwilliam laughed. "How I wish I had seen it! She stripped his pretensions away and flayed him with nothing more than her tongue and the force of her wit. What an excellent woman she is!"

"She is that, indeed," murmured Darcy.

"Does this change your intentions?"

"Not at all," replied Darcy. "As I already knew of it, the opinion I stated included these sentiments."

"Then what is holding you back?"

Darcy considered his cousin's question. "At present, I am unaware of her feelings, as I have already stated, and I am not quite certain of my own. Miss Elizabeth has given me no hint of her regard."

"As I informed you before, Darcy, that is something you may discover."

"I understand that. The other matter that holds me back is Lady Catherine's presence. Against all I might have expected to the contrary, Lady Catherine appears to approve of the Miss Bennets. How long will her approbation last if she sees me making love to Miss Elizabeth?"

"Then wait until Lady Catherine departs," said Fitzwilliam with a shrug. "She will not stay here forever."

"That is a possibility," agreed Darcy. "But the same as you, I will not be at liberty to make my addresses for at least three months. Further, visits to Longbourn will be sparse and the Bennets will not attend events. There will be no occasion to win Miss Elizabeth's regard. For that reason, I wonder if it might not be better to depart from Netherfield and return in the spring."

Fitzwilliam frowned at Darcy's suggestion and turned his attention to the first part of Darcy's statement. "Then wait until they are in half mourning to make your attempt. As you so succinctly suggested, Miss Elizabeth is not going anywhere in the meantime.

"I will make one suggestion to you," added Fitzwilliam, as he rose to depart. "Follow whatever path will make you happy, Darcy, and do not allow Lady Catherine to deter you. You have already told her many times—including yesterday evening—that you have no intention of marrying Anne. Given that, Lady Catherine cannot complain if you choose Miss Elizabeth."

"There are many reasons I think she could use to complain," replied Darcy.

Fitzwilliam chuckled. "Perhaps you are correct. But you have never allowed others to determine your path before. Now is not the time to start."

Then Fitzwilliam bid him good night and left the room. Perhaps Darcy should have sought his bed at once. But thoughts of his cousin's words mixed with memories of Miss Elizabeth kept him in the darkened study until the wee hours of the morning.

CHAPTER XVI

****

$\mathcal{T}$he stark, somber presence of the new hatchment on Longbourn's door was a reminder of the Bennets' recent travails. As Darcy alighted from the carriage with his family and regarded it, it reminded him of his own father's passing and the more distant memory of his mother. More than anything else, the news brought by Lady Catherine or the knowledge of events of the previous day, the hatchment brought a somber cast to Darcy's mind, the reminder of how fragile life could be. In some strange way, it also bolstered him. Having informed his cousin the previous evening that he was uncertain about Miss Elizabeth, the reminder of the brevity of life suggested he should take the chance of happiness at once and hold it for as long as possible.

The housekeeper once again showed the signs of the house in mourning, her dress more somber than it had been the other times Darcy had visited. She greeted them, her manner kind but reverent, and guided them into the house, a maid appearing to accept their outerwear. Then she led them into the sitting-room where the Bennet sisters were all gathered.

"Oh, Lizzy, Jane!" exclaimed Charity, Anne following close behind her. "What a tragedy for you all! Please accept our condolences;

though we did not know your mother well, I believe we all understood her to be an estimable lady if nothing more than for her rearing of five excellent daughters!"

"Thank you, Charity," said Miss Elizabeth, as Darcy's cousin enfolded her into an embrace. "I believe it will take some time, but we will be well again."

The words of condolence from the rest of the company were offered and accepted, many tears shed. Georgiana, Darcy knew, had grown close to the youngest Bennet sisters and was engaged in her greetings and expressions of sorrow for them, while Fitzwilliam fixed his attention on Miss Bennet. Darcy watched Miss Elizabeth and Charity speak, drawing close and offering his regrets, while Lady Catherine watched them all, her sense of affection for this family palpable.

Then Charity caught sight of the small cradle situated to the side of a sofa and cried out with interest. "Is this your brother?"

"It is," said Elizabeth.

Her elder sister went to the small bed and, noting the heir of Longbourn was awake and gazing about the room, retrieved him, settling him into her arms as if he was her child. The ladies gathered around, cooing at the child who was much too young to speak back to them, exclaiming how handsome he was, how his eyes were so bright, his hair so soft, among other expressions of delight.

When Darcy drew close, he noted the child was, indeed, bright of eye, rosy of countenance, and blessed with a resemblance to his sisters that was marked even at this early stage of his life. His head was adorned with dark wisps of hair, and his tiny fingers were curled into a fist in one hand, while the other grasped Georgiana's finger.

"He is a handsome child, Miss Bennet," said Lady Catherine. "Of course, I already knew that when I held him last night. Have you given him a name?"

Miss Elizabeth and Miss Bennet looked at each other, the former responding to Lady Catherine's question. "We have called him Joseph Edward Gardiner Bennet, Lady Catherine. Joseph was my father's middle name, Edward my uncle and his father's name, and Gardiner is my mother's maiden name."

"An excellent name, Miss Elizabeth, and perfectly chosen, I should say. With such examples as you and your sisters to look up to, he cannot fail to become an exceptional man."

The company then sat to visit, Jane holding the child while most of those remaining gathered about them to coo and exclaim over him. Miss Elizabeth sat a little apart with Darcy and Lady Catherine in attendance. Darcy noted, given her diverted glance in his direction, that Miss Elizabeth had realized that Lady Catherine liked to be of use. Then again, her actions of the day previous had already informed her of that facet of the lady's character.

"Let us discuss the practicalities first, Miss Elizabeth," said she, ignoring Darcy's glance of surprise. "Have you received a reply from your uncle yet?"

"We have not," replied Miss Elizabeth. "But we expect he will join us this morning. As Uncle Gardiner lives only four hours away, there is little reason to suppose his response will be anything other than his arrival here."

"A sensible plan," said Lady Catherine. "What of the need to inform Mr. Collins of these events?"

"That duty fell to my Uncle Phillips, the family solicitor," said Miss Elizabeth, stifling a smile. It seemed that Lady Catherine wished to distract her, for Darcy knew she was aware of their uncle's position. Miss Elizabeth's look at Darcy suggested she had realized the same thing. "Uncle Phillips was here for a brief time this morning, and he promised to handle the matter at once."

"That is good. As you are aware, Mr. Collins's state of anxiety for these events is high. It would be best to ensure he understands the situation as soon as may be."

Miss Elizabeth paused, and Darcy thought she was considering how much she should say. Mr. Collins was, after all, Lady Catherine's parson, and she could not know how the lady would accept any criticism of the man. The lady noticed her hesitance, however, and nodded for her to speak.

"It is only that I wonder what Mr. Collins's response will be. He has been so insistent that he will inherit, and some of his actions have led my uncles to threaten him with a legal response if he does not desist."

"And you think he will not?"

"Our history with him suggests it is unlikely," replied Miss Elizabeth. "Given some of his letters, I wonder at his ability to reason, for he is most unhinged about the situation."

"Oh?" asked Lady Catherine, a flinty look of displeasure in her eyes. "I do not believe I have heard the details, Miss Elizabeth. Will you share them with me?"

Heartened by the lady's manner, Miss Elizabeth related their difficulties with Mr. Collins, including his claims of fraud, his declarations of the inevitability of his inheritance, and more recently, his suggestion he marry one of them and provide them with a home when Longbourn eventually became his. Lady Catherine listened without comment, but her darkening countenance and the firming of her lips spoke to her displeasure.

"I had no notion Mr. Collins was behaving in such a reprehensible manner, Miss Elizabeth," said Lady Catherine. "Please know that I shall speak to him when I return to Rosings. If he should dare to come here and confront you, please call me from Netherfield. I shall set Mr. Collins to rights."

"Thank you, Lady Catherine," replied Elizabeth. "Your aid is, again, most appreciated."

Lady Catherine nodded and began inquiring again of the state of matters at Longbourn, including the details of the funeral for Mrs. Bennet, for which she pledged Darcy and Fitzwilliam's attendance. Darcy would have attended regardless, and he knew Fitzwilliam had also planned to show his respect for his neighbors' mother. Miss Elizabeth answered Lady Catherine's questions, even those that might have appeared intrusive, with calmness, though perhaps not perfect composure. The aplomb with which this impressive young woman met Lady Catherine's questioning filled Darcy with more respect for her. She was truly an excellent woman!

Of Miss Elizabeth's perception of Lady Catherine's words, Darcy could determine nothing. The lady's comments and questions were a little more invasive than Darcy might have wished, but underneath it all, he caught a subtle hint of encouragement that appeared to bolster her confidence.

"That is excellent, Miss Elizabeth," said Lady Catherine at the end of her inquiry, nodding with approval. "It appears you have matters well in hand for the present. The improvements you have planned for the estate this coming spring should pay off handsomely for your family's future prosperity."

"Thank you, Lady Catherine," replied Miss Elizabeth. "My steward says the same. I am eager to put the improvements to the test."

"And your father could not have chosen a better guardian of your brother's inheritance," replied Lady Catherine. "It appears you know your duty, so I shall say nothing further of that.

"Of course," continued the lady, her manner more offhand, "when you marry, your husband will take over responsibility for the management of the estate, and your sister's husbands will assist. Given my perception of your character, however, I suspect you will wish to continue to involve yourself in it."

"I cannot say you are incorrect, Lady Catherine," replied Miss

Elizabeth. "I love Longbourn and wish to do whatever I can to ensure my brother inherits a prosperous property."

"Excellent. Then you have made a good start of it." Lady Catherine paused and looked about the room. "For the present, I believe we have stayed long enough and should depart."

Before the lady could rise and instruct all the party to exit the room, the door opened, and a gentleman entered, regarding them all with some interest. He was not tall, a little stocky, had dark brown hair with nary a hint of gray, and possessed a strong resemblance to the late Mrs. Bennet. Clearly, this was the uncle of whom Miss Elizabeth had spoken so kindly.

"Jane, Lizzy," greeted the man, and while he presented a somber mien, he was in control of his emotions. "I apologize it has taken me so long to arrive, for I was required to make arrangements for my absence."

"Uncle," said both ladies, approaching him and allowing themselves to be drawn into his arms. Knowing precedence dictated that Mr. Gardiner, as the man lower in society, wait for the higher to request an introduction, Darcy waited until the man greeted all his nieces before making the request.

When the introductions were offered and comments of pleasure exchanged, Mr. Gardiner regarded them with great interest. "My recent letters from my nieces have overflowed with comments concerning their new neighbors at Netherfield Park. I thank you all for the support and friendship you have shown them in these difficult times."

"It was no trouble, Mr. Gardiner," said Fitzwilliam, speaking for them all. "I think we all agree that your nieces are excellent women. We have been happy to make their acquaintance."

A brief conversation ensued, and Darcy found himself impressed with Mr. Gardiner. In particular, the man turned to him and addressed him with words that surprised Darcy in both their content and their delivery, which was not intended to ingratiate.

"Of you, in particular, I have some intelligence, Mr. Darcy. My dear wife informs me you are the Mr. Darcy of Pemberley in Derbyshire."

"Yes, that is correct," said Darcy, curious how this man could know of him.

"It is a place of which I have heard much, sir, for Mrs. Gardiner was raised in a small town called Lambton. I am certain you must have heard of it."

"Heard of it?" echoed Darcy. "Why, Lambton is not five miles from

Pemberley. Most of the business of the estate is conducted in that town, though we attend worship services in Kympton, as the living there is under my patronage."

"That much I have heard, sir. To hear my wife speak of it, Lambton is the dearest place in the world. She very much wishes to return to visit it someday."

Mrs. Bennet had been a woman of uncertain temper and an excitable nature, and Darcy had not thought much of her intelligence. Unintelligent was not an adjective that could be ascribed to Mr. Gardiner. If Darcy had not already heard of him from the Bennets, he might have thought the man was a gentleman, his manners better than many men of Darcy's acquaintance. For a few pleasant moments, they stood speaking, Darcy becoming more impressed by the moment.

At length, however, propriety dictated that the Netherfield company depart. Darcy could not disagree, even if he wished to speak to Mr. Gardiner more. Thus decided, they offered their condolences once again and took themselves from the room, content that the family, though beaten down by the events in their lives, would recover.

"Well, girls," said Mr. Gardiner, turning to regard them when the visitors had departed, "it seems you have fallen in with illustrious people."

"You would never know it to speak to them, Uncle," said Elizabeth. "I have little experience with those of high society, but they are not pretentious or above their company. I have enjoyed knowing them very much."

Mr. Gardiner nodded, and then the smile ran away from his face. "I can scarcely believe my sister is gone, though I am gratified her final efforts provided some security for you all."

"As am I," said Elizabeth, tears welling up in her eyes again, noting her sisters were in the same straits. "It does not seem real, Uncle."

"I expect to hear Mama calling for her salts," said Kitty.

"Or exclaiming about the next assembly or the possibilities for marriage offered by our new neighbors," added Lydia.

"Yes, girls," said Mr. Gardiner, showing them a sad smile. Then he turned back to Elizabeth. "And the new heir of Longbourn?"

Elizabeth showed her uncle to the little cradle they had set up in the room. Their brother was sleeping at that moment, his little hands twitching to something he saw in his dreams. Uncle Gardiner inspected him with some approval before turning to the sisters.

"He seems healthy and shows a marked resemblance to your father,

I dare say. Did your mother inform you of her wishes for his name before her passing?"

The sisters exchanged glances. "She did not, Uncle," said Elizabeth. "Mama was barely lucid by the time they called us into her room. We have named him Joseph Edward Gardiner Bennet."

Mr. Gardiner nodded, clearly pleased. "Joseph was your father's second name, was it not? His name is an excellent way of honoring both of your families." Mr. Gardiner paused and grinned. "I shall assume his second and third names are for my father."

"And for you, Uncle," said Jane. "You shared your father's name, and we thought it only appropriate."

"And I thank you for it," said Mr. Gardiner. Then he sighed and said: "Please show me to your mother, girls, and then we can sit and discuss what happened."

Elizabeth obliged him with Jane in tow, Mary, Kitty, and Lydia remaining in the sitting-room. Elizabeth could understand her sisters' reluctance to go to the room where their mother lay in repose, the same her father's remains had occupied after he had passed only six months before. At the door, the sisters stopped, allowing their uncle to go in alone, unwilling to enter in as the sight would prove without any doubt that they were now parentless.

"I hope Uncle does not think the worst of us for not entering," murmured Jane.

"I cannot imagine he does," replied Elizabeth, taking her sister's hand and grasping it in a tight grip. "Mr. Gardiner would prefer not to view our mother himself I should say."

"But he must pay her his respects," murmured Jane.

When their uncle rejoined them some moments later his cheeks were suspiciously moist and his voice hoarse. "Let us go to the study, for I believe we have some matters we must discuss."

Nodding, Elizabeth led him away down the hall toward the room her father had occupied so recently. Entering therein, a pang again entered Elizabeth's heart, the duller ache of her father's passing brought into focus again by her mother's untimely death. They eschewed the desk and sat near the fireplace which was roaring with a cheery fire, no doubt set by the ever-faithful John upon Mr. Gardiner's arrival, knowing they would need to use the room.

"Now," said Mr. Gardiner, regarding them each in turn, "I wish to know what happened. I hate to dredge up painful memories, even if they are still fresh. But I wish to know what led us to this point. The last information I had suggested everything was proceeding as well as it could."

"That is what we all thought, Uncle," said Jane. "The midwife said the birth was hard, but whether it was because of her age or other factors of which she was not aware, we cannot be certain."

"I did not notice until later," said Elizabeth quietly, "but Lady Catherine's dress was sprinkled with Mama's blood."

Mr. Gardiner looked at them with interest. "I might not have thought a woman of Lady Catherine's lineage would concern herself with the birthing of a woman of the minor gentry."

"And yet she has been a wonderful help," said Elizabeth. "And this after only making our acquaintance two days ago."

"Then you have been fortunate."

For the next several minutes, Elizabeth, with Jane's support, did their best to inform their uncle of what had happened the previous day. Their tale was riddled with holes as was to be expected, as neither sister had been present in the birthing room. Their uncle, however, did not press them for details they did not possess, focusing on what they could tell him rather than indulging in useless speculation.

When they finished, Mr. Gardiner leaned back in his chair and sighed, rubbing his temples as if his head ached. "I can scarcely believe what has happened. I feel as you do, girls, that the sound of her insistence that Mrs. Hill attend her will ring throughout the house within moments. It seems impossible we shall never hear it again."

"I feel it too," said Elizabeth. "I only wish we had not ignored my mother's complaints before we left for the ball."

"Her time was approaching, Lizzy," said Mr. Gardiner, his tone chiding. "I am a father several times over, and I can tell you that all women experience something similar. The midwife, I am certain, was aware of the situation. No blame can be attached to you."

"As Lady Catherine has already informed us, Lizzy," said Jane. So rare was the occasion that Jane had words of disapproval for Elizabeth that she was surprised by it. But Jane did not give an inch. "This self-censure is not helping, Lizzy. There was nothing we could do. We should look to the future and not forever reprove ourselves for the past."

"You speak sense, Jane," said Uncle Gardiner. "Let us have no more talk of this.

"Now," said their uncle after Elizabeth nodded, feeling no small measure of embarrassment, "we must discuss the practicalities. As you are aware by your father's wishes, your Uncle Phillips and I are joint guardians to all but Jane, who is now of age. And it is a good thing that she is of age, for we need not concern ourselves with that aspect of your situation. Phillips and I have agreed he will take responsibility for legal matters and your day-to-day needs, and that I will be responsible for financial issues, and handle the approval for anything extraordinary, such as proposals of marriage."

Mr. Gardiner paused and grinned at them. "It has been my opinion, given the progression of your letters of late, that it may not be long before there is such a request for Jane. Am I correct?"

"I do not know, Uncle," said Jane, attempting her usual measure of self-effacement. "It is possible, but Colonel Fitzwilliam has yet made no overt statements of interest."

"What do you think, Lizzy?" asked their uncle with a wink for Jane.

The look Jane shot at Elizabeth promised retribution, but Elizabeth contented herself with a grin at her sister before turning back to her uncle. "Jane has the right of it in essentials, Uncle. I suspect Colonel Fitzwilliam is further along the path of proposing to Jane than she will allow, but I will own I have no evidence to support my supposition."

"I suspected as much," nodded their uncle. Then he became serious. "At present, of course, you cannot entertain any notion of courtship or marriage, and I suspect that Colonel Fitzwilliam understands and respects this. Should he make overtures once your half mourning has passed, you may send him to London. You do not need my permission, Jane, but I should very much wish to give you my blessing, nonetheless."

"Of course, Uncle," said Jane. "If he proposes, I would not wish to proceed without your blessing."

"You are a good girl, Jane. I know your father said that often, but it bears repeating. Even those few moments I spent in company with the gentleman informed me that he is an excellent man, one who will make you a happy woman.

"As for the immediate future," continued Mr. Gardiner, "I am only at liberty to stay until the funeral tomorrow, then I must return to London the following morning. I trust you have everything in hand with the estate?"

"There is no need to concern yourself for that, Uncle," said Elizabeth. "Mr. Whitmore has matters under control and informs me of everything of which I must be aware. It is in excellent hands. Now that we know my brother shall inherit, we may implement the improvements we have planned when planting begins."

"That is very good, Lizzy," said Mr. Gardiner. "For as you know, I know nothing about estate management. I shall have a word with Mr.

Whitmore before I depart.

"The last matter of which we should discuss," said Mr. Gardiner, "is your aunt's intention to come to Longbourn to assist you in this difficult time."

"Aunt Gardiner is to come here?" asked Jane.

"She is, Jane." Mr. Gardiner fixed them with a mock stern look. "I shall lose my dear wife for several weeks, but she has insisted she must come and stay with you in your time of need. The exact time of her arrival is yet to be determined, but I suspect it shall be next week. I shall join you for Christmas and return according to my usual schedule, and then your aunt will return to London in the New Year."

"That is excellent news, Uncle," said Elizabeth, giving him an impudent smile. "Though I pity you for your loss, having Aunt Madeline here will be a great boon."

"Trust me, Lizzy, of that I am well aware. She is my partner in every sense, for not only does she manage our home and see to our children, but I value her advice and insight. I shall sorely miss her while we are parted."

Uncle Gardiner then seemed to shake such thoughts off in favor of matters of current importance. "Let us speak of this no more for the moment. I must go and speak to the parson at Longbourn church, for I suspect his is the task of seeing to your mother's funeral. When I return, I hope you will allow me to dine, for I am famished."

"I shall see that luncheon is ready to be served, Uncle," said Jane.

With a few more words and a smile of affection, their uncle departed. For all that Elizabeth had been put in control of Longbourn's operation, it was a welcome relief to have him here, for Elizabeth trusted her uncle above all men. The shock of their mother's passing was still upon them, but Elizabeth hoped they would recover in due course.

CHAPTER XVII

$\mathcal{M}$rs. Margaret Bennet was laid to rest the next day in the small churchyard by the church building, interred next to her husband. Elizabeth declined to focus on the difficult relationship between her parents and instead fixed on the happy memories she had of them. That her parents were gone, a circumstance she could not have imagined only a few months ago, was now a stark reality. It was now the duty of Elizabeth and her sisters to carry on the Bennet name, to prosper the estate and their family fortunes. All their hopes rested in the person of one small infant.

As Elizabeth and her sisters sat waiting for the return of their uncles, Mrs. Phillips sniffling into her handkerchief, she could not help but wonder what the future would hold for them. Such thoughts were morbid in the extreme, but Elizabeth knew mortality was an affliction they would all suffer, and there was no guarantee their brother would ever reach his adult years. Precarious was their situation, even with an heir to the estate.

Not formed for such thoughts, Elizabeth shook them away, eager to espouse happier feelings, to watch her brother grow, to teach him everything her father taught her, to nurture his love for the land so he would one day become an excellent master and provider for the family he would someday have himself. Elizabeth's father, she knew, had attended Eton and Cambridge, and she was determined her brother would do the same, have all the privileges one of his station could expect. That would require hard work and Elizabeth would do as she must to provide for him. Had her father had a son, she liked to think he would have done better in managing his estate, would have wished to pass his legacy to him with as much advantage as he could. Elizabeth could do no less.

At length, their uncles returned, their manner solemn and regretful. They spoke some few words of the funeral service but did not belabor the point, much to Elizabeth's appreciation. The Phillipses stayed for dinner, Mrs. Phillips's continued sniffles testament to her distress. It was distress that Elizabeth thought exceeded that of even Mrs. Bennet's daughters, for while they were all sorrowful, they managed it better than did their aunt.

The following morning, Mr. Gardiner took his leave and returned to London, complete with renewed promises that their aunt would soon attend them. "We shall finalize Madeline's plans and send you word as to the particulars. As she was eager to be with you, I suspect she will travel early next week. In the meantime, I hope I can trust you to manage matters."

"Of course, Uncle," said Jane, Elizabeth nodding by her side. "We shall be adequately protected here, and as we shall not go out much, I foresee little trouble."

"What of this Mr. Wickham of whom I have heard?" asked Uncle Gardiner, turning his attention to Elizabeth. "The fact of your stewardship over Longbourn still may present a temptation to him, though he would not be at liberty to do what he wished even if he should marry you."

"I have little fear of Mr. Wickham importuning me again," said Elizabeth. "There has not been even a hint of his presence, and even if he comes, we shall deny him entry."

"Yes, that is for the best. It may be best if you were to ask your friend, Charlotte Lucas, to keep you informed as to the doings of the regiment and this Mr. Wickham in particular. She may glean little from his activities, but she might hear something of his doings which will either bring you relief or put you on your guard."

It was a sensible suggestion and one Elizabeth would put to her friend as soon as may be. With these and a few other comments, Mr. Gardiner departed, promising to see them again at Christmastide. Thus, the sisters settled in for their second period of mourning that year.

All was well for those few days that were to elapse before Mrs. Gardiner was to join them. As the season was late, there was little estate business to conduct, and Elizabeth often found herself at liberty to do as she wished. While she might have preferred to resume her habit of walking, the weather did not permit it and it would not be considered proper, regardless. The gardens and the wilderness behind the house were available, however, and Elizabeth availed herself of them, sometimes in Jane's company, but more often in solitude.

As for their sisters, it appeared to Elizabeth that they were coping as well. Kitty and, in particular, Lydia, often became a little teary for their departed mother, accepting comfort from their elder sisters when they might have disdained it before. Mary was her usual stoic self, comforted in her religious treatises which often seemed to encompass the subject of the afterlife. On several occasions, Mary persuaded them to read the family Bible together, and the passages she chose, speaking to the comfort of the Lord to the deceased, brought them all comfort, even those who had decried Mary's suggestion.

Of more pertinence to the family was a circumstance that Elizabeth became more aware of as time passed. Mrs. Campbell, as Lady Catherine had suggested, had come to live at Longbourn, given a room in the servants' quarters. At night, should Joseph fuss, she would feed the child and see him asleep again, and she attended to his feedings during the day. It was good the child was quiet and good-natured, for she had an infant of her own who was fussier.

"I wish my own David were such a happy child," said she to the eldest sisters a few days after she arrived. "David often fusses two or three times a night. But Joseph does so once and settles back to sleep again when I have fed him and does not stir until the morning."

"Is there any problem feeding him?" asked Elizabeth. The anxiety for the young master of Longbourn was such that the sisters were painfully attuned to every cough, every cry the child made.

"Not at all," said Mrs. Campbell. "He is a lusty eater and is satisfied at once. I dare say he is no trouble at all."

"Then we thank you, Mrs. Campbell," said Jane. "Please know that your husband may visit you here at any time convenient. We understand what you are sacrificing to be of use to our brother."

"I am happy to do it, and you have compensated me well. I dare say the money will assist David in the future, though I hope he will someday have siblings to play with him."

This was welcome news, for it helped settle the sisters' concern for their brother. The other aspect of his care was a matter surprising for both Jane and Elizabeth.

"Jane," said Elizabeth that Sunday when they were sitting together after their first church service without their mother. "Does it appear to you that Lydia seems to be eager to care for our brother?"

"It has been growing on my mind for several days," said Jane, observing her youngest sisters, who between them had Joseph in their arms and were cooing at him much as a young mother might for her child. "Did you note her changing his soiled linens this morning before church?"

"I might never have thought it of her," said Elizabeth. "Instead, I thought she would decry him as a smelly, loud bit of annoyance and bemoan the additional months of mourning ahead of us."

Jane shot Elizabeth a look which informed her of her sister's displeasure. "Come, Jane, tell me you thought she would be so . . . maternal toward him."

"No, I suppose you are correct," said Jane with a sigh. "It seems these events have provoked our sisters to mature faster than we might have expected."

"I still believe we should hire a nurse."

Pursing her lips, Jane regarded her siblings and nodded. "Yes, that would be for the best. Even if Lydia wishes to see to his care, she will not always be at liberty to do so."

"The notice has gone out," said Elizabeth. "Once Aunt Gardiner arrives, we can interview applicants."

Jane nodded, and they dropped the subject. Until there was a nurse, their brother's care would fall to Mrs. Campbell and the sisters. As they all considered their brother a piece of their mother left to them after her passing, they were all content with the task. Elizabeth wondered if Lydia's maternal instinct would last for any length of time, but she did not voice her opinion out loud. Not only would it be unfair to Lydia, but she suspected at least some changes in her sister's behavior of late would be long-lasting.

And then trouble reared its ugly head again.

"What is that missive, Aunt Catherine?"

Lady Catherine looked up from the brief letter she was perusing and addressed Darcy's question. "It is a letter from Miss Elizabeth Bennet. Trouble has arisen with a tenant of Longbourn, and she writes to beg the help of my nephews."

Darcy shared a significant look with his cousin, remembering the confrontation between Miss Elizabeth and Mr. Bates. That he would choose now, with the family newly bereaved, to cause trouble suggested a greater penchant for mischief than he might have expected. Fitzwilliam, too, remembered, for his countenance darkened in response.

"Given your looks," commented Lady Catherine, "I suspect you have some knowledge of this man."

"Not long after we came to Netherfield," said Darcy. "The man manages Longbourn's herd of cattle; it seems his charges cause problems periodically with the other tenants. What has he done this time?"

"A dispute with a neighbor," replied Lady Catherine, handing him the letter, "though the cattle do not appear to be the cause of it this time."

Darcy glanced over the letter, noting Fitzwilliam looking over his shoulder while the ladies looked on. It was typical of the man, Darcy suspected, for he had impressed Darcy as one who would struggle to get on with anyone.

"Do you mean to offer your assistance?"

Looking up at his aunt, Darcy noted the intensity with which she regarded him, and he nodded. "I think it would be best. What I know of Mr. Bates suggests he chose this time to make trouble for a purpose of his own."

"I might have expected as much," said Lady Catherine. "Then if you are to go brave all this man's displeasure, perhaps I shall go to Longbourn to visit the Bennet ladies and see how they get on."

Such a declaration was certain to prompt entreaties from Darcy's sister and cousins to be allowed to join her. This led to a round of discussions on the propriety of visiting a house newly in mourning, Lady Catherine suggesting it was not proper, while Charity and Anne—and to a lesser extent Georgiana—argued they were better acquainted with the Bennets and had become good friends. In the end, Lady Catherine allowed it.

"Very well. Darcy, Fitzwilliam, we shall depart within thirty minutes. Will you join us or return to Netherfield?"

"It may be best to stop at Longbourn for a short time at least," said Fitzwilliam. "Miss Elizabeth will wish to know the results of our discussion with Mr. Bates."

"Then we shall await your coming there. Do not delay, for while a visit is acceptable, we should not stay long."

Thus decided, the men retired to their rooms to change into riding clothes while the ladies departed to prepare for their visit. It was not long before Darcy and his cousin were astride their horses, cantering down the road which led through Netherfield's lands to the estate and the cattle farm in the distance. The house was as Darcy remembered, the lowing of the cattle accompanied by the soft rustle of the wind through the branches bare of their summer bounty.

They had just ridden up to the house when the door opened, and Mr. Bates stepped outside. It seemed he had not noticed their company, for he regarded them, his surprise turned to fury.

"Ach, I should have known she would dispatch you louts," growled the man, spitting on the ground to signal his disdain.

"Your behavior makes you more deserving of the moniker," said Fitzwilliam, stepping down from his horse and standing before the shorter Mr. Bates. "Keep a civil tongue in your head."

Darcy, who had dismounted behind his cousin, stepped forward and presented a united front before the man, who eyed them with equal parts distaste and wariness. "Well, what is it to be? Will you tell me to behave meself again?"

"Perhaps you should explain the situation before we convict you," said Darcy.

The man peered at him, a hint more respect than he had before. His following explanation was more than a little disjointed, made little sense in parts, and glossed over in others, leading Darcy to believe Mr. Bates had acted as Darcy thought—perhaps provoking this confrontation with his fellow tenant was premeditated. The question was, what did he have to gain from it?

"It seems to me, Mr. Bates," said Fitzwilliam, echoing Darcy's thoughts, "that you thought to cause trouble knowing the family has been recently bereaved." The man scowled but did not respond. "The question is what we are to do with you. Therefore, I shall ask you a question: would you like to be pensioned on the estate and cede the care of the herd to another?"

Mr. Bates gaped at Fitzwilliam in astonishment. "Leave me herd? Why would I do that?"

"It becomes more difficult to manage them as one ages," said Fitzwilliam, seeming to possess an instinctual understanding of what would persuade him. "You have no one to assist you. When we visited you last, Miss Elizabeth mentioned this possibility."

"We must ratify it with her, of course," said Darcy. "But she is not opposed to the notion. You would live out your retirement in peace, and another would take your position and the care of your charges."

The man regarded them, his belligerence now gone in favor of interest for their proposal. "And I could hunt as I wish? Mr. Bennet did not keep a gamekeeper."

"Perhaps that could be arranged," said Fitzwilliam. "The position of gamekeeper carries the responsibility of managing the wildlife on the estate."

"And I might look in on the herd from time to time." Mr. Bates directed a wistful look at the barn in which the cries of his charges still reached them. "These old bones find it more difficult to move of late, but me cattle have been me companions for many years."

"As long as you do not infringe on the rights of the new tenant to manage his affairs."

Mr. Bates seemed to consider this for a moment before giving them a curt nod. "Then if Miss Elizabeth agrees, I will accept."

"Very well. We will carry word to her of what we discussed. Given the family's current situation, I suspect the steward will negotiate the specifics."

"That's bad business, that is," said Mr. Bates, a look of mixed brooding and reflection on his countenance. "I lost me own wife and child in childbirth many years ago." The man paused in thought, and after a moment said, though grudgingly: "I doubt this cousin who was to inherit would be so generous with me. I will thank Miss Bennet when I have the chance."

"Excellent," said Darcy. "Then we will depart."

When they left the man, he was seated in a chair near the door of his house, regarding his domain, his absence of manner speaking to contemplation. As well he might have, given his length of residence there. Mr. Bates's sour nature was, in part, explained by what he had informed them before they left.

"You have good instincts, Cousin," said Darcy as they cantered toward the manor to the south. "I had not remembered Miss Elizabeth's suggestion."

"It is little different from dealing with a dilatory officer," was Fitzwilliam's jovial reply. "Give them a way of saving face and a course of perceived benefit, and they will not hesitate to accept."

Darcy chuckled and shook his head. "When you decide to purchase, I am certain you will do well, indeed."

Relieved as she was by the solution the Netherfield gentlemen had posed, Elizabeth was effusive in giving her enthusiastic approval. "I shall have Mr. Whitmore speak to Mr. Bates and make the arrangements. Longbourn had a gamekeeper when I was a girl, but when old Mr. Crenshaw died, Papa saw no need to replace him."

"An estate the size of Longbourn can likely do without one if necessary," said Darcy, not wishing to dredge more of her father's failures in keeping the estate. "It seems fortuitous he did not replace the man, for it provides a neat solution to the problem of Mr. Bates."

"Then again," said Elizabeth with a laugh, "it is possible Mr. Bates will terrorize my other tenants rather than just the Johnsons, for he will have the run of the estate."

"In that case, Miss Elizabeth," said Colonel Fitzwilliam, responding with a grin of his own, "at least he will not be bothering the other tenants with his cattle."

"And the opportunity to shoot a fox or a few birds might sap the aggression from him," said Darcy.

"Oh, I know he will be well in his new position," said Elizabeth. "Mr. Bates is so unsociable that the other tenants will likely see neither hide nor hair of him once he does not need to associate with them."

"That may be for the best," said Darcy. He paused and eyed her. "Do you know anything of his past and the wife and child he lost?"

"It happened before I was born," said Elizabeth with a sigh. Considering how she felt now, she wondered if she did not understand and empathize with Mr. Bates more than she ever had before. "I have heard the tale, but that is the extent of my knowledge."

The gentlemen nodded, for there was no reason to belabor the point. The subject resolved, Colonel Fitzwilliam turned his attention on Jane, and Mr. Darcy continued speaking with Elizabeth. Lady Catherine and the three ladies from Netherfield had joined their younger sisters and were engaged in exclaiming over the new heir to Longbourn in the nursery, and Elizabeth expected them back momentarily. For the next several moments, they continued in this attitude, and all seemed well.

Then there arose a commotion outside.

"What can that be?" asked Elizabeth to no one, rising and going to the sitting-room window. When she pulled the curtains aside and looked out on the drive, what she saw shocked her.

"What is it, Lizzy?" asked Jane as Elizabeth turned and made for the door.

"Mr. Collins," said Elizabeth over her shoulder as she exited and hurried toward the front door.

As Elizabeth approached the entrance, she heard Mr. Collins shouting in a loud voice, his words unfit for a parson, let alone the ears of a gentlewoman. When she reached the stoop, Elizabeth took in the situation. Mr. Collins was not a small man, though he was all spindly arms and knobby knees, and he was attempting to fight his way past John and Mr. Whitmore to enter the house. John, as Elizabeth knew, was a powerful man, and was fending the parson off with ease, while Mr. Whitmore assisted him, attempting to talk some sense into him.

"Cousin Elizabeth!" shouted Mr. Collins when he caught sight of her. "You urge your lackeys to deny me my right, I see."

"You have no right here, Mr. Collins," said Elizabeth, her tone cool and unyielding. "As my uncles informed you, my mother bore a son. He is now the heir and will become the rightful master of the estate when he comes of age."

"I know not with whom your mother cavorted to cheat me from my birthright, but I require you to depart from the estate at once. Longbourn is mine, and I will have it!"

"That is enough from you, sir," said Mr. Darcy.

Elizabeth had not realized it, but the two gentlemen and Jane had followed her from the house, and now joined her in confronting the parson. John had released Mr. Collins now that he was not trying to enter the house, but he had not relaxed his vigilance, and Mr. Whitmore appeared ready to spring into action at a moment's notice.

"And who are you?" asked Mr. Collins, disdain coloring his voice. "I might have thought my cousins would bring in men to enforce her claim. But she can give herself to every man in the country and it will avail her little. I shall have my due!"

"Mr. Collins!" rang out Lady Catherine's voice before Elizabeth could do more than gasp at his disgusting insult.

The parson positively started, his gaze whipping around to see the lady, having exited the manor with her relations and the remainder of the Bennet sisters in tow. They now had a veritable audience, a fact Mr. Collins was not so concerned over, except for the unexpected presence of his patroness.

"L-Lady Catherine!" stammered he. "I-I had n-not expected to s-see you here."

"That much is obvious," said the lady, her gaze boring down on the man like a bludgeon. "What do you mean by coming to a house inhabited by ladies and attempting to enter amid slurs and slights that would make a common soldier blush?"

It was clear Mr. Collins did not know what to say. Elizabeth saw the man for what he was, this evidence in addition to what she had endured since her father's death. Mr. Collins was a bully, one who persecuted those he considered weaker than himself. Now that his patroness was here, a woman he could not browbeat, he could not muster a response.

"Your disgusting claims also included my nephews," said Lady Catherine when he did not respond, "sons of my late brother, the Earl of Matlock, and my dearest sister. What have you to say for yourself?"

Mr. Collins became green at the thought of offending such high personages and his mouth gaped open for a moment. Trust Lydia to break the silence with an observation designed to belittle.

"It appears Mr. Collins is adept at capturing flies. No doubt he draws them to him."

The parson's mouth snapped shut, and he glared at her. This spurred him to action.

"Lady Catherine," said he, resorting to pompous tones, "I know not what my cousins have told you, but they are attempting to defraud me. I know my rights. They must leave so I can take my rightful place."

"Do you suppose they can fool me, Mr. Collins?" demanded Lady Catherine. "I was present when Mrs. Bennet gave birth to the heir who was, until your display disturbed him, sleeping above stairs."

"We cannot know who the child's father is," was Mr. Collins's dismissive response.

"Do you have any proof of that charge, Mr. Collins?"

The question came from Mr. Darcy, his tone all that much more dangerous in that his words were quiet and menacing. Mr. Collins seemed to understand Mr. Darcy's displeasure, and his knowledge the man was Lady Catherine's nephew gave him greater respect.

"Of course, he does not," said Colonel Fitzwilliam, raking his gaze over Mr. Collins in clear contempt. "He wishes it to be true, so in his minuscule mind, it is true. He does not concern himself with whatever does not support his supposition."

"That is a harsh assessment, Nephew," said Lady Catherine, her scrutiny of the parson causing the man to sweat, even in the coolness of the late November day. "But it appears to be true.

"There are laws against slander, Mr. Collins," said Lady Catherine, now speaking to her parson. "And there are rules against extorting that which does not belong to you. If you had proof of Mrs. Bennet's infidelity, you would have presented it. That child in the house is Mr. Bennet's son. There is nothing you can do to change it. You had best return to Hunsford and not return."

"But—"

"Now, Mr. Collins." Lady Catherine's voice was firm and

198 %L Jann Rowland

unyielding. "I am not in the habit of enduring disobedience. Return to Hunsford at once. If you do not depart and cease to bedevil the Miss Bennets, I shall discuss your conduct with your bishop."

Had Mr. Collins been secure in his claims of ownership of Longbourn he might have discounted Lady Catherine's threat. His mouth worked for a moment as if attempting to summon a response. Nothing issued forth, and Mr. Collins instead turned and departed, his haste to leave them behind unseemly. Elizabeth breathed a sigh of relief.

"Thank you for your support, Lady Catherine," said Elizabeth when he had disappeared. "I do not think he would have been so readily induced to leave had you not been here."

"It is no trouble, Miss Elizabeth. I cannot imagine what has come over him, for the man is the worst sycophant I have ever met. His conduct here is quite astonishing."

"Perhaps it would be best to discover what has made him so insistent," said Mr. Darcy. "His actions speak of more than a simple disappointment in being passed over as the heir of the estate."

"That may be best," agreed Lady Catherine. "When I return to Rosings, I shall speak to him." Lady Catherine turned her attention back to Elizabeth. "Should he come again, it may be best to call the constable. I shall do what I can to prevent him from importuning you again."

"We shall do so, Lady Catherine," said Elizabeth. "My uncles have given me the same instructions."

The matter of Mr. Collins dealt with for the moment, they returned to the house. The visit only lasted a short time longer before their guests gave their regrets and departed.

CHAPTER XVIII

"Come, Darcy, we must speak."

Jolted from his thoughts, Darcy looked up and regarded his aunt, wondering if she wished to provoke another argument about his supposed engagement with Anne. The entrance of his cousins following Lady Catherine into the sitting-room, where Darcy had been sitting and thinking in solitude gave the lie to that supposition. Unless she meant to bring it up before them all.

"Speak, Aunt?" asked he. "Of what?"

Lady Catherine turned and directed Fitzwilliam and the ladies to their nearby sofas and sat, considering before she spoke. The events of the morning as Darcy had been considering them faded to the background as he regarded his aunt. The lady had been remarkably quiet since their return from Longbourn, and Darcy suspected her parson was the focus of her thoughts. Mr. Collins, they had learned after, had traveled to Hertfordshire by mail coach, without taking thought for any of his own needs, such as changes of clothes or other such necessary items one requires when traveling. The man would say but little when they found him in Meryton, his fear for Lady Catherine such that he had already purchased a return ticket to Kent and had been waiting by the inn for his departure, which would not occur for several hours.

"I meant to assure myself of my cousins' situation," muttered Mr. Collins when pressed. "I still suspect them of cheating me."

"They are not cheating you, Mr. Collins," Lady Catherine had told him after the third or fourth time he had repeated himself, her tone allowing no opposition. "I shall not speak further of the matter at present. However, I will require that you stay in Kent where you belong and do nothing to further disturb the peace of the Miss Bennets. Do I make myself clear?"

"You do," had been Mr. Collins's short, unhappy reply.

Thinking back on the confrontation now, Darcy could not help but wonder about the parson. Disappointing though having one's expected future snatched from before one's very eyes at the last moment was, a normal man did not press forward with accusations of such a vile nature to gentlewomen. Darcy made a mental note to remind his aunt to discover what was motivating him.

"We must decide what we are to do," said Lady Catherine, drawing Darcy's attention back to the present.

"I assume you mean something particular, Aunt," said Charity.

"Whether we shall stay in Hertfordshire," clarified Lady Catherine.

"What you mean to do I have no notion," said Fitzwilliam. "But I have no intention to depart from Netherfield."

Lady Catherine cast a shrewd look on him. "Might I suppose you wish to stay because of Miss Jane Bennet?"

"And if I do?" asked Fitzwilliam, his tone challenging. "What is it to you?"

"Cool your temper, Fitzwilliam," said Lady Catherine. "It is not my intention to slight the Miss Bennets, for I like them very well. All you informed me of them was not in error, for they are excellent young ladies.

"But you must own that they are not our level of society."

Fitzwilliam snorted. "If you think that concerns me even a jot, you do not know me."

"No, I would not suppose it did." Lady Catherine paused and considered him. "In this opinion, you are much like my brother."

"And my brother," said Fitzwilliam. "James no more cares for the status of another than do I."

"Which is to your credit. As you know, I am a little more concerned with matters such as status and rank, but I can find nothing amiss in the Miss Bennets. Should you make a choice and your choice be Miss Bennet, I cannot gainsay you, nor would I wish to try."

"Then what are you suggesting Lady Catherine?" said Darcy, trying to move the conversation along.

Lady Catherine sighed. "The Miss Bennets have suffered enormous loss these past six months, and they are newly in mourning again. As is the custom, they will not be in society until they reach half mourning, and that will not be for another three months. Thus, I believe It would be best if we returned to London for the duration of their deep mourning."

"Return to London?" demanded Charity.

"Charity," said Lady Catherine, her tone softer than the lady usually employed, "I know you wish to support your friends, and that is laudable. But you must consider the proprieties of the situation. While it is acceptable to visit a house in mourning occasionally, it is not proper to do so as often as we have. It is my understanding that the Bennets' aunt will join them, and their uncle will return at Christmas, so they shall have the support they require."

Lady Catherine then turned her gaze on Fitzwilliam. "While Fitzwilliam claims his attachment to Miss Bennet, and I do not question the strength of his regard, the fact remains that you all have only known the Bennets for a matter of two months. I believe it would be best to remove ourselves to London, spend the Christmas season there, allow the Bennets to grieve in peace, and if your regard remains strong, return in the spring after their mourning."

Silence descended after Lady Catherine's statement. A glance at his cousin suggested Fitzwilliam was troubled, his wish to stay as clear as his suspicion it might be best if they did not. The three ladies, Darcy knew, wished to support their friends. It was evident, however, that Lady Catherine had hit upon a pertinent point, that they had visited too much since the death of Mrs. Bennet. It might be best if they pulled back for a time.

"What do you all think?" asked Fitzwilliam, breaking the silence.

"I believe the more relevant question is what you think, Brother," said Charity. "I suspect we all wish to stay and provide support to the Miss Bennets. But Aunt Catherine brings up an excellent point too. The real question is whether you intend to further your connection with Miss Bennet."

"I . . ." Fitzwilliam trailed off. He struggled for something to say but the words, it seemed would not come. At length, he gave them a helpless shrug. "Yes, I believe I wish to offer for her, Charity. But I had not resolved in my mind that I would."

"What of Miss Bennet?" asked Anne quietly. "It is my observation that her affections are engaged. Shall you leave now with no warning and perhaps break her heart?"

"Of the state of Miss Bennet's heart, I have no notion," said Lady Catherine, "so I will bow to your greater knowledge of her. Please understand it is not my purpose to suggest you simply leave without a backward glance and forget about her."

"If we do go, we should ensure we take our leave of them."

"Yes, yes, that is the proper thing to do," said Lady Catherine, impatience coloring her tone. "Again, I was not suggesting we steal away like thieves in the night. Time away from her, however, will firm your feelings, I suspect. We can visit them and inform them of our decision, and you can make clear your intention to return. They will understand."

"And Charity, Anne, and I can continue to write them," said Georgiana. Though her lack of eagerness to depart was in evidence, it was clear his sister was putting the best face on it.

"Yes, that would be acceptable," said Lady Catherine. "Through continued correspondence, you would show them we do not mean to allow the acquaintance to drop, which should give Miss Bennet some comfort. If you inform her of our decision correctly, she will also have the time to determine the contents of her own heart. I suspect you will both be the happier for it."

"Then when should we depart?" asked Darcy.

It appeared they were all decided for they exchanged looks meant to determine the opinions of the others.

"Perhaps two days from now?" said Anne. "We may visit tomorrow and take our leave, then depart the day after."

"Then let us prepare," said Fitzwilliam. He turned a serious look on them all. "But be aware that I intend to return as soon as may be. It is true I may not have made the final decision, but my heart is engaged."

"Trust me, Fitzwilliam," said Lady Catherine, "I would have expected nothing different."

"Brother! Brother!"

Bingley, sitting in his study as he was, more to find relief from his sister's presence, winced at the sound of her strident voice ringing throughout the halls of Pulvis Lodge. Hurst, seated in the chair across the desk from Bingley, looked at him, his expression blank. Bingley knew his brother still did not appreciate the way he dealt with his sister, but at the same time, Bingley knew he had made strides. He still abhorred confrontation, but he would not allow his sister to direct the course of the family any longer.

Soon his sister's staccato footsteps reached the study door, and she entered with nary a request for permission. Louisa, he noted, followed behind, her gait unhurried as her sister's had been the opposite. Caroline's face, flushed with more satisfaction than excitement, broke into a wide grin upon seeing him.

"Brother, I have just heard the most excellent news. It seems the Netherfield party are to depart for London on the morrow."

Bingley frowned at his sister. "I am surprised, though I know not why it would be excellent news or why it would affect us at all."

"Why," said Caroline, peering at him as if she thought him deficient, "it shows they have finally tired of this insignificant town."

"Or it could mean something else altogether," said Hurst. "They have been closest to the Bennets, and now that their society will be limited, perhaps they return to London for the Christmas season only."

Caroline shot Hurst a withering glare. "I suspect they have finally realized there is no one in this town who is of consequence and do not wish to be associated with them any longer. Regardless of the reason, their departure means we need not remain any longer."

"Again, I do not know why their departure affects us," replied Bingley to his sister's scowl. "In fact, in some ways, it may even benefit us."

"Do not be ridiculous!" snapped Caroline. "Surely you cannot be thinking of Miss Bennet, Brother."

"What if I am?" asked Bingley. "She is all that is amiable and lovely."

"And Colonel Fitzwilliam has been paying her an excess of attention," observed Hurst.

Bingley shot his brother a look, but Caroline spoke before he could muster a response. "And the colonel has decided he will not continue his attentions. Would you swoop in and snap up a woman rejected by a man of high society? For heaven's sake, what can you be thinking?"

"I am thinking of my happiness," rejoined Bingley, "without respect to you or anyone else."

"Bingley," said Hurst, his even tone drawing Bingley's attention. "Whatever Caroline says, I suspect Fitzwilliam is not abandoning Miss Bennet. It makes sense for them to leave to spend Christmas with family. Given what I have witnessed of the man's affections, I cannot imagine he will not return."

Deflating a little, Bingley nodded, though his heart constricted within his chest. Bingley could not say he was in love with Miss Bennet. However, he was painfully aware that she was the sort of woman he found irresistible. Colonel Fitzwilliam, however, was a large obstacle to any designs on her, and Bingley had witnessed much the same as his brother. He would not think kindly of any infringement on his interest in Miss Bennet.

"When he returns to town," said Caroline, shooting a dark glance at Hurst, "I have no doubt he will realize what a mistake it will be to offer for such an insignificant country miss."

"A country miss who is the daughter of a gentleman," reminded Hurst. "And do not make comments about her status." Hurst fixed her with an unfriendly glare, a warning to remember her place; not that Caroline was capable of remembering any such thing. "Recall that her family owns their land. Your brother is an excellent man, as was your father, but neither has ever owned land. You would do well to remember that."

Caroline shot him another hard glance before returning her attention to Bingley. "With the Netherfield party withdrawing, there is nothing left for us here. You have gleaned some experience in the running of an estate; now it is time to return to the city where we may be more comfortable, and next year you can search for a larger estate in a more appropriate neighborhood."

"I do not know what neighborhood would suit you, Caroline," muttered Bingley. "One containing the Duke of Devonshire himself?"

"All I wish," said Caroline from between clenched teeth, "is to mingle with those who are of excellent manners and taste. I do not know what you saw while we were here, but there is little of any such virtues."

"Perhaps Caroline is correct for the moment," mused Hurst. Bingley regarded him, uncertain why his brother would agree with his sister, so at odds had they always been. "If we returned to London now, we could always return in the spring if you feel you require more experience."

"I have not even experienced the planting or the harvest," muttered Bingley.

Hurst waved him off. "A good steward can handle such things, and the man employed here is competent. Oversight is good, but personal involvement is not always necessary. If it were, most of those who attend the season would not be there."

"If you must return later, then do so," said Caroline, though Bingley knew from the gleam in her eye she meant to persuade him against ever setting foot in Hertfordshire again. "For now, however, I long to be in town. Let us go, Brother."

Bingley considered his sister's plea. The image of Jane Bennet rose in his mind, tempting Bingley to deny her application. The reality, however, of Colonel Fitzwilliam's recent actions toward her and the lack of enthusiasm with which she had greeted Bingley himself informed him there was little to be gained from pursuing her. And it would not be bad to be back in town. It may even be a boon, for Bingley would have excuses to be out of his sister's company. That was a desirable outcome, indeed.

"Very well, Caroline," said Bingley, capitulating at last. "Let us return to London."

"Thank you, Brother," said she with a triumphant smile. "I am certain we shall all be much more comfortable in town with good friends."

Then she swept from the room, Louisa following behind. A snort of laughter caught his attention, and he turned to regard his brother.

"You know she means the Darcys and Fitzwilliams, right?" asked Hurst when he noted Bingley's scrutiny.

Bingley's response to Hurst's claim was akin to his own a moment before. "It will avail her little. I am more acceptable to Darcy than Caroline, and it appears he has little desire to forward a friendship with me."

"Yet in Caroline's mind, I believe she already considers herself engaged to one of them." Hurst paused and shook his head. "Or perhaps she means to use them as stepping-stones to the Earl of Matlock. He is unmarried yet, is he not?"

"Or so I have heard," replied Bingley. "Caroline is delusional. If she thinks she has a chance of attracting Colonel Fitzwilliam's brother, she is fit for Bedlam."

Hurst nodded but did not respond. His wine glass was of more interest to him at that moment.

The surprise the sisters all felt on learning the Netherfield party was to depart was acute. Elizabeth, however, realized that she should have expected it. Lady Catherine was a woman attentive to all matters of propriety, and their friends had visited more than they should have. It was fortunate, in Elizabeth's opinion, that they made their reason for withdrawing clear, for Jane understood at once and did not become distressed.

"We will join my brother for Christmastide," said Colonel

Fitzwilliam, ostensibly speaking to the family, though his gaze never moved from Jane's visage. "But I intend to return to Netherfield in the spring, for I would like to see to the planting this year, and I doubt I could bear to be parted from dear friends in this neighborhood for much longer than that."

"Then we hope you will have an excellent season with your family there," said Jane, her composure not cracking for an instant. "Do you have other family besides your brother with whom you will visit?"

"My elder sister, Rachel, will also be there," said Charity with a smile for Jane. "Rachel has several dear children. I believe we are all eager to see them again."

"Then we wish you joy," said Elizabeth.

The conversation turned more private after that, Colonel Fitzwilliam, as always, by Jane's side, while Anne and Georgiana spoke with Elizabeth's sisters. Lady Catherine was, as was her wont, a font of advice for Elizabeth, and had she found the lady more officious, she might have objected to her constant stream of words.

"It may be best," said Lady Catherine, "if you were to hire another footman or two. As you are a family of young ladies without the benefit of a male relation for your protection, you require the greater protection more male servants would provide."

"Theodore is new to the estate," said Elizabeth, reflecting that her Uncle Gardiner had been of the same opinion only months before. "We now have two footmen, the steward, and all the stable hands. My uncles have promised to consider the matter and will discuss it further when they arrive for Christmas."

"Your uncles appear to be conscientious men, Miss Bennet," said Lady Catherine, giving her an approving nod. "If you hire someone, will they be of the neighborhood and known to you?"

"Meryton is not a large town, so I imagine we will have some knowledge of them."

"That is well. If they are familiar to you, they are more likely to possess a certain level of loyalty, which cannot go amiss. I believe you mentioned your aunt was to come from London to stay with you. When does she come?"

"On Tuesday, your ladyship," replied Elizabeth.

"That is well, for you will have a woman of experience at hand to assist. How is your Aunt Phillips coping with the loss of her sister?"

"It is hard," replied Elizabeth, her eyes finding Jane, considering what it would be like if she lost her dearest sister. "Mama and Aunt Phillips were very close throughout her life. I believe Aunt Phillips is feeling more than a little lost."

"Yes, Miss Elizabeth," said Lady Catherine, her tone quiet and introspective. "That is a sentiment I understand very well." The lady paused, as if in consideration, and said: "As you know, Darcy's mother was my sister, and a better sister I cannot imagine. I feel her loss keenly to this very day."

Lady Catherine fell into contemplation, leaving Elizabeth to speak with Charity and Mr. Darcy, only adding a comment here or an observation there for the rest of their stay at Longbourn. Between the three they carried on a pleasant enough conversation, though Elizabeth was often distracted, considering the events of the previous months and the effect it had on her equanimity. The future often preoccupied her these past days, for it was set with the birth of her brother. For him, Elizabeth wished to do everything she could to ensure Longbourn was a prosperous estate when he inherited.

At length, Charity turned to Anne and Mary's conversation, leaving Elizabeth with Mr. Darcy's sole company. The gentleman who had seemed so quiet and withdrawn when she had first made his acquaintance, had grown in Elizabeth's estimation these past days. So much so that Elizabeth now felt him among the best of men.

"How is Mr. Bates, Miss Bennet," asked he after a few moments of speaking.

Elizabeth smiled and said: "I have not met with him, but Mr. Whitmore informs me he almost seems like a new man. I cannot imagine he will become affable, but I suspect he will take to the duties of a gamekeeper with tolerable ease."

"Do you suppose it will be difficult to find a new family to take over his lease?"

"No," said Elizabeth. "Mr. Whitmore has already begun inquiries. Mr. Bates will continue to care for the herd until we find a new tenant. I hope to have someone in place before the spring."

"Then I wish you luck. The replacement of a tenant is always a major undertaking. But there are always families looking for placement, so it should not be difficult."

They continued to speak in this manner for a time, Mr. Darcy asking her about the doings of the estate, showing his knowledge in every word he spoke. Then after a time, the tenor of his conversation changed.

"It must be agreeable to be in a position to assist your family. Had I been underage when my father passed, I do not know that I would have had such an excellent steward for our lands."

Elizabeth blushed, but she managed to say: "It is my pleasure, Mr. Darcy. I am happy that my family line will continue here. I only wish my father were here to see it."

"He would have been proud of you, I am certain." Mr. Darcy paused, caught in reflection. "I suppose you will not be required to look after the land for long, for when you marry, your husband can take an active hand."

"Yes, that is possible," said Elizabeth, distracted. "But I think I wish to have some continued input into how the estate is managed, and I suspect I shall not marry for some time."

"Your future husband cannot fail to understand how valuable you are to the continued operation of the estate, Miss Elizabeth. Do you have any wishes in particular?"

Surprised by his forthright nature, Elizabeth regarded him. "In a husband?" At his nod, Elizabeth said: "Jane and I have always determined we shall only marry for love. That may sound like a quaint notion, but I have never thought it undesirable."

"My parents, Miss Elizabeth, married for affection," said Mr. Darcy, his tone and looks as serious as Elizabeth had ever seen. "I do not see it as quaint. Such a situation is to be sought after, I think. I hope to find something similar myself."

It seemed to Elizabeth that something significant had just passed between them, but she could not determine what it was. Soon after, the Netherfield party departed, amid well wishes and promises they would return. Jane was serene at their going, her countenance shining in the hope that Colonel Fitzwilliam would return, and all her dreams would come true. Elizabeth was happy for her sister and wished very much that it would be so. For herself, she would not consider much, for she had no notion of what her future life would be like.

If she were to find a husband, a man tall, handsome, desperately in love with her, with a sense of duty was what she wished for. A man such as Mr. Darcy. But she could not consider such things at present, not with her current responsibilities.

Chapter XIX

*L*eave taking, Elizabeth knew, was an important part of polite society, particularly among the lower gentry, who rarely had a house in town or a cottage in some popular location. Whenever they would embark on travel, those traveling would call on their closest friends to bid them farewell and express their eagerness to be reunited, to inform them of their destination and when they expected to return. It was especially important if the traveler either did not expect to return for some time or not at all. To depart without taking leave could be considered gauche, a lack of manners and breeding, and a black mark upon one's name in the society so snubbed.

After the Netherfield party's departure, Elizabeth could not help but contrast the two families that had recently been in the neighborhood. Colonel Fitzwilliam's family, though descended from a noble line, was everything friendly and obliging, not given to airs or an excess of pride, nothing wanting in their behavior to the people of the small town who had rarely had such eminence in their midst. Then when they departed, they visited the Bennets, the Lucases, and a few other families with whom they had been friendly, fulfilling their obligations. Had they chosen not to do so, there may have been some talk, but it would have been minimal, their actions attributed to their being so much higher than the local society.

The other recent arrival, however, was another story altogether. Elizabeth had observed that Mr. Bingley had been eager to put himself in the presence of Elizabeth's eldest sister, notwithstanding Colonel Fitzwilliam's assiduous attentions. And yet, according to Elizabeth's dear friend Charlotte, they had slunk away, taking their leave of no one, with no word of when — or if — they would return.

"The talk is all over Meryton," said Charlotte when she visited several mornings after Colonel Fitzwilliam and his family departed. "Yesterday the Bingley carriage was seen proceeding through Meryton to the road toward Watford."

"Returning to London?" asked Elizabeth.

"So it seems," said Charlotte. "The rumors in Meryton are that the house has been closed and servants let go. I suspect we will not see the Bingleys again soon."

"That is unfortunate," said Jane. "I liked them very well, indeed. They shall be missed."

Elizabeth shared a look with Charlotte that spoke volumes. "Perhaps that is true of Mr. Bingley, for he is an amiable man. But I cannot imagine anyone will feel the same about the rest of his party."

"Especially after they have decamped with nary a word," said Charlotte.

Jane appeared shocked. "I am not surprised they would not visit Longbourn, but surely they have visited others to take their leave."

"No, not a one," said Charlotte. "Even their closest neighbors did not receive the courtesy of a call."

"If you expected more of Miss Bingley, I cannot imagine why." Elizabeth shook her head. "Miss Bingley made it clear that this town was not to her taste, for we were all too provincial for her to condescend to pay us the compliment of her attention.

"Do not suggest differently, Jane," said Elizabeth when it appeared Jane would protest. "Miss Bingley always behaved as if she was better than we were. I know you try to see the best in others, but you must own that Miss Bingley has portrayed herself as nothing more than a reprehensible creature the entirety of our acquaintance."

Jane, it appeared, could not bring herself to repeat such words, and contented herself with a noncommittal murmur, after which she fell silent. As she had no wish to belabor the point, Elizabeth directed the conversation to other matters. Of the Bingleys, she had never thought much, and as a result, she had no difficulty in pushing them from her mind.

Soon, there were much more pleasant matters with which to occupy herself, including the coming of a most beloved aunt and her children. On the appointed day, Mrs. Gardiner's carriage rolled up Longbourn's drive and halted, its passengers disembarking amid exclamations of welcome. The Gardiner children were well-mannered, two boys and two girls, their exuberance appreciated over the recent desolation. That day they were a little subdued as was to be expected, the youngest not quite understanding why their uncle and aunt were not there to greet them.

Mrs. Gardiner followed the Bennet sisters inside and settled in, seeing her children into the nursery, her calm presence a balm to the sisters. When she had refreshed herself and her children, she gathered again with them in the sitting-room, young master Bennet displayed for the introduction. Her children were enchanted with their new cousin, for they fussed over him, the eldest pleading to be allowed to hold him.

"Very well, Jessica," said Mrs. Gardiner with a smile for her eldest. "But you must be careful with him and support his neck, which is not yet strong enough to hold up his head."

The girl nodded, her mien solemn with the responsibility, and soon she was seated on a sofa, her cousin in her arms, her brothers and sister gathered around her, with Mary in close attendance.

"He appears to be a happy child," observed Mrs. Gardiner to Elizabeth and Jane. "And a healthy one. You have been blessed, even amid the tragedy of your mother and father's passing."

"Yes, I believe we have been," said Elizabeth. "The wet nurse tells us that he is content, and rarely fusses."

"That will change with time," said Mrs. Gardiner with a laugh. "When he walks, you will wonder how you will ever control him."

"I believe that is something we did not wish to hear," said Elizabeth with a wry smile at her aunt.

"And yet, it is true of every child. As you and your sisters must be surrogates for your mother, his care will fall to you."

"Lydia appears to have taken up his care to a large degree," said Jane.

Mrs. Gardiner turned an interested look on her. "That is interesting, for she has always concerned herself about other matters. Then again, with all that has happened of late, it should not be a surprise that Lydia has matured."

"I suppose not," conceded Elizabeth, "though I have wondered if she would ever mature. If there was some good from our father's death, it was that Lydia and Kitty were not at liberty to run amok with the officers of the regiment. The behavior to which they subjected us was enough."

"Speaking of the officers," said Mrs. Gardiner, abjuring any further mention of Lydia's behavior, "I recall something from your letters about an officer paying an inordinate amount of attention to you. Whatever happened of that?"

It would have been the subject of one of her letters, had the evening at Netherfield not ended so chaotically, with their brother's birth and their mother's passing. Therefore, Elizabeth told the story of Mr. Wickham's actions and what had happened at the ball, finishing with what Mr. Darcy and Colonel Fitzwilliam had said of the man. When she had finished, Mrs. Gardiner was shaking her head.

"It is painful for me to think that a young man that hails from Derbyshire could be so worthless, but it appears this Mr. Wickham is just such a man. It is fortunate you had men such as Mr. Darcy to assist you in putting him off. What have you done about him?"

"Colonel Fitzwilliam told me he and Mr. Darcy had a word with the colonel of the regiment," said Jane. "I believe the shopkeepers were also told to take care when extending credit to the officers."

"Mr. Wickham's name was not mentioned in particular," said Elizabeth. "But they warned the shopkeepers, insinuating there were those in their ranks whose dependability may be in question."

"That should be enough," replied Mrs. Gardiner with a nod. "That gives them enough information to be on their guard but does not destroy Mr. Wickham's reputation needlessly."

Mrs. Gardiner regarded Elizabeth again. "Let me say that you were masterful in deterring Mr. Wickham, Lizzy." Her aunt laughed. "I should like to have been there to see it! His expression must have been indescribable!"

"I suspect he had never had anyone speak to him that way before," acknowledged Elizabeth. Pausing, Elizabeth returned her aunt's look. "Do you remember Mr. Wickham? He is not much younger than you, I think."

"But I left Lambton when I was a girl," replied Mrs. Gardiner. "Lady Anne Darcy I knew by sight, and I believe I remember seeing her son occasionally. But the son of a steward? I would not have given him much attention, nor would I have been much interested in him if I had.

"Of Mr. Darcy, I remember little, but I know more of him. Others universally speak of him as a man who possesses great discernment and intelligence, a man of soberness and strength. The elder Mr. Darcy had an excellent reputation, and his son is of the same character."

"I can well believe it," said Elizabeth. "Mr. Darcy has always seemed to me to be an honorable man, for if he is of a quiet disposition, he is friendly when he speaks, and his intelligence shines through every time he opens his mouth."

Mrs. Gardiner regarded Elizabeth for a long moment. "If I am not mistaken, I believe you admire Mr. Darcy very much, Lizzy."

"It is unfathomable to think that anyone can disapprove of him, Aunt," said Elizabeth. "As I said, he is an excellent man."

"And as a man?" asked Aunt Gardiner.

"Do you suggest I am in love with him?" asked Elizabeth with a frown.

"Perhaps not," said Mrs. Gardiner. "But your warm words of him certainly speak to respect beyond the common sort. Has he given any indication of admiration of you?"

"Mr. Darcy rarely has any attention for anyone other than Lizzy," interjected Lydia, unhelpfully in Elizabeth's opinion. "Why, I have seen them spend an entire visit together, speaking of subjects I cannot even fathom!"

Grinning, Mrs. Gardiner turned back to Elizabeth, arching an eyebrow in challenge. Elizabeth, annoyed with her youngest sister, glared at Lydia; the girl only smirked back at her and turned back to the children, who were still cooing with awe at Joseph.

"I am not in love with Mr. Darcy," said Elizabeth at length, much to her aunt's disbelief. "Mr. Darcy, as I have said, is a good man, and he and his cousin have been of extraordinary assistance to us. Other than that, I can see nothing of admiration in his eyes. Yes, we have been good friends, but I have no expectations otherwise."

For several moments, Mrs. Gardiner watched her, as if trying to determine the veracity of her statement, the strength of her convictions. Confident as she was about her understanding, Elizabeth returned her stare, feeling she had nothing to hide, nothing for which to feel embarrassment. At length, Mrs. Gardiner nodded, though she did not allow the subject to lapse without another comment.

"Very well, Lizzy; I shall not tease or attempt to press a point that I know nothing about. However, I shall appeal to you to keep an open mind about your future. You cannot know what it holds, Lizzy. What I can tell is that I expect it will hold more than simply to manage Longbourn until your brother comes of age. There is more for you than this, but you may miss it if you close yourself off from the possibility."

214 *❧ Jann Rowland

Having had her say, Mrs. Gardiner turned her attention to other matters. Elizabeth, however, continued to think about her aunt's words for some time after.

As it turned out, Mr. Wickham was not a concern for long. Before Christmas arrived, Charlotte—who served as the primary source of news for the Bennet family in those days—arrived at Longbourn to inform them of the fate of the militia officer who had so shamelessly attempted to use them to gain their security for himself.

"Mr. Wickham has left the regiment?" asked Elizabeth when Charlotte imparted the news.

"Yesterday morning," replied Charlotte. "It seems he visited several shops trying to obtain credit. The merchants took Mr. Darcy's warning seriously and would not allow it. Denied the ability to accumulate debt and looked on with suspicion by his fellow officers and those of the town, he resigned his commission, departing as soon as he could."

"I shall have to inform Charity the next time I write to her. Mr. Darcy and Colonel Fitzwilliam will be pleased to learn of the efficacy of their words."

"And yours," said Charlotte with a laugh. "I am not surprised you do not know of it, Lizzy, but several of our neighbors overheard you speaking to him the night of the ball. Not only were the merchants warned of him, but the gentle families knew as well."

That was something Elizabeth had not known. The event, she knew, did not reflect ill on her, and would have put a listener on their guard with Mr. Wickham, so she decided she would allow the matter to rest.

As Elizabeth was to learn, her confrontation with Mr. Wickham had become infamous, and as she had apprehended, Mr. Wickham was the villain, while she was the woman who had courageously stood up to his perfidy. As visitors were scarce, the Bennets heard little gossip; even so, every time someone paid a call, they commented on Elizabeth's intrepid set down of the pernicious militia officer who might have done much more damage if not for her. Not knowing what to make of it, Elizabeth would thank the one who commented, assure them that she had acted to ensure her and her sisters' protection, and change the subject.

That year's Christmas was a quiet, subdued affair. The Bennet sisters could not, of course, attend events of the season, and therefore remained at home with their aunt and her children for company. As he had promised, Uncle Gardiner joined them at Longbourn for the holiday, and the Phillipses came for their muted celebrations. Aunt Phillips, it seemed, had calmed from the hysteria she had suffered at Mrs. Bennet's death; there was still more than a hint of melancholy about her, and Elizabeth thought her aunt suffered more than she and her sisters did, but it appeared she would mend. There was little of greenery and no seasonal games of which to speak, but Elizabeth felt heartened by the understanding of the season's meaning and hope for the future. She also hoped that her parents were happier where they were than they had been together in life.

During her uncle's stay and after, he consulted with Elizabeth concerning several estate matters, not the least of which was the plans the steward had developed for the coming planting season. Mr. Gardiner was not a gentleman, and while he had some of the gentry in his ancestry, he had never been trained and had no experience in land management. What he was, however, was an intelligent man, well-read and sensible, and Elizabeth could see he had put these strengths to good use, likely abetted by the purchase of books on the subject. Elizabeth was grateful, for while Mr. Whitmore was a priceless treasure of knowledge, she knew it was the owner's responsibility to oversee the steward. That she could go to Uncle Gardiner with questions and know she could trust the advice he gave her would be nothing less than a boon.

"It appears we have finally induced Mr. Collins to desist," observed Mr. Gardiner one day just after Christmas.

Elizabeth regarded him with interest. "Did Uncle Phillips receive a response from his letter instructing Mr. Collins to refrain from approaching us again?"

"No, and I would not have expected it." Mr. Gardiner shook his head, his disgust for the parson manifest in his hard eyes and thin lips. "However, it has been nearly a month since he departed with his tail between his legs, and you have received nothing since. Had I known this Lady Catherine of yours was the key to inducing him to sense, I might have asked for her intervention some time ago."

"Lady Catherine has been a great help to us," murmured Elizabeth.

"So I understand." Mr. Gardiner returned to the previous subject. "You know what to do should he come again."

"Yes," replied Elizabeth. "Now that it is proven in the eyes of the law that he has no claim to the estate, we shall treat him as a trespasser."

"Good. I should relish the ability to have him thrown into prison after all he has done to interrupt your peace. If he comes while I am here, I shall see him incarcerated myself."

Mr. Gardiner hesitated and eyed Elizabeth. "What of Colonel Fitzwilliam? Your aunt has told me something of what has happened, but I would prefer to hear it from you, for I know Jane will not be capable of answering with honesty."

"The account you shall receive from me," said Elizabeth with a grin, "is little different from what Jane might have said, though I suspect she would refrain from claiming he has any interest in her out of the common way."

"And you think he does?"

"Rarely have I seen such a promising inclination. Yet, Colonel Fitzwilliam is happy and civil to all and does not act as if he were the son of an earl. And I have Jane's account of his promise to return for her. I cannot say that he wishes to propose, but I suspect he will know his heart before long."

"Good," said Uncle Gardiner with a nod. "Jane has agreed to send him to me, though as an adult, she does not need my permission. Still, I would appreciate the opportunity to offer my blessing in your father's stead."

"I cannot imagine Jane would demur," said Elizabeth.

"Nor could I," replied her uncle. "Now, your steward has collected the rents for the quarter, has he not?"

"Yes, Uncle. And I am eager to discuss what we shall do with them."

Mr. Gardiner regarded her. "Much may be returned to the estate to make it more profitable."

"I would agree with that," said Elizabeth. "But I also wish to augment my sisters' dowries. As you know, we each received our equal share of our mother's five thousand pounds on her passing, and then there is the additional money Papa saved before his passing and the little we have accumulated since. But that is a paltry sum to entice a young man to pay attention to a woman."

"It is interesting to hear you say that, Lizzy," said Mr. Gardiner. "I might have thought you would decry a man for focusing on such material matters."

"If that is all he cares for, I would advise a rejection, should he offer his hand. But you know as well as I do, Uncle, that such considerations must be part of a man's calculation. A wealthy man may ignore the point altogether if he chooses, for he can provide for a wife regardless of the lack of fortune a wife would bring."

"Such as Colonel Fitzwilliam," observed her uncle.

"Yes," replied Elizabeth, "though I will own I do not know the extent of his fortune."

"If his affections toward Jane are what you say, it must be sufficient."

"That is what I think. Either way, a man who is not wealthy must be more judicious in making that choice, for a wife's dowry will go a long way toward providing dowries for any daughters they might have."

Elizabeth leaned back in her chair and sighed. "It is for this reason I wish to ensure my sisters have as much dowry as we can manage. As we have no connections of sufficient standing to attract a suitor—no insult intended, Uncle—we must concentrate on dowries."

"I shall not take offense, for it is nothing less than the truth," said her uncle with a grin. "Personally, I consider such attitudes of society silly, though I know we must live with them. For myself, I am not ashamed of what I am.

"However," continued he, regarding her with some seriousness in his manner, "I will bring up two points. The first is that Jane's marriage to Colonel Fitzwilliam, if it should take place, will increase you and your sisters' marriageability because of the connection."

"That is true," affirmed Elizabeth. "It is a matter I had given some consideration. It is also, I think, prudent to refrain from counting the marriage as a fait accompli and concentrate on the factors we can control."

"Yes, that is prudent, indeed. Now, the second question I should like to ask you pertains to your dowries. More particularly, I wonder at your insistence on increasing theirs while making no mention of yours."

"You have spoken with Aunt Gardiner," said Elizabeth, feeling a little testy and wondering if her uncle would urge her toward Mr. Darcy.

"I have," said Mr. Gardiner with a laugh. "But you may put away your claws, Lizzy, for I have no intention of speaking concerning a specific gentleman. I have no direct knowledge of the man's behavior and suspect men such as Colonel Fitzwilliam may be nearly unique.

"More of concern to me is your apparent insistence on ignoring your own needs. I would not wish you to sacrifice your future in favor of your sisters'."

Elizabeth sighed and looked away from him. While she had no interest in discussing this with him, knowing he would press her on it, she had also known the discussion was inevitable. Thus, there was little reason to defer it to another time.

"I am not ignoring my own needs, Uncle," said she at length. "Rather, I prefer to face the reality that my father has charged me with looking after the estate. My attention will be fixed on Longbourn for a time, and I doubt I will consider a suitor for at least some years. All I suggest is that we consider my sisters' dowries first and then turn our attention to mine."

"Lizzy," said Mr. Gardiner, his tone faintly chiding, "that is not sensible, and I suspect you know it."

When Elizabeth made to protest, her uncle held up his hand to prevent her. "Given your ages, it makes much more sense to focus on you and Jane, as the eldest, before your younger sisters. Jane may be engaged before long, so her situation will pass from our concern. That leaves you.

"As you are not yet one and twenty, you still have several years before you will be deemed unmarriageable by society's estimation. Yet, by about seven and twenty you would be considered on the shelf. Thus, you only have six years until you reach that fateful age, while Lydia is yet twelve years away from it."

"This I understand," said Elizabeth, feeling annoyed with his insistence.

"Then you must agree it is best to augment your dowry and Jane's, along with Mary's, first, and attend to Kitty and Lydia's later. Remember, Lizzy, less money in Kitty or Lydia's dowry will benefit them more, as the interest will have more time to grow. None of you will be fabulously wealthy, but even another one or two thousand pounds would help. Trust me, my dear: I am familiar with business and investing and I understand how we can best use what funds we have available.

"Even so," continued Uncle Gardiner, "your sisters will have much more dowry than you and Jane ever will. Thus, please allow me to manage your funds as I see fit, for I believe we can assist you all and leave no one behind."

Elizabeth sighed, knowing her uncle was correct. He was the one with the knowledge. It was silly for Elizabeth to attempt to direct him when she could not claim the same.

"Very well, Uncle. I shall trust your judgment."

"Excellent! Now, let us discuss the rents and the monies you have available, so I may make plans upon my return to London. Perhaps we should also see if there are adjacent lands near to Longbourn for purchase, for such an investment will pay off handsomely in the future."

And so they sat together for much of the afternoon. Elizabeth became ever hopeful their situation would improve with time.

CHAPTER XX

*D*ealing with sycophants was part of Lady Catherine's daily life. The fault for this was something that could only be laid at her feet.

Catherine knew of her family's opinion of her preferences. Contrary to what they believed, however, she did not wish to be surrounded by those who would glorify her name or praise her to the skies. Rather, she knew what she wanted and how she wished to manage her domain and had no patience for others gainsaying her edicts. This had led, in large part, to her doing as she would and sometimes making mistakes—well-meaning advice might have come in handy at times. Yet, Catherine was prepared to put up with these minor lapses, for the annoyance of receiving advice for every decision she made would irritate her so much she thought it was not worth the bother.

Managing a sycophant, however, had never seemed so difficult as it did that moment, when Mr. William Collins sat on the sofa across from her, his scowling countenance so far from the man who would never have dared contradict her not many months ago. Recalling those days, Catherine remembered the amusement the man had provoked, how he would venerate her to the skies and say nothing contradictory to her opinions. It had also been annoying, but she had put up with it as he was a part of the well-ordered operation of her domain.

This matter of Longbourn, however, had changed him, and Catherine could not understand what was at play. The Mr. Collins she had first met would have accepted her wisdom and continued at Hunsford, assured that his inheritance had simply not been meant to be. Catherine had not seen him in some months now, other than that unfortunate scene outside Longbourn. The silly, toadying specimen had been altered into this brooding fool, seriously displeasing Catherine in the bargain. She could not understand him, and she did not like the feeling.

"So," said she, for it seemed like the hundredth time since this interview had begun, "you will not tell me of why you are so insistent on this matter of your cousin's estate."

The man turned mutinous eyes on her but subsided when her fierce countenance informed him that she would not accept insolence from him. "The estate should be mine, Lady Catherine." His tone was surlier than it had been before if that was even possible. "My cousins are attempting to defraud me."

"Mr. Collins," said Lady Catherine, her patience with him at an end, "there is no deception in the matter of your cousin's estate. His son takes precedence over you. If you take the matter to court, you will be laughed out of the courtroom, even if you could find a solicitor foolish enough to represent you.

"Furthermore," said she, her annoyance rising when he scowled in response, "you invite a slander lawsuit by continuing to make such claims. The estate is not yours. You remain the heir, but you will not inherit unless something unfortunate happens to Joseph Bennet. As a man of God, I cannot imagine you would wish such things on one of your blood."

"Of course not," said Mr. Collins, more a response to her tone demanding an answer than any conviction on his part. On the contrary, Catherine thought the man would cheerfully wish all manner of calamity to fall on his cousins should it only gain him what he wished.

"But perhaps it would be best if I married my Cousin Elizabeth and took over management of Longbourn." He slipped into the pompous tones that had been so much a part of his conversation when he had first come to her notice. "She is naught but a woman and is entirely unsuited for the role she fills. She needs the touch of a man to manage the estate properly for her brother's future prosperity."

"Do not be foolish!" snapped Lady Catherine. "As far as I can determine, Miss Elizabeth does very well. Furthermore, I am a woman. Do you consider me unsuited for the role I fill?"

"Of course not," mumbled the parson. Six months previous he would have fallen all over himself denying he had meant any such thing.

"Have you heard nothing I have said?" said Lady Catherine, ensuring she had his full attention. "The Bennets and their relations are on the verge of filing suit against you. Should you show yourself at Longbourn, they will call the constable. I do not believe I need to remind you of what that will do to your position in the church if they have you taken away to prison."

Mr. Collins's grimace informed her he knew exactly to what she referred.

"Then let us end this discussion," said Lady Catherine, tiring of his silliness. "Do not presume to approach your cousins again, for if you do, it will go ill for you. Stay away from them and do not write. Should circumstances change and you inherit the estate, the Bennets' solicitor will contact you. Until such time as that should occur, tend to your flock and preach your sermons. I do not wish to be required to speak of this matter again."

With ill grace, Mr. Collins gave her a clipped nod, and he stood, his bow sloppy, and excused himself. Catherine rubbed her temples, wondering if there was something she was missing in his behavior. In the end, she decided it was Mr. Collins's silly petulance and let the matter be.

"Do you think Mr. Collins will obey?"

Telling Anne of the confrontation when she returned to London was not a matter of choice, for her daughter had accosted her as soon as Catherine had arrived. As her journey to Rosings had been short— only two days to see to a few matters that had arisen in her absence— she knew Anne had been waiting with impatience to hear about Mr. Collins. How she had become so close to the Bennet ladies in such a short time was almost beyond Catherine's comprehension. Another time she might have disapproved, but the Bennets were excellent, genteel ladies who had suffered far more in their young lives than anyone should.

"It is difficult to say," allowed Catherine. "I do not recognize the man Mr. Collins has become. When he first arrived, he never would have thought to gainsay me, but this matter of his cousin's estate has changed him."

"It might almost be better if he did go to Longbourn," said Anne. "If the constable carted him off to prison, perhaps his bishop would remove him."

"A point I made to him myself."

"Pity," said Anne.

Catherine turned her full attention on her daughter. "If you do not mind, I would like to speak of something else." Anne's look of studied innocence nearly overwhelmed Catherine's control, but she swallowed the bark of laughter in favor of a firm look. "Yes, Anne, I wish to know of you and Darcy."

"What of Darcy?" asked Anne.

"Please do not consider me bereft of wit, Anne." Catherine huffed with annoyance. "You had two months in Hertfordshire with Darcy and there is not one hint you have come closer to an agreement with him. Moreover, you should know I was not blind to Darcy's interest in Miss Elizabeth."

"That is interesting, Mother," said Anne, chuckling and shaking her head, "for I am not even certain Darcy is not blind to his interest in Miss Elizabeth."

"Darcy understands his feelings," said Lady Catherine. "But he is cautious, as always, and he is as closed a man as I have ever known. What I wish to know is what you mean to do about it."

"Nothing," was Anne's quick reply. Catherine's glare intensified, but Anne shook her head. "Mother, Darcy made it clear we do not wish to marry. I have never had any interest in him. He is a cousin and dear to me because of it, but I have no wish to have him for a husband."

"Darcy has informed me, but I am curious why you have never made your sentiments known."

"Would you have listened?" Anne's pointed question provoked an emotion Catherine had rarely felt: abashment. "If you recall, you would never hear of anything else. Thus, I allowed Darcy to speak for us both. He was the difficult one in your eyes, the one you could not control, while I was the obedient daughter. It made our lives easier that we were not at odds."

"But it was the favorite wish of both your mothers," said Catherine.

It was clear her plea had not moved Anne in the slightest. "Perhaps it was, though I wonder if Aunt Anne wished it or merely agreed to placate you."

"We spoke of it often," said Catherine, defending herself.

"And I am certain you did. In the end, however, the matter was ours to decide, and Darcy and I have decided we do not wish to wed. I believe, Mother, that Aunt Anne would have accepted it. I ask you to do the same."

The sigh with which Catherine responded all but signaled her defeat, though she did not wish to confess it. Darcy, Catherine knew, was a man impervious to her attempts to induce him to do something he did not wish, even if she could persuade Anne, and that was now more uncertain than it had ever been before. Thus, it seemed there was little reason to continue to belabor the point.

"Very well," said she at length. "I hope you know what you are doing, Anne, for we shall be besieged by fortune hunters when society learns you are not to marry Darcy."

"Do not concern yourself. I can handle them."

And Catherine decided that was the best for which she could hope. Anne was her daughter, and as Catherine had been capable of putting off overeager suitors, her daughter may prove just as capable.

Dispensing with a leech was often difficult, for, by their very nature, they held on longer than they had any right to believe they should. In a person such as Miss Bingley, this trait was multiplied tenfold. Darcy suspected it was because the woman was desperate to climb the heights of society, little likely though it was that she would ever achieve her goal. Persistence, Darcy supposed, was a quality she had to a large degree; he must give her credit for that much.

When the woman entered the room, Darcy noted she was mercifully alone, her sister possessing more sense than the greater fortune hunter that was Miss Bingley. The way Miss Bingley's eyes gleamed as she regarded both Darcy and Fitzwilliam, the way she cast her eyes around the room, as covetous as Wickham at his worst, informed him that she meant to have one of them at all costs. This knowledge firmed Darcy's resolve to disabuse her of the notion altogether.

"Good morning to you all!" exclaimed Miss Bingley as she entered, her manner insinuating a connection that simply did not exist. "How lovely it is to see you, for it has been far too long. How do you do?"

Charity, taking the responsibility for their response on herself, given Georgiana's shyer nature, eyed Miss Bingley with some distaste. "We do very well, Miss Bingley. To be honest, we had not thought to see you here."

"My brother prefers town to his estate," said Miss Bingley. Darcy was certain the woman had willfully misunderstood Charity's meaning. "Since we became such dear friends in Hertfordshire, I wished to visit again to continue the acquaintance. How fortunate it is that we are all together here in town."

"Fortunate is one way to put it," said Fitzwilliam, the laughter in his voice not hidden from any of them.

Miss Bingley again proved herself adept at ignoring anything she did not wish to hear. The visit continued for some moments after, the conversation carried by Miss Bingley, while no one else said anything of note. Lady Catherine, Darcy noted, watched Miss Bingley, her air displeased, and he felt more than once she was about to deliver a stinging rebuke to the pretender. But she maintained her silence; perhaps she believed in the old axiom of allowing others enough rope with which to hang themselves. Miss Bingley had coiled a sufficient length when she spoke of the season.

"I hope you are all anticipating the season as much as I am." Miss Bingley paused and simpered. "There is nothing like society in London, for there is nowhere on earth one can be assured of such refinement, sophistication, and excellence. Do you not agree, Mr. Darcy?"

"Actually, I do not," replied Darcy, having no interest in trading words with this woman. "London is a nest of vipers, each person behaving with more depravity than the last, many of these so-called leading lights, immoral, uncultured, and degenerate. While there are good people among them, I care little for society and less for the amusements of the season."

Darcy's response took Miss Bingley aback, unable to explain away his words, given the bluntness with which he had stated them. "Then I hope you find yourself among those whose friendships you cherish," said Miss Bingley, attempting to change the direction of the conversation. "And I hope I find myself in company with you all often, for I have no doubt you are shining lights. I do love to mingle, and I hope you will come armed with the determination to show those of whom you disapprove how to behave. I am ready to do my part, to assist and participate with you in whatever activities you enjoy."

"Your wish is vain, Miss Bingley," said Fitzwilliam shortly. It was clear he was losing patience with her. "There will be little society for me, and I suspect for the rest of my family, for I mean to return to Hertfordshire as soon as the Bennet family's mourning period has elapsed. Thus, you will not find me in the dens of iniquity that exist in London during the season."

Astonished, Miss Bingley gaped at him. "Return to Hertfordshire?

That is singular, sir, for I had the impression you were eager to quit that insignificant speck."

"Again, you are mistaken," said Fitzwilliam. "I have always meant to return and shall do so before long."

"And what is there for you in Meryton?" asked the woman, her lip curled with disgust. "The machinations of a family without fortune, standing, connection, with only the most modest of support. Surely there are those in London who can meet your needs, ones who are closer to your status with whom to connect yourself."

At that moment Lady Catherine stepped in, fashioned the noose, and hung it in the gallows. "Miss Bingley, you truly astonish me. Do you truly think that you, the daughter of a tradesman, is closer in status to my family than a gentle family?"

Miss Bingley colored in mortification and anger. "I have a substantial dowry and have been educated at the best seminary."

"Irrelevant," snapped Lady Catherine. "Birth, Miss Bingley, will always be of more importance than fortune, except to those who have fallen on hard times, usually due to their profligate ways. Perhaps you have a fine dowry. We have no need of it, for we can provide for ourselves more than adequately.

"Let us come to the point," continued Lady Catherine, as Darcy noted with satisfaction as Miss Bingley's face reddened. "There is little you could give us. Connections? We possess far higher than you and do not need what connections you might bring. We have already touched on your dowry. You cannot even offer yourself as a member of the gentry."

"I—" attempted Miss Bingley, but Lady Catherine cut her off.

"Furthermore, as the family of greater standing in society, it is up to us to decide whether we wish to continue the acquaintance. As we have been in town for two months without visiting, that should have been enough to inform you that we have no desire to know you. When you leave today, please note that we will dispatch no invitations, will not visit, and will not deign to acknowledge you should we attend the same function, unlikely as you have no access to the circles we inhabit."

Miss Bingley shot a desperate look at Darcy, but he only shook his head.

"It is beyond my comprehension how you could have missed our disinclination for your company, Miss Bingley. Your brother is tolerable, but your charms are in no way sufficient to tempt me to anything other than civility. Expect nothing from me, for I have no intention of being caught in your web."

"Now," said Lady Catherine, leaving no room for argument. "This has gone on long enough. Please depart at once, Miss Bingley, and do not return. We will bar you from entering if you attempt it."

Little though she seemed to understand it and with unmistakable resentment, Miss Bingley rose and stalked from the room, head held high as a queen. Those left behind exchanged looks and shaken heads, but it was Lady Catherine who spoke with obvious satisfaction.

"And that is how you dispose of a social climber."

The opportunity to speak to the lady's brother presented itself only two days later. Darcy and Fitzwilliam had stopped in at their club for drinks and conversation with a few friends they had not seen in some time. After their friends departed, Darcy, left with his cousin's company, regarded him, wondering if his cousin had come to any decision about Miss Bennet. Fitzwilliam, as was his wont, anticipated him.

"Yes, Darcy," said he, a hint of a grin playing about his lips as he sipped from his glass. "I believe I return to Hertfordshire with a purpose; if you do not know that purpose, I must think you are daft."

"So, you have decided to offer for her."

"It is strange," said Fitzwilliam, a seeming non sequitur as he leaned back in his chair, "but my affection for Miss Bennet has grown the longer I have been away from her. I shall return to Netherfield as I promised, and if my affection for her is confirmed when I see her, I cannot imagine I will do anything other than offer for her."

"What is strange about it?" asked Darcy. "The longer I am away from Georgiana the more I long to see her."

Fitzwilliam laughed. "Yes, I suppose you are correct. What of you, Darcy? Have you decided about Miss Bennet's lovely sister?"

"I have not," replied Darcy, "but I feel much the same as you."

"Then you will accompany me?"

Darcy paused to consider the matter. "It is a difficult decision to make: the charms of Miss Elizabeth and our friendship with the family or the endless drudgery of the season, all the insincere flattery, the mockery of good manners, and the extended claws of the fortune hunters. I know not how I shall decide."

By the time Darcy finished speaking, Fitzwilliam was roaring with laughter. "Only you could refer to the season as drudgery, Darcy."

"And yet you do not disagree."

"But I do not have your skill of expressing myself."

Shaking his head, Darcy settled for confirming his attendance when

Fitzwilliam returned to the country. "Name the date, Fitzwilliam. If we race, I shall be within the carriage ready to depart before you have even thought to move."

"I am not surprised, Darcy. Then we shall go together."

Before Darcy could reply, a shadow fell over their table and they looked up to see Bingley regarding them.

"Fitzwilliam, Darcy," said he in greeting, his manner giving no indication of whether he had overheard their banter. "I trust you are well."

"We are, indeed, Bingley," replied Fitzwilliam. He sat back, looking up at Bingley, a hint of distaste in his manner.

"I hope you do not mind my approaching you, but I thought to stop and speak, for I wish to ask you a question."

"By all means," said Fitzwilliam, gesturing to a chair.

Bingley sat, but Darcy watched his cousin, wondering at his manner. Rarely had he known Fitzwilliam to be anything other than friendly, yet his conduct suggested dislike for Bingley. Darcy thought he knew why.

"We received the visit of your sister the other day," said Fitzwilliam in a conversational tone. "I hope she has carried our greeting back to you and your family."

However he had expected this conversation to proceed, it was clear it shocked Bingley to hear of his sister's visit. "Caroline approached you in your home?" demanded he aghast.

"Darcy's home, to be precise," said Fitzwilliam, waving in Darcy's direction.

Bingley winced, for he must have some inclination of how such a visit might have gone. "I hope she did not cause affront," said Bingley after searching for a response.

"I have no wish to offend, Bingley," said Darcy before his cousin could make another inflammatory statement, "but the act of calling on us as if we were acknowledged friends and acquaintances is akin to an insult."

"You have my apologies," muttered Bingley, swallowing thickly. It was clear he understood, as his sister had not, how her misstep could affect his family's standing in London. "Hurst and I instructed her to refrain, reminding her it was your prerogative to encourage a connection if you wished it."

"A fact of which my aunt reminded her," replied Darcy. He attempted to keep the dryness out of his voice, but given Bingley's flinch, he knew he had been unsuccessful. "I apologize, Bingley, but your sister should be in no doubt of our sentiments now."

"That must be why she has been so difficult of late," said Bingley. "We did not know what caused her such upset. Given what I know of your aunt's frankness, her set down of my sister must have been a sight to see."

"It was rather . . . spectacular," said Fitzwilliam, his voice filled with a measure of his own dryness.

Bingley nodded and squared his shoulders. "Then I cannot repine the results, for I believe Caroline understands for the first time that all her pretensions are worth little. Though I cannot imagine she would return to the scene of such humiliation, I pledge my brother and I shall not allow her to trouble you any longer."

"Thank you, Bingley," said Darcy. "We appreciate it."

Bingley nodded then turned to Fitzwilliam. "I ask your forgiveness in advance, Fitzwilliam, but I wish to understand the full measure of the situation in Hertfordshire. Do you mean to return, and do you have any intentions toward Miss Bennet?"

When Fitzwilliam's nostrils flared in anger, Bingley hurried to say: "No, I am not her guardian, and I will not be so crass as to attempt to claim her. I am well aware of your previous interest in her, and I would not step on any toes if I can avoid it. If you have decided against pursuing her, I mean to pay her the compliment of my attentions. But you have the greater claim on her affections. I merely wish to know if I should refrain."

Fitzwilliam, though he still looked at Bingley, suspicion alive in his gaze, allowed his anger to drain away. "I thank you, Bingley, for not making a cockfight of this affair with Miss Bennet. I had always intended to return to Hertfordshire and gave Miss Bennet my promise to do so before I left. It is my intention to come to know her better and offer my hand to her when the time is right. There is, I believe, an excellent chance of success."

It was clear to Darcy that Bingley had harbored hope against hope that Fitzwilliam would deny any further interest in Miss Bennet. His countenance appeared pained for a moment, but then he squared his shoulders and offered his hand to Fitzwilliam.

"There is, I think," said Bingley as Fitzwilliam accepted his hand, "little chance of her refusing you, Fitzwilliam. Please accept my early congratulations and my best wishes for your future happiness."

"I appreciate the sentiment, Bingley," said Fitzwilliam.

Having canvassed the weighty subjects, they made some slight effort at conversation thereafter, even as there were long periods of silence in between. When Bingley excused himself and went away, Darcy watched him go, wondering if there had ever been any chance of friendship between them. Given what he knew of Bingley's character, Darcy thought it unlikely he would pay much attention to his leased estate, and as the circles in which he moved differed greatly from Darcy's, he suspected he would see the man but little.

"Do you suppose Bingley will make a go of it?" asked Fitzwilliam, drawing Darcy from his thoughts. "It seems he has had enough of his sister. If he could remove that millstone from about his neck, he would become more attractive as a friend and connection."

"Perhaps," said Darcy. "But I suspect Bingley will ever remain too frivolous for my taste."

"I do not know, Cousin," said Fitzwilliam. "He seemed as serious as he ever has. To speak to me concerning my plans, as improper as it was, is better by far than attempting to turn Miss Bennet away from me. Had he instead come to Hertfordshire to vie for her hand, I would not have been so polite with him as I was."

"No, Cousin," said Darcy with a chuckle. "I cannot imagine you would have."

CHAPTER XXI

*S*pring is the season of renewal, the return of a dormant world to life, the promise of warmth and light to those oppressed by darkness and despair. The spring of that year was especially poignant to the ladies of Longbourn, for it presaged a newness to their own lives, that they could overcome the losses of the last year, that sorrow would not forever rule them. Forever after, they would remember the year 1811 as the worst of their lives; 1812, however, was the year they began to live again, that the family recovered, and joy returned to their lives.

A visit one morning, one long promised and long anticipated, symbolized the family's return to life. It happened only a few days after their deep mourning ended, again allowing them to don gowns of more colorful, though still muted hues. That their visitors arrived soon after it was permissible to do so was missed by none of them; teasing would ensue, though they would wait until their visitors departed before allowing their wit free rein.

"Colonel Fitzwilliam and Mr. Darcy," announced Mrs. Hill as she led the gentlemen into the room.

The beaming smile with which the colonel regarded them all — and more especially Jane — spoke to his pleasure at having returned. Mr.

Darcy was, as always, the more muted of the two, his delight displayed in the way he greeted them, the warm felicitations he spoke, his smile at the welcome the sisters heaped on him. The greetings completed, the gentlemen sat with them, Colonel Fitzwilliam as ever by Jane's side, while Mr. Darcy sat near Elizabeth as was his wont.

"First things first," said Colonel Fitzwilliam, nodding to Lydia, who was holding Joseph in her arms. "How is the young heir to Longbourn?"

"I cannot believe how much he has grown already!" exclaimed Lydia, holding the young master for the gentlemen to see. "It is odd to think he was such a tiny thing when he was born, for he is so much larger now."

"And a handsome fellow, too," said Colonel Fitzwilliam. He made a face at the baby, and Joseph rewarded him with a wide, toothless grin at the sight.

"He appears to be active and happy," observed Mr. Darcy.

"Mrs. Campbell informs us she has never seen such a contented baby," said Elizabeth. "When he begins to crawl, and thereafter walk, I declare we shall have a difficult time keeping him under control."

"Then he must be like you, Lizzy," said Jane, fixing her with a wry grin. "Mama often spoke of how you were determined to cause mischief and adept at escaping your minders."

The sisters laughed, to Elizabeth's chagrin, the gentlemen joining with them.

"He is much more like Jane, then," said Mary, "for Mama also commented on how quiet Jane was as a child."

"When he runs," countered Jane, "I have little notion his current quietude will survive his energy."

"Then he will be no different from any other boy," said Colonel Fitzwilliam. "A little mischief is a part of the characters of all such children."

"Now that we have canvassed the subject of Joseph," said Elizabeth, "might we move to the subject of importance to us? How are your sisters and cousins? How is Lady Catherine?"

"Ah, cut to the quick!" cried Colonel Fitzwilliam, putting a dramatic hand to his breast. "It appears we are not wanted, Darcy, for the ladies care only for our relations."

"And well they might," said Mr. Darcy. "How anyone could hold such a reprobate as you in esteem is quite beyond my understanding."

"Will you continue as actors in a Shakespearean drama, or will you answer my question?"

Colonel Fitzwilliam winked at her. "The former has its charms, but I am pleased to answer the second. Our relations are still in London for the present. But I should not wonder if we will see them in Hertfordshire before long, for they have spoken many times of their wish to see you all again."

"Then you must invite them to make haste," said Elizabeth, "for we long to see them."

"Perhaps I shall, Miss Elizabeth. One word will likely bring them flying to Netherfield."

"I believe I speak for my sisters when I say I am anticipating it very much."

Colonel Fitzwilliam nodded and his mien turned serious again. "How are you all? I hope you are all coping with your loss?"

The sisters shared glances, and Jane spoke up to answer for them all. "I will not say it has not been difficult. But I believe we are as well as we can be. The turn in the weather to spring has also been a benefit, especially for Lizzy, who endures winter, and does not enjoy being confined to the house."

"I love nature," said Elizabeth simply when the gentlemen turned to regard her. "How can the inside of a house, even the finest in the land, compare with the glories of a dew-covered meadow when the first rays of the sun kiss it in the morning?"

"It cannot, of course," said Mr. Darcy. "Pemberley, my home, has a surfeit of such vistas. I hope you can see it someday, Miss Elizabeth."

Taken aback by his quiet statement, Elizabeth peered at the gentleman, wondering as to his meaning. Further consideration was impossible, for Kitty spoke up of a matter near and dear to her own heart.

"We are now out of mourning!" exclaimed she, picking at the lavender dress she wore that morning. "And just in time, for there is an assembly to be held next week!"

"Oh, I cannot wait!" added Lydia. "It has been so long since we have had an opportunity to dance."

"And I am certain your friends must have missed you very much," said Colonel Fitzwilliam. "And the gentlemen, to be certain."

"It is my friends I long to see," said Lydia, showing the maturity she had recently attained. "I am happy to dance, but there are few gentlemen of any interest in the neighborhood."

"What of the officers?" asked Colonel Fitzwilliam. "I seem to recall you were fond of their society."

"We have had little of their society," said Kitty. The way she

234 Jann Rowland

glanced at her sister suggested she hoped for Lydia's approval of her words, but she did not wait to obtain it. "Some of them are good men, but I find I can do without their company."

"Because we have had no choice but to do without it," said Lydia, making a face at the thought. "But I agree with Kitty. I am happy to speak with them, but I know they will depart before long, and none of them is anything other than pleasant company, anyway."

Elizabeth saw the glance Mr. Darcy and Colonel Fitzwilliam shared. Had Elizabeth not witnessed her sisters' transformation, she might not have believed it herself. As it was, the three eldest appreciated their youngest sisters' progress, for none of them had relished trying to control them in the absence of their father. Then again, without Mrs. Bennet present to provoke them to greater heights of folly, perhaps they could have exerted some control over them. That it was not needed as much as she might have expected was a relief.

"Shall you attend the assembly too?" asked Elizabeth of the gentlemen, eager to push away such thoughts of her sister.

Colonel Fitzwilliam looked to Mr. Darcy, who shrugged to signify he had no dislike for the scheme. "I believe, Miss Elizabeth, we should be happy to attend and reacquaint ourselves with all our neighbors." Then the man turned his attention to Jane and there it stayed for the rest of their visit.

Regarding the colonel, Elizabeth reflected with happiness that a proposal might be in the offing. Perhaps he would wait until the end of their mourning before he did so, but Elizabeth was certain that her sister's future was assured. She could not be happier with the prospect.

"It appears you are contemplating something with great pleasure, Miss Elizabeth."

Smiling, Elizabeth turned her attention back to Mr. Darcy. "How can I not be happy, Mr. Darcy? My sisters and I have a wonderful home, a young brother to dote on, and excellent friends. It seems there is every reason for cheer."

"Then perhaps you should inform me of your recent doings. How is Mr. Bates in his new role?"

Elizabeth could not help the laugh that bubbled up from her breast. "Taking to it as if he was born for the role. The only problem is his tendency to advise Mr. Sutton, the man Mr. Whitmore brought in to manage the herd, of how to care for them. It is fortunate Sutton is of an easy temperament, else I suspect I might have another problem on my hands."

"That is excellent. Perhaps I shall see him during our stay here."

"If you do, I believe he will appreciate it. Mr. Bates often retreats to his cottage and eschews contact with others, but when he is among others, he is eager to praise the two gentlemen from the north who suggested his current fortunate situation."

After the allotted time, the gentlemen expressed their happiness and departed, leaving an excited group of ladies behind. As Elizabeth had thought, the teasing began soon after they were alone.

"Well, Jane," said Kitty, fixing her sister with a sly smile, "it seems Colonel Fitzwilliam is as ardent as ever he was."

"And so handsome and easy in company!" said Lydia. "Perhaps I shall take on Mama's role and encourage him in his pursuit of you. Someone must do it!"

"I think, Lydia," said Mary, "that Colonel Fitzwilliam needs no one to spur him on. There is nothing of indecision, for he appears to know what he wants with no one informing him of it."

"What he wants appears to be our Jane!" exclaimed Lydia, much to the mirth of them all.

Jane, by this time, was sporting pinked cheeks, her glare informing them all she was not amused. Then she responded in a manner Elizabeth might not have expected.

"You all tease me, but it seems you missed just how much attention Mr. Darcy was paying to Lizzy."

"Oh, to be certain!" cried Lydia before Elizabeth could find a response. "Why, he could not be moved from Lizzy's side the entire time they were here."

"I am certain Mr. Darcy meant nothing by it," protested Elizabeth. "Mr. Darcy prefers rational conversation. All he will receive from you is silliness."

"That, I suspect," said Kitty, "is part of your appeal. Mr. Darcy strikes me as an intelligent man, one who would find interest in a woman of equal intelligence." Kitty paused and gave them all a crooked smile. "I suspect Papa was the same, more is the pity, as Mama was not the most scintillating conversationalist."

It was a surprising observation from Kitty, for Elizabeth had not thought her sister was that observant. "That may be true, Kitty," said Elizabeth settling a look of fondness on her sister. "Regardless, I suspect Mr. Darcy is not looking for a wife—at least, he is not looking for one in Hertfordshire, of all places."

"If Colonel Fitzwilliam can look for a wife 'in Hertfordshire, of all places,'" insisted Lydia, "why can Mr. Darcy not do the same?"

"I have said nothing against Mr. Darcy's character, Lydia. Should there be a lady in Hertfordshire who would fill his desire for a wife, I am certain Mr. Darcy would not hesitate to approach her."

"And he has. Many times."

Shaking her head with exasperation, Elizabeth decided there was little reason to argue. Lydia had gotten it into her head that Mr. Darcy admired her and protesting against it would do nothing more than provoke her continued teasing. Thus, Elizabeth decided it would be best to drop the subject.

"I do anticipate the ladies' arrival," said Jane. "It will be good to see them again."

"That much is certain. Perhaps we may ask Colonel Fitzwilliam to hurry them along the next time we see him."

Jane laughed. "Yes, perhaps we might."

At that moment, Charlotte followed Mrs. Hill into the room and sat down to visit with them. Pushing thoughts of the gentlemen aside, Elizabeth attended to their guest, eager to acquaint Charlotte with the visit they had received that morning. And in this pleasant manner, they passed the time until luncheon.

"Well, Cousin? What do you think?"

"I think I am in love and shall go distracted if I cannot propose as soon as may be."

Darcy laughed at his cousin's words and spurred his horse on ahead. "I never thought I would see the day when my stalwart cousin was so lost in the thrall of a woman. Your mother would weep with happiness if she could see you now."

"Yes, Mother would be happy," said Fitzwilliam. "But she would still be aghast at my brother, two years older and yet unmarried!"

The cousins laughed as they rode to the doors of Netherfield, dismounted, and handed their mounts to a pair of grooms waiting nearby. Striding into the house, they went to their separate rooms, each changing from their riding clothes into something more suitable for an afternoon. They had ridden out the morning before going to Netherfield, inspecting a few minor items the steward had brought to their attention, before making their way to Longbourn. Now that they had returned to Netherfield, Darcy was quite uncertain what they would do with themselves for the rest of the day.

"I find myself cursing these silly notions of polite society," said Fitzwilliam, echoing Darcy's thoughts after they retired to his study after luncheon. "How is a man to come to know a woman well enough to know if he wants to marry her when restricted to half-hour visits and a few evenings in company?"

"I cannot say," said Darcy, regarding his companion with amusement. "But you seem to have managed it with tolerable ease."

"That is because Miss Bennet is such a desirable woman," rejoined Fitzwilliam. "Any man who does not understand her worth within moments of making her acquaintance must be a simpleton. Then again, I suppose it is to my benefit that simpletons abound, else she would not have been available when we came!"

"That is true," said Darcy. He turned to his cousin and watched him as Fitzwilliam lost himself in his thoughts.

"It is quiet here, is it not?" mused Fitzwilliam. "If the ladies were present, it would be far livelier, but with only you and I, the estate is akin to a mausoleum."

"Perhaps it would be best not to compare the estate you are leasing to a crypt," quipped Darcy.

Fitzwilliam chortled. "Perhaps you are correct. And though the estate is quiet, that is nothing a good wife will not fix."

"So, you have made your decision?"

"Without a doubt," was Fitzwilliam's firm response. "I shall offer for Miss Bennet at the first opportunity. Of course, I believe it will be best to wait until her mourning is complete, but I shall present myself at her door at the first available moment after with my hat in my hand."

"There is no doubt she will accept you."

"Of course not!" exclaimed Fitzwilliam. "What woman would not feel fortunate to receive my proposal!"

"Miss Bingley would have accepted with alacrity."

Fitzwilliam made a face. "I suspect she would have, not that there was ever a chance of proposing to her." Turning to Darcy, Fitzwilliam grinned at him. "I hear she has an excellent dowry. Perhaps you should give her a go."

"I would prefer to marry Zeus."

"And your horse would make a better wife, to be certain!"

The cousins laughed together and lapsed into companionable silence. Fitzwilliam, Darcy noticed, was looking around at the study in which they sat, and soon he rose and went to the window, pulling the curtains aside to look out.

"Netherfield is a fine property," said he after a moment of inspecting his domain. "It is not Snowlock or Pemberley, I know, but it is solid and of a good size. I might wish for something a little larger, yet Netherfield is an excellent estate."

"I sense a 'but' in your words, Cousin."

With a shaken head and a wry smile, Fitzwilliam turned away from the window. "You know me well, Darcy. While Netherfield is a good bit of land, I do not believe I wish to live here forever."

"Not even with its proximity to Longbourn?" asked Darcy. "It will be convenient in the future to be close to Longbourn, with its master yet a babe in arms. I imagine you will be called on to assist with the management of the estate."

"Is Longbourn not managed by a capable hand now?" asked Fitzwilliam. "Unless you mean to have something to do with that situation . . . ."

"Yes, Longbourn has a competent hand at the helm," said Darcy, ignoring his cousin's statement. "But that will change, I suspect. I will own interest in her, though it is too early to say for certain what will happen there. Even if I decide against her, I cannot imagine she will remain unmarried."

"True," said Fitzwilliam. "But an estate may be managed from a distance, as you well know, and the proximity to town means we may stay here whenever required. While I appreciate Netherfield's worth, I believe I do not wish to settle here. Better to purchase in the north. Perhaps near to Pemberley?"

"There should be estates for purchase," said Darcy with a nod. "I should be happy to offer my assistance. Did you have anything particular in mind?"

The cousins sat for some time, debating the merits of this enterprise or that facet of estate management, and Darcy had the distinct impression his cousin wished an estate similar to Pemberley. Darcy did not think it was hubris to suggest few estates in England could match Pemberley. While it might not be possible to find one as diverse as his home at a reasonable price, he thought his cousin could purchase a property at least the consequence of Netherfield with tolerable ease.

"Can I assume these ruminations about your future home do not mean your purchase is imminent?"

"I have no intention of leaving Hertfordshire soon. First, there is the matter of Miss Bennet and my engagement to her to which I must attend, and then we must actually marry. I have the lease on Netherfield until September, so we can attend to those two matters while I am still here. Then we can repair to the north to search for an estate."

"That sounds reasonable," agreed Darcy. "It may be best to engage a man to compile a preliminary list of what is available. That way, when we go north, we can look at properties at once."

"Excellent advice, old boy. I shall write to James and see if he knows of anyone we can engage."

"Do not bother," said Darcy. "I know of such a man in Lambton. I shall write to him at once."

As Darcy went to the desk to attend to the task, his cousin remained in his chair, and to Darcy's eyes, he was considering something. When he had written the letter, Darcy handed it to the care of the butler with instructions to post it at once and returned to his cousin.

"What of Miss Bennet's sisters and brother, do you think?"

"It depends on what happens with Miss Elizabeth," said Darcy. "If she remains at Longbourn, I imagine she will wish her brother to remain there too."

"Do you know when she comes of age?"

Darcy shook his head. "I do not, though I suspect it will be soon. I believe she was already twenty when we arrived last autumn."

"Then if she is of age, there will be no trouble with her living here with her brother."

"That is certain," said Darcy. "As for her sisters, I would imagine they will remain here too, though Miss Bennet may wish to host her sisters occasionally."

"Which I will certainly not oppose," said Fitzwilliam. "It will be a pleasure to have them with us."

"And the boy will benefit from a man to look up to," said Darcy. "He will be old enough to attend Eton before you know it and will benefit from some training before he is to go."

"That is not something Miss Elizabeth cannot attend to," said Fitzwilliam, "but I agree with you. As he is my future bride's brother, I would count it an honor to be entrusted with a measure of his upbringing."

"Methinks you are putting the cart a little before the horse."

"Did you not say you did not think she would refuse me?"

"I did, but it is still premature."

Fitzwilliam nodded easily, then turned to Darcy, speculation alight on his countenance. "As for you, I suspect your usual hesitance and careful nature afflicts you.

"No, there is no need to deny it, Cousin," said Fitzwilliam, waving his protests away. "I know you too well, Darcy. If I might give you a bit of advice, I would suggest you put such thoughts away and allow yourself to feel and decide based on those feelings. If you were to offer for a woman based on fortune and connection, it would be a business transaction, one easy to determine by pure logic. But the heart is not a logical organ, Cousin. Feelings cannot be explained. Court her, put your heart at risk. I do not think she will disappoint you."

"I cannot imagine she would ever disappoint me," said Darcy, reflecting his cousin's advice was as good as any he had ever received.

"Then your path is clear." Fitzwilliam paused and gave him a wicked grin. "Perhaps I should write to our relations and convince them to come at once. Charity and Anne wish to have her for a relation. They would provide an excellent prod to you in your quest to secure the lovely Miss Elizabeth."

"I believe, Cousin," said Darcy dryly, "that I can conduct my wooing well without their interference."

"Perhaps you can," said Fitzwilliam. "But I think I shall write to them, anyway. This place is too quiet for my taste; I would appreciate the presence of the ladies to brighten it up."

Their positions then switched, for Fitzwilliam went to his desk to compose his letter while Darcy remained in his chair, deep in thought. The thought of baring his heart to Miss Elizabeth had entered his mind and would not be dislodged. But it would have to be done with care. A man did not enter a woman's home, blurt out his love for her, and demand she accept his hand in marriage.

And love, Darcy decided, he had aplenty. It was only the state of Miss Bennet's feelings he had to determine. If he thought she held him in affection, his path was as clear as his cousin's.

CHAPTER XXII

*C*harles Bingley was not happy.

It was a strange condition for a man who was amiable to all, one who enjoyed society in whatever form it took. Bingley had often found himself as comfortable in the society of his home, that of London whether high or low—not that he had experienced much of the former—as he was in small society towns such as Meryton. Rarely had he found himself at odds and ends, for he was adept at finding something to do and being happy doing it.

That is why the current situation was so odd. For some reason Bingley could not define, he was restless, unable to settle himself into the demands of society, impatient with activities that once brought him pleasure. And Bingley could not understand why, for it was so unlike him. Then again, at least part of the reason was unmistakable.

"It is wonderful to be in London again for the season," said Caroline one early March morning as they were discussing what events they would attend. "Lady Diane has invited us to an afternoon tea at her home, and I cannot wait, for her parties are always so interesting!"

The lack of eagerness in Hurst and Louisa's faces was not unsurprising to Bingley. Lady Diane Montrose was an old "friend" of Caroline's, the daughter of a baron, and perhaps the haughtiest woman Bingley had ever had the misfortune to meet. The lady was also their sole means of entrance into Caroline's higher society, such as it was, for Bingley found Lady Diane's friends as distasteful as the woman herself. But Caroline leapt at every opportunity she could to put herself in Lady Diane's society, never seeing the snide looks she received from those with whom she associated. Bingley was not so blind as his sister, and not being ashamed of his background, he had no interest in mingling with such objectionable people.

As Caroline prattled on, Bingley thought of his situation with a certain moroseness of mind, wishing he were anywhere else. Caroline was, he had determined, a large part of his disquiet. She had always been ambitious, had always longed for a greater level of society than that which she could reasonably strive to attain. The business in Hertfordshire had been the latest in Caroline's attempts to curry favor with those of a higher sphere and, if possible, snare a wealthy husband to guarantee her entrance to those circles she craved. Had Fitzwilliam's brother been present, Bingley had no doubt her behavior would have been that much more mortifying.

Since their return to London, it had gotten worse. Caroline had been breathless with anticipation, certain Fitzwilliam and his family intended to keep up the acquaintance, regardless of what anyone else said on the subject. Her disappointment, when they had not come, had been acute. After her ill-fated visit to Darcy's townhouse, Caroline had been snappish and surly, but the past few days she had seemed to have recovered some of her equilibrium. Bingley and Hurst had agreed against speaking to her about it, not wishing to provoke an argument that appeared unnecessary, but they had watched her, leaving instructions to the driver of their carriage that he was, under no circumstances, to take her to Mayfair again. Perhaps it was cowardly of them—Hurst had been in favor of confronting her, Bingley had to own—but the greater harmony in their home had been worth it, in Bingley's opinion.

For some moments Bingley wallowed in his thoughts, wondering what he could do to rid himself of his sister. The obvious solution was marriage. Marriage, however, was difficult as Caroline insisted on wedding a man of high society and great wealth, certain she could attract such a man when it was obvious there was little chance of it. Caroline had never been known to be reasonable, and several men who were eligible matches, she had dismissed without a thought. It was a pity, for Bingley wished to cede her care to another as soon as may be.

A comment from his sister pricked the bubble of Bingley's thoughts, and he looked up, wondering if he had heard her correctly. A glance at Hurst revealed he was looking at Caroline, his countenance overset by mixed fury and disbelief, and when he looked at Bingley, his gaze suggested he had best do something, or Hurst would himself.

"Caroline," said Bingley, breaking into her continuous flow of words, "can you elaborate on your comment? What did you say about new acquaintances?"

A shadow passed over his sister's face, one Bingley would not have seen had he not been watching her closely. She shook whatever thought crossed her mind like a dog shakes water off its coat and fixed him with a bright smile.

"Why, only that our new acquaintances will certainly wish us to be comfortable in their level of society. I suspect they will wish to greet us like old friends should we meet them at some event."

"Even after Lady Catherine chased you from Darcy's home in disgrace when you presumed to call in defiance of accepted social mores?"

Caroline turned white. "Wh . . . How . . . ?"

Giving her a slow nod, Bingley returned: "Yes, Caroline. I am aware of your escapade at Darcy's house. I am also aware Lady Catherine informed you of the presumption of your actions, though I am certain you did not need to be told. Is that not true?"

Turning white and then red, Caroline shook her head to deny it. Bingley kept his pitiless gaze on his sister, not allowing her to deny her social misstep.

"Oh, Caroline," said Louisa, shaking her head, her countenance desolate. "Why would you do such a thing?"

"Because," snapped Caroline, "someone had to attempt to keep up the acquaintance. It would do us so much good in society should families such as the Fitzwilliams and Darcys accept us."

"Would it not be better to retain something of their good opinion, even if we must keep our distance?"

The question caught Caroline by surprise and she again turned red at the reminder of what she had accomplished. Hurst, as angry as Bingley had ever seen, spoke to Caroline with contempt flowing through his words.

"Now that family considers us ill-bred social climbers, though I suppose they already knew very well what you are."

Heat entered Caroline's eyes, and she directed it at Hurst. He, however, appeared to be in no mood to listen to her, for his glare soon destroyed whatever retort she had mustered. Her glare of self-righteousness, however, never abated. Then she made a comment that made her situation all that much worse.

"It matters not, for they mean to return to Hertfordshire," Caroline spat the word with such venom as Bingley had rarely heard, "and the Bennets. They will not be in town and will know nothing of what happens here."

"Good heavens, you mean to imply an acquaintance with the Darcys and Fitzwilliams to gain us invitations to society events!" Bingley's exclamation contained more alarm than sense. Hurst and Louisa both understood the implication at once.

"Are you mad?" demanded Bingley, unable to repine that his question had come out as nearly a yell. "Can you not understand what that would mean for our family when they discovered your trading on their name for entrance to society? What can you be thinking?"

"Why would they discover it?" asked Caroline. "They will not be here!"

"I find it difficult to credit how senseless you are, Caroline," said Hurst. The man was shaking with fury. "Do they not have acquaintances in town? Insinuating a connection to one of them could see a letter dispatched soon after, to say nothing of how they might discover it when they return."

"Do not forget that Colonel Fitzwilliam has a brother in town even now," added Bingley. "That brother is no less than the Earl of Matlock. Do you suppose he will not discover it? Do you think he would appreciate someone of whom he knows nothing using his brother's name for entrance into such society as he inhabits? He would rightly berate us for our sins and declaim all acquaintance with us."

"Do you think your social ambitions would survive being cut by an earl, Caroline?" asked Hurst. "Surely you cannot be so blind as to misunderstand this."

Caroline glared at them, mutiny alive in her countenance. It was well she made no further attempt to speak, for Bingley was on the edge of slapping her and confining her to her room until she gained a little sense.

"Let me be rightly understood, Caroline," said Bingley, "the names 'Fitzwilliam,' 'Darcy,' and 'de Bourgh' shall not cross your lips when you are speaking to anyone in town. Lady Catherine and her family made it quite clear when you imposed upon them that we are not their friends, and Colonel Fitzwilliam and Mr. Darcy were not appreciably friendlier to me when I met them at my club. If you disobey my instructions, I will have you on a coach to Scarborough before you can say 'high society' and will not allow you to return. I will not have you destroy what standing we have gained. Do I make myself clear?"

When Caroline did not respond at once, Bingley rose and loomed over her, looking on her with all the contempt he felt. "Do I make myself clear?" repeated he, enunciating every word.

"You do," spat Caroline at length.

"Good," said Bingley at length. "Do not test me, Sister. You will not like the result if you do."

So saying, Bingley spun and walked out of the room, eager to be out of her company. What his sisters did for the rest of the evening Bingley could not say, for he requested a tray to his study and remained there, unwilling to so much as look on Caroline again. The dinner that was delivered to his room was not much comfort, for Bingley found he had little appetite, doing little more than moving the food around the plate in a listless attempt to muster some interest in it. He saw no one else in the house until Hurst found him again late that evening and entered his study with nary a by your leave.

It was unlike Hurst to be so sober that late in the day, for the man was fond of the bottle and indulged whenever he could. His eyes, however, were keen, and he regarded Bingley with interest as he sat across the desk, his mien faintly demanding.

"I have never seen you act that way with your sister," said Hurst in his characteristic bluntness after a few moments of silence.

"Is it not what you have urged me to do?"

Hurst chuckled and shook his head. "I apologize if I gave the appearance of criticism, Bingley. In fact, it was long overdue and seemed to get her attention, for which I believe we can all be grateful. Sorry, old man, but your sister cannot become many degrees worse without having to lock her up in Bedlam to avoid the ruination of our family."

"Well do I know it," muttered Bingley sourly.

"It is more than this," observed Hurst. "I have noted your dissatisfaction of late, Brother; it has not all been caused by Caroline. Will you not share what is bothering you?"

Bingley sighed and rested his head back against his chair. "Caroline is a large part of my recent malaise," said Bingley, "but you are correct. To be honest, I do not know exactly what is bothering me. I have little interest in the season at present, and I feel restless besides. It is as if I were stuck in York in the dead of winter and had nothing to do."

Eyeing him, Hurst nodded his understanding of Bingley's words.

"If you will forgive me, Bingley, I suspect you are attaining a little of that maturity that has been lacking in your character."

Stung, Bingley glared at Hurst. "Then I have always been a source of amusement for you with my childish ways?"

"Peace, Bingley. You know I have always esteemed you. Yet, there has always been a hint of unseriousness about you, a desire for the next society event, the next pretty face, rather than the concerns we all, as adults, must attend to."

Bingley sank back down in his chair. "Yes, I suppose you are correct."

"It is unfortunate about Miss Jane Bennet," said Hurst in a conversational tone. "I suspect that had Colonel Fitzwilliam not been there before you, she might have been the making of you."

A nod was Bingley's only response. Given the current subject, Bingley did not wish to inform his brother of the true state of affairs. Much as Hurst might be correct in his assertion, Bingley was uncomfortably aware of the reason Miss Bennet drew his immediate attention—it was her beauty, nothing less. Bingley did not actually know her well, for he had spent little time in her company. For that, he had Caroline to thank, for her insult of Mrs. Bennet had prevented them from spending as much time in the Bennets' company as he might have wished.

For some time, they remained in that attitude, neither speaking. What Hurst was thinking, Bingley had no notion, for he was absorbed in his thoughts, reflecting on the conundrum in which he found himself. When he realized what he wanted, he blurted it out without further thought.

"I am in no mood to be in London at present. I should much prefer to return to Pulvis Lodge."

"Return to Pulvis Lodge?" asked Hurst with some surprise. "Do you suppose it is wise to return Caroline to that place? She offended everyone with whom she came into contact."

"I have no notion of taking Caroline with me," muttered Bingley.

Surprise quickly turned to anger, and Hurst glared at him. "So, you would abrogate your responsibility for your sister and leave her to me to manage?"

"No, Hurst," said Bingley, feeling abashed for what was, in his opinion, a concise translation of what he had been thinking. "I know I have responsibilities here and must see Caroline safely married, though how it may be accomplished is beyond my comprehension at the moment. I know my responsibilities and shall not abandon them to you."

Hurst watched him for several moments, considering before he gave Bingley a slow nod. "Actually, I think you might have hit on it, Bingley. If you wish to go to Hertfordshire, I shall not oppose you, though I have a few conditions for my cooperation."

Surprised, Bingley was quick to say: "I do not mean to abandon you, Hurst. Caroline is my responsibility."

"I dare say she is." Hurst paused and regarded him. "Though I mean no slight, you must own that you are not of a forceful disposition, Bingley. You tend to endure your sister's poor behavior, becoming more frustrated, until you finally explode in anger as you did earlier today. That is not the way to handle Caroline, for she needs a firm hand at all times."

Bingley grimaced, but he nodded. "I do not dispute your assertions. Then you mean to provide that firm hand?"

"If you cede to me the right to full control over her and her finances, then yes. Caroline is of age and does not need our permission to accept a caller. It is the opposite that is the problem. Once you depart, I shall speak with Caroline, inform her that she cannot reject an eligible suitor, and I will ensure that she considers him should one present himself. If this is agreeable to you, I shall keep her here and do my utmost to ensure she is engaged by the end of the season. But I must have full control to approve, on your behalf, any offers of marriage and sign the articles when her betrothed presents them. Only when she understands the power I wield over her, will she comply with my dictates. Is this acceptable?"

"Do you truly wish to take this task upon yourself?"

"In all honesty, I do not," said Hurst. "I have no doubt your sister will make matters as difficult as she can. I may not possess much hair by the end of the season for dealing with her. But I will act to remove this millstone from about both our necks."

"Then I accept," said Bingley, feeling an immense weight lifted from his chest. "Thank you, Hurst. I cannot begin to say how grateful I am that you are willing to step in."

"You are a good man, Bingley," said Hurst as he rose from his chair, his voice gruff. "I have always been very fond of you. Go and find yourself in Hertfordshire; I suspect you will be a better man for it. I shall deal with Caroline."

Then Hurst departed from the room, leaving Bingley to his thoughts. It would not be difficult to pass control of Caroline's fortune to Hurst's control, and his verbal agreement would suffice for the rest.

Caroline would not appreciate it, but what did she appreciate these days? With any luck, Bingley could depart for Hertfordshire before the end of the week. And he could not wait to get away from London.

Agony and ecstasy, Darcy learned, were two sides of the same coin. And both were sensations with which Darcy became intimately familiar those days after he and his cousin returned to Hertfordshire.

The ecstasy was, of course, the person of Miss Elizabeth Bennet. While parted, Darcy had known she attracted him, for his thoughts returned to her often, drawn to her in a way he could not deny. But the memory of her had been nothing compared with the sheer force of her presence, and being back in her company, he imagined what could be, to consider just how he might make her his.

There was very little not to like about the woman, for she was, in a word, exquisite. The deep, mahogany hair, always with a few unruly curls escaping from her coiffeur; the dark, expressive, intelligent eyes peering at him from behind long, lustrous lashes; the light and pleasing figure which, though she was dainty, hinted at delightful curves beneath her dress all spoke to her desirability. Many times, Darcy had to remind himself that he was a gentleman, and gentlemen did not look on a woman to lust after her. Darcy contented himself with the thought that she would be a passionate partner, should he convince her to marry him.

And it was not only her physical appeal that drew him to her. Her mannerisms could only be called adorable, from the way she laughed with delighted abandon, though never loud or raucous, to the way her eyebrow would arch during a debate about literature. The intelligence shining in her eyes was also an irresistible lure, for Darcy had always wished for a woman who would challenge him intellectually, who would become a partner, rather than an adornment for his arm. Darcy had not been in Hertfordshire for two days before he realized he was hopelessly in love with her and wished nothing more than to make her his wife.

That was where the agony came into play. Darcy was under no illusions as to his appeal. Many ladies, he knew, considered him handsome, and he had no few examples of this by the number of ladies who had let him know it would be agreeable to them to begin an affair with him. But Darcy had never wished for such an arrangement, for such things were superficial, a means of slaking base lust rather than achieving the connection he wished. Darcy had always known his position in society and his estate would draw ladies of the kind with whom he did not wish to associate. Miss Bingley was neither the first nor the worst in this respect.

Whatever the reason, Miss Elizabeth appeared to be unaffected by him. They could sit together for hours, talking, debating, exchanging opinions about whatever subject caught their fancy. But never once did Darcy catch her looking at him with anything more than the interest of a woman with what she considered pleasant company. Her wit, so delightful and sparkling, her open and teasing manner seemed somehow diluted with him. Darcy could not quite explain it, but he thought Miss Elizabeth was unaffected by whatever charms he possessed.

This was amply demonstrated the day before the assembly. Fitzwilliam and Darcy had visited Longbourn as was their wont, their presence a daily occurrence under the watchful eye of Miss Bennet, who was the only lady of age and seemed to have taken something of a mother hen position over her younger siblings. As was his wont, Darcy found himself drawn to Miss Elizabeth, and they sat together for some time, speaking of various subjects. One matter of which Darcy found Miss Elizabeth could speak without ceasing was the estate and her plans for the future. As such subjects interested Darcy, there was rarely a silence between them.

"Those are excellent plans, Miss Elizabeth," said Mr. Darcy after she had informed him of some thoughts she had for the future of the estate. "Your brother is blessed to have such a conscientious elder sister managing his affairs until he comes of age."

Miss Elizabeth's cheeks became rosy, as they often did when he praised her. "I have a very good steward, Mr. Darcy. And my uncles look over my decisions and concur with them.

"Your uncles, Miss Elizabeth, are men of trade and the law. Those professions are honorable, and I have no doubt they are both knowledgeable in their fields, but managing an estate is a different matter altogether. It is clear to me that you have learned much in the brief time since you have taken control and have made wise decisions for the disposition of the estate. The plan to augment your sisters' dowries and the improvement of the estate is prudent. Your father would be proud of you."

"I hope so, Mr. Darcy," said she.

"I would hope that you believe me," said Darcy. "If I had fared half so well as you when I had been the master of my estate for less than a year, I would have been well pleased."

Miss Bennet regarded him with interest. "You were not prepared to inherit?"

"I believe few are," replied Darcy. "My father's passing was unexpected, you see, and I was still only two and twenty when I came into my inheritance. Pemberley is a much larger and more diverse property than Longbourn, it is true, but I had received training at my father's knee. I believe you have performed your duties as well as might be expected, given the circumstances. Many men who claim a deep knowledge could learn from you, I am certain."

Again, she appeared abashed at his praise, but she turned it to interest, regarding him with a frank appraisal. "Then are there any further improvements I have not considered that you might suggest?"

Darcy paused to contemplate her question. "Perhaps. The new tenant caring for your herd is a welcome change, considering the irascible nature of the man who previously held that position." They shared a warm grin at the mention of Mr. Bates. "You might look at adding parcels of land if there is anyone nearby willing to sell, though land prices might be dear at present. You could also investigate the possibility of diversifying your holdings."

"Such as adding sheep or perhaps selling timber," said Elizabeth. "There are enough strands of trees that we could easily fell some and either use the newly cleared land for farming or plant more for the future."

"Both would be worthy additions." Darcy paused and regarded her. "Excuse me, Miss Elizabeth, but do you know what form of crop rotation you use?"

"That is a subject that has come up much of late," said Elizabeth. "My father did not use the most modern practices, and Mr. Whitmore and I have discussed a new system to replace the old. I have also discussed it with Lady Catherine."

"Then might I suggest the Norfolk system? My father instituted it at Pemberley, and by his account, it accounted for a substantial increase in the yield of our fields."

"That is what Mr. Whitmore has been considering. Can you tell me something about it? I have some knowledge, but I would benefit from hearing of it from one who has utilized the system."

They spoke at length of the rotation that Darcy was, by now, familiar with, explaining the details of the rotation and the benefits Darcy had observed by using it. By the end of their discussion, they had agreed on a rough outline of how Longbourn might adopt the method in the coming year, Miss Elizabeth contributing her knowledge so that there would always be several fields in each stage of the four-part course. In this way, they would always have food crops and feed for the livestock, as well as further improvement in Longbourn's income generation.

"I thank you for this, Mr. Darcy," said Miss Elizabeth, standing with him when the time of his visit had elapsed, her eyes shining. "I cannot express my gratitude for your advice in this matter. Tomorrow, I shall speak with Mr. Whitmore, for while I believe his plans resemble what we have discussed, I believe we have created a plan more comprehensive by far." Miss Elizabeth laughed. "And just in time for spring planting too!"

"Your tenants may not appreciate change," said Mr. Darcy, fixing her with a smile. "Tenants often view change as an anathema, for they worry over their ability to provide for their families."

"If we explain the benefits to them, they will come to appreciate the greater prosperity it will give them."

"There is no one who could better explain it to them," said Darcy, meaning every measure of his praise.

Again, she blushed and nodded. Departing in the company of his cousin, Darcy spent the distance to Netherfield thinking about her. There was something intrinsically estimable about her, something that continued to draw him. But he always wondered if he would ever have more than her friendly regard. For though her gratitude was welcome, and Darcy felt happy to have assisted her, more than her gratitude, he wished for her love.

CHAPTER XXIII

As the Bennet sisters prepared for the assembly, Elizabeth was struck by the sense that this had happened before. All her sisters, she thought, were affected, for there was little of the banter, the exclamations of excitement from her youngest sisters, or the moralizations Mary so often thought necessary on such occasions.

And there were several similarities to the last assembly they had attended, similarities that no doubt caused their disquiet. Both assemblies they had attended soon after emerging from half mourning, the first for their father and this one for their mother. They were all as excited for their reemergence into society as they had been last time, regardless of the unease they all felt.

Of course, there were differences, among the most striking of which was the composition of the family. While their numbers were the same, Mrs. Bennet had passed on to her eternal reward, replaced by the bright-eyed, tiny person of the long-awaited heir of the property. Even the characters of the two were completely different, though Elizabeth could confess her brother's character was not at all formed. Mrs. Bennet, however, had been a nervous woman, while the heir to Longbourn was a contented young man, more apt to yawn and fall asleep than cry out his displeasure.

It was surprising, as they prepared to leave, that the one among them who professed concern at their going was the youngest among them. Or perhaps it was not, given Lydia's continued affinity and care for her infant brother.

"What if something happens while we are away?" fretted Lydia as they gathered in the vestibule preparing to depart. "Perhaps it would be better if I stayed behind with him."

"I never thought I would see the day when Lydia Bennet would suggest she stay home from an assembly," said Kitty, poking a bit of gentle fun at her sister.

Lydia shot her sister a sour look, but Elizabeth took up the standard of teasing from her sister. "I might have expected to hear her demanding we leave earlier so that we will be assured of not missing the first dance."

"You and Jane have your first dances assured," muttered Lydia. "If the rest of us do not go, I am certain no one will miss us."

"What of Maria and your other friends?" said Elizabeth, wondering what Lydia meant about stating with such confidence that she would be engaged for the first. "It would be best, I think, if we all attended, Lydia."

"It will do us all some good," added Jane.

"Do not concern yourself for Joseph," said Elizabeth, taking her sister's hand and squeezing it to provide comfort. "We have hired an excellent nurse to see to his needs, and Mrs. Campbell and Mrs. Hill are also here. There is no need to concern yourself."

"I know there is not," said Lydia, in frustration. "It is just . . ."

"I believe we all feel it," said Mary, stepping close to them. "There is no suggestion that Joseph is in any way frail. We may safely leave him for an evening."

Mary had pulled back the veil on a cloud that had been hanging over the sisters. None of them, Elizabeth knew, thought their brother would expire if they were not there for an evening. But their recent losses had led them to question what they knew; a realization had settled in that life was fragile, something they had never considered, given the invulnerability of youth. In time, Elizabeth thought their equilibrium would return, but at present, their confidence was a tenuous thing.

"No, I suppose he shall not," said Lydia. Then she brightened. "Shall we not leave then? I cannot wait for tonight, for we have been stuck at home these past months. Mama would wish us to enjoy ourselves!"

Having said as much, Lydia set about her preparations for their departure, her excited chatter with Kitty reaching Elizabeth's ears. Elizabeth shared a glance with her other two sisters, each of them shaking their heads, diverted at this evidence of Lydia's youthful resilience.

"It seems Lydia has recovered," was Mary's dry comment. "I have never been so certain as I am now that she is our mother's child."

Jane and Elizabeth stifled laughter at Mary's observation, which was as apt as any they had ever heard. "Then let us depart before her nerves make a return," said Elizabeth, provoking further mirth.

Within moments, the five ladies made their way to the Bennet carriage, and they were off into the evening for the brief journey to Meryton and their entertainment. The excited chatter of their youngest members informed Elizabeth that Lydia's recovery would continue throughout the evening. Elizabeth suspected a return of her concern when they departed the assembly for the return journey; there was nothing they could do but deal with her concerns when they made a reappearance.

Much the same as their last attendance, the neighborhood welcomed the Bennet sisters with open arms, accompanied by many expressions of pleasure at their return. The gentlemen from Netherfield were already present, offering their greetings with as much fervency as the sisters' friends of longstanding. Colonel Fitzwilliam immediately secured Jane's first dances as expected, proving himself an ardent suitor in the way he regarded her. What surprised Elizabeth was the realization of Lydia's prediction of Elizabeth's status for the first dance.

"Miss Elizabeth," said Mr. Darcy with a bow as he greeted her. "If you are not engaged, will you do me the honor of dancing the first with me?"

So surprised was Elizabeth that for a moment she could not respond to him. The sight of his uneasiness, however, provoked her to action, and she thanked him for his invitation and agreed to his request. Mr. Darcy, it seemed, was a little discomposed because of her hesitation, for he bowed and moved away to speak to Sir William for the few moments before the dancing was to start.

"Lizzy?" Charlotte's voice interrupted her thoughts. "What did you do to poor Mr. Darcy?"

"I am certain I did nothing," replied Elizabeth, her eyes refusing to leave the form of the handsome gentleman from the north. "He asked me to dance, and I accepted."

"Were you surprised by his application?" asked Charlotte.

"Very much so."

"And why would it be that much of a surprise?"

Elizabeth, her attention diverted from the gentleman, turned to her friend with a questioning glance. "Because I had not anticipated it. Mr. Darcy strikes me as a careful gentleman, and I seem to remember him commenting that he does not enjoy dancing and rarely stands up for the first."

"Perhaps that is true," said Charlotte, "but it seems to me that he enjoys your company very much, regardless of his feelings for dancing."

"Mr. Darcy does enjoy my company," said Elizabeth, wondering what her friend was saying. "He often speaks to me. I will own that I enjoy his company as much as he does mine."

Charlotte regarded Elizabeth, her manner seeming to suggest she wondered if Elizabeth were telling the truth. "Elizabeth," said she after a moment, "do you not suppose that Mr. Darcy is interested in more than someone with whom he can have an engaging conversation?"

Prevented from responding by the sound of the music floating over the company, Elizabeth regarded her, wondering if Charlotte were speaking nonsense. Mr. Darcy came to escort her to the floor, and Elizabeth was left without the ability to question her friend. She allowed herself to move along with him and began to dance with Mr. Darcy when the set started.

The first thing that Elizabeth noticed was that Mr. Darcy was quieter than was his wont. Their one dance at the Netherfield ball had been an experience of clever repartee and interesting conversation. During this dance, however, Mr. Darcy appeared content to regard her, an undefinable expression on his face, one that seemed intense and complacent altogether, his eyes measuring, judging, perhaps even questioning. Had Elizabeth thought she possessed the answer to his question, she might have endeavored to offer it.

For a time, the world faded away, leaving Elizabeth alone in the company of Mr. Darcy, the music, and the sounds of the tread of many steps on the floor, the scent of Mr. Darcy's musky cologne when she drew close, and the sheer physical presence of the man. And for a moment, she wondered what it might be like to inspire the love of such a man, to bask in the warmth of his approval and meet him as a lover.

Then reality asserted itself. Mr. Darcy was a man who felt deeply, she thought, but he had never directed his feelings at Elizabeth or given her any reason to suspect he was in love with her. Regardless of what Charlotte had said, Elizabeth knew Mr. Darcy was more interested in her management of the estate than in making love to her. Moreover, Elizabeth was occupied with her duty to Longbourn and her brother; there was no room for a gentleman's attentions in her life at present.

These thoughts, more than anything, prompted Elizabeth to break the silence that had become uncomfortable for her. "This is strange, Mr. Darcy."

The gentleman, appearing surprised she had spoken, turned to regard her, a question in his gaze.

"Why, I do not believe we have ever spent so much time in each other's company saying nothing. Usually, we have more to say to each other than time to express ourselves."

While surprised at first, Mr. Darcy's gaze turned amused with a hint of tenderness. "And such long silences are not palatable for you, is that correct?"

Elizabeth laughed. "Do you paint me as a young lady who chatters to avoid uncomfortable moments of quiet?"

"I think anything but that, Miss Elizabeth," replied Mr. Darcy, his gaze fixed on her as if she were the only woman in the world. For a moment, she wondered if her determination was incorrect. "I have the highest opinion of your intelligence."

"But that says nothing of my ability to endure quietude," replied Elizabeth, feeling her cheeks heat at his praise.

"No, I suppose it does not. Then I shall be explicit: I have the highest opinion of you, whether you have much to say or little. There is nothing that could change that, for I believe I have taken somewhat of your measure."

"Somewhat?" asked Elizabeth, arching an eyebrow at him.

Mr. Darcy grinned, delighted with her reply. "A character as intricate as yours, Miss Elizabeth, must forever provide some new aspect, some facet unseen, as to render taking the fullness of it impossible. I can claim to know as much of you as most acquaintances of six months, but more is quite impossible unless I am provided the opportunity to study you for a lifetime."

Something tugged at Elizabeth's senses, something whispering to her that her understanding to which she had committed herself only moments ago was faulty. What man spoke of studying a woman for a lifetime if he did not mean to pay her the compliment of his addresses?

Yet Elizabeth could not believe it. There was something earnest about the gentleman, something that made promises she did not think she was ready to accept. As such, Elizabeth searched for a way to respond, to diffuse the sudden tension between them.

And then she found it.

"Mr. Bingley?" asked she, startled by her sudden sight of the gentleman.

"Bingley?" asked Mr. Darcy, their previous subject now forgotten. "Where?"

As Elizabeth took Mr. Darcy's hand to dance around him, she gestured to the side of the dance floor with her other hand. "Right there, Mr. Darcy, standing with Sir William. Did you know he was in Meryton?"

Mr. Darcy followed her gaze and his eyes alighted on Mr. Bingley, though what he was thinking Elizabeth could not determine. Surprise, for certain, was palpable in his eyes, though at the same time she thought he was assessing the other man; what he wished to determine, Elizabeth could not be certain.

"I did not know," said Mr. Darcy. "He said he did not—"

It was impossible not to wish to know what Mr. Darcy mean to say before he broke off, the abruptness of the action suggesting he thought he should refrain from saying whatever had crossed his mind. Instead, he glanced at her, then directed his gaze back at Mr. Bingley.

"You would not know of what happened in London."

"Not unless you tell me, sir," said Elizabeth, feeling amused in spite of herself.

Mr. Darcy replied with a hint of a smile. "No, I suppose not. Miss Bingley took it upon herself to visit my townhouse, hoping to continue her acquaintance with us. As my Aunt Catherine was present, I believe you can imagine the scene that ensued."

Grimacing, Elizabeth nodded her understanding. "I cannot imagine Miss Bingley left without your aunt taking her to task."

"In that, you would be correct," confirmed Mr. Darcy. "Thereafter, Bingley chanced to meet Fitzwilliam and me in our club. Upon hearing of the matter, he apologized and went away, promising to prevent her from bothering us again. I have not seen him since."

"And I assume you have not seen Miss Bingley either?"

"Mercifully, no."

"Given your reaction to seeing him, can I assume you did not expect him to return to Hertfordshire?"

Mr. Darcy gave her a sharp nod. "The Bingley I know has ever been enamored of society. I could not have imagined he could be pried from the season an instant before it finished. Bingley's interest in his estate must be less pressing than the charms of the season."

"Then I assume we shall learn of the reason for his presence soon enough," said Elizabeth.

The gentleman nodded his agreement and fell silent. It proved the end of their conversation that dance, for the music soon ceased and Mr. Darcy escorted her to her sisters and bowed, taking his leave. That he went to his cousin, who had also noted Mr. Bingley's presence, did not surprise her. Elizabeth attempted to ignore them when they moved to confront Mr. Bingley, for she knew their disagreement was none of her concern. But that did not prevent her curiosity.

Preventing Fitzwilliam from making a scene was a matter high in Darcy's thoughts during the final moments of his dance with Miss Elizabeth. That it should be interrupted with such a matter Darcy viewed with no small amount of exasperation, for Darcy had thought matters were proceeding better than they had ever before. It seemed she was responding to him, more open than ever, her heart beginning to be touched. But Darcy knew he needed to push it to the side to deal with the matter of Bingley and his cousin.

Though Miss Elizabeth had noted Bingley's presence and had seen something of Darcy's concern, he suspected she had seen nothing of Fitzwilliam's countenance upon seeing the man. Darcy, with a long association to help understand his cousin, knew he was not pleased with the sight. For that matter, Darcy was concerned himself, for if he had not said as much to Miss Elizabeth, he still knew the only thing that could draw Bingley away from the season was the smiling face of a pretty woman.

"He said he had no intention of pursuing her," spat Fitzwilliam as soon as Darcy reached his cousin, proving Fitzwilliam understood Bingley's character well enough himself. "And now he appears in Hertfordshire again? What is he playing at?"

"I cannot say, Cousin," said Darcy in a low tone, hoping it would induce his cousin to lower his voice. "Ranting about it, however, will draw attention. We should speak to him, but quietly, as we do not wish to cause gossip."

"Would it cause gossip if I threw him from the hall?" muttered Fitzwilliam, shaking his head in his anger.

"I suspect it might," quipped Darcy.

This drew the anger from his cousin more than any cajoling would have accomplished, for Fitzwilliam chuckled and glanced at him. "It is usually my role soothe the savage breast with a jest."

"It was my understanding that only music had that power."

Fitzwilliam continued to chuckle and shook his head. "I shall take your word for it, Darcy, for I have little interest in poetry."

Darcy decided against illuminating him as to the true origin of the quote. Taking a quick look around, Fitzwilliam noted—as Darcy did soon after—that Bingley had separated from Sir William and was looking about the hall as if trying to find someone. Darcy suspected he knew for whom Bingley was searching.

"Come," demanded Fitzwilliam. "Let us take this opportunity now that it has presented itself."

Fitzwilliam was moving almost before Darcy nodded his agreement. They weaved between the denizens of the neighborhood, with a nod here and a greeting there, his cousin refusing to allow himself to be pulled into conversation. Fixed on his goal he was, determined that he should confront Bingley before the man could occupy himself with someone else. Bingley saw them before they arrived, and he regarded them with a welcoming smile, apparently misunderstanding or not seeing Fitzwilliam's pique.

"Darcy! Fitzwilliam! How are you today? I was a little late, else I would have greeted you when I arrived."

"Bingley," said Fitzwilliam, mercifully keeping his voice low, "I had not known you were coming to Hertfordshire."

A shadow passed over Bingley's face as if he realized that something was amiss. "It was a split-second decision." Pausing, Bingley glanced about at those assembled and added: "I have nothing against telling you about what brought me here, but I think I should refrain until we can speak in private."

Fitzwilliam's jaw worked in his anger. "No, Bingley, I believe we should speak of it now to ensure there are no misunderstandings. Before you charge in and insert yourself where you should not, I would have you know I am firmly committed to offering for Miss Bennet and shall do so the moment her mourning has ended."

Startled, Bingley peered back at Fitzwilliam, his jaw slack for the barest instant. "You think I am here to pursue Miss Bennet?"

"Are you not?" asked Fitzwilliam, his voice laden with suspicion.

"I am not," replied Bingley in as firm a tone as Darcy had ever heard from the man. "It appears I did not consider how you might interpret my coming, and I apologize for that. I have no intention of interfering in your romance with her, Fitzwilliam. I shall pledge not to dance with her at all if that is what you prefer."

That Fitzwilliam was surprised was beyond question. Darcy,

however, was not, for he realized the moment Bingley reacted that he had nothing nefarious in mind. The question remained, however, why he had left London during the season.

"Anyone who sees Miss Bennet with you must understand the true state of affairs," said Bingley when Darcy and his cousin failed to speak at once. "I saw it the moment I spied you dancing with her. Should I attempt to turn her away from you, I doubt she would give me even a hint of notice. I have no chance with her and shall not make a fool of myself trying to replace you in her affections."

"Then why did you come to Hertfordshire?"

It was a blunt question, one more than a little presumptuous. Bingley, however, took no offense, instead earnestly attempting to assure them he was no threat.

"The truth is I have tired of London." Bingley paused and laughed, with little genuine mirth, but a rather rueful quality inherent in it. "You must both know enough of me to be shocked at such an admission, but there it is. Though I enjoy society as much as I ever have, the situation in London, the frivolity with no thought to serious matters has drained me of any desire I might have had to stay.

"When the opportunity arose to return to Hertfordshire, I will own I jumped at it. I leased Pulvis Lodge, intending to gain experience, and the planting is fast approaching. It would be preferable to spend my time here, engaged in meaningful tasks and mingling with people who are far more genuine than those one might find in London."

"I have often felt the same myself," said Darcy, shocked that Bingley would say what he did.

Bingley grinned at him. "Yes, I have heard as much. Perhaps we can meet to discuss estate matters at some point. I would not command all your time, but as I am new to this, your experience would be quite welcome."

"If I can assist, I should be happy to do so," Darcy found himself saying.

"Thank you," replied Bingley, beaming at him.

"And your family, Bingley?" asked Fitzwilliam. "They are all well, I hope?"

"All very well, I thank you." Bingley paused and glanced about as if attempting to determine if there was anyone near enough to overhear. "Again, any further details I believe should wait until we are at greater liberty to speak."

Bingley shook off his momentary caution. "And your family? I do not see them present tonight."

"They are all well," replied Darcy. "We expect their arrival in the next few days, for they are eager to visit with the Miss Bennets again."

"As I might have expected," said Bingley with a nod. "It was plain when we were here in the autumn that your family esteemed the Bennets greatly."

They spent some moments conversing pleasantly, the tension of the previous moments pushed to the side. While Fitzwilliam had shifted to his usually genial manners, Darcy knew his cousin was not yet mollified by Bingley's capitulation. The second sets had already begun, leaving them speaking by the side of the floor while the dancing continued.

When the music ceased, the Bennet ladies congregated nearby, and the gentlemen went to greet them, to stand and speak, Bingley greeting them and the ladies welcoming his return. Miss Elizabeth cast a look in Darcy's direction, her manner questioning, but Darcy smiled, a slight shake of his head informing her all was well for the moment. Darcy could see the concern in her eyes lessen, though it did not disappear. And he understood for she would not wish her sister to become the prize for warring parties.

"Your sisters are not present?" asked Miss Bennet of Bingley, the woman ever taking the role of the gracious hostess.

"No, they remain in London," said Bingley, though he appeared as if he did not wish to discuss the matter. "I do not expect them to join me either. I apologize, but you must endure me without the company of my sisters."

"Not at all, sir," said Miss Bennet. "I believe we are happy to have you."

It appeared to Darcy that while Bingley had pledged he would not attempt to turn Miss Bennet's attention from Fitzwilliam, he had not completely overcome his fascination with her. Fitzwilliam seemed to understand it too if his scrutiny was any sign. Even given that fact, it was still a surprise to see Bingley turn to Miss Mary and address her.

"Miss Mary, might I claim the honor of dancing with you for the next sets?"

Miss Mary's hand, Darcy knew, was not solicited for a dance as often as her sisters, and she started at his request. It appeared she was not uninclined, for she smiled and nodded her acceptance. When the music for the next sets began, she allowed Bingley to escort her onto the floor.

"That was a surprise," said Miss Elizabeth, stepping close to him. "Can I suppose Mr. Bingley has promised not to interfere with your cousin and my sister?"

"Yes," said Darcy, still watching the couple as the dance began.

"That is well then," said Miss Elizabeth. She regarded her sister critically and added: "I suspect he requested Mary's hand to remove himself from Jane's presence. I hope he knows better than to fix on her to avoid Jane and raise her hopes."

"I believe, Miss Elizabeth, that you have nothing to worry about. This Bingley is much more thoughtful than I have ever known him to be. He is still the same man in many respects, but I believe he has learned a little caution."

"That is good news," murmured Miss Elizabeth.

CHAPTER **XXIV**

*P*reparing to journey with Lady Catherine de Bourgh was a situation fraught with consequences. Charity esteemed her aunt as she did anyone else in her family, though privately she would own that Lady Catherine's singular character often made her unlikable. But Charity had always known that regardless of how her aunt directed, commanded, and dispensed her advice as if she were the most authoritative voice on any subject, she possessed a good heart and an interest in the family's welfare one could not challenge.

Living with her in the same house often came with the same drawbacks, yet the lady was usually more personable in the company of her family than with those she believed beneath her. Having resided with her in Darcy's house since the autumn — other than the lady's brief sojourn to Kent — Charity found herself satisfied with her society. That she would have it again when they returned to Hertfordshire was a matter she accepted with an unusual philosophy. Lady Catherine had taken it into her head to like and approve of the Miss Bennets, and as her opinion was so like Charity's, she appreciated her aunt's need to feel useful. Still, sometimes her aunt's need to be of use could be irritating.

"No, Charity," said Lady Catherine, when she had looked in on her to assure herself that preparations for their departure were proceeding apace. No doubt she had subjected Anne and Georgiana to the same attention. "That is not the proper way to fold your dresses, for they shall become wrinkled, unfit to be seen, creating additional work for your maid. Let me show you."

Everyone in the family knew when to allow Lady Catherine to have her say, and when she was attempting to impart her wisdom was one of those times. While Charity might not have credited the thought of her aunt involving herself in such a menial task as folding gowns for a journey, she set to it with a will, explaining every step of the process as she attended to one of Charity's dresses. It was, Charity noted, amusement mixing with exasperation, not so different from what she had done herself.

"There," said Lady Catherine, her task completed, "do you see now?"

"Oh, to be certain," said Charity, noting that Anne had slipped into the room and was watching them, her mouth turned up at the corners. "I had not thought of that, Aunt. I shall be certain to attend to my packing properly from this time forth."

"Excellent," said Lady Catherine in the tone she always used when she felt she had made her point. Then she spied her daughter standing by the open door and added: "I hope I need not demonstrate this to you, Anne. We have spoken of the subject enough."

"Without a doubt," said Anne, her expression schooled so she betrayed not a hint of a smile. "I have already prepared my trunks and shall be ready to depart on the morrow. I anticipate seeing Elizabeth and Jane again!"

"As do I," said Charity, scarcely less eager than her cousin. "And I know Georgiana wishes for Lydia and Kitty's company again."

"Yes, well," said Lady Catherine, intent upon not appearing excited. "They are good girls, I suppose, though the younger are not the equal of their elder sisters."

"As is often the case with young ladies who are still at an awkward age," agreed Anne. "Elizabeth's last letter spoke of how much her youngest sisters have matured in a short time, so I suspect we will find them much altered."

"That is not surprising," replied Charity. "They are at an age where maturity swiftly approaches, and their trials of the last year must affect them to a great degree, I think."

"One would hope," said Lady Catherine. "Still, they will need guidance, especially if Fitzwilliam is to offer for Miss Bennet. Heaven knows there is a fine enough line of behavior that should they cross it, they will make our family the laughingstock of society."

"I think all will be well," soothed Charity. "They are young yet — Miss Lydia is only fifteen — so there is enough time to teach them what they must know. And their behavior is not so bad they must be firmly taken in hand."

Lady Catherine huffed but said nothing, allowing Anne to interject. "I am surprised, Mother; I might have thought you would oppose Anthony's choice rather than speak of molding the girls into acceptable connections."

"Do you suppose I possess the necessary influence to direct him?" demanded Lady Catherine, appearing annoyed she did not. "Fitzwilliam has always gone his own way. He would not even listen to his father, his years in the dragoons ample proof of that stubbornness."

"No," replied Anne. "I suppose he does not."

Anne did not mention that everyone in the family would have expected her to protest, regardless. It must be a measure of her esteem for the Bennet ladies that she would put her objections to the side to this degree. Then again, Lady Catherine actually approved of Jane Bennet. There was little enough of the woman that invited disapproval, Charity mused, so that was as likely as not.

"Then I should go and see to Georgiana's packing," said Lady Catherine, bringing Charity's attention back to her aunt. "I suspect she requires my guidance."

"Georgiana is in the sitting-room at present," said Anne. "My purpose in joining you was to let you know James has come to visit."

"My brother is here?" asked Charity.

"Why did you not inform us?" demanded Lady Catherine at the same time.

"Because you drew me into your conversation," said Anne, glancing skyward where Charity could see her, and Lady Catherine could not.

"Then let us join him at once," replied Lady Catherine.

"Ah, there you are," greeted James when the three ladies entered the room.

Standing, he approached Charity and kissed her cheek, then doing the same with his aunt and cousin. James was as tall as Anthony, though perhaps not as broad shouldered, meaning he towered over Charity, who was not a small woman, and Anne, who was. With a brilliant grin, she sat down to speak with him, leading Charity to reflect that his character was also not unlike his brother's, though tempered with the responsibility of his position.

"I hope you will forgive the imposition," said he, "but I thought I would visit you all before you depart. It is my understanding you are for Hertfordshire on the morrow."

"We are," replied Lady Catherine. "Your sister and cousins are eager to reunite with a family of young women whose acquaintance we made during our stay."

James nodded, fixing them all with a knowing look. "The family of the young lady Anthony is pursuing."

"Yes," said Charity. "What do you know of the matter?"

"Only what my brother has told me," replied James, chuckling under his breath. "Of that, Anthony had plenty to say. If I did not believe it impossible for angels to walk among us and appear in earthly form, I might have thought the woman was far too good for this mortal world."

"Jane Bennet is an excellent woman," said Anne, Charity nodding to agree with her cousin. "It may be wise for you to make her acquaintance before Anthony proposes to her."

James nodded. "Yes, that would be advisable." After a pause, James continued and said: "What of this other family of which I have heard of late? According to Darcy and Anthony, the man was a university acquaintance who has leased an estate nearby."

"The Bingleys," said Lady Catherine, though the sneer with which she said it informed all within range of her voice how little pleasure she took in the acquaintance. "A most disobliging and utterly contemptible family. And the youngest! A more shameless fortune hunter and social climber I have never had the misfortune to meet."

Lady Catherine continued for some moments in this manner, her invectives about the Bingleys something they had all thought at some point. At least Miss Bingley had retreated when Lady Catherine had sent her scurrying from the house with her tail between her legs. Then again, their disinclination for her company had been quite apparent before, and the woman remained blind to their lack of affinity for her. That her misunderstanding had been of the willful variety was a fact lost on none of them.

"In fact," said Anne, when Lady Catherine's diatribe had finally wound down, "I thought the family was not so disagreeable as mother suggests. Miss Bingley is difficult to endure, but her brother and sister were amiable, though perhaps Mr. Bingley is a little too unserious for my taste."

Lady Catherine agreed with a wave of her hand. James, Charity thought, had known what he would provoke from their aunt, and was watching her now with marked amusement.

"Then perhaps I should pay this Bingley fellow a call. His sister would, no doubt, welcome me with open arms."

The rolling of the ladies' eyes was in near unison, such that it provoked both Georgiana and Anne to giggles. "And begin shopping for her trousseau at once," was Charity's ironic reply.

"There is a benefit in such a character," said James. "I will not need to go to the bother of proposing to her, for Miss Bingley will assume that I have already done so. If I but show myself at the church at the appointed time, I may avoid all the hassle!"

"James!" barked Lady Catherine while the other ladies laughed at his jest. "Do not suggest such a thing. I shall not have Miss Caroline Bingley as a niece. Every proper feeling rebels against such an odious connection!"

"Ah well," said James in a sigh of mock regret. "Then I suppose I must search for my future wife in the traditional manner."

"You have never cared much for that search before," observed Charity.

"No, but now that I am the earl, I suppose I must take thought for such things." James paused, showing them all a grimace of distaste. "Mother would abuse me for still remaining unmarried. At least Rachel gave her a grandson before her passing."

"She is correct," said Lady Catherine. "It is an unconscionable dereliction of your duty that you have yet to marry and sire an heir. If something should happen to you, what will become of the earldom?"

"Anthony has the succession well in hand," said James, disinterest in his tone. "For that matter, since he is considering marriage, I have little doubt he will have his own heir not long after, so perhaps I may avoid the business altogether."

Charity knew her brother was not opposed to finding a wife. However, his opinion of most young debutants was like those espoused by Anthony and Darcy, and he did not wish to marry an empty-headed woman for the sake of siring an heir. There were several young ladies of the nobility that might suit, but he had not sought a connection and had declined several invitations to enter an understanding based on dynastic considerations.

"Then again," said James, the twinkle in his eye suggesting mischief, "perhaps I should journey to Hertfordshire with you all. Anthony did say his lovely lady had four younger sisters. Perhaps one of them would do."

It was to the surprise of them all that Lady Catherine contented herself with a weary sigh and a shake of her head. James, it seemed, had thought to provoke her, and he looked on her with interest when it became clear she would protest no further.

"Well, for that I must wait, for my duties in parliament must take precedence for the moment. I believe I should like to go into Hertfordshire, but I shall content myself with the pompous blowhards and their simpering progeny I must endure here."

"Your long-suffering astonishes us all," said Charity, prompting a laugh from her brother.

"I am certain it does, dear sister," murmured he in response.

Their discussion turned to other matters, and they persuaded James to stay and dine with them. Having seen little of her brother of late, Charity was pleased to be in his company again.

Of his matrimonial prospects, Charity thought on them with some interest throughout the evening. If Darcy had not been so besotted with Elizabeth, Charity might have entertained the notion of putting her forward as a potential match for her brother, for if anyone of her station would possess the capability of handling society with aplomb, Charity declared it was Elizabeth. As it was, however, she suspected Darcy's future happiness rested with her dear friend, and she would not deny him that happiness.

"What do you think of Bingley?"

Unexpected though the question was, Darcy knew exactly to what his cousin referred. Or perhaps it was not so unexpected, considering what he had witnessed from Fitzwilliam the previous evening and his introspection that morning.

Adjusting his seat on his mount, Darcy looked out over the fields and woods of Netherfield Park, noted the life leaping out after its long winter sleep. Spring had come to Hertfordshire and Darcy thought it was an agreeable location, even when compared to Pemberley. His estate, Darcy knew, would wake more slowly, tentatively greeting the warmer weather, wary for storms which sometimes swept through in April and May.

"If you ask if I think he is here to cause trouble," said Darcy turning to meet his cousin's gaze, "I do not."

Fitzwilliam's eyes narrowed, and he glared at Darcy, demanding an explanation. Darcy was happy to oblige.

"The Bingley I knew in Cambridge—and I will acknowledge I

never knew him well—was a man who abhorred conflict. If I am honest, I believe that may be some of the trouble he has had with his sister, for she is of a more forceful disposition than he is himself."

"Miss Bingley herself must carry a part of the blame for her downfall," said Fitzwilliam.

"And I do not deny it," said Darcy, noting with some mirth that his cousin had placed himself in the position of defending Bingley. "Even so, to my original point, Bingley does not like conflict, and I believe he retains enough respect for you and your position that he would not interfere, particularly when he has given his word that he will not."

Considering this, Fitzwilliam nodded and said: "Then you believe his promise."

"I suspect, Cousin, that there is no choice but to do so until he proves himself false. Last night he did not approach Miss Bennet other than the original greeting between them. He was eager that you did not suspect him of ulterior motives."

"And yet, I did not miss the times he looked at her."

Darcy chuckled. "No, nor did I. I did not suggest he had lost his fascination with her, and for that, you must pardon him, I think. Miss Bennet is a beautiful woman; she receives long looks wherever she goes. At the same time, however, his behavior was circumspect. Even if you doubted Miss Bennet's regard for you, I would not think you have anything over which to concern yourself."

A grunt was his cousin's response, for Fitzwilliam appeared deep in thought. In truth, Darcy found his cousin's suggested lack of confidence diverting, for it was unlike him to worry like this. It must be a mark of his regard for Miss Bennet and his eagerness that everything proceed according to his design.

While his cousin thought as they rode, Darcy looked out over the land again with appreciation. Netherfield was, he had noted, an excellent estate, for all that it had sat neglected for some years, its owner only peripherally involved in its operation. There had been a few deficiencies, but they had handled those when they had arrived in the autumn. This year, Darcy thought, the fields would yield quite a bounty, bringing extra funds to the tenants, who were always eager for that extra bit of security.

Darcy enjoyed being here, and there was a particular reason he was staying with his cousin, beyond the need to assist him, which Darcy thought was a fiction at this point. Pemberley called, for he had not visited his property since the previous summer. But he would not leave now with his interest in Miss Elizabeth unresolved. The woman would make him a happy man, he thought, if only he could convince her of it.

"You know," said Fitzwilliam, drawing Darcy's attention again, "perhaps it may be best to purchase here after all."

It appeared Fitzwilliam had come to some resolution about Bingley, for he would have continued to speak of the matter if he had not. At present, he was looking about with interest, much as Darcy had done only moments before.

"Oh?" asked Darcy. "So now you prefer Hertfordshire to Derbyshire?"

"I do not know if I prefer it," replied Fitzwilliam. "Rather, I remember all the times you and James—not to mention my father— complained about how much more difficult it is to grow in the north. Netherfield might be preferable due to the milder climate and richer soil."

"Perhaps," said Darcy, "but owning an estate in the north has its rewards. I can only agree that the soil here is better than in the north, and the growing season is a little longer, though the difference is not profound. Estates in the north also tend to be more diverse, which is a benefit in times of uncertainty."

"True," replied Fitzwilliam. "Times are uncertain at present, with the war on the continent."

"Which has driven prices of land and produce higher," replied Darcy, agreeing with his cousin. "In fact, it may be best to wait until the end of the war before you purchase. Prices will almost certainly plummet after the tyrant falls."

Fitzwilliam grimaced but acknowledged Darcy's point with a nod. "That may be best. But I would wish to offer Miss Bennet a home, not a temporary situation."

"Do you suppose she will complain?" asked Darcy.

"No, I do not," replied Fitzwilliam. "But a man wishes to have his own abode."

"That is your pride speaking," replied Darcy. "I shall not tell you what you must do, Fitzwilliam, but I shall note that Miss Bennet is not the kind of woman who would object to living at a leased estate, and she will understand your reasons for delaying your purchase should you choose to wait. The only issue here is your pride. Do not act with that in mind; rather, do what is best for your future."

"Sage advice," murmured Fitzwilliam. He seemed to shake off his introspective mood and turned back to Darcy. "I think my future with my Bennet sister is all but secured, though I will wait until she is out of mourning. What of you and Miss Elizabeth?"

Darcy paused and considered his cousin's question, reflecting he had thought of little else since their return to Netherfield. "Are you asking if I mean to propose or whether I think she returns my regard?"

"Both, I should imagine. Do you suppose she will refuse you?"

With a sigh, Darcy shook his head. "I know little of what she will do. I esteem Miss Elizabeth very much, Fitzwilliam, for she is a woman without equal. There is little I wish more than to propose to her."

"But?"

"But it has always seemed to me that she does not respond as a woman who esteems a man. She has always seemed . . . cold somehow. Sometimes she is animated and lively, which I suspect is her true character. Then she withdraws and is quiet. And there is her lack of response to my overtures to her."

"I would not have expected it of her," mused Fitzwilliam. "It seems the changes they have endured these past months have affected them all and not only Miss Lydia."

Darcy nodded; they had spoken of the changes in the youngest Miss Bennets, astonishing alterations even given their previous knowledge through Miss Bennet and Miss Elizabeth's letters to Anne and Charity.

"Perhaps she has changed," said Darcy. "But if she has, I do not know how to compare it. We met after her father's death, after all."

"If you will pardon me," said Fitzwilliam, "it seems to me that the birth of her brother has wrought further alterations in her. What they might portend, I cannot say. It reminds me of you when you assumed control of Pemberley.

"One thing I will say," said Fitzwilliam, preventing Darcy from considering his observation any further, "is that I believe you should not allow her to slip through your fingers if you truly esteem her."

"I will not stay where I am not wanted," averred Darcy. "If she has no interest in me, my only recourse is to retreat."

"That is true. At this point, however, you only have your observations as evidence. Trust me, Darcy—if you love her, you should do everything in your power to induce her to love you in return. Happiness, I think, is not a matter of chance. You must seize the opportunity when presented and do your utmost to ensure you attain it. The prize is a life of happiness with a woman you love, a woman who loves you in return. Do not allow it to pass you by."

Fitzwilliam spurred his horse on ahead, Darcy following. Within his mind, his cousin's words whirled about, dancing through the possibilities of love and life, happiness such as Fitzwilliam had suggested might be his. Darcy was still concerned about Miss Elizabeth and her response to him, but something in what Fitzwilliam had said, his observation of Miss Elizabeth and her stewardship over Longbourn struck Darcy. He badly needed to regain his room and reflect upon what Fitzwilliam had said.

It was not to be, however, for as they rode up to the estate, they noted a carriage stopped by the front door. It was a carriage with which they were both familiar.

The cousins dismounted and by common consent went into the house, searching for their relations. They found them in the sitting-room by the simple expedient of following their Aunt Catherine's voice.

"Darcy! Fitzwilliam!" boomed Lady Catherine's voice as they entered the room. "Why were you not here to greet us?"

"Probably because we arrived so early," said Charity before they could muster a response. "We are more than an hour ahead of our time, after all."

"That you are," said Fitzwilliam, stepping forward to greet his sister.

That burst the dam and they all exchanged their pleasure at being in company yet again. Even Lady Catherine, Darcy thought, appeared pleased to be there, and Darcy thought he knew the reason.

"Need I ask why you hastened to join us?" said Fitzwilliam, fixing them with a knowing grin.

"Of course, you do not," was Anne's prim reply. "As we are here with plenty of time left in visiting hours, we can visit Jane and Elizabeth today." Anne paused and wrinkled her nose. "If you and Darcy remove the stink of horse from your person we may depart at once."

"We must change also," observed Lady Catherine. "These traveling clothes will not do for a morning visit."

"Then we had best be about our business," said Charity, a crispness in her tone bespeaking her determination. "I do not mean to wait even another day to visit our dear friends."

The other ladies chorused their agreement, prompting Fitzwilliam to turn a look on Darcy. "I suppose we must oblige them, though I will note we informed the Miss Bennets we would not visit today."

"Elizabeth and Jane will not protest," said Charity.

"I would hope they are as eager to see us as we are them," added Anne.

"I also missed Lydia and Kitty," said Georgiana, her voice filled with shyness.

"Then we should prepare," said Lady Catherine. "I am eager to see how the little master of Longbourn has grown."

"Much changed from when you last saw him," said Fitzwilliam with a laugh.

"Enough speaking," insisted Charity. "Let us prepare.

And so, they did, and within thirty minutes, two carriages had departed Netherfield bound for Longbourn.

CHAPTER XXV

*E*lizabeth had some notion that the newly arrived ladies would wish to visit that day, even as the gentlemen had suggested they would delay the visit until the following morning. Still, it was something of a surprise when the two carriages pulled onto the drive, for Lydia and Kitty, who had gone to the window as was their wont, squealed in their excitement.

"Georgiana has come!" exclaimed Kitty.

"Along with Charity and Anne," added Lydia. "And Lady Catherine is with them."

Uncertain as she had been regarding Lady Catherine's attendance, Elizabeth exchanged a look with Jane, noting her sister's nod of determination. It seemed unlikely that Lady Catherine would oppose her nephew's attentions to Jane at this late date, especially with how she had taken to the sisters when she had been here in the autumn. But the lady was of such a forceful character that Elizabeth could well understand her sister's reason for bracing herself.

Soon the visitors arrived with many exclamations of pleasure and happiness at being reunited. Elizabeth noted that Lady Catherine appeared as pleased to see them as her younger relations and that as much as anything else calmed Elizabeth's concerns. When they sat down to visit, Lady Catherine was the first to speak.

"If you please," said she, her tone a mix of her typical authoritative command and eagerness, "I should like to see Longbourn's heir if he is available."

"Of course, Lady Catherine," said Elizabeth. "I shall have him summoned if he is awake."

Pulling the cord, Elizabeth issued the instructions when Mrs. Hill appeared and turned back to their guests. "Mrs. Hill and Mrs. Campbell claim he is a placid child who sleeps much."

"Compared with Mrs. Campbell's son, he is a veritable angel," said Lydia with a moue of distaste. "He is always fussing and is rarely content."

"Some children can be that way," said Lady Catherine. "Anne was much like your brother, though our Georgiana was the opposite."

Georgiana colored and directed a mock glare at her aunt, even as laughter rose about them.

"It did not make us love you any less, Georgiana," said her brother. "In fact, I believe you had us all wrapped around your little finger from the moment you opened your eyes. Father adored you, saying you were the image of Mother."

This bit of information changed Georgiana's frown to a shy smile. At that moment, the nurse entered the room with Joseph in her arms, and Lydia was quick to rise and take the precious bundle from his nurse. Elizabeth arranged with her to return in fifteen minutes and dismissed her as the Netherfield ladies gathered around.

"Oh, what a beautiful child!" exclaimed Charity as she caught sight of him. "He is so alert and awake. I dare say he can see right through any of us straight to our hearts."

It was a bit of a silly observation, Elizabeth thought, though she had always thought he was a bright child when he showed his deep brown eyes. Charity stuck her hand into the blankets and Joseph grasped it tight, and for a few moments, he cooed at the assembled faces peering down at him, appearing pleased to be the center of their attention. The ladies returned his coos amid much laughter, and they coaxed Joseph to smile widely at them more than once.

"He is a sharp-eyed child," said Lady Catherine from her place surrounding Joseph with her relations. "There have been no problems with his health?"

"None whatsoever," replied Jane. "Then again, Mama birthed five healthy children before him, so I suppose it is not a surprise that Joseph is like we all were."

"Then your mother comes from sturdy stock," said Lady Catherine. "That bodes well for his future. It is fortunate you have been so blessed."

Elizabeth nodded, agreeing with her ladyship and for more than one reason. After a time of the ladies' exclaiming over the child, the nurse returned and gathered her charge, returning him to the nursery. Joseph protested his removal from so many interesting visages, but as was his wont, the nurse soon quieted him as she left the room, singing him a lullaby Elizabeth was certain would lull him to sleep before long.

Elizabeth found herself with Charity and Anne, and they fell into a conversation as animated as any they had before their return to London as if no time had passed and no separation had occurred. Finding Charity as lively and Anne as wry as ever, Elizabeth soon lost herself in their accounts of their recent doings in London, including some anecdotes of events they had attended during the early days of the season. It was amusing, Elizabeth noted, that Charity wished to speak of an unlamented loss to the neighborhood party.

"I am certain Anthony and Darcy informed you of Miss Bingley's visit to Darcy's house," said Charity when the subject of the woman had come up.

"They did," said Elizabeth with a shake of her head. "I can scarce believe she was so blind as to think she could flout society's expectations without consequence."

"Of consequence in society, I think there has been little," said Charity. "She has never been near the first circles, all her pretenses to the contrary. Her claim to the second circles is tenuous at best."

"Even so, we have some news of her," said Anne.

Elizabeth looked on with interest. Mr. Bingley's coming to Hertfordshire had suggested to Elizabeth that something had happened concerning his sister. Elizabeth was far too well bred to question Mr. Bingley about his sisters' remaining in London, but she had been curious all the same.

"I have a few friends who mingle with people who know Miss Bingley," said Charity.

"It seems the woman has thrown herself into the season," said Anne.

Charity shook her head. "I suspect it is more likely that Miss Bingley's brother demanded that she try to find a husband, for a friend reports she has been in a dour mood of late. There are some rumors of a man calling on her, but who he is or how interested he is, I cannot say."

"Mr. Bingley is here in Hertfordshire," said Elizabeth, uncertain if her friends knew that bit of news. It was clear from their reaction they had not.

"That is a surprise," said Charity. "The last intelligence I had of Mr. Bingley was that he had escorted his sister to a ball last week."

"I do not think he has been here long," said Elizabeth. "Last night he appeared at our assembly. Mr. Darcy and your brother spoke with him, but other than a dance with Mary, we saw little ofhim."

"Mr. Bingley danced with Mary?" asked Anne, with an interested look at where Mary was attending the conversation between Georgiana and the youngest Bennets. "Can we assume this was nothing more than a simple dance?"

"I cannot imagine he means anything by one dance," said Elizabeth with a frown. "In all honesty, I suspect he asked her to take himself out of Jane's company." Elizabeth shot an affectionate look at her elder sister who was, as was her wont, in Colonel Fitzwilliam's company, along with Lady Catherine. "I do not suppose your cousin would appreciate it if Mr. Bingley put himself in Jane's way such as he did before."

"No," said Charity, her affectionate gaze falling on her brother. "Anthony would not be at all pleased should Mr. Bingley put himself forward in such a manner."

"And Anthony's attention to Jane continues unabated."

"I cannot be happier for her," said Elizabeth, deciding there was little reason to demur. While some might prefer to avoid appearing presumptuous or avaricious, Elizabeth was confident in the affection of these ladies and knew there was no reason to refrain. Their reactions vindicated this opinion.

"None of us expected anything different," said Charity. "While in London, he was akin to a caged lion, chafing against the restrictions of your mourning. Had matters been different, I suspect a wedding would be in their near future."

"There are none so deserving as Jane," murmured Elizabeth. She grinned at her companions and added: "You may consider it nothing more than hubris, but I have long thought Jane was the best person of my acquaintance. That she has found a man who esteems her as she deserves is a matter of much happiness to me."

"I dare say you are correct, Elizabeth," said Charity. "I suppose that you, being so close to Jane, will not be content to be long outdone by your sister. Shall there be a man in your future too?"

Taken aback, Elizabeth regarded her friend, noting that Anne was watching her with equal interest. "Perhaps there shall be," said Elizabeth at length, uncertain what her friend meant to say. "But I do not believe there will be a man soon. At present, my focus is on Longbourn; I do not believe I have time for anything else at present."

"You do not mean to marry?"

The image of Mr. Darcy entered Elizabeth's mind, and she darted a look at the gentleman, noting he was attending to Georgiana and Elizabeth's youngest sisters. Tempted to shake her head in denial, Elizabeth instead turned back to her friends, whom she noted were watching her closely, having the distinct impression they had not missed her impetuous action.

"It is not that I do not mean to marry," dissembled Elizabeth, keeping her voice calm and objective. "Jane and I grew to become adults promising each other we would marry for love and nothing else. I hope I shall attain that when the time is right. At present, however, it is only that my concentration must be on Longbourn."

Her companions regarded her as if wondering at her determination. "I think, Elizabeth," said Charity at last, "your wish is closer than you suspect, if only you will open your eyes to the possibilities."

Annoyance bloomed in Elizabeth's mind, for there were those of her acquaintance, of late, who wished to pair her with Mr. Darcy. The gentleman had been attentive, to be certain, but Elizabeth had seen nothing of particular regard. A little voice at the back of her mind whispered to her, speaking to her of the untruth, but she quashed it without thought. Longbourn needed her. Joseph needed her, and she would not betray the trust her father put in her.

Anne introduced another topic at that moment, much to Elizabeth's relief, for it allowed her sudden anger to drain away. Having come to esteem her, Elizabeth supposed it was not unusual her friends would wish to promote her to their dearest relations. What would come of it, Elizabeth could not say, but she was not about to allow herself to be pushed. As they seemed content to allow the subject to rest, Elizabeth decided there was no reason to belabor the point.

Darcy found himself preternaturally aware of Miss Elizabeth Bennet's presence. Though he sat with his sister and the youngest Bennets, the woman's every move caught and held his attention, every smile, every frown burned on his memory. Of what they were speaking, Darcy could not say, though their glances in Fitzwilliam and Miss Bennet's direction provided a clue. Then they began speaking of something else and Darcy caught a glance or two in his direction.

Could his relations be promoting his interests to Miss Elizabeth? While the thought might have Darcy annoyed in other circumstances, his ostensible lack of any success in provoking a response from her convinced him to reconsider. He had never spoken of his admiration with his female relations, but he knew they were aware of it on some level. That they would like to have Miss Elizabeth as a relation was unmistakable; Darcy knew he would have no firmer supporters than they.

After a time, Darcy tired of the excited chatter of the youngest members of the party and drifted away from them. As was common in such situations, he was drawn into Miss Elizabeth's orbit. A comment from Charity brought him into their conversation.

"Do you not agree, Darcy?"

Surprised, as he had not been close enough to hear them, Darcy looked at her askance. Charity was happy to oblige his unspoken request.

"We were speaking of the sights one can see in England," explained Charity. "Anne has said how much she loves Kent, and I will own that it is a beautiful county. However, if one wishes to see the beauties of nature, Derbyshire and the north are the better options."

"You know what Darcy will say," said Anne, much to Miss Elizabeth's amusement. "Do you suppose he will claim that anywhere is superior to Derbyshire? Why, I declare Darcy could visit fabled Olympus and say it was nothing to his home."

Anne and Charity shared a laugh while Miss Elizabeth looked on with interest, her gaze finding Darcy. "Well, Mr. Darcy? Is your cousin's portrayal a faithful one, or can you deny it?"

"In some respects, it is faithful," replied Darcy, charmed by her arch look. It was one he had not seen as often directed at himself as she had shown it to others. "Then again, I suppose Anne loves Kent because it is her home; by that standard, we are all in the same position."

"It is a question of what one prefers," said Charity. "The beauties of Kent are in its woods, its abundance, the wonders of the sea at places such as Ramsgate and Brighton. Derbyshire, not bordering next to water, must rely on the Peaks and other such beauties."

"And it is lovely, indeed," said Anne. "For my part, I find the Lakes as beautiful as anything found in Derbyshire."

"Oh, I should like to see the Lakes," said Miss Elizabeth. "My aunt and uncle have spoken of journeying to the north, for as you know, my aunt was a girl in Derbyshire. I suspect they will not travel this year, given the trials we have had, but perhaps they will go next year. If they do travel, they may go as far as the Lakes."

"There are wonders aplenty there," said Darcy, warming to the subject. "My family has long owned a lodge on Lake Windermere, and I remember traveling there when I was a boy."

"You have not gone in many years, Mr. Darcy?" asked Miss Elizabeth.

Darcy paused and considered what he might say. Given her losses the past year, he did not wish to reopen wounds that might have a thin scar over them holding in the pain. Then again, he knew as well as anyone that speaking of the dead can have the opposite effect, to make that skin stronger and less apt to reopen a wound, the bereaved more able to bear the melancholy that sometimes entered the heart and mind.

"After my mother's passing," said Darcy, "my father did not wish to return. Georgiana and I have visited twice since my father's passing. Other than that, we have employed a man to oversee the property, and it has largely been let out to gentlemen who wished for a holiday."

Far from responding with sorrow, Miss Elizabeth nodded. "Yes, I can see that, Mr. Darcy. I hope I am fortunate enough to see the Lakes someday."

"They are well worth the effort," replied Mr. Darcy.

"Come, Darcy," said Charity, her countenance shining with suppressed mirth, "you are ruining my portrayal of you as a man who cares for nothing but his own home."

The ladies tittered at Charity's jest, and Darcy allowed himself a smile. "There are beauties aplenty in Derbyshire, as you well know, Charity, as your brother's estate is also in Derbyshire."

"It is," said Charity, "but it is in the south on the border with Staffordshire."

"That does not make it any less estimable," said Darcy.

"I sense there is something serious in this teasing," said Miss Elizabeth, observing them all. "You have spoken something of your estate, Mr. Darcy, but I do not believe you have spoken much of its exact location."

"Pemberley is in a broad valley a little to the south and east of the Peak District. If you were to ride to the rim of the valley in the far northwest of the estate, you can see the peaks on a clear day in the distance. You can travel to Dovedale and return to Pemberley in a single day if you are of a mind to do it."

Miss Elizabeth appeared impressed with this intelligence. "Then I venture to suggest it is a beautiful estate, indeed."

"To me," said Darcy quietly, "it is the dearest place in the world."

As a group, they continued to speak of Derbyshire, the Lakes, and other such topics, Charity appealing to Elizabeth to visit them in the north, suggesting they convene at Darcy's house near Lake Windermere. Darcy was not of a mind to refuse such a notion, for the thought of Miss Elizabeth at the Lakes, the image of her at Pemberley, making his house a home, filled him and fired his imagination.

Yet, for all this, Darcy was not unhappy that he did not have her to himself. As he had noted that she often became more serious with him, in the company of his cousins she appeared as lively as ever, and Darcy enjoyed this side of her. Several times she turned a raised eyebrow in his direction or made a mischievous comment, and Darcy wondered that he had not fallen at her feet and begged her to be his wife.

In time, the visitors rose to depart, amid expressions of pleasure at being in one another's company again and promising to gather often. That Fitzwilliam had an intimate farewell with Miss Bennet did not escape Darcy's attention, but strangely, he did not regret that he had not had the same with Miss Elizabeth. The past moments in her company had been enough, he thought. There would be plenty of time for lovemaking later.

"It seems the Bennets are getting on well," said Lady Catherine when they had arrived back at Netherfield.

"Life goes on after tragedy," observed Fitzwilliam. "Those ladies are as resilient as any I have ever met."

Lady Catherine regarded him, choosing silence as they walked back toward the sitting-room. Arriving there, Charity gave the order for the staff to provide tea, and they all sat, all seeming aware they were on the cusp of a conversation of some import. Fitzwilliam, Darcy thought, was safe, for even if Lady Catherine might have wished for a bride of greater prominence in society for her nephew, she liked and approved of the Bennets. As for Darcy himself, should he succeed in wooing Miss Elizabeth, he wondered if Lady Catherine might object; the thought she would not wish the position that had belonged to her daughter filled by a young lady of so little standing flitted through his mind.

"Then I suppose I must conclude you have made your decision regarding Miss Bennet."

Fitzwilliam cocked his head to the side and regarded his aunt. "If you recall, I made my sentiments known before I left London."

"You did," affirmed Lady Catherine. "I had not thought you would reconsider, but the chance still existed. The evidence of this morning's visit, however, gives the lie to any such thoughts."

"Then I shall reiterate, and we need not speak of the matter again. I mean to offer for Miss Bennet and shall not be moved from my course. The only thing that holds me back is her mourning."

Lady Catherine nodded as if she was not surprised. "The only thing left is to wish you joy."

It was a surprise that Lady Catherine subsequently turned her attention to Darcy. "And what of you, Nephew?"

Nonplused, Darcy stared at his aunt. Lady Catherine noted it and huffed her exasperation.

"You children all believe me bereft of wit; I cannot say why, for I believe I have proved my powers of observation many times. Your interest in Miss Elizabeth is obvious, Darcy, for while you sat with Georgiana and the youngest Bennets, I did not see your eyes leave her the entire time we were at Longbourn. Now, I ask you again: what of you?"

"If you will excuse me, Aunt," said Charity before Darcy could respond, "the fault is yours, for you have often displayed a preference for seeing what you wish rather than the truth."

The annoyance in Lady Catherine's huff could not be mistaken, nor was the flashing of her eyes as she regarded Charity. "It is not seeing what I wish, Charity. It is merely confidence that my wishes are for the best. Of late I have had little choice but to relinquish my desires, for you children have declared you will not oblige me. But I still believe they are for the best, though I know I shall not have my way."

To Darcy, Lady Catherine's assertion little resembled the truth, and the grins his cousins displayed informed him that he was not alone. Knowing Lady Catherine would not appreciate such an observation, he refrained; she probably knew what they were all thinking, regardless.

"Let me say, Aunt," said Darcy, "that whatever my wishes, I will prove as impervious to persuasion as my cousin."

"Of that, I have little doubt," was Lady Catherine's sour reply.

Darcy nodded. "The fact is that I have not yet reached Fitzwilliam's level of certainty, but I believe I wish to have Miss Elizabeth for a wife. I know you may wish for a more prominent woman of society for me, but I find myself indifferent to such considerations. Miss Elizabeth is everything I ever wanted, and that is the most important point."

Lady Catherine considered him for a long moment, and Darcy realized with a start that the lady had changed in the past months as much as any of them. Not long ago, Darcy could not have imagined that she would think so highly of a family such as the Bennets, would never lower herself to offering such friendship to them. Even without considering her wishes, she would have broken into a loud harangue if the mere thought of Darcy's interest in Miss Elizabeth had crossed her mind.

"Then you shall have my support," said Lady Catherine at length, again surprising them with her easy capitulation. "Miss Elizabeth and, indeed, Miss Bennet," Lady Catherine nodded to Fitzwilliam, "will require a sponsor in society, not only to make their curtsey to the queen but also to ease their way. For that, I pledge myself."

"Thank you, Aunt," said Fitzwilliam, Darcy nodding his agreement. "We shall count on your counsel and support."

"Very well," said Lady Catherine. "Now, if you will excuse me, I believe I shall retreat to my chambers for a time."

Once she had left the room, those remaining regarded one another, bemusement upon every face. It was Georgiana who broke the silence.

"Was that truly Aunt Catherine?"

"Do not question it, Georgiana," said Fitzwilliam, his chuckles displaying his mirth. "It is better to simply accept it."

It was a bit of sage advice, Darcy thought. He meant to follow his cousin's advice and never broach the subject again.

CHAPTER XXVI

*W*ithin days of the ladies' return to Netherfield, the situation was much as it had been the previous autumn. The families at the two estates were constantly in each others' company, both through visits — which happened almost daily — and at events in the neighborhood. What the rest of Meryton society thought of their comfort together, Darcy could not say, but the lack of envy was marked, and Darcy was content that at the very least their neighbors believed the Bennet family's recent trials were recompensed in some small part by their friendship with a family high in society.

While Darcy continued to confine his attention to Miss Elizabeth as often as he could, he was coming to appreciate her sisters more than he had before. Miss Bennet was, as ever, angelic and kind; Miss Mary, level-headed and intelligent; and even the youngest sisters appeared to have learned to temper their high spirits into something better, resembling the behavior of a young lady of gentle breeding. Their livelier natures were also drawing Georgiana from her shell, doing what Darcy had never quite managed himself.

The surprise addition to their party was Bingley, who had proven true to his promise to avoid pursuing Miss Bennet as he had before. That did not mean Bingley still did not look at her often, but such instances of wistful or interested glances were becoming fewer, and it seemed his attention was becoming more fixed on Miss Mary. Darcy was not quite certain what to think of that development, but it was not his place to speak with Bingley or attempt to discover his intentions.

"It is yet early, Mr. Darcy," Miss Elizabeth had said when he had made some small comment on the subject. "Jane and I have noted Mr. Bingley's increasing easiness with Mary, but he has not pushed propriety and genuinely seems interested in her."

"It is not a match I might have expected," confessed Darcy. "Bingley has always seemed so . . . unserious, and your sister . . ."

Miss Elizabeth's eyes crinkled with amusement. "Oh, yes, Mary possesses an abundance of gravity. But if you look at them both, Mary has loosened a little, and Mr. Bingley has attained a hint of solemnity. In a certain sense, they balance each other well."

"So, you suggest I should withdraw and allow them to come to their meeting of minds," said Darcy.

"You and your family have been godsent, Mr. Darcy. We appreciate everything you have done for us. Jane and I are careful with our sisters, and while we welcome your support, I have every confidence in Mary's ability to choose for herself."

That exchange had raised Darcy's hopes, for Miss Elizabeth had confided in him, had looked upon him with eyes filled with affection and trust. It was not the look of love Darcy dreamed of receiving, but it was a beginning. Provoking her returning regard for him had never seemed so attainable.

It was some days before Darcy learned of the truth of the matter of Bingley's family, and while the knowledge might have caused him concern again for Bingley's character, in the end, he was satisfied. It happened on a day when Darcy and Fitzwilliam had gone to Pulvis Lodge to assist Bingley, to help him become accustomed to being a landowner during the planting season. After spending some time on the estate, they had retreated to the house where Bingley had invited them in for a drink. As often happened, the effects of drink and time spent in one another's company loosened their tongues and allowed for easier conversation.

"Pulvis Lodge seems to be an excellent estate," observed Fitzwilliam after a time of inconsequential conversation.

"There is nothing wrong with the estate," confirmed Bingley, a look of unusual concentration on his features. "My sister might disagree, but it is a good investment in the short term, an early test of my abilities. I hope I am not failing that test."

"It seems to me," said Darcy, ignoring the mention of Bingley's sister for the moment, "you have matters well in hand."

"Even so," said Bingley, "I do not believe I wish to purchase this estate. When the lease ends in September, I shall allow it to lapse and look for a more substantial property. Pulvis Lodge is a little small."

"So it is," said Fitzwilliam. "For my part, I think I agree with you regarding my lease. It is not where I wish to settle."

"Oh?" asked Bingley, fixing an interested look on Fitzwilliam. "I had not thought you were reconsidering Netherfield as a long-term purchase."

"I never seriously considered it. There is little wrong with Netherfield, and the society in the neighborhood is friendly. My family, however, are all from the north; I believe I would prefer to return to my roots rather than settling at such a distance."

"That is understandable," replied Bingley with a nod. "That is a consideration for me too. As you know, I am from York and have many relations there. Pulvis Lodge is almost four days' journey to my relations."

"Do you have any notion of where you wish to settle?" asked Darcy.

"Darcy and my brother can likely assist, should you wish to settle in Derbyshire, Staffordshire, or even Nottinghamshire."

It was a mark of how Fitzwilliam had become warmer with Bingley of late that he would suggest Bingley might look in Derbyshire. Bingley seemed to understand, for he flashed them a grin and nodded.

"At present, I have no notion of where I might purchase. Should the opportunity present itself, however, I should be happy to accept any guidance you may wish to offer."

From there, the conversation turned to a discussion of the benefits and drawbacks of estate ownership in Hertfordshire, Derbyshire, and near Bingley's home in York. As was his wont, Darcy remained quieter, allowing Bingley and Fitzwilliam to carry the conversation while he observed and considered the men before him.

In particular, Darcy was struck by how much he liked the Bingley that had returned to Hertfordshire without his sisters. Darcy could confess to himself that there were times when Bingley's behavior had not always pleased him, for he had been superficial, eager to pay attention to the next pretty face, content to dance and flirt and engage in activities, which, though Darcy did not think they were immoral, could only sustain a man for a short time. Unless that man were George Wickham, of course.

The thought of his former friend provoked a moue of distaste, though Darcy hid it from his companions. That Wickham had retreated from Meryton soon after learning he could not engage in his usual activities had been a welcome development. Wickham's time in England, Darcy thought, was coming to a close, for he had made himself unwelcome in so many places; many would like to lay hands on him for his past deeds. If he did not achieve his goal of a marriage to a woman of wealth—and Darcy had always thought that was unlikely—it would not surprise him if Wickham took ship for the New World, to find new people to defraud, new ladies to ply with his charms. Darcy hoped he would, for he had no desire to be in Wickham's company again.

Shaking his head clear of unpleasant memories, Darcy turned back to his original thoughts. This Bingley was a man he thought he could call a friend, a man who would lighten the mood of anyone with whom he associated, yet a man who knew when to be serious, when to roll up his shirt sleeves and work for his bread. In many respects, he was now like Fitzwilliam, though he did not have Fitzwilliam's sense of the absurd, his finely honed sense of irony.

"No, Fitzwilliam, my sisters shall not join me. Of that, you may be certain."

Darcy focused on Bingley, realizing his attention had wandered. "Your sisters do not wish it?" asked Darcy.

Bingley sighed and sat back in his chair, sipping the drink he held in one hand. "After speaking with you both at the club, I returned home with a greater understanding of why Caroline had been so out of sorts the previous days."

Chuckling, Bingley shook his head. "It will not surprise you to hear that my sister has a greater impression of her position in society than she possesses."

"No, Bingley," said Fitzwilliam. "With all due respect to your excellent sister, I have no illusions as to her impression of her worth. Her behavior toward the Bennet sisters illustrated her opinion without the possibility of misinterpretation."

The grimace with which Bingley responded showed his distaste for his sister's behavior, but Darcy thought he was not angry with Fitzwilliam's less than diplomatic words.

"Much of the problem stems from her association with Lady Diane Montrose. Lady Diane is of age with Caroline, and they attended the same seminary together. Having made an acquaintance she considers acceptable so easily led Caroline to the assumption that all of society would accept us with equal ease.

"Then again," Bingley's lip twisted with disgust, "I have my doubts that Lady Diane feels any genuine friendship for my sister."

"Lady Diane is the sort of woman who feels nothing for anyone but herself," muttered Fitzwilliam. "My brother has had some dealings with her and was forced to all but cut her in society before she would desist in throwing herself at him."

"Yes, that sounds like Lady Diane," agreed Bingley. "The pathetic thing is Caroline does not see Lady Diane's selfish disdain for anyone of a lower social stratum, and she does not exempt Caroline from her contempt. I suspect Lady Diane accepts her presence and others of her circle so that she may congratulate herself on her position as their highest member. Cruelty is in her blood. But Caroline insists it is how the upper classes behave and will not hear a word against her."

Darcy shared a look with Fitzwilliam and sighed. "In this instance, your sister is correct to a large degree. Many in society behave like Lady Diane, and some are much worse."

"If you will pardon my saying," said Bingley, "I would not wish to associate with that set even if I did concern myself at all for rising in society."

It was something akin to what Darcy might have said, informing him that Bingley possessed a core of goodness in him, one hidden underneath his frivolous manners. Darcy felt his regard for the man growing apace.

"Returning to the subject of my sister," said Bingley, "it will also not surprise you to learn that she feels her means of rising to the level of society she craves is through marriage to a man who inhabits that level. If she could manage such a coup, she would inhabit that level by the right of her husband."

"In that, she is not as correct as she believes," said Fitzwilliam. "Many will still treat her with contempt, feeling she is an interloper who bought her way into high society by virtue of her dowry, that she still stinks of the shop."

"Well do I know it," said Bingley with shaken head. "But Caroline cannot see that. Or she does not wish to acknowledge it—either way, there is little difference. Even with such ambitions and a friend so advantageously placed, Caroline has never had the opportunity to set her sights on a man who would meet her needs until she met you both. Even those men who will associate with Lady Diane would not give my sister a second glance.

"Her failure made her waspish," confessed Bingley. "There have been several men who have looked on Caroline as a potential wife in the past, but she rejected them out of hand for they were not high enough for her. This season, however, refusing to allow eligible suitors to court her will come with a price."

"You have informed her she must marry?" asked Fitzwilliam.

"Yes," replied Bingley. "If she does not, she is at an age where she may take control of her dowry and set up a residence of her own. It will not be enough for her to live in London, which means she would be confined to York or Scarborough, and most likely end an old maid. Hurst and I believe she fears remaining unmarried more than she wishes for a society marriage."

"Then I salute you both for coming to that determination," said Fitzwilliam. "Forgive me for being blunt, but if that is so, why are you here?"

Bingley looked down and responded with a self-deprecating chuckle. "Because I am aware of my strengths and weaknesses. Hurst and I delivered the ultimatum together, but I am not of a forceful character, and Caroline believes she may rule me. She has a better chance of attracting a husband in the circles Hurst frequents without my presence, for she believes she can sway me to her side. Since I retreated, Hurst now has full control, and whatever else Hurst is, he will not allow her to misbehave.

"Besides," said Bingley, "London society had lost much of its charms for me. I leased this estate to acquaint myself with estate management, and I am much better served to see to it rather than playing the gentleman in London. The sooner I attend to the business of behaving like a gentleman, the sooner I will become one in truth."

For a moment as Bingley explained his reasons for absenting himself, Darcy wondered if he should hold his flight from his sister against him. There was more than they were being told, he was certain, and he did not think it would paint Bingley in a good light. Then again, it was clear he understood his limitations. Perhaps it was better if Hurst handled Miss Bingley. Disposing of his sister in marriage would surely be a boon for Bingley's future, for the woman did him no credit as she was now.

"It takes an intelligent man to know his limitations," said Fitzwilliam, and Darcy agreed with his cousin. "I wish your brother all the best in finding some poor sod willing to take your sister off your hands!"

The two men guffawed together, and Darcy could not restrain his chuckles.

"Thank you, sir!" exclaimed Bingley. "For the moment, I feel as free as a bird! And the excellent company does not hurt either!"

The serious topics at an end, they lapsed into desultory conversation thereafter until Darcy and Fitzwilliam returned to Netherfield.

It was some days later when a persistent problem, one that had gone dormant for some time, again reared its ugly head.

It was a beautiful spring day and the Longbourn ladies were expecting the Netherfield ladies to join them for a day in each other's company. Elizabeth had noted that their neighbors were more often at Longbourn than the reverse, a fact she attributed both to their continued mourning status and their infant brother, whom they were loath to leave behind. On this day, Elizabeth had also invited Charlotte to join them, for her dearest friend had made a favorable impression on the Netherfield ladies and had become friendly with them.

"Lizzy!" greeted Charlotte when she entered the study a few minutes before the Netherfield ladies were to arrive. "I see you have closeted yourself in your father's study again, looking over the estate books."

Elizabeth grinned at her friend and closed the ledger she had been inspecting. "I had thought to finish whatever work I had for today before our guests arrived. You are ahead of your time."

"Perhaps I am," said Charlotte. "But I think you are not so busy at present as you would have me believe."

Laughing, Elizabeth agreed and returned the book to its place on the shelf. "You are correct, my friend. I had finished what I was doing and was looking over it to ensure there were no errors."

"Then let us leave this room. I hope you have many amusements planned for our pleasure today."

"Of course. Let it not be said that Longbourn stints in providing for our guests' enjoyment."

With much banter, the friends made their way from the library and out into the hall. Elizabeth thought to lead her friend to the sitting-room, but the sound of a masculine voice rent the peace of the estate.

"Cousin Elizabeth! How fortunate I am to have found you."

Turning, Elizabeth blanched when her eyes found the tall, thin person of her father's cousin standing just inside the entrance. The man's appearance was unwelcome, but it was the sight of the unkempt nature of his hair and clothing, the way his gaze fell on her with a fanatical intensity that caused her to shiver.

"Here, what is this?" the voice of John, the footman interrupted them.

"He pushed his way past me," said Mrs. Hill, Elizabeth belatedly noting the housekeeper was just behind the parson, her fidgeting informing them of her agitation.

"Well, he can turn around and walk back out the door," said John, taking the initiative when Elizabeth did not speak at once.

"A mere servant shall not remove me," said Mr. Collins, sniffing in disdain. "I have come to speak to my cousins and will not be evicted."

"This is a house of young ladies and you are a man alone," scolded Mrs. Hill.

"That is correct," said Elizabeth, finally finding her voice. "Please step outside and you may say whatever you wish."

"I shall not," snarled Mr. Collins.

The parson started forward, but John intercepted him neatly, grasping his arm and in one smooth motion twisting it around his back. The parson seemed so shocked to be manhandled in such a way that he could not respond, his momentary inactivity providing John all the opportunity he required to remove him to the stoop beyond the door. Then the parson began to shout insults, swearing in a manner unbecoming a common laborer, let alone a parson.

"Mrs. Hill," said Elizabeth, "please send for Mr. Whitmore and Theodore at once."

Nodding, Mrs. Hill turned away to summon the steward and the new footman they had hired. Then Elizabeth squared her shoulders and stepped toward the door where John stood toe to toe with an incensed Mr. Collins.

"Take great care, Eliza," said Charlotte, her tone low with warning. "There is something at work here beyond a man's desire to own an estate."

Elizabeth acknowledged her friend's counsel with a tight smile and stepped from the house, Charlotte trailing her. Jane appeared from behind them, her frown inferring her own disquiet, though she did not shirk from providing a united front with Elizabeth and Charlotte.

As she stepped out, Elizabeth noted two things. The first was that her younger sisters were watching the spectacle through the sitting-room window, their mouths agape with astonishment. Elizabeth motioned for Mary to keep Kitty and Lydia there. The second was that Mr. Collins was shouting some rather vile insults at John, who stood there impassively, eyeing Mr. Collins with evident disdain. John, Elizabeth knew, was a capable protector, one who could handle the likes of William Collins without issue.

"When I am the master of the estate," intoned Mr. Collins as the ladies approached, "I shall dismiss you without reference and ensure you never work in this neighborhood again."

"Do as you will," said John. "Until that day, you have no say in my employment. I should not wish to work at an estate where you were the master."

Beyond infuriated, Mr. Collins turned to Elizabeth, seeming to believe it was best to ignore the footman. From around the corner of the house, Theodore appeared and hastened toward them, and Elizabeth felt a little better, knowing there was another man to help protect them should Mr. Collins become more belligerent than he already was.

"Why are you here, Mr. Collins?" demanded Elizabeth. "You are trespassing; my uncles have advised me to call the constable should you bother us again."

"My dear cousin," said Mr. Collins, his voice taking on an unctuous tone, though one belied by the glittering of his hard stare, "I have come to offer an olive branch to mend the distance between us."

"Any olive branch you could have offered via a letter," said Elizabeth.

"Oh, no, Cousin," said he, "I could only present this in person. For I have decided it would be best if I assumed my responsibility of caring for the family as the only man remaining. To do that I must, of course, wed one of you, for then I may take my rightful place as the master of this estate and save it from the ruin of being managed by a young woman unsuited for such a task."

Charlotte snorted at the parson's words, but Elizabeth could spare no thought of her friend's opinion, even if it mirrored her own. "Mr. Collins, please remember that being the master of Longbourn is not your rightful place. That place belongs to my brother when he comes of age."

Elizabeth might not have thought it possible, but Mr. Collins's look became even darker. "Of course," said he from between clenched teeth, "I do not seek to usurp your brother's place. But it is clear Longbourn needs a man's guiding hand, and I mean to take up that position. That way his birthright will remain solvent if he reaches his majority."

Whether it was a trick of her distaste for this man, Elizabeth wondered if he had not placed a slight emphasis on the word "if," and the thought bred further anger. For the first time, the notion that Mr.

Collins might mean her brother harm passed through her mind, fed by the man's irrational behavior. Just what would this man do in his need to grasp at the property which was not his?

"I am sorry, Mr. Collins," said Elizabeth, "but for my part, I must decline. My younger sisters are not an option either, for they are all underage. My uncle will countenance none of us marrying you."

"It matters little," said Mr. Collins. "I may have your elder sister."

"No, you shall not," said Jane, her voice unusually firm. "Nothing in this world will compel me to marry you, Mr. Collins."

"You shall have me!" spat the parson.

When he stepped forward to reach for them, the immovable wall that was John intercepted him, and assisted by Theodore, they barred his way forward. Mr. Collins shouted at them to stand aside, and when they would not, he attempted to force his way past. Finally, pushed beyond endurance, Mr. Collins made a clumsy swing at John, who sidestepped neatly, caught the man's arm, and wrenched it behind his back again, this time with more force than he had before.

The sound of carriage wheels on packed gravel interrupted the conversation, though Mr. Collins cried out and swore and tried to free himself from John's grasp. The carriage shuddered to a halt at the imperious command from inside the box, and Lady Catherine stepped out before the footmen could assist, her blazing eyes fixed on the person of Mr. Collins. With a slack jaw and fear-filled eyes, Mr. Collins stopped struggling, and John released him.

"L-Lady C-Catherine!" stammered the parson. "I th-thought you were in London."

"It appears you did," was the lady's deceptively mild reply. "If you recall, I expressly forbid you from coming to Longbourn again, did I not? Why are you here?"

Mr. Collins's eyes darted to where Elizabeth stood glaring at him, and the sight of her anger seemed to provoke him. "I wish to offer marriage to Cousin Elizabeth, so the estate can have the guiding hand of a man again."

"You should reconsider your story, Mr. Collins," said Elizabeth, disdain falling on him like the blow of a hammer. "A moment ago, you were intent upon marrying Jane."

"It matters little which of you I have," said the parson. "That I shall be master of Longbourn is what is important."

"That is perhaps the most senseless thing I have ever heard you say," said Lady Catherine. "And that is saying something, as sense rarely passes your lips."

Mr. Collins's lips curled in anger. "This does not concern you, Lady Catherine," said he in a bit of daring Elizabeth might not have expected. "I must deal with my cousins. You may return to wherever you are staying."

"That is enough, Mr. Collins! I am involved because of my friendship with these ladies and by my position as a woman of sense and compassion. While it is understandable you are disappointed with how matters have ended, they have done nothing that is against the law. Joseph Bennet is the future master of this estate, and nothing you say will change that fact."

"But my cousins require—"

"Your cousins require nothing more than your immediate absence!"

Lady Catherine stared at Mr. Collins, daring him to speak, and for the moment, the man was silent. "Good. Now, go back to Hunsford, Mr. Collins. I shall not tell you again to refrain from contacting your cousins. I believe it is time to speak with your bishop concerning your actions. You should know that I am on excellent terms with him."

For a moment, Elizabeth thought Mr. Collins would continue, even in the face of his patroness's obvious displeasure. More than once, she thought he would speak; his mouth worked, and his eyes darted in Elizabeth's direction, seeming to blame her for his situation.

Then in a smooth motion, he turned and departed. But he would not leave before making one last statement.

"This is not over! I shall have my due!"

CHAPTER XXVII

*T*he carriage stopped before Longbourn, and the men stepped out, hurrying into the house in response to the summons they had received. The house was calm as if nothing had upset the morning, belying the concise demand for their presence, together with the news that Mr. Collins had come, written in a careless hand most unlike his aunt. Sparing little time for the niceties of divesting hats and gloves, Darcy followed Fitzwilliam into the sitting-room, Bingley following—Bingley had been at Netherfield that day when the summons arrived.

"Miss Bennet," said Fitzwilliam as he stepped into the room, going to Miss Bennet at once. "Are you well?"

Darcy was scarcely less eager to hear the answer to his question, though he looked to Miss Elizabeth. Approaching, Darcy sat close to her, examining her for any damage, noting she appeared as calm as ever. A faint smile hovered around her mouth, though nothing compared to the open amusement displayed by Darcy's female relations.

"We are all well," said Miss Bennet as Darcy inspected her sister. "The footmen forced Mr. Collins to depart."

"This insistence of his is troubling," said Miss Elizabeth. "What sort of a man attempts to gain that to which he has no right, trampling the wishes of others underfoot as he does so?"

"A man without sense," growled Lady Catherine. "I hardly knew him, for he has always bowed and scraped and venerated every word that proceeded from my mouth."

"Perhaps it would be best to relate what happened." Bingley, Darcy noted, had set himself near to Miss Mary, assuring himself that she was well, much as Darcy and Fitzwilliam had done with her elder sisters. "It would be better than guessing and flailing in the dark."

"You have kept your head when the rest of us have not," said Lady Catherine, nodding in Bingley's direction. "Yes, let us explain what happened. Miss Elizabeth, I believe you were witness to it all from the beginning?"

With a nod, Miss Elizabeth retold the tale in simple language, descending but little into speculation or useless clarifications. Miss Lucas, who Darcy had not noticed was present, assisted her in the telling, as she had been with Miss Elizabeth when the fool Collins arrived. Darcy became angrier the longer they talked; it was only a few moments, but by the end of them, Darcy found himself in a towering fury.

"What possessed you to give him Hunsford, Lady Catherine?" demanded Darcy when Miss Elizabeth fell silent.

"At present," said Lady Catherine, "I wonder that myself."

"Regardless of that," said Miss Elizabeth, "the question at hand is what to do about him. The longer he continues in this obsession, the more fearful I become of what he might attempt to do in his apparent desperation. And I thought . . ."

Miss Elizabeth trailed off and appeared ill at ease, unable to continue her thought. It took Lady Catherine's gently stated: "What is it?" to induce her to explain herself.

"A thought that occurred to me as he was speaking," confessed she. "The inflection in his voice when he said he would take control of Longbourn and keep it solvent for Joseph to inherit 'if' he reached his majority. I wondered if Mr. Collins somehow meant my brother harm."

Silence reigned, and several of the company gaped at her. Into the shock, Miss Lucas spoke: "To own the truth, I considered that myself."

Lady Catherine shook her head. "Mr. Collins is a fool, one who seems to believe he is owed the position that is now lost to him. But I cannot believe he is a violent man who would stoop to murder the innocent to gain what he feels is his."

"You may be correct, Aunt," said Fitzwilliam. Darcy almost started at the sight of Fitzwilliam's hand holding Miss Bennet's as if he never meant to let go; that the woman allowed it was a testament to her returning feelings. "But let us not be hasty in ruling out that possibility. History is littered with legions of men who have become unreasonable over such matters as wealth and privilege. Some of them have been good men driven to evil acts by such lusts."

"Wickham," said Darcy. Fitzwilliam caught his eye and nodded.

Lady Catherine shot him a look. "As I recall, he attended the ball at Netherfield."

"And left as soon as Miss Elizabeth confirmed she did not own Longbourn," said Darcy, resting a warm gaze on the woman and remembering how magnificent she had been that night. "Soon after, he resigned his position and left, as we had ensured he could not accumulate debts and toy with the young ladies of the neighborhood."

"His story is instructional," said Fitzwilliam. "I suspect whatever good George Wickham possessed burned away in the fires of his envy when he reached an age where he understood the difference between his position and Darcy's. Mr. Collins's circumstances are not identical, but there are similarities. He is a man who thought nothing was standing in the way of his inheritance, only to have it snatched away at the last instant. Is it surprising to any of us that he has reacted in the way he has?"

"Loath though I am to disagree with you," said Miss Elizabeth, "I believe there must be something more to his obsession than disappointed hopes."

"On the contrary, we do not disagree, Miss Elizabeth," said Fitzwilliam.

"For my part," said Miss Lydia, her hands protectively around her infant brother as she gazed at them all in defiance, "I care little for his motivations. I only want him to stop threatening my sister. I shall claw his eyes out if he attempts to harm Joseph!"

Darcy suppressed a chuckle, and he was not the only one in the same straits. It appeared a vicious protective instinct had overtaken Miss Lydia, and her sister, folding her arms and nodding by her side, appeared similarly infected.

"That is the key, Miss Lydia," said Fitzwilliam, giving the girl a warm smile. Then he turned to Darcy and arched a brow. "Then what shall we do?"

"For one," said Miss Elizabeth, her manner businesslike, "we should inform our uncles. This most recent incident will exhaust their patience. Mr. Phillips has threatened to bring suit against Mr. Collins since he first began pestering us after Mama's condition came to light."

"Yes, you should let your uncles know," said Darcy. "Also remember that if you sue Mr. Collins, his legal troubles may lead to the loss of his ordination, which would leave him even more desperate."

"Perhaps it will, Mr. Darcy," said Miss Elizabeth. "But to keep threatening him and never acting on those threats is like crying wolf, is it not?"

"It is, and I would not suggest your uncles do not pursue that path. However, I suggest we pursue a more direct method of silencing him at the same time."

Fitzwilliam gave Darcy a long look and nodded, even as Lady Catherine said: "Even I have failed to silence him, and I have his adoration."

"Given the way he behaved to you," said Miss Lucas, "I am suspect that is not true any longer."

While Lady Catherine scowled at her, she gave a curt nod.

"You have not considered the benefits of Fitzwilliam and I lending a hand," said Darcy; there was nothing of lightness in his tone. "While he may revere you, he will not fear you. In this instance, I believe fear may work to our advantage."

"And perhaps we may call in additional support," added Fitzwilliam. "My brother is to come to Netherfield soon. By this time, I suspect he is eager to depart London. If we send him an express tonight, I expect he will eagerly accompany us to Kent tomorrow. Will Collins defy not only the nephews of his patroness who promise retribution but the Earl of Matlock too?"

"Unfortunately," said Lady Catherine, "I find myself unable to predict what Mr. Collins will do. This whole situation is beyond my understanding of him."

"Then I suggest we pay him a visit," said Darcy.

"Do you require my support?" asked Bingley.

"At present, I should think not," replied Darcy after a moment's thought. "I suspect it will not be necessary, and I should be relieved if you were to remain in Hertfordshire and watch over the Bennet ladies."

"Perhaps we should make a party of it," said Miss Elizabeth. She looked around to the other ladies and continued: "Would you like to stay at Longbourn? We should love to have you with us as we wait for the gentlemen's return."

"I should be delighted," said Miss Lucas with a warm smile for her friend.

"As would we," said Charity. Darcy noted she spoke quickly before Lady Catherine could speak otherwise.

"For my part," said Lady Catherine, "I have no objection." The lady paused and grinned, adding: "It has been many years since I took part in such frivolity. I believe I shall anticipate our revelries keenly."

"Then it is settled," said Miss Bennet.

The next few minutes were filled with a flurry of discussion, the ladies talking of what they would need for their stay, while they prepared notes for their maids and servants at Netherfield, which Darcy and Fitzwilliam pledged to deliver when they returned to the estate. Miss Lucas, her home being much nearer, wrote a quick note to her mother and tasked a footman with seeing it to Lucas Lodge and returning with her effects.

"What of Thompson?" asked Fitzwilliam.

"Thompson is my most trusted footman," said Darcy when the Bennet ladies looked on him for an explanation. "He is also the largest man I have ever met, one who can intimidate with nothing more than a look. In answer to your question, Fitzwilliam, I believe we should take him to Kent with us. The ladies have adequate protection here, and one harsh look from Thompson may well put Collins in fear for his life."

Fitzwilliam laughed. "That is true. Then he accompanies us to Kent."

With those words, Fitzwilliam turned to Miss Bennet, fixing his attention on her for the final few moments of their stay. Darcy followed his example, turning his attention to Miss Elizabeth for the same purpose. Heartened by the way she responded, Darcy exchanged a few words.

"It may be best if you all remain in the house, Miss Elizabeth," said he.

"Do you suppose there is any danger?"

"No, I should not think so. But it would be best to be cautious, all the same."

Miss Elizabeth sighed and fixed him with a slight smile. "This business of Mr. Collins has been . . . difficult to endure, Mr. Darcy. I thought we had persuaded the man to desist, and yet he comes to the estate again and forces his way past our housekeeper and engages in fisticuffs with our footman. Part of me wonders if we can ever reason with him."

"It is my opinion," said Darcy, "that the time for reasoning with him is over. We now must take other measures to deter his ambitions."

The sigh with which she responded was deeper, but she nodded. "And I thank you again. Your family has been good to us, Mr. Darcy, in our time of need. We shall not forget it."

"There is no need to thank us," said Darcy, a powerful feeling again welling up in his breast. "Nothing could have prevented us from offering our support."

It was as bold a statement as Darcy thought he could offer at that moment when he was so uncertain of her returning regard. The tender look with which he regarded her would tell her the rest, he hoped.

To his dismay, her gaze found Fitzwilliam and her sister, and she said: "Yes, I suppose Colonel Fitzwilliam would never have allowed a man to all but claim Jane without making his sentiments known."

"Do you suppose that is the only thing that motivates us? That motivates me?"

The demand slipped from Darcy's lips before he had time to consider what he was saying, even as he meant every word. Miss Elizabeth appeared astonished, for she regarded him, her bafflement for his meaning written upon her face. And suddenly Darcy could not stand her indifference any longer. It was time to retreat.

"Fitzwilliam," said he, rising and drawing his cousin's attention to him, "it is time to depart. I suggest we go to London today and make an early start for Hunsford in the morning from there."

"Yes, that would be for the best."

His cousin, Darcy knew, had seen something of his sudden desire to depart; counting on him to hold his tongue in front of the ladies, Darcy turned and bid his goodbyes, his eyes not quite meeting Miss Elizabeth's. Darcy feared what he might find within them. Or rather, what he would not find.

"Perhaps I shall call tomorrow morning," said Bingley when the carriage rolled into motion toward Netherfield.

"It should not be necessary," said Fitzwilliam. "But your vigilance is welcome, nonetheless."

As the carriage rolled on toward the estate, Darcy allowed his companions to carry the conversation and focused on his thoughts, morose reflections, indeed. The question of helping the Bennets did not even materialize in Darcy's mind—whenever Miss Elizabeth stood in need of succor, Darcy would not hesitate to offer it. Yet, the appeal of remaining in Hertfordshire had waned, for the matter of Miss Elizabeth's indifference was becoming unbearable. Perhaps it would be best to return to Pemberley where the evidence would not always be before him.

Fitzwilliam Darcy was a man who prided himself in his determination, his knowledge of what he wanted, and his tenacity in the pursuit of those desires. It was one reason he accounted himself a competent master of his estate, for he would allow the solution to no problem to elude him.

But he had never been a man in love, had never felt the pain of rejection. Or the worse and ongoing pain of knowing the woman he loved was unmoved by him. A gentleman did not force his attentions on a woman who did not wish for them; those were the actions of a lout. And Miss Bennet would not feign affection for him if she did not feel it, and Darcy would not wish her to come to him under such circumstances, anyway. A selfish being, Darcy wanted her love and devotion, and if he could not have it, he could not have her. It was simple but difficult to bear.

At Netherfield, Bingley bid them farewell and departed for Pulvis Lodge, leaving Darcy and his cousin to request his carriage for an immediate departure and return to their rooms to gather what effects they would need. Darcy gave Snell, his longtime valet, the orders, and Snell gathered his master's effects efficiently.

"Do you wish me to accompany you to London, Mr. Darcy?" asked he.

Darcy thought for a moment and shook his head. "For one night, I believe I shall be fine. I expect we shall return by tomorrow."

"Very good, Mr. Darcy."

Within a half-hour of arriving, the cousins had returned to the road in Darcy's carriage, instructing the driver that they were for London, and as there was ample time left in the day, that he need not hurry. Darcy did not miss his cousin's eyes on him as they traveled, but he determined it was best to ignore him and concentrate on the scenes they were passing.

"Are you well, Darcy?" asked Fitzwilliam at length.

"Perfectly so," replied Darcy.

"Is that so?" asked his cousin. "If you recall, I know you as well as any man alive, Darcy, and I suspect you are not well at all."

"Please leave it alone, Cousin," said Darcy. "Let us concentrate our energy on putting the fear of God into Mr. Collins. We may deal with anything else later."

It seemed to Darcy that his cousin wished to pursue the matter. But he must have seen something in Darcy's countenance that warned him to desist, and he did, though not without a sigh. Thus, they continued in silence, Darcy brooding about his situation.

At Longbourn, the ladies settled in for the day, chatting as was their wont, all formality between them lost as it was between the best of friends. It was quickly determined that Lady Catherine would stay in the master's chambers, while Charity and Anne shared the adjoining chambers of the mistress. Georgiana would stay with Kitty, while Charlotte would inhabit their guest room. While it was a tight squeeze, for Longbourn was not large, the ladies were happy with their company and there were no complaints.

Or most of them were happy with their company. Elizabeth could not say she was unhappy, for she esteemed these ladies more than she ever had anyone else. Rather, she was struck with an absence of mind, or more correctly, her mind was engaged in other matters. For she had seen the sudden change in Mr. Darcy and did not know what to make of it.

Could the gentleman be opposed to his cousin's interest in Jane? The thought beggared belief, for Mr. Darcy had never appeared to be a gentleman who looked down on them. His friendly countenance was a reason she anticipated the visits of their neighbors so much, for he was both interesting and intelligent, and Elizabeth enjoyed speaking to him very much.

Then why had he been so eager to be out of her presence? The answer, Elizabeth felt, was just out of her grasp, akin to a puzzle she could not quite make out or a word on the tip of her tongue she could not call forth. There was something that told her he would feel foolish for her inability to understand, that confirmed she would wonder how she had ever missed it when she finally realized the answer to her question. But clarity did not come, though Elizabeth spent much time that evening thinking on the subject. The answer came from a most surprising source.

Late that evening, later than had been the sisters' wont these past months, the ladies dispersed to their rooms to ready themselves to retire. Elizabeth accomplished her nightly ablutions and donned her nightgown, hoping the matter she had considered that day would not keep her awake that night. Pulling her hair into a braid, her preparations were complete when her door opened and in stalked her youngest sister, preventing Elizabeth from blowing out the candle.

"Lydia?" asked Elizabeth, noting her sister's displeasure, wondering what she was about.

"Lizzy," said Lydia, stopping just inside Elizabeth's door, her arms folded while she tapped her foot in displeasure. "I should like to know what you think you are doing, Sister."

Elizabeth felt like her head was encased in molasses. "What I am doing? I am certain I have no notion of what you are talking about."

Releasing a frustrated snort of exasperation, Lydia shook her head and spread her hands out as if to please for patience. "I have always considered you the most intelligent of us all, Lizzy, and I dare say I am not incorrect about that. But these last days have made me wonder, for you appear as dense as Mr. Collins!"

Startled to anger, Elizabeth glared at her sister. "I do not appreciate you comparing me to that odious man."

"And I might not have expected my sister would play with a man's heart the way you seem to be doing to Mr. Darcy."

Shocked at Lydia's assertion, Elizabeth could do little more than gape at her. "Mr. Darcy? Of what do you speak?"

Lydia looked skyward. "Must I spell it out for you, Lizzy? Given how observant you are, how much you rely on your vaunted ability to sketch characters, I might not have credited such blindness if I did not know you.

"Do you not see how Mr. Darcy is extending his hand and his heart to you? Can you not see how he is pained when you do not respond? Lizzy, you are doing everything but trampling on the poor man's heart, and it pains me to see it. Can you not either give him some encouragement or end his hopes altogether? Surely informing him you have no interest would be easier than to string him along, forever hoping, but coming no closer to what he desires."

"Mr. Darcy . . ." attempted Elizabeth, desperately striving to bring sense to her jumbled thoughts. "But . . . but I never . . ."

With a sigh, Lydia stepped forward and grasped Elizabeth's hands. "Sister, you should believe me. Indeed, I cannot account for your blindness in this matter. Mr. Darcy is in love with you, but he all but fled from the room when you did not respond to him."

"You heard what we said?" replied Elizabeth, though in a voice so faint she could hardly hear herself.

"Of course, I did not," said Lydia. "But I can observe and understand much from what I see.

"Lizzy, please listen to me. Mr. Darcy is deeply in love with you. For myself, I cannot imagine a better man to love me than he, but if you do not favor him, let him know and end his suffering. For myself, I cannot but think you mad if you refuse him, but I shall not attempt to direct you. This cannot continue. You must either acknowledge his love or reject it. Nothing else will do."

With a last squeeze of her hands, Lydia turned and retreated from the room, leaving Elizabeth to her thoughts. Could it be true? Could Lydia have seen what Elizabeth had not? Mr. Darcy had been polite and interested, but not in love. Or had he? A few moment's thought on the subject informed Elizabeth that her sister, a young woman with dreams of romance, might be completely incorrect about Mr. Darcy. But then another interruption entered the room, one whose powers of observation Elizabeth trusted much more than Lydia's.

"She is correct, you know."

Starting at the sound of another voice, Elizabeth looked up to see Charlotte in the doorway, regarding her. On her face was a soft smile, one Elizabeth knew Charlotte reserved for only those who were dearest in her heart.

"You have not been in Mr. Darcy's company," said Elizabeth, as much to break the uncomfortable silence as anything else.

"A few moments are all that is required, my friend," replied Charlotte. "At any other time, I would have thought you would recognize it long before I have. Perhaps it is because you are a participant that you are blind.

"It was marked in everything Mr. Darcy did today, Lizzy. Did you not see how he went to you at once, how his concern was for you, how the poor man could hardly take his eyes from you?"

"He has always preferred my company."

Charlotte's eyebrow rose, and Elizabeth blushed. Such a silly response. Was the essence of love not the desire to be in the exclusive company of the object of one's affections? Was that not evidence of his regard?

"Yes, Lizzy," was Charlotte's simple reply. "I dare say the gentleman prefers your company and has always preferred it. The question is, what do you mean to do about it?"

Then, with a significant look, Charlotte turned and departed, closing Elizabeth's door behind her. It is not to be wondered that Elizabeth's fears for her ability to sleep that night were well-founded. Rest was impossible given the revelations of her two visitors.

CHAPTER XXVIII

A sigh escaped Darcy's lips as those in the carriage spied the bulk of Rosings Park rising in the distance. Their journey was almost complete, the confrontation with Mr. Collins loomed. How they would deal with him, Darcy could not quite say; if canvassed, Fitzwilliam would suggest ways of dealing with him that would cause laughter, or a shaken head, or both. What Matlock thought, Darcy could not say, but the man had been eager for this excursion, and if he did not have familiarity with the Bennet sisters to motivate him, he still abhorred poor behavior, which Collins displayed in spades.

The house, Darcy noted, was situated on a bit of high ground, and thus was visible long before anything else in the area, including the parsonage which lay on the other side of the lane. It was, Darcy thought, a superior property, one many would call him mad for not scooping up with Lady Catherine's previous insistence he marry Anne. The house was not, he thought, the equal of Pemberley, but few houses were. But it was fine and prosperous, and Lady Catherine's stewardship had made it more so than the reverse.

And Darcy did not want it. Rosings was the legacy of the de Bourghs, the family of Lady Catherine's daughter. It was fortunate that

Anne could inherit it, for Darcy knew there had been some talk of instituting an entail in the time of Anne's grandfather. No, Darcy did not need Rosings, and he was content to leave it to Anne. She was his cousin, and he had no wish for a closer relationship with her. Darcy knew what—whom—he wanted. It seemed he was destined to be disappointed.

"I must once again voice my skepticism."

Darcy turned to his cousin, noting he had repeated the same refrain several times in the course of their four-hour journey from London. Matlock, as his brother had suggested, had been eager to leave town, forsaking the concerns of parliament behind, even as he informed them he could not be away for long. The notion of interceding on behalf of Fitzwilliam's lady appealed to him, and he had been ready to depart early that morning. Given the number of his trunks and how he had sent his valet ahead to Netherfield, Darcy might have thought he was ready to stay for a month complete.

"When you make Mr. Collins's acquaintance," replied Fitzwilliam, "you shall understand."

"Lady Catherine always has interesting lackeys to do her bidding, to say the least," said Matlock. "The man you describe is so ludicrous as to suggest a caricature."

"I will remind you that neither I nor Fitzwilliam is well acquainted with the man," said Darcy. "I have met him but once, and those few moments told me all I need to know."

The reminder did nothing more than provoke a wider grin from his cousin. "So you say. Then your opinion is heavily colored by Lady Catherine's word, and as *she* placed in him the position he holds, her opinion must be suspect."

"If it was only Lady Catherine, I might agree with you. But I trust the Miss Bennets, who have met him more than once *and* endured his continued bleating, and Anne and Charity were also present when he arrived yesterday."

"Then what do you mean to do?"

"This problem seems like one a little old-fashioned intimidation will resolve," said Fitzwilliam, the cracking of his knuckles punctuating his present thirst for blood.

While Matlock grinned at him, he turned his mind to the practicalities. "While I am certain you will enjoy threatening him, you know that will not be a long-term solution. A man forgets after a time, the immediacy of fear becoming less until he fools himself into believing the consequences would not be as he fears, or that he might avoid them altogether."

Darcy nodded slowly; that was something he had considered himself.

"There must be a more permanent solution for this issue," continued Matlock. He turned to look at his brother. "Given what I have heard from you, I assume you are set on Miss Bennet?"

"I intend to propose to her as soon as her mourning is complete in late May."

Matlock nodded and Darcy knew he had expected it, though Fitzwilliam had not told him of his plans in so many words. "That will help, as you will be closely connected to the family. But you will not always be at their estate, as you will have your own to manage. Miss Bennet is also not the daughter managing the estate."

"No, that task falls to her next younger sister, Elizabeth," replied Fitzwilliam.

"Then the best you can do would be to see her married as well. I do not suppose she has any prospects at present?"

Fitzwilliam's gaze flicked to Darcy, who willed him to be silent with a look. It was to his relief that his cousin did nothing to embarrass him.

"They are just out of deep mourning for their mother, before which they spent six months in mourning for their father. It can hardly be supposed she has a suitor at this point."

"Her sister has you," said Matlock.

Fitzwilliam nodded but did not reply, allowing Darcy to interject. "That may not be a solution, anyway. According to Miss Elizabeth's account, Mr. Collins does not care who he weds. As the sole man in the family—or so he supposes—he believes he would take on the management of the estate no matter which daughter he married."

"Yes, I can imagine such a man would believe what he will," agreed Matlock. "Then the ultimate solution involves the parson directly. Have you investigated him to determine why he is behaving so?"

"We spoke of that before," said Fitzwilliam, "but I do not think Lady Catherine did so when she was last in Kent."

"That is a good point," said Darcy. "It may be best to ask the butler at Rosings if he has heard anything, and to engage a man to investigate, regardless."

Matlock nodded. "His current behavior may be enough to expel him from the clergy, and if you can do that, his situation may be such that he can no longer remain in England. I pledge my support if it comes to that. Removing him from England altogether would best see to the family's safety, I should think."

"Perhaps you are correct," said Fitzwilliam. "But there remains the simple problem of finding a way to accomplish it."

The grin with which Matlock regarded him was feral. "My influence will assist, and I shall not even consider it an abuse of my power. If we can find something deceitful that is provoking his behavior—and I suspect there is something—removing him from these shores would be the best for all concerned."

"I cannot disagree," said Darcy. "But the parsonage approaches, so we should concentrate on the task at hand."

Hunsford, Darcy thought, was an excellent prospect for a man of the cloth. It stood in a pretty grove of trees, a spacious house that had been built in the time of Sir Lewis's father. For a single man without a family, it could be considered far too large, something he knew Lady Catherine appreciated as she felt it expedient for a parson to set the example of matrimony in his parish. Had circumstances been different, she might have pushed him toward his cousins for a wife, regardless.

When the carriage stopped in the drive, they exited and stretched their legs, the miles of road from London coupled with the presence of three large men within leaving them stiff and cramped. Within moments, they had righted themselves and approached the house to confront a man with whom they could claim no acquaintance.

It was a long moment before a maid answered their raps, a bit of tardiness that would have provoked a severe reprimand at Rosings Park. The woman was young and thin, and looked at them with wide eyes, sensing their positions in life.

"Good morning," said Matlock, taking the lead. "We are here to see Mr. Collins. Can you please have him summoned?"

Despite his congenial tone, the maid seemed to sense there was nothing of friendship in his application. Then her response was most surprising.

"I beg your pardon, sirs, but Mr. Collins is not at home."

"Do you know when he will return or where he went?"

"I do not know," said the woman, "nor do I know where he went. Mr. Collins left yesterday morning and did not inform us of his destination or when he would return."

"Yesterday morning?" demanded Darcy, bringing the woman's eyes to him. "He did not return at all last night?"

"No, sir," replied she, clearly cowed by his forceful manner.

"Then thank you," interjected Matlock. "We shall be on our way. If Mr. Collins returns, please inform him that the Earl of Matlock, his brother, Colonel Fitzwilliam, and his cousin, Mr. Darcy, have called on him. We are relations to Lady Catherine de Bourgh."

The woman nodded, her eyes suddenly wide. Then Matlock stepped away, drawing Darcy and Fitzwilliam with him, returning to the carriage before he looked at them. Darcy noted the woman was still in the door to the parsonage watching them, her mouth wide open in shock.

"Collins has had plenty of time to return from Hertfordshire," said Darcy, concern flooding him at the man's absence. "The confrontation happened soon after mid-day."

"But you did not confirm he had returned."

Darcy exchanged a look with Fitzwilliam. "It never occurred to me that he might not."

"I believe we erred in that, Darcy," replied Fitzwilliam. "If he is not in Kent, I suspect he is still in Hertfordshire. There is no telling what he means to do."

Darkness descended over Darcy's eyes, fury at the notion that Collins may have some devilry in mind. Darcy was not certain he had Miss Elizabeth's esteem and could not say if she would ever love him, but he would be damned before he would allow anyone to hurt her or force her into that which she did not wish.

"Then we had best return with all speed," said Matlock. "I suspect he is up to no good."

As one they returned to the carriage, Darcy instructing the driver to proceed with all haste to London and from thence to Hertfordshire. Then he climbed into it with his cousins.

"Even at speed," said Matlock, "it is several hours to London and several more north to Hertfordshire. We can change horses in London."

"I have a better idea," said Fitzwilliam. "When we reach London, we can leave the carriage and proceed north on horseback. We will make better time that way."

Darcy nodded his agreement. "Then that is what we will do. Heaven help Collins if he harms the Bennets."

"I could not have said it better, Cousin," growled Fitzwilliam.

Not only did thoughts of Lydia and Charlotte's words plague Elizabeth throughout the night, but they rendered her inattentive the next day. A part of her wished to deny what they had told her, to cleave to her belief that there was nothing of truth in them, but try as she might, she could not.

Duty. That was a thought foremost in her mind during those hours. Was it not her duty to look after Longbourn and ensure its solvency for her brother when he came of age to inherit? It was, she decided, and that firmed her resolve to think on the matter no more. Then the words of her uncle and aunt returned to her mind, and she knew it was silly to deny herself happiness on such grounds. It would not be difficult to manage an estate such as Longbourn from afar, provided she had a good steward in place. And a husband could assist—Mr. Darcy was a man possessing deep knowledge of what was to be done. Could he not manage the place better than she could ever hope to herself?

When those thoughts failed to resolve Elizabeth's inner turmoil, she turned to the man himself. Mr. Darcy had been pleasant, civil, had conversed with her intelligently, his opinions interesting and provoking her to consider her own. What she had never seen from him, however, was the depth of attraction or affection Elizabeth had always thought a man should show for the woman he favored.

Or had he? The longer Elizabeth thought on the matter, the more she believed she had been blind. Or not blind, precisely, as she had noted something of it. Duty, however, had pushed such considerations to the back of her mind, for she had not wished to consider them. And for what? For a misguided desire to fulfill her father's wishes and see to her brother's future? What of her future?

The more Elizabeth thought on the matter, the more she realized that Mr. Darcy's affections for her had been in plain sight, certainly since he had returned to Hertfordshire, but also before. He was not an open man like Mr. Bingley, and he was not a jovial man like Colonel Fitzwilliam. But in his quiet way, with his attention, his deference to her opinions, a touch here or a look there, he had informed her in words as loud as any man had ever spoken of his esteem for her.

That provoked the next and perhaps most important question: was Elizabeth in love with him too? A lengthy consideration of this question informed Elizabeth that she was not in love with him. How could she be? She had spent so much time focused on her duty, pushing her notice of his affection away from her that she had no time to rise to that blissful state. Along with this conviction, however, came the realization that it would take very little for her to bridge the distance. Allowing herself to feel his love, to consider the possibility of it herself would be enough to push her over the edge and meet him with as much affection as he held for her.

It could not be supposed that a day spent in the company of her sisters and the ladies of Netherfield could pass without someone noticing her introspection. Indeed, Elizabeth was certain they were all aware of it, and several comments proved her supposition.

"You have been dull, today, Lizzy," said Kitty as they sat down to luncheon. Kitty, Elizabeth thought, was not as observant as Lydia, had likely not seen as much of Mr. Darcy's actions, and was thus ignorant of the reason for her behavior.

"Perhaps there is something on her mind," said Charity, fixing Elizabeth with an amused look.

"Or someone," said Anne in a tone just audible to the rest of the diners.

The general laughter did not bother Elizabeth in the slightest, though she could not help but wonder that most of her friends and sisters had realized the truth long before she had herself. It did not speak well to her powers of observation as Lydia had pointed out the previous evening.

Those were not the only comments she endured that day, but they were the most blatant. Elizabeth ignored them as best she could and after luncheon, she found herself better able to focus on their guests rather than worrying the problem over in her mind.

Mr. Bingley came to call soon after, the gentleman's jovial spirits lightening an already ebullient mood. It did not escape Elizabeth's notice that the man focused his attention on Mary once he had assured himself that they were all well. Elizabeth might have observed them together if it were not for a brief encounter with Lady Catherine that further clarified her thoughts.

"It seems Mr. Bingley is intent upon your sister, Miss Elizabeth."

"It is something we have all noticed," replied Elizabeth. "I have no notion what he means by it, but he seems to take care for her feelings."

"Yes, I would expect nothing else of him." Lady Catherine turned her attention away from Elizabeth's sister. "How are matters on the estate?"

"I have nothing for which to complain," replied Elizabeth. "Mr. Whitmore is an excellent steward, and the planting is complete. I hope, with the improvements Mr. Darcy suggested, our profitability will further improve."

Mentioning Mr. Darcy proved to be a mistake, for no sooner had the words left her mouth than thoughts of the gentleman filled her yet again. That Lady Catherine noted it was apparent in the long look she gave Elizabeth, a look which caused her to blush.

"I might speak of anecdotes of my experience in estate

management," replied the lady after a moment, "but I suspect there are other, more pressing matters to consider. It seems your eyes have been opened to the reality of the situation with my nephew, though I will own I was quite diverted that it was your youngest sister who took you to task."

By this time Elizabeth's cheeks were burning. "You heard?" asked she, though she knew it came out as little more than a squeak.

"Not by design," replied Lady Catherine. "I had occasion to speak to Anne, and I was near enough to your room to hear a little of what your sister said, and then Miss Lucas after."

Shaking her head, Elizabeth sighed and shook her head. "I am so confused."

"And I am not the one to relieve that confusion," said Lady Catherine. "After all, for many years I wished for Darcy to make a match with my Anne, and if I am honest, I will confess that desire has not left me."

"It is not my intention to impose myself," was Elizabeth's quiet reply.

"No, I do not suppose it is." Lady Catherine paused and sighed, her mien now appearing a little moody. "As my daughter has made it clear in no uncertain terms that she does not mean to marry Darcy, it seems I have little influence in the matter. It is not a case of you inserting yourself where you are not wanted, Miss Elizabeth.

"The important factor for you to consider is the contents of your own heart." The smile with which the lady fixed her was unfeigned. "I hope you will not take offense when I suggest that connections or fortune are not matters to consider, for you have little to give."

"Not at all," said Elizabeth. "Of this, I am well aware."

"I am certain you are," murmured Lady Catherine. "Then that leaves nothing other than matters of the heart. I cannot tell you what to feel, nor would I attempt to do so. Yet I ask you to be certain, for my nephew is a man who feels deeply. With the example of his parents' close relationship, I am certain he wants the same. Do not break his heart. At the same time, do not allow anything else to stand in your way—not the situation at Longbourn, the opinions of others, or anything else unconnected with you. Act based on what you feel for him. If you do so, I shall be content."

It was advice Elizabeth might not have expected from Lady Catherine, yet excellent counsel all the same. It also had the effect of pushing Elizabeth back into her thoughts. After a time, Mr. Bingley rose, saying he should return to his estate, but Elizabeth only gave him a cursory farewell as the gentleman departed. When he was gone, Elizabeth rose herself, intending to remove from them all for a time to allow her thoughts time to settle. There had always been one activity that more than any other allowed her to think.

"It would be best if you did not walk out, Lizzy," said Jane with some concern when Elizabeth made her intentions known.

"I do not mean to go far, Jane. Only to the back lawn and only for a short time." To the rest of the ladies, she smiled and added: "I find my thoughts are a jumble today, and walking has always helped me bring some sense to them. I shall not be long."

The grins to which they subjected her informed Elizabeth they all knew of what she wished to think, and there were no more objections. If they kept to their original schedule, the gentlemen had already taken Mr. Collins to task, and her Uncle Phillips was preparing a lawsuit against the parson. Besides, she was not walking country lanes that morning and thought she would be safe enough.

Before long, Elizabeth was engaged in her favorite pastime, and if the gardens were not her beloved paths, the sunshine on her face soothed her and pushed her worries to the side. The calming effect of the wind on her face removed her harried thoughts, and she reveled in the simple pleasures. And then she decided there was nothing to do on the matter of Mr. Darcy.

Or perhaps there was. When the gentleman had departed the previous day, Elizabeth had witnessed a tightening of his guard, distress about him that spoke to his dismay for her lack of response to him. That must be corrected, she knew. How she would go about it, Elizabeth could not say, but she knew she needed to show him she was now open to the possibility of a future with him. To leave him in suspense was unconscionable, as Lydia had pointed out.

"At last, I have you alone."

Startled by the sound of a voice so near, Elizabeth turned to see Mr. Collins step from the woods at the back of the property out onto the grass. He was dirty and unkempt as if he had rolled about in the dirt of the forest, his eyes crazed and fixed upon her. Elizabeth took an involuntary step back in alarm, an action which provoked a cruel smile from her father's cousin.

"You have been most disobliging, Cousin, you and your family. But you shall not cheat me of my due. If I cannot have Longbourn, at least I can have control over it until your *brother* is of age."

The way he spat the word filled Elizabeth with anger. She squared her shoulders and glared at him. "You shall have nothing of

Longbourn or any of us. You repulse me, Mr. Collins, for you are no man of the clergy."

The man's eyes narrowed. "If I cannot persuade you, compromising you will do the trick."

At that moment, another man emerged from the trees behind Mr. Collins. "Here, what is this? Why are you bothering the mistress?"

The sound cause Mr. Collins to spin around with a muffled oath, and he looked into the countenance of Mr. Bates, who was watching him with disdain.

"It is none of your concern," spat Mr. Collins. "Return to your farm, or I shall remove you when I am master of the estate."

"A position you shall never hold," said Elizabeth.

"Oh, in that you are incorrect," replied Mr. Collins. "I shall have it soon. And you are my means of having it."

Unable to endure anymore, Mr. Bates moved forward and put himself between the parson and Elizabeth. "No, you shall not. The mistress requires you to leave, *sir*. You shall do so at once."

"Out of my way!" screamed Mr. Collins, all pretense at control now gone.

"You shall not harm the mistress," repeated Mr. Bates.

The parson stepped forward and attempted to remove Mr. Bates from his path, but the gamekeeper was immovable as a mountain. The relative sizes of the gentlemen made it impossible for Mr. Collins to dislodge the man, for while he was taller, Mr. Collins was all knobby knees and spindly appendages, whereas Mr. Bates was a stocky man, likely weighing several stone more than Mr. Collins.

At last, Mr. Collins, seeming so incensed he could hardly see, swung out with one fist to strike Mr. Bates. The man only laughed and stepped to the side, allowing an overbalanced Mr. Collins to tumble to the ground.

It seemed the confrontation had not gone unnoticed from the house, for around the corner Mr. Bingley appeared, with the footmen and all the ladies in tow. The men quickly surrounded Mr. Collins, who gave them uneasy looks as he got to his feet. It appeared four to one odds were too much for him to attempt to get to Elizabeth again, though his hateful look at her spoke of his anger.

"Miss Elizabeth," said Lady Catherine as she eyed her parson with no little distaste, "did your uncles instruct you to call the constable should Mr. Collins return to Longbourn?"

"They did," confirmed Elizabeth.

"Then I suggest you do so now. It seems nothing else will prevent him from importuning you. For my part, I mean to speak to his bishop, for I would not have a man such as he continue to oversee the spiritual wellbeing of my parish."

"But Lady Catherine!" cried the parson.

"No, Mr. Collins, I am done speaking with you. By your actions, you have proven yourself unfit for that collar you wear. When my nephews return, we shall discover your reasons for acting as you have. Until then, I suggest you do not make matters worse for yourself."

With wild eyes, Mr. Collins started forward, though Elizabeth could not determine what he was about. John, however, put his hand on the man's chest, preventing him from moving again.

"Do not make me subdue you, *sir*. You will not like the result."

The determined countenances of the rest of the men, including Mr. Bates's glower and Mr. Bingley's hard glare seemed to convince him he had best behave. Mr. Collins's shoulders slumped, a clear signal of his defeat.

CHAPTER XXIX

*T*he clatter of the carriage's wheels on the gravel road provided cover to Elizabeth's thoughts at that moment. While she might have thought her mind would be fixed on the confrontation that afternoon with Mr. Collins on Longbourn's back lawn, such was not foremost in her mind. Indeed, little other than Mr. Darcy could hold her attention. The gentleman appeared to have that effect on her.

The memory of his return flitted before her eyes, the concern flowing from him in waves, washing up against her like the gentle caress of a tide on a calm beach. His eyes fixed upon her had both warmed and confused her, the confusion stemming from how she had not seen his regard before. Elizabeth wondered how she had missed it.

"Then you are well," confirmed the gentleman when they had related particulars of the events to him.

"I am," replied Elizabeth, her tone quiet, for she was still uncertain how she should behave toward this man. "Mr. Bates protected me, and Mr. Bingley and John assisted to bring Mr. Collins to heel."

"And we shall need to thank Bates when we see him again," said Colonel Fitzwilliam. "And you too, Bingley."

"It is no trouble," replied Mr. Bingley with a grin. "I had departed for Pulvis Lodge, for I had thought there was no danger. As I went, however, I happened to see a figure passing through the trees and wondered who it could be. I returned to the estate and rousted the footmen to see who it was."

"It seems you guessed correctly," observed Mr. Darcy.

"As I say," replied Mr. Bingley, "I was happy to help."

"Now that you are here," said Lady Catherine, "I believe it is time to brave my parson's silliness and discover what has made him act in the way he has. For this, I pledge myself, for I believe we have a greater chance of inducing him to answer my questions than anyone else."

"He will answer," muttered Colonel Fitzwilliam. "If he wishes to keep his teeth, he will answer whatever question we put to him."

"While your bloodlust is understandable," said Lord Matlock, a man Elizabeth was certain was much like his brother, "a softer approach might be desirable over a blunt instrument in this instance. To make this Mr. Collins aware of the implied threat, however, I shall offer my support, for I suspect my position will intimidate him."

"I also wish to go," said Elizabeth, her elder sister nodding by her side. "Mr. Collins owes us an explanation for why he has continued to torment us these past months."

That, predictably, brought a chorus of requests to accompany them from her youngest sisters. A look at Lydia confirmed her sister wished to scream in the parson's face for behaving in such a manner, an opportunity Elizabeth had no intention of allowing.

"No, Lydia," said Elizabeth into the noise a moment later. "Jane and I shall go. You, Mary, and Kitty will remain here."

"Listen to your elder sister," said Lady Catherine, not unkindly, when Lydia made to protest. "With myself, my nephews, and your eldest sisters present, that will be more than sufficient for the moment."

"It will," said Elizabeth. "I have not frequented our town's prison, but given what I know of it, I suspect it will be difficult to fit us all in."

This had led to Elizabeth's current position, ensconced in the de Bourgh carriage with Jane and Lady Catherine, the gentlemen traveling in Colonel Fitzwilliam's conveyance. It could not be said that her younger sisters were sanguine about being prevented from going with them, yet Lady Catherine had such a manner about her as to be impervious to any entreaties to the contrary. To her credit, Lydia had made little further protest and had agreed to stay at Longbourn, with Charity, Anne, and Georgiana, Mr. Bingley remaining to watch over them all.

Within moments, the carriage rolled to a stop in front of the prison and the footman opened the door and handed them out. The man was, Elizabeth knew, a trusted retainer of Mr. Darcy's, a large and intimidating man, one she knew Mr. Darcy had tasked with looking after them. Elizabeth presumed he would be present for Mr. Collins's interrogation, his fearsome visage a deterrent against Mr. Collins's misbehavior.

The constable was not present at the moment, the prison being watched by one of his deputies. When they asked the man to retrieve Mr. Collins from his cell, he complied readily enough with a grunt and no other response. The ladies seated themselves in a few sparse chairs the building boasted, while the gentlemen stood nearby, the final chair reserved for the unfortunate parson, to better be able to intimidate him, or so Elizabeth thought, though the small size of the room also played a part.

The cells were located a short distance down the hall from the constable's office, and the man soon escorted the parson into the room. Mr. Collins's countenance blanched at seeing the array of faces glowering at him and made no protest when the deputy led him to the chair and saw him seated. Then he turned to the gentlemen.

"Begging your pardon, but the constable would like to know how long we must hold him here."

"That is yet to be determined," said Mr. Darcy, "but I suspect it shall not be long. When we know what has motivated him, we shall better understand what to do with him."

Mr. Collins blanched, but the deputy just nodded and took himself from the room. For a moment, silence settled over them all. For the parson's part, he seemed to feel the effects of their scrutiny, for he fidgeted, appearing the schoolboy called into the headmaster's office for some misbehavior.

"Well, Mr. Collins?" asked Lady Catherine, the first of their number to speak. "What do you have to say for yourself?"

A spasm of anger passed over the parson's face, but a rustle of movement from the large footman removed any further defiance from him. Instead of answering, Mr. Collins grimaced and did not speak.

"Mr. Collins," said Lady Catherine in a voice of exaggerated patience, "I believe I asked you a question. Can you justify your actions?"

"My cousins—"

"Owe you nothing and have not wronged you," interrupted the impatient voice of Mr. Darcy. "Do not continue to use that grievance,

Collins, for we all know the truth of the matter. Do not mention your supposed complaint again or it will go ill with you."

"It has long been my opinion," interjected Elizabeth, "that there was some motivating factor behind your refusal to accept what happened, beyond your disappointment at not inheriting Longbourn. When you appeared yesterday, your words and actions suggested you meant my brother harm; no rational man would threaten an infant."

"B-But . . . I never . . ." sputtered the parson, turning indignant.

"I am highly insulted you would think that of me, Cousin!" spat he when he had regained control over his wits.

"Do you not think she had cause?" demanded Colonel Fitzwilliam.

Mr. Collins turned a sour look on him and refused to respond.

"Mr. Collins," said Lady Catherine again, bringing the man's attention to her. "It is apparent that I erred when I did not take the time to investigate you when I returned to Rosings in January. Miss Elizabeth is correct, I suspect—there is something beyond disappointment motivating you, and I wish to know what it is. You will inform me now."

Elizabeth might not have credited it, but Mr. Collins turned away and shook his head, refusing to speak to her. Lady Catherine's lips tightened in response, and Lord Matlock spoke into the void.

"Mr. Collins, do you know who we are?"

The parson studied him for a moment. "Based on the resemblance, I suspect you are a relation to her ladyship. Perhaps her nephews?"

"You are correct, Mr. Collins. My brother, Anthony, I believe you have met before; he is leasing the estate neighboring Longbourn. My cousin Darcy has been staying with him—I believe you might have seen them when you trespassed on Longbourn lands after the death of the Miss Bennets' mother. What you do not know is that I am Anthony's elder brother, and also the Earl of Matlock."

Eyes widened with astonishment and encroaching horror, Mr. Collins gaped at him.

"As you did not know," said the earl, his tone conversational, "I shall not take offense at the way you have addressed me." Lord Matlock paused and his gaze turned hard. "You should know, Mr. Collins, that I am now very much in control of your future. If you wish to have any hope of future prosperity or freedom, I suggest you answer our questions. I can have you on a ship bound for Botany Bay by next week. Either there or a scaffold to send you to hell. I suggest you tell us what we wish to know."

It was several more moments before Mr. Collins's open-mouthed stare of astonishment turned to abject fear. Little though he wished it, the moment of his capitulation arrived in his downcast and sullen glare down at his feet. It appeared his lordship understood the man's surrender himself, for he glanced at his aunt and cheerfully motioned for her to continue her interrogation.

"Little pleased though I am at your unwillingness to oblige me," said Lady Catherine with a sniff, "the question Miss Elizabeth posed remains. Why were you so intent upon procuring Longbourn for your own when lawfully it was not?"

The man squirmed in his seat, but at length, he responded: "I had little choice. I have . . . accumulated some small amount of debt and have no means of repaying it at present. Longbourn was to be my means of dispensing with that debt."

"Debt?" asked Lady Catherine with a frown. "What do you mean, Mr. Collins? Hunsford is not an insignificant living. How could you have amassed such debt as to render you unable to repay?"

A movement caught Elizabeth's attention, and she looked up to see Mr. Darcy gazing at Mr. Collins, his intensity enough to intimidate any man. It was to Mr. Collins's fortune that he was still gazing down at his feet and did not see it, and his misfortune that Mr. Darcy spoke when he was reluctant.

"They are debts of honor, are they not? Gaming debts."

The way Mr. Collins's eyes darted to Mr. Darcy suggested disbelief. It also removed any doubt about the truth of the matter.

"You are an idiot, Collins," said Colonel Fitzwilliam. "We have had experience with those who allow themselves to succumb to the lust for the gaming tables. Even if you gained Longbourn, I have little doubt you would have bankrupted the estate due to an inability to refrain from returning thither, for it is an insidious habit."

"What I would like to know," interjected Elizabeth, "is how much you owe. Longbourn is not a large estate and cannot sustain such habits for long. How much did you mean to take from the estate to fund your immediate debts?"

Mr. Collins regarded her, unwilling to respond. Elizabeth thought the only reason he did was because Lord Matlock cleared his throat and, when Mr. Collins glanced at him, fixed him with a stern look, suggesting he reply.

"I owe about five thousand pounds."

Shocked silence reigned for a moment before Elizabeth's anger exploded. "You witless worm! Longbourn produces two thousand pounds per annum. It could never support such debts. How did you suppose you could have funded such debts on such a small estate? What manner of man are you?"

"A wicked man," interjected Colonel Fitzwilliam.

"I would like an answer, Mr. Collins," said Elizabeth, her voice frigid, her look no less than a bludgeon. "Even if you gained nominal control over the estate through marriage to me, we do not have the capital to make such an expenditure. How did you suppose you could pay off that debt?"

"Mama's dowry."

Stunned, Elizabeth turned to her sister, who she noted was glaring at Mr. Collins in a fashion most unlike her. One look at the parson informed Elizabeth that her sister had the right of it, for the parson's mien screamed his guilt, his look back down at his feet confirmed it.

In a rush, Elizabeth stood, bringing Mr. Collins's eyes back to her. "I restate my opinion, Mr. Collins: I know of no more contemptible, selfish man than you. I have no wish to lay eyes on you again and hope that Lord Matlock sees fit to punish you in a manner which you deserve. But I shall stay and trade words with you no longer."

With a final glare of contempt, Elizabeth marched from the building. Once outside, she looked up and down the street, wishing to stalk the length of it as an outlet for her fury and frustration. There were, however, still people present, and as she did not wish to draw attention to herself, she contented herself with kicking at a nearby rock and folding her arms around her own frame, still feeling the shock of what Mr. Collins had revealed. Then Jane was there, folding her in an embrace, one that Elizabeth returned fiercely.

"I could never have imagined he was so loathsome," said Elizabeth, clinging to Jane, feeling she was about to burst into tears. "To scheme to remove Longbourn from its rightful heir, to plan to use our mother's dowry to save himself—what manner of man is Mr. Collins?"

"A man apparently without morals," replied Jane. "Given some of what Father said of old Mr. Collins, I suppose it cannot be much of a surprise."

That was an aspect Elizabeth had not considered before. "I suppose you must be correct. There is also the matter of his intentions for Joseph, which I am still not convinced were not malevolent. At least, I suspect they might have turned to evil if he had insinuated himself into our midst."

It was a mark of Jane's disgust with the man that she did not attempt to gainsay Elizabeth. They stood in silence for some moments, each relishing the other's company. When they separated it was to stand close to each other, each lost in their thoughts.

Elizabeth thought it was perhaps fifteen minutes later that the door opened, and the gentlemen, in Lady Catherine's company, exited the building. Then she looked up and, noting the position of the sun, thought her estimate might be a little low, considering how far it had descended. It seemed she had been lost in the wilderness of her thoughts for longer than she believed.

"There are a few other specifics we must explain," said Lady Catherine when she reached them, "but the main street in Meryton is not the place for them. Let us return to Longbourn, and we shall attempt to convey what Mr. Collins told us."

To the general agreement of all, they made their way to the carriages and entered for the return journey to Longbourn.

When they arrived at the estate, Jane went to Mrs. Hill to see about dinner, the invitation to dine with them extended in the carriage. Lady Catherine accepted on behalf of the Netherfield party, and Jane informed them she would invite Mr. Bingley when she entered the house. The sight of Mr. Bates loitering near the entrance of the estate, however, prevented Elizabeth from following her sister.

"Mr. Bates," greeted Elizabeth upon seeing him, noting the man knuckled his forehead with far more respect than Elizabeth had ever seen him offer. "Thank you for your help today with Mr. Collins."

"Ach, it is nothing, Miss Bennet," said he. "I am only happy he weren't successful in compromising you. I hope we can all expect he will not inherit should something happen to your brother."

"That chance has all but evaporated, Mr. Bates," said Mr. Darcy. "Your assistance today was essential, sir. We cannot express our gratitude enough."

"It were no trouble," replied the groundskeeper. "I tracked his progress through the estate when he confronted you. He spent the night in one of the derelict cottages, and I knew he was up to no good. You have been good to me, Miss Bennet—I couldn't allow him to harm you."

Elizabeth's eyes met Mr. Darcy's, noting the tenderness she had missed before, and then returned to Mr. Bates. "Then I thank you again, sir."

With a gruff nod, Mr. Bates turned and departed, leaving those remaining watching after him.

"It seems Mr. Bates has proven his mettle," said Colonel Fitzwilliam. "But who would have believed the way he did it?"

"There is something estimable in all god's creations," said Lady Catherine. Then she paused and a look of distaste came over her face. "Except perhaps in the person of my former parson."

"Let us go inside, Lady Catherine," said Mr. Darcy. "It is time we addressed this business of Mr. Collins and then put it behind us forever."

Her ladyship nodded, allowing her nephews to lead her and Elizabeth into the house. When they had divested themselves of their outerwear, they followed the sounds of conversation into the sitting-room, where they found the rest of the company already assembled. Jane informed Elizabeth that dinner would be served in thirty minutes, and she smiled gratefully at her sister.

Elizabeth took it upon herself to explain what had happened at the jail, detailing the offenses Mr. Collins had contemplated against them. The indignation of her sisters was the equal of what Elizabeth had felt, though even Lydia refrained from railing against the parson for his black deeds.

When she had finished explaining what she knew, Elizabeth turned to the gentlemen. "Shall you not inform us of what happened after Jane and I left?"

"In essence, Miss Elizabeth," said Mr. Darcy, "it was more of the same as what you witnessed. Mr. Collins, it seems, felt his defeat, for he made no further attempt to defend himself. He confirmed his intention to use your mother's dowry to pay off his immediate debts and insisted he intended to give up his gambling ways."

Colonel Fitzwilliam snorted his disdain. "I have seen enough men caught in the vice to suspect that Mr. Collins would have succumbed again. It is more likely he would have ended in debtors' prison, given he could not sell a part or all of the estate should he accumulate more debt."

"Unless he meant my brother harm," said Elizabeth.

The gasps from her sisters told Elizabeth that they had not considered such a possibility, and Kitty, who was holding Joseph, drew the babe close to her breast.

"That is something Mr. Collins denied and would not recant," said Mr. Darcy. Then the gentleman grimaced and shook his head. "But we all know that desperation can push a man to actions he would otherwise not contemplate."

"Regardless," said Lady Catherine, "Joseph is safe, so there is no reason to belabor the point."

"Is there anything else?" asked Elizabeth, bringing the discussion back into focus.

"Nothing of consequence concerning Mr. Collins," said Lord Matlock, who had heretofore remained silent. "In the end, I think that is more than enough to convict him. Therefore, I shall arrange for Mr. Collins to depart on a ship bound for Botany Bay. There, he will work off his debt, for he has no means of ever paying it back."

"And for that, I have pledged myself," said Lady Catherine.

While Elizabeth gawked at the lady, Mr. Darcy gave her a disapproving glare. "I still do not agree with your determination, Lady Catherine."

"I did not ask for your approval," said the lady with a sniff. "Mr. Collins is my responsibility. I should have looked more closely into his activities, and in that, I failed. If I had done so, I might have prevented this."

"It seems to me you have little ground to stand on, Darcy," said Colonel Fitzwilliam. "If you consider all the times you insisted on paying Wickham's debts, for you to take Aunt Catherine to task for the same thing is more than a little silly."

Mr. Darcy grimaced, but he did not respond, allowing Lady Catherine to speak again. "If I do not, Mr. Collins will waste away in Marshalsea for the rest of his life. I feel some responsibility for him and mean to pay his debts. That way, we may safely send him across the ocean and put him forever beyond the ability to stir up more trouble here." Lady Catherine paused and her lip curled in a moue of distaste. "It is unfortunate, indeed, that Mr. Collins is in debt to one of the worst gamesters in all Kent, but I shall meet his obligation, nonetheless."

There was little more to say on the matter, and no one else attempted it. Elizabeth thought to ask after the identity of the man to whom Mr. Collins was indebted, but she remained silent, for knowing his name would accomplish little.

Mary then turned to the next question, one that had occurred to her too. "Then what becomes of the entail? It is still in force until Joseph is old enough to inherit."

"That I do not know," confessed Elizabeth. "As far as I am aware, Mr. Collins was the last possible heir under the terms of the entail. What happens when he is sent to a penal colony, I am afraid I cannot say. That is a question we must ask of Uncle Phillips."

"In most instances," said Mr. Darcy, "I believe it reverts to the will of the most recent of age master, which would be your father. I suspect there is a provision in his will should there be no remaining heirs."

Elizabeth made a note to herself to ask her uncle for his opinion when next she saw him. Regardless, she would need to speak to him the following day and acquaint him with what had happened with Mr. Collins that evening.

"Is there anything else?" asked Elizabeth after a moment.

"Nothing of any note," replied Lady Catherine. "Mr. Collins truly is a silly man underneath his malevolence. Until the end, he kept informing us he would not give up his right to Longbourn—and Hunsford, for that matter—for he said it would be difficult to find another parish. Beyond the obvious blindness he displays in thinking we would allow him to keep his status as a parson, let alone ever acting in that capacity again, he was slow to understand that he will leave these shores, never to return."

"You should not believe it, Aunt," corrected Lord Matlock. "I am certain Mr. Collins understood it well enough. He simply did not believe I was in earnest when I spoke of my determination to see him transported."

"I dare say he is in no doubt now," said Colonel Fitzwilliam.

Lord Matlock snorted his disdain, appearing every inch the haughty noble. "I hope so. Had the idiot said a single word more I might have run him through."

"Then that is the end of our troubles with Mr. Collins," said Elizabeth with a sigh. "Thank you all for all you have done to assist. It has been invaluable."

As the call had not yet come for dinner, the party remained where they were, discussing the events of the day. Charity and Anne sat close, seeming to wish to assure themselves that Elizabeth was safe, rendering her grateful for their unstinting support and friendship.

But while her friends chattered, Elizabeth's thoughts returned to Mr. Darcy. The gentleman sat on another chair, one distant from Elizabeth's, unlike his custom of situating himself close to her. Elizabeth wondered what the gentleman was thinking, imagining she played a large part in his thoughts. But he did not look at her and remained separate throughout the evening.

The thoughts and feelings she had considered the previous night and throughout the day until the business with Mr. Collins forced it from her mind returned to Elizabeth, distracting her for the rest of the evening. Elizabeth did not know what to do about the gentleman, what she should do about the intelligence Charlotte, Lydia, and Lady Catherine had imparted to her.

What was clear was that she would need to act quickly, whatever she meant to do. Elizabeth did not know how she knew this, but some sense informed her that she must do something quickly.

CHAPTER XXX

*S*o, you mean to return to Pemberley?"

Contemplating his breakfast plate before him, Darcy had not been attending his cousin, as Fitzwilliam had been quiet since they had sat down that morning. Matlock had not yet joined them, allowing the two cousins to speak in private. The matter was one he had been considering, however, and if Darcy was not yet certain of the answer, he was not averse to speaking of it.

"I do not know," said he, opting for a candid reply.

Fitzwilliam eyed him, curiosity written upon his brow. "It is unlike you to be so indecisive, Darcy."

"Perhaps it is. But I have never been in a situation such as this." Darcy paused and gave his cousin a wry smile. "As you know, I am much more apt to flee from ladies. I find myself at sea now that I have found one I can tolerate."

"More than tolerate, I should say," replied Fitzwilliam with a snort. "The question is whether you are willing to fight to gain her favor."

"A gentleman does not push his suit where there is no welcome."

Fitzwilliam cocked an eyebrow. "Are you certain she does not wish for it? And furthermore, it seems to me that such a stodgy response is more likely to condemn you to a lonely and miserable life when you could have so much more."

The observation was apropos, such that Darcy could not muster a response. A response was not something Fitzwilliam required.

"It seems to me, Cousin, that you have two options open to you. You could return to Pemberley and remain miserable, or you could be more open with Miss Elizabeth, inform her of your feelings, and ask if you may earn her regard. The second is, of course, a viable path to happiness."

Considering his cousin's suggestion, Darcy nodded, albeit slowly. "Yes, that is possible, I suppose. Part of me fears her answer, however."

"But then you would have an answer," replied Fitzwilliam, fixing Darcy with a pointed look. "If you leave, you will have nothing but supposition for what she might have said, whereas if she rejects you, at least you will no longer live in doubt.

"In my opinion," continued Fitzwilliam, rising from the table, raising his napkin to his mouth, "I suspect there is something else at work with Miss Elizabeth, though I will own I cannot say what it is. Regardless, I do not think she is indifferent to you. But the choice, of course, is your own to make."

Then Fitzwilliam excused himself, citing a need to see to some tasks in his study. Whereas Darcy might have accompanied him to attend to such tasks most mornings, his cousin did not invite him, likely knowing Darcy needed to consider matters and arrive at a solution to his dilemma. It may have been a welcome distraction, but Darcy knew his cousin was correct, that he should consider his words and come to his own decision.

The question was, Darcy decided when he had situated himself in the library, leaving his half-eaten breakfast, whether he should take the chance his cousin had suggested. There was no question as to Miss Bennet's worth—she, the one perfectly suited to him, he thought, a woman any man would be fortunate if he could only provoke her regard. Similarly, there was no question about Darcy's fortitude— again, his cousin had hit on the crux of the matter, for knowing the answer once and for all would either set him on a path to his happiness or forever put her out of his reach.

No, the question, and he was still uncertain of the answer, was whether it was proper for him to speak openly. Darcy thought long on that question, and in the end, he had to confess there was nothing improper about it. If the situation were different, if Darcy were pursuing a society match, he would approach her father—or herself, in this instance—and discuss the possibility of an alliance without hesitation. The courtship—official or unofficial—would follow. Then the difference between this situation and the one he considered was his feelings.

The clinical manner in which he thought of the different options available to him firmed Darcy's resolve. Darcy had always been a rational being, one for whom careful consideration of any decision had always come naturally. Affairs of the heart were by no means rational, but the decision to approach Miss Bennet was. Thus decided, he arose, determined to repair to Longbourn at once.

Before Darcy could take more than a step or two, however, the door opened, and the housekeeper ushered Miss Elizabeth into the room. Surprise filtered through Darcy's consciousness, and he stopped and stared at her, wondering what she was about. The other ladies were still at Longbourn after having stayed the night, rendering her sudden appearance inappropriate. But Darcy could not repine it, since it brought her into his presence that much sooner.

"Miss Elizabeth to see you, Mr. Darcy," said Mrs. Nichols, as these thoughts were passing through Darcy's mind.

"Thank you, Mrs. Nichols," replied Darcy with an absence of thought, the more part of his concentration on the woman before him. "You may leave us, but please leave the door open and station a footman outside."

Mrs. Nichols curtseyed and departed, though not without a significant look at Miss Elizabeth. For her part, the young woman appeared embarrassed at the scrutiny, as if she had suddenly realized the impropriety of her actions. To some extent, the realization heartened Darcy, for it spoke to some absence of mind on her part, an impulsivity behind her coming that might bode well.

"I am surprised to see you here, Miss Elizabeth," said Darcy when they were alone again. A rustle of movement beyond the door informed him that Mrs. Nichols had done as he asked, and there was now a footman there. "The ladies at Longbourn are all well, I trust."

"All very well," replied she, nervousness in her manner appearing past her embarrassment.

"And Lady Catherine?" asked Darcy, allowing a hint of jesting to appear in his tone. "I might have thought the lady would make her displeasure at your appearance here alone known to anyone within hearing distance."

Far from inducing the woman to laughter, her embarrassment worsened so much that her cheeks were flaming. For a moment, Darcy thought she could not respond until she plucked up her courage and looked at him.

"I hope to keep this matter from Lady Catherine's notice. I informed the company I would walk for a time."

That surprised Darcy. "You walked to Netherfield?"

"It is but three miles to Netherfield," said Miss Elizabeth, lifting her chin, her self-possession restored for the moment. "Less if one does not go through Meryton. I have often walked two miles to Oakham Mount and back, so I am well capable of it."

"Never would I have dreamed of suggesting otherwise," said Darcy, pleased to have put her more at ease. "Then shall we sit? Having traversed three miles to Netherfield to speak to me, I must assume a weighty reason for your coming."

Again, Miss Elizabeth blushed, though he was pleased when she took her place on the sofa. Sitting nearby, Darcy regarded her, noting her nervousness had returned if the twisting of her gloves in her hands were any indication. Seeing such a confident woman reduced to this state bemused Darcy, for he had never thought to see its like. It also gave him hope, such hope as he had never felt before. Surely, she would not be in this state for a mundane matter.

"Miss Elizabeth?" asked he gently after they sat for a moment in silence. "You have come to speak to me; might I know what you wish?"

Darcy was thinking she might not respond when she suddenly looked up at him and blurted: "Is it true you are in love with me?"

The question hung in the air between them, for her sudden question shocked him to silent, and Miss Elizabeth, when she realized what she had just said, blushed crimson, her color reaching heights Darcy had never thought to see. Then she looked down at her hands and seemed to take hold of herself, take in several deep breaths, and then looked up at him again.

"I apologize for my unseemly question, Mr. Darcy. Perhaps you will allow me to restate what I discovered?"

"By all means," said Darcy.

Another deep breath and Miss Bennet said: "In coming here today, I am aware that I am breaching propriety to an enormous degree. But when I thought on the matter, I decided if I did not act at once I might lose . . . something . . . precious, something I might never recover. The thought of that consequence filled me with consternation and would not allow me to remain silent, which is why I have come.

"It has . . . come to my attention that I have been . . . blind in my relations with you, that I have seen less than I should have. Indeed, as a woman who prides herself on a keenly honed ability to observe others' behavior, I must own that this has unsettled me. Even so, I must own that I suspect I have not seen everything there is to see in your conduct toward me, and I must clarify your meaning before I will know what to do."

Miss Elizabeth looked up at him, determination in her gaze, and said: "Thus, I ask you, sir, though I know it is improper, what are your intentions? Is there something to my sister and your aunt's assertions about your feelings for me?"

Pausing for a moment, Darcy considered how best to respond. The impulse to restrain himself, to answer with words guarded as was his custom was strong, for he had ever been a careful man. But then his cousin's words from that morning at the breakfast table rang through his memory, and Darcy knew only an open and honest answer would do. It did not appear he would feel the sting of disappointment if he only took a chance.

"There is little, I think, that your sister or my aunt might have said that could have exceeded the truth of my feelings for you."

Miss Elizabeth stared at him, shock etched upon her features. The only response she seemed capable of making was an ineloquent: "Oh."

"Oh, indeed," said Darcy, feeling amusement steal over him again. "Then am I to guess from your question that my attempts at lovemaking have been so inept as to escape your notice altogether?"

"No!" exclaimed Miss Elizabeth. Then she to realized she had burst out again, and she calmed herself with a visible effort. "I think, Mr. Darcy, that you must allow me to accept the blame, for I have been foolish." She paused and gave him a bashful smile. "I have long known you preferred my company, but the thought that you might be interested in me as more than a conversation partner never crossed my mind."

Miss Elizabeth paused and appeared embarrassed all over again. "Or rather, I believe I had noticed, but I dismissed it. My folly, I think, has been equal parts duty and an inability to accept what was staring me in the face."

"Duty I understand," said Darcy. "At times it can seem like a mountain. If you will pardon me, I suspect that in this instance you have allowed your sense of duty to blind you, to prevent you from entertaining such thoughts."

"There is a certain measure of truth in that," said Miss Elizabeth. "Having the management of Longbourn, I am determined to do well by my brother and ensure the estate, when it passes to his control, is as profitable as I can make it."

"That is a sentiment I can well understand. I feel it every time I look on my home and think of the ancestors who made Pemberley what it is today."

Smiling, Miss Elizabeth nodded but did not reply.

"If you still consider it an impediment," said Darcy, "you should remember that marrying will not make it impossible for you to continue to manage Longbourn. Yes, it makes it more difficult, but I have several satellite estates that I manage and only visit occasionally. Longbourn would become the same."

"Yes, that is true."

"And you should also remember that your husband would assist in those tasks, for he would not wish for anything other than the most profitable enterprise for your brother."

With a nod, Miss Elizabeth agreed before turning serious again. "The other question is about my brother's upbringing. Should he not be raised in the home he will eventually inherit?"

Darcy smiled, realizing that Miss Elizabeth was now attempting to make excuses for herself; Darcy was not about to allow it.

"That is not sound, Miss Elizabeth. What does it matter where we rear your brother? To me, the important points are that he is brought up to do you—and your father—credit and grows to adulthood knowing his heritage and his future.

"Furthermore, have you appointed yourself his guardian? Should Fitzwilliam, for example, purchase this estate and marry your sister, will raising him here not satisfy the need to raise him near his home?"

"I thought . . ." Miss Elizabeth paused and after a moment gave him a wry smile. "I supposed that as my father put me in control of Longbourn, that his care would fall to me. Then again, I was thinking I would remain at Longbourn at the same time."

"Then your thinking may be laced with fallacy," said Darcy, grinning, to which she responded without hesitation.

"When you put it that way, I suppose I have no choice but to capitulate."

"Excellent," said Darcy.

Then he leaned forward and looked her in the eyes, noting how gloriously lovely they were, as was everything about this woman. With a bit of daring, Darcy reached out and brushed the back of his fingers against the silky softness of her skin, prompting her to lean into his touch.

"The only question that remains, Miss Elizabeth, is whether you are as much in love with me as I am with you."

Miss Elizabeth gave him a little laugh. "Having fooled myself all these months, you can hardly expect that my feelings are the equal of yours."

"Perhaps not," replied Darcy, though in the confines of his mind he thought her feelings were more developed than she believed. "If you are not yet ready to confess undying love for me, I suppose I can afford to be patient for a time. At present, if you can assure me you are open to the possibility, I can be content."

Again, she crimsoned under his touch, but she plucked up her courage and said: "I believe it is possible, Mr. Darcy. In fact, I wonder I had not considered the prospect before."

"Then we shall discover it together, Miss Elizabeth," replied Darcy. "We have all the time in the world."

They stayed that way for some time, Darcy feathering light touches along her cheeks, wondering at the softness of her skin, at the possibilities that now seemed open to them, opportunities that had seemed closed only moments before. And as he did so, Darcy realized he could never have walked away from this woman until she had made it clear he had no chance of gaining her regard. To even attempt to do so would have been foolishness of the highest sort.

"Well, I must say that it is about time you realized it," said Colonel Fitzwilliam, for not the first time since their return to Longbourn. "I am certain everyone else saw it before you did, which leads me to wonder if you have had your eyes closed these past months."

The laughter at her expense did not bother Elizabeth in the slightest; she rather thought she deserved it, for it was nothing less than the truth.

"You may be correct, Colonel Fitzwilliam," replied Elizabeth, giving him a helpless shrug. "I will note that I have been distracted these past months."

"Yes, yes," interjected Lady Catherine, "you have not been thinking clearly. As a woman excessively attentive to all matters of propriety, I wonder at the audacity which led you to approach my nephew and apply to him in defiance of all common decency."

Elizabeth gave the lady a shrug. "Given how blind I had been, I feared I would lose all if I did not act at once. If that action was unorthodox, at least I have the chance of happiness I might not have otherwise had."

"Only you, Lizzy," said Lydia.

Giving her sister only the barest of her attention, Elizabeth instead focused on Mr. Darcy, noting how pleased he was that she had acted. Never had she felt like she might love him as she did at that moment.

"If you want my opinion," said Lord Matlock, "I think it is charming that Miss Elizabeth acted the way she did. Darcy has long decried ladies of society and their Machiavellian attempts to draw his attention. Had it been any other woman, I suspect he would have run for the hills."

A burst of laughter met his lordship's jest, and Elizabeth noted that Mr. Darcy laughed as much as anyone else. Lady Catherine, her sense of propriety offended, huffed and did not speak into the general merriment.

"I am curious," said Elizabeth as the laughter died down. "Did you all see what I could not?"

"It was clear to us all," said Jane, though Kitty's slightly bewildered look suggested that she, at least, had not suspected it as much as the rest.

"I certainly knew," said Charity. "Then again, with my inscrutable cousin, it was easy to see. The walls Darcy has built around himself prevent any woman from having any hope of scaling them, and yet he was as comfortable with you within moments of meeting you as he was with any of us."

"It was easy to see," added Anne. "I suspect that had you stepped back and allowed yourself to see beyond what was immediately before you, you would have noticed the same."

"Perhaps I might have," said Elizabeth, thinking back on the previous months. "I remember thinking a time or two that Mr. Darcy seemed to pay me more attention than I might have expected, and his behavior the day of Mr. Collins's coming confused me. Had you left me long enough, I might have puzzled it out for myself."

"But you did not," said a gleeful Lydia. "Thus, I shall always remember how I saw it first and had to confront you for you to see the truth!"

Again, they laughed, though Elizabeth contented herself with glaring at her sister, promising retribution. It was no surprise that her warning did nothing to remove the grin from Lydia's face.

"For my part," said Lord Matlock, "I must own that I am shocked and bemused by what has happened here in Hertfordshire." The earl paused and winked at Elizabeth. "It seems my family has found the Bennets irresistible, and if what I see before my eyes is correct, Bingley here is in the same conundrum."

Mr. Bingley, who had arrived some time earlier, grinned from where he sat beside Mary but made no other response.

"It appears you have all been infected by the same affliction, one that has led you all to become enamored with the ladies of a certain family. I struggle to account for it."

"If this is an infection," said Colonel Fitzwilliam, "I submit myself willingly to it." Then he shot a grin at his brother. "You should try it, James. Long have you and Darcy complained that ladies of society are not genuine and have nothing more than capturing a man of fortune on their minds. There are, you must see, two more Bennet sisters yet unattached."

"And the cats of London will howl if I should snatch one of them up!" rejoined Lord Matlock.

"Do not suggest such a thing!" said Lady Catherine, apparently horrified.

Though she supported Mr. Darcy and Colonel Fitzwilliam, it appeared a Bennet marrying the Earl of Matlock was a bridge she could not quite cross. Kitty and Lydia, rather than being insulted at the vehemence in her ladyship's exclamation, appeared instead diverted by it. Elizabeth noted Lydia did throw a saucy look in his lordship's direction, one that provoked him to release his mirth again.

"With all due respect to the youngest Miss Bennets, I suspect they are yet too young for me." Lord Matlock sighed and said: "Thus, I must continue to sift through the debutants in London to find that one woman who is not a shark in disguise."

"Then may I present my dearest friend as a potential bride?" asked Elizabeth, fixing Charlotte with an amused grin.

"Lizzy!" exclaimed Charlotte, who had sat quietly enjoying the banter.

"Do not allow her to fool you, your lordship," said Elizabeth, ignoring Charlotte's reproof. "Charlotte is an excellent woman, practical and intelligent, and would do you proud as your wife. And she is not as young as my youngest sisters."

The ladies—with the notable exception of Lady Catherine and Charlotte herself—tittered at Elizabeth's words. His lordship fixed her with an appraising look, causing her to blush, and then nodded to himself.

"Then perhaps we should allow nature to run its course. It would be music to my ears to hear those in London crying out their distress that a country miss has succeeded where they have failed."

Charlotte glared at Elizabeth and then turned a similar, though not as heated, expression on the earl. "I am practical, Lord Matlock, but I do not suppose I am that practical. The desire to befuddle society does not seem like a good foundation on which to build a marriage."

With a chuckle, his lordship shook his head. "I think you must be correct, Miss Lucas. And with those words, you have proven yourself more worthy than anyone in London. I cannot think of half a dozen young ladies there who would have refused me for any reason I chose to favor them with my attention."

"I can well imagine it," murmured Charlotte.

"Well, all is well that ends well," said Lydia, ignoring the fact that matters between Elizabeth and Mr. Darcy had not yet been settled. "I must wonder what my mother might have said if she were here to see this gathering. Hosting not only the sons and daughters of earls but an actual earl himself would have sent her scurrying for her salts!"

The Bennet sisters, having known their mother, responded to Lydia's jest with a melancholy sort of laughter. It was apropos, Elizabeth knew, for her mother could never have dreamed of hosting an earl.

"I hope I do not affect you in that way, Miss Lydia."

"Not at all," said she with a smile. "Had you not informed me of the matter yourself, I would not have known you were anything other than a gentleman."

Lord Matlock, to Elizabeth's eyes, was considering this information with some interest. As a man who had been subjected to others currying favor with him, while every woman he met would throw herself at him hoping to catch his fancy, she thought he had become somewhat jaded. Perhaps this visit to the country would do him good, though Elizabeth had no notion he would find a wife here.

The discussion turned to other matters, though there continued to be exclamations aplenty amid the excited comments of what had occurred that day. As she sat in the company of beloved family and friends, Elizabeth wondered if this was a scene that would continue throughout her life. And one look at Mr. Darcy told her it would. Mr. Darcy would not give her up, would not accept failure to provoke her regard. And Elizabeth knew she was not opposed to giving it to him. In fact, she felt she already had in many respects. For who would be cold enough they would not love him? It was unfathomable.

EPILOGUE

*L*ongbourn, on that day of all days, was anything but quiet. The house was abustle, servants moving this way and that while the young ladies who comprised the family were aflutter with excitement preparing for the day.

It was unlike that day more than a year ago now, the day Elizabeth had sat at her father's desk waiting to discuss what she and her sisters could expect from the future. Waited for the detestable Mr. Collins to come to Longbourn and claim his birthright. As Mr. Collins had been sent to Botany Bay and was gone from their lives, there was no further need to think of him. Occasions such as this, however, brought the recent past to mind, and with it the specter of Mr. Collins. So much had changed in the intervening year, so much had happened that had Elizabeth not lived it, she might not have believed so much could transpire in the space of twelve short months.

"What are you thinking, Lizzy?"

A warm smile formed at Elizabeth's lips and she turned to regard her sister, careful not to disturb the maid who was styling her hair for this, the most important of days.

"How much has happened. How much has changed. And above all, how fortunate we have been this past year despite our trials. I can hardly believe that I shall marry before the end of the day, when I thought not long ago my future, for at least the short term, comprised managing Longbourn against the day of Joseph's inheritance."

Mary smiled, her nod tempered with her usual seriousness of mind. "Yes, we have been blessed, indeed."

"What of you, Mary?" asked Elizabeth, curious, for her sister had spoken little of her future, being both reticent and intensely private. "Do you suppose Mr. Bingley will propose to you, and if he does, will you accept?"

The pause was wholly Mary, for Elizabeth knew she was uncomfortable speaking of herself. "Do you suggest I should think twice before accepting him?"

"I suggest no such thing," replied Elizabeth. "You are capable of choosing your path in life, Mary; if it comes to that, Mr. Bingley appears to be a very good sort of man. I only speak of certain . . . drawbacks associated to his situation."

Far from misunderstanding, Mary nodded, a pensive frown attached to her face. "That is a matter of which Mr. Bingley has already spoken."

"Oh?" asked Elizabeth, surprised to hear as much.

"No, he has not proposed, nor do I suppose he will do so soon. It seems, however, that Miss Bingley is now engaged, so the problem of his sister is moot."

That was a bit of news Elizabeth had not yet heard.

"As you know," continued Mary, "Miss Bingley stayed in London with Mr. and Mrs. Hurst with the explicit instructions that she was to find a husband. It seems she did not believe they were in earnest and continued as she was."

"And how did this lead her to being engaged?" asked Elizabeth.

Mary shook her head, as close to disdain for another that Mary would ever show. "It seems she made the mistake of informing a highborn friend of her brothers' demands for her future. The lady responded in a way that Miss Bingley could not misinterpret, and all but disabused her of any notion of her dream of marrying a man of high society to raise herself to that level. As I understand, the experience was humiliating for Miss Bingley as it occurred in front of many other friends."

"I can imagine it was," said Elizabeth. Given how her friends had spoken of the behavior of those with whom they mingled, Elizabeth could understand how Miss Bingley might have felt.

"That event seems to have made her more docile. The man she is to marry is a gentleman, but he is not on Mr. Darcy's level. I understand he owns an estate in Devon, but as it is much smaller than your future home and the man rarely comes to town, they expect to be in her company but little."

"That is a shame," murmured Elizabeth. Mary only grinned. "I am curious, Mary, for Mr. Bingley seems to have informed you of much that is unknown in the neighborhood."

Pinking at the observation, Mary ducked her head. "Well, I informed Mr. Bingley that I required complete openness from him. I was concerned he had turned to me because of some misguided notion of my being Jane's sister. I do not wish to be his second choice because he could not have Jane."

"That was well done, Mary," replied Elizabeth, filled with affection for the sister with whom she had never been close. "Anyone would wish for the same. Has he proven himself?"

"To a large extent, yes," replied Mary, raising her head, and regaining her composure. "He has told me he would often focus on what he considered the prettiest girl in any company with no thought given to her character or anything else. This business with his sister has, he feels, provoked him to mature. While he has yet to make any promises to me, I feel he knows me better than any woman with whom he has ever been infatuated. I feel, Lizzy, I have reason to hope, though a proposal is not imminent."

"Then I am happy for you, Mary," replied Elizabeth warmly. "I hope everything works out to your satisfaction."

With a smile, Mary excused herself to see to her preparations. It was a moment before Lydia replaced her, sweeping into the room without a word of warning as was her wont.

"Lizzy," said Lydia. "Please speak to Uncle Gardiner and make him stop."

"What has he done now?" asked Elizabeth, hiding a grin from her sister.

Lydia gave a little cry of annoyance. "He told me, again I might add, that we will not attend any society when we are at Pemberley and that I am not yet out. It is most annoying, for I have been out since before Papa passed away!"

"He is now your guardian, Lydia," said Elizabeth, trying to be reasonable with her sister. "You shall be at Pemberley for three weeks with only Georgiana and Uncle and Aunt until William and I join you. How would you attend society without someone to introduce you? Georgiana is not out yet, and Uncle and Aunt Gardiner are not known there."

"Aunt Gardiner is from Lambton," grumbled Lydia. "She must know some of those who live there."

"Of a certain level of society, yes. But Aunt is the daughter of a parson, one who departed Lambton before her own coming out. She does not know the gentlemen and their families."

With a huff, Lydia dropped on Elizabeth's bed and gazed at her with exasperation. For all that they had recognized a change in Lydia's behavior, in many ways she was still the same headstrong girl she had always been, though now seasoned with a little more sense and a slight hesitation that had not been there before. Lydia, Elizabeth knew, would always be lively, would always wish for society and amusement, even as she could also now be content with quieter activities and the society of her sisters and close friends.

"It is so unfair!" whined Lydia. "I am two years younger than Kitty and shall be held back and stifled in boredom while Kitty dances at balls and I know not what."

"Given those two years difference," replied Elizabeth, "you should recall that Kitty may very well be married by the time you make your debut. Thus, you will have the attention all to yourself. You should also remember that my marriage to William and Jane's to Anthony will mean you shall have a season in London, where we never did."

That reminder set Lydia to imagining future delights, as it always did. Lydia was not the silliest girl in England, as her father had often said, but she sometimes gave the appearance of it.

"Is Joseph ready?" asked Elizabeth, deciding to change the subject.

It was fortunate Lydia was in a mood to allow herself to be distracted. "He is already at the church with Lady Catherine and the other ladies. I only hope we can keep him quiet."

With that, Lydia rose and departed the room as suddenly as she had entered it. Elizabeth watched her go, amused at how the mention of their brother could always distract Lydia. It was not the custom for children as small as Joseph to attend the weddings of his elder siblings, but Elizabeth felt his presence was somehow appropriate. Whether she felt him a representative of their absent parents she could not say, but to have all her family present was fitting in a way she could not explain.

When the maid was finished with her hair, Elizabeth rose to don her dress, with the help of the maid, when a third sister—Kitty— entered the room. The girl took one look at her and stepped forward to assist her with the gown, looking on with appreciation once it was draped over Elizabeth's form.

"How lovely you look, Lizzy," said she shyly as the maid fastened the buttons.

"Thank you, Kitty," replied Elizabeth, giving her a soft smile. "Are you as disappointed as Lydia that you shall stay quietly at Pemberley until we arrive?"

Kitty blushed, giving Elizabeth the answer to her question. However, Kitty was not so headstrong as Lydia and much more easily led.

"I shall not make myself unhappy about it, Lizzy." The girl paused and smiled, adding: "Georgiana has said so much of Pemberley that I suspect there will be much with which to occupy ourselves. Perhaps I might even take up walking, such as you do, for there will be much to see."

Elizabeth laughed and drew her sister in for an embrace. "Yes, I can imagine there will be."

Nodding, Kitty fell silent for a moment and then ventured: "Is it not odd for us to stay at Pemberley when Mr. Darcy is not there?"

"Not when his sister will also be present," replied Elizabeth. "And we shall be family, shall we not?"

To that, Kitty smiled her agreement. "Then we shall all anticipate your return. Making our home at Pemberley will be different, will it not?"

"Different, indeed," said Elizabeth. "But remember, we will also return to Longbourn, and when Jane and Anthony settle, you might also live with them for a time."

"Do you suppose they will settle close to Pemberley?" asked Kitty.

"I know Jane wishes to be near me," replied Elizabeth. "And Anthony wishes to be near his cousin and brother. I imagine they will search with that in mind, though it depends on the availability of estates."

Kitty smiled and nodded. "What an excellent day this shall be. Two of my sisters have found their hearts' desires; I only hope I am one day so fortunate."

With those final comments, Kitty left the room, leaving Elizabeth thinking on the truth of her words. When their parents had still been with them, Elizabeth had known the chances of finding a good man who would take her, knowing of the drawbacks of her situation, had made it unlikely she would marry. After her father's passing, she had thought any chance had passed, and the subsequent events had fixed her attention on her duty. In some ways, Elizabeth was still almost shocked at how matters had ended.

Loving William, however, had not been an onerous task, as Elizabeth had known it would not be. Simply altering her attitude to be open to the possibility had been enough, and she had always known what an excellent man he was. What had surprised her was the depth and fervency of her feelings. William was the best man she had ever known. How she could have remained in ignorance of her feelings was a source of continued confusion.

At that moment, the maid walked around her and inspected her handiwork. "You are ready, Miss Elizabeth."

"Thank you, Sarah," said Elizabeth, giving her a brief embrace of thanks.

As Mrs. Hill had requested leave to retire, Elizabeth had agreed and arranged for her to be installed in a cottage to live out the remainder of her days. Then she had promoted Sarah to the position of housekeeper, as both the longest-serving and most capable of Longbourn's maids, and as a young woman who had often been as much a friend as a servant in the years of her residence at the estate. She would perform her duties with the house empty for most of the year when the family was not in attendance, but Elizabeth knew Sarah loved the estate almost as much as she did herself and would keep it running efficiently against the periodic return of the family and the future inheritance of the heir. Between Sarah and Longbourn's steward, Mr. Whitmore, an admiration had sprung up; it would not surprise Elizabeth if they married before long.

As for the rest of the servants, they would not replace Sarah as a maid, the absence of the family making it unnecessary, and the other two maids would continue as they were. As for the footmen, John was to travel with Elizabeth to Pemberley and take up a position in William's house, while Theodore was to remain at Longbourn to assist Mr. Whitmore.

"You shall be the most beautiful bride, Miss Elizabeth," said the girl after they separated.

"I should think that title will belong to Jane," replied Elizabeth. "But I thank you, nonetheless."

With a few words of pleasure, Elizabeth excused herself from her longtime maid and crossed the room to the door, letting herself out into the hall. The sounds of her sisters preparing themselves reached her ears, Kitty and Lydia together in Lydia's room, giggling over some bit of nonsense. Elizabeth smiled and shook her head, recalling her father's words concerning them, how they were silly and ignorant like all girls. That had changed, she reflected, though they could still be silly at times.

At that moment, Jane walked out of her bedroom, another maid trailing her, her face lighting up with pleasure at seeing Elizabeth. Mindful of the need to avoid undoing their maids' efforts, they came together in a brief embrace, and then clasped hands together, joining in their happiness.

"Did you ever think this day would come, Lizzy?"

"It has been a journey with some twists and turns," acknowledged Elizabeth. "But at the risk of sounding like our mother, I knew you could not have been so beautiful for nothing."

Jane laughed and shook her head. "And I knew you could not have been so clever for nothing. It is only fortunate you used that vaunted cleverness and see Mr. Darcy for the man he is."

"It is not that I did not know what a good man he is," said Elizabeth with a chuckle. "I shall not bore you with a retelling of how it all came about, but I will own that I cannot be happier."

"As you should be," replied Jane.

They descended the stairs to where Mr. and Mrs. Gardiner were waiting for them, the former exclaiming over their beauty, while the latter smiled and informed them how proud their parents would have been. Soon the other three Bennet sisters joined them, and they all set off for Longbourn church in the distance, arriving only a few moments later.

"Uncle," said Elizabeth, "may I have a moment with my sisters?"

"A moment only," replied her uncle with good-natured humor. "That is all we can spare unless you are confident your grooms will not flee when you do not appear at the precise moment you are supposed to."

The girls all laughed at his jest, Mrs. Gardiner exclaiming: "That is something my Brother Bennet might have said!"

"And I am taking his place this morning," replied Mr. Gardiner. "I take my office most seriously, my dear."

With an exasperated snicker, Mrs. Gardiner grasped her husband's arm and pulled him to the side, leaving the Bennet sisters standing together. Elizabeth gathered all her sisters in, and they all embraced each other. It struck Elizabeth that they were closer than they had ever been when their parents had lived. And it was as it should be.

"Well, my dears," said Elizabeth, fixing them all with a misty smile, "we have come to the end of our long journey in the night."

"And we have grown because of it," said Mary.

"I dare say I am blessed to have such a wonderful group of sisters," said Jane.

"And we are counting on you to introduce us to society," said Lydia, much to the amusement of the rest.

"I, for one, cannot wait to see Pemberley," was Kitty's shy addition to their happiness. "And so, you shall," offered Elizabeth to her sisters. "I do not suggest that life shall not bring more storms our way, but we have weathered those that have beset us. Let us move forward into the future, only remembering the past as it pleases us."

The sisters chorused their agreement and separated, the younger three joining their aunt and slipping into the church, where Elizabeth knew they would join Lady Catherine, Charity, Anne, and Georgiana, who had charge of Longbourn's young heir. Remaining behind, Mr. Gardiner approached the two remaining sisters as they checked their appearance over one last time to make certain everything was in order. Behind that door, Elizabeth knew, was her destiny and that of her sister, with the Earl of Matlock standing up for his brother and cousin.

"Well, my dears?" asked Mr. Gardiner. "Are you ready?"

"Yes," said Jane and Elizabeth.

Then they stepped to the door together and entered the church.

A most auspicious day it was, and Elizabeth ever after would remember it as the best day of her life. Once vows were exchanged and the wedding breakfast passed, Elizabeth and her husband traveled to the lakes to the lodge William owned, where they spent their honeymoon. Jane and Anthony's steps also took them northward, where they stayed in similar accommodations amid the glories of the peaks. The lakes were beautiful and Elizabeth enjoyed staying there. She extracted a promise from William they would explore the wildness of the peaks, and William, eager to please her, agreed without hesitation.

After this time of bliss, the couples once again gathered at Pemberley, spending the rest of the summer in the company of beloved relations amid the beauty of the estate. Elizabeth soon fell in love with her new home, its hills, valleys, streams, woods, and fields becoming as dear to her as that of her former home. At length, the Gardiners returned to London and their lives there, but they often gathered throughout the years, Mr. Darcy's family coming to esteem them as much as Elizabeth and her sisters did.

It should not be a surprise that the Bennet sisters all lived at Pemberley for many months, for while Colonel Fitzwilliam was eager to purchase a home for himself and his wife, he also wished to be prudent, to choose an estate with care. It was six months before they found an estate to lease, and several years before he finally made the purchase. That Jane would be situated within an easy distance of Elizabeth's home was a source of joy for both sisters.

Mary also stayed at Pemberley for some time, continuing to grow in maturity and confidence, and receiving Mr. Bingley's calls whenever he was in the area. Their courtship was lengthy, Mr. Bingley seeming content with that for many months. It was only after he, with William and Anthony's advice, also purchased an estate in Derbyshire, that he finally proposed to Mary. It was a most curious pairing, for Mary, though she had softened over time, could still be rigid and moralizing, and Mr. Bingley was a man gregarious and civil to all. But they made it work in love and esteem, having several children to raise and nurture.

The youngest Bennet sisters spent the chief of their time at Pemberley, though when their elder sisters married, they often stayed at their homes as well. As expected, Kitty came out first and married first, and as Georgiana delayed her debut a year, she and Lydia came out together, cutting a swath through the hearts of the young men in London. Soon they too found themselves husbands, and all the sisters settled within a shire of each other, and ever after remained on the most intimate of terms.

By contrast, Miss Caroline Bingley married her gentleman and settled in Devon, and she was rarely in the company of her siblings, a circumstance which did not cause distress to any of them. Mrs. Hurst proved herself more amiable than her sister, retaining her connection with Mr. Bingley and, through the Bingleys, to the rest of the family. In time she and her husband produced children, and Mr. Hurst inherited his estate, much to his satisfaction and relief.

As for the extended family, Anne and Charity each found gentlemen to marry, and if Anne was situated further away in Kent, still they found occasion to meet as often as circumstances permitted. Lady Catherine, the last of the previous generation, proved her longevity, for she lived to a hale old age. She never lost her imperious manners or her penchant for dispensing advice, often when least wanted, but she was viewed by all as a beloved elderly aunt and saw them all—even the other Bennet sisters' children—as her grandchildren.

As for the Bennet family's youngest member, he also primarily made his home at Pemberley, and with such excellent examples to hand, he became an exceptional young man, attending Eton and then Cambridge when he attained the necessary age. With Elizabeth's eldest son, named Bennet, with whom he was of age being less than two years older, he was the closest of friends, and if the younger boy sometimes cheekily called him "uncle," he would respond by using his title of "nephew," resulting in much laughter between them. As he turned one and twenty while he was at Cambridge in his final year, he waited until he had completed his studies to claim his birthright, though his ownership was confirmed and the entail ended on that late November day. His brothers-in-law had seen to the details. Thereafter he journeyed with the family to claim his inheritance and take his place as his father's heir.

The town that appeared before him was little changed from the last time Joseph Bennet had visited, which had been only the previous year. It was a quaint little collection of homes, shops, an inn, and a few other sundry buildings such as the town office and the assembly halls. In the recent two years, the main road had also received a welcome renewal, for the road had been paved with cobblestones, the dirty, muddy street of the past now a memory.

As Joseph rode through town, he noted the people engaged in their business, a few wearing the clothes of the gentry, though most were townsfolk. The shops were, he knew by the testimony of his sisters, much as they ever were, though a hint of fresh paint or the shine of new windows spoke to improvements in their appearance. The people too, Joseph knew, were many of the same characters as those known to his family, together with children who had grown to adulthood. Had matters been different, he might have grown with them.

There was no one he knew by sight, so he passed through the town, noting with an absence of mind that his passage created something of a stir. Whether these people knew him, knew of his family's imminent return, or just gawked at the sight of a well-dressed gentleman, he could not say. Among them were several young ladies, a few quite pretty, though Joseph did not pay them much heed. He would become acquainted with them in time, he knew, as he began to take part in the neighborhood's society. There was no thought in his mind of seeking a wife at present, though he had his eye on one or two young ladies in Derbyshire, for he knew there was much work ahead of him as he took control of the reins of the estate.

Joseph could not state why, with any surety, he had ridden on ahead of the company. Somehow it seemed fitting that he did, a sign that the next generation of Bennet masters of Longbourn should arrive alone to take possession of his home. The rest of the party—a large one, including all his sisters and their sundry families—would arrive on the morrow. It would be possible for them to come today, but they had informed him of their plans, and Joseph appreciated it, knowing they had done it to allow him his time alone.

The road forked at the end of the village, and Joseph took the left path he knew led to Longbourn. As he entered the trees, the road once again became a gravel path, winding through trees and crossing a stream or two. After a few moments, he came upon a path that led off to the right, to the estate of Longbourn's closest neighbors. And there, by the side of the road, stood a man, elderly, but still hale and active.

"Joseph Bennet," greeted the man, prompting Joseph to dismount. "I had it from my Charlotte that you would arrive soon."

"Sir William," replied Joseph, accepting the man's proffered hand in his own. "How do you do, sir?"

"Oh, I am well," replied he, showing that elevated sense of civility for which he was infamous. "Samuel chafes under the restrictions of still having a father to watch over him, but I do not feel these old bones will fail me yet."

Joseph grinned. Samuel was an excellent fellow, one Joseph knew loved his father very much. Lady Lucas, Joseph knew, had passed in the intervening years, and Sir William's other children had all moved away from the home, his sons to various professions, his daughters to their own homes. The eldest, Charlotte, of whom Sir William had spoken, was Lizzy's particular friend, he knew and had married into the family, becoming the Countess of Matlock only a year after his family had departed from Longbourn. Though Joseph was too young to have any direct knowledge of it, stories of the shock and chagrin of the ton—and infamously Lady Catherine—had been on the lips of his sisters since he could remember.

"And I shall be glad to see Charlotte again," continued Sir William, his words recalling Joseph to the fact that the earl would join them. "We will be glad to have you in residence at Longbourn. Your steward has maintained the estate very well in your absence, as I am certain you know, but having a master in residence is always welcome."

"And I am pleased to take up my duties here," said Joseph. "Perhaps we should meet to discuss matters of mutual concern."

"I should like that, and I know Samuel will be agreeable. I know you will be an excellent master, given the men who trained you. Please send around a card or come to visit us. Your brothers are all welcome, of course."

Joseph smiled and agreed, and then mounted his horse, riding off after a final farewell. The fact was that he agreed with everything Sir William had said. His brothers were excellent men, though he was closer to Fitzwilliam, Darcy, and Bingley than the others, having largely been raised in their homes. And everything about the estate would be well in order, for those same men had watched over his inheritance, and Mr. Whitmore was himself an excellent man, one who had the estate well in hand.

He also knew that the Longbourn he had inherited was something more than the estate his father had left him. As the family was not in residence, Lizzy had taken the profits from the estate yearly and invested them with Uncle Gardiner or used them to make improvements. Though it was not a matter of which he was supposed to be aware, Joseph also knew that his brothers had used their own funds for the purchase of a field here, or an improvement of a part of the estate there. Longbourn now, he knew, was almost double the size of what it had been.

By contrast, Netherfield to the west had largely fallen into disrepair, the owner content to gather whatever profits he could and ignore the place. Much of Longbourn's recent prosperity had come at the expense of Netherfield, its borders now reduced, the house a dusty mausoleum of its past grandeur. The disorder of the estate was an opportunity, Joseph thought, for the owner would almost certainly wish to be rid of it once and for all. The next months, Joseph knew, he would spend acclimatizing himself to be the new master of Longbourn, after which he would consider what he might do to acquire the rest of Netherfield. That was a task for a later time, but one he had considered for at least several years.

At length, the tiny village that sat outside the gates to the estate rose in the distance. It was nothing more than a small collection of houses, a blacksmith, a church, and a few other sundry structures, their appearance much the same as Meryton's had been. It was but a moment before he had passed through and onto the drive of the estate beyond.

The feelings coursing through Joseph's heart as his horse placidly walked on the drive, its hooves crunching on the gravel below, could not be described. Pemberley and Thorndell, Fitzwilliam and Jane's home, and even Hazelwood, Bingley and Mary's estate, had long been his place of residence, and his diverse homes for all his life. But Longbourn . . . Longbourn had always been his home, his inheritance.

The house was in no way comparable with those venerable properties, its recent additions notwithstanding. But it was his by right of birth and the long line of Bennets that had held the estate for generations. Joseph had never met the man, but he had vowed long ago to make his departed father proud, to see Longbourn flourish under his stewardship.

Upon dismounting, a woman appeared in the door, her face lighting up in a brilliant smile at the sight of him. She stepped forward to him and dropped into a perfunctory curtsey, her beaming grin never dimming a jot.

"Master Joseph!" exclaimed she. "I suppose it should not surprise me to see you here today, though we were informed you were to arrive tomorrow."

"I rode on ahead, Mrs. Whitmore," said Joseph, feeling unaccountably abashed. Mrs. Whitmore was now five and forty years of age if she was a day, but Joseph could remember being infatuated with a younger Mrs. Whitmore when he had been a boy.

"Well, we are pleased to have you returned to us," continued Mrs. Whitmore. "I shall inform the cook you have arrived for dinner and call for Mr. Whitmore, for I am certain you have much you must wish to discuss."

"That will not be necessary, Mrs. Whitmore," said Joseph. "Is your husband out on the estate?"

"Visiting the Suttons at present."

"Then I shall speak to him tomorrow," replied Joseph. "For now, I believe I wish to rest from my journey."

"I shall instruct the footman to provide bathwater."

"Thank you, Mrs. Whitmore, you are a treasure."

The woman curtseyed and moved away again, leaving Joseph to follow her into the house. There, a maid waited to take his hat and gloves, which he passed to her with an absence of mind. The vestibule was the same as he remembered, and the hall beyond, he knew, led deeper into the house, to the sitting-room, the stairs to the second floor, the secondary parlor at the back of the house, as well as the kitchens and the servants' quarters. None of these were of interest to Joseph for the moment, for his thoughts were fixed on the other door in the hall, the one leading to his father's—his—study.

The room was light and airy, the walls lined with bookshelves groaning with the weight of the bounty that had been his father's solace, all lovingly preserved, the room kept clean by the maids' and Mrs. Whitmore's diligence. In front of him, before a large, open window, stood his father's dark cherry desk, recently polished, so bright was the shine of the light beyond on its surface.

Joseph made his way around the desk, his fingers trailing along the grains, feeling the stories he knew were a part of the wood of the desk, of every item in the room. At length, when he had rounded the desk, he sat in the comfortable chair, the very chair occupied by his father all those years ago, and by Lizzy and Darcy, Fitzwilliam and Bingley, and all the others when they had visited to manage the property in his stead.

At length, his eyes found the bookshelves and a particular title caught his eye. Leaning forward, he plucked the book from its shelf, knowing it was of special significance, not only to Lizzy but to his father. Opening the front cover of Paradise Lost, Joseph noted the bookplate with the name "Henry Bennet" emblazoned in gold. Joseph lightly brushed his fingers over the letters of his father's name, feeling the tightness of emotion well up in his breast. Then Joseph set it on the desk, wishing to read the familiar passages from the book his father and sister had perused before he was born.

Looking again around the room, Joseph Bennet knew. He had come home. At last, the Bennets of Longbourn had returned.

The End

MORE GREAT TITLES FROM ONE GOOD SONNET PUBLISHING!

PRIDE AND PREJUDICE VARIATIONS

By Jann Rowland

Acting on Faith
A Life from the Ashes (Sequel to Acting on Faith)
Open Your Eyes
Implacable Resentment
An Unlikely Friendship
Bound by Love
Cassandra
Obsession
Shadows Over Longbourn
The Mistress of Longbourn
My Brother's Keeper
Coincidence
The Angel of Longbourn
Chaos Comes to Kent
In the Wilds of Derbyshire
The Companion
Out of Obscurity
What Comes Between Cousins
A Tale of Two Courtships
Murder at Netherfield

Whispers of the Heart
A Gift for Elizabeth
Mr. Bennet Takes Charge
The Impulse of the Moment
The Challenge of Entail
A Matchmaking Mother
Another Proposal
With Love's Light Wings
Flight to Gretna Green
Mrs. Bennet's Favorite Daughter
Her Indomitable Resolve
Love and Libertine
In Default of Heirs Male

By Lelia Eye

Netherfield's Secret
A Sister's Sacrifice

By Colin Rowland

The Parson's Rescue
Hidden Desires

PRIDE AND PREJUDICE SERIES

By Jann Rowland

COURAGE ALWAYS RISES: THE BENNET SAGA

The Heir's Disgrace
Volume II Untitled*
Volume III Untitled*

NO CAUSE TO REPINE

A Tacit Engagement
Scandalous Falsehoods
Upstart Pretensions
Quitting the Sphere

BONDS OF LIFE

Bonds of Friendship
Bonds of Love*

* Forthcoming

OTHER GENRES BY
ONE GOOD SONNET PUBLISHING

FANTASY

By Jann Rowland & Lelia Eye

EARTH AND SKY SERIES

On Wings of Air
On Lonely Paths
On Tides of Fate*

FAIRYTALE

By Lelia Eye

The Princes and the Peas: A Tale of Robin Hood

SMOTHERED ROSE TRILOGY

Thorny
Unsoiled
Roseblood

* Forthcoming

About the Author

Jann Rowland

Jann Rowland is a Canadian, born and bred. Other than a two-year span in which he lived in Japan, he has been a resident of the Great White North his entire life, though he professes to still hate the winters.

Though Jann did not start writing until his mid-twenties, writing has grown from a hobby to an all-consuming passion. His interests as a child were almost exclusively centered on the exotic fantasy worlds of Tolkien and Eddings, among a host of others. As an adult, his interests have grown to include historical fiction and romance, with a particular focus on the works of Jane Austen.

When Jann is not writing, he enjoys rooting for his favorite sports teams. He is also a master musician (in his own mind) who enjoys playing piano and singing as well as moonlighting as the choir director in his church's congregation.

Jann lives in Alberta with his wife of more than twenty years, two grown sons, and one young daughter. He is convinced that whatever hair he has left will be entirely gone by the time his little girl hits her teenage years. Sadly, though he has told his daughter repeatedly that she is not allowed to grow up, she continues to ignore him.

Please let him know what you think or sign up for their mailing list to learn about future publications:

Website: http://onegoodsonnet.com/
Facebook: https://facebook.com/OneGoodSonnetPublishing/
Twitter: @OneGoodSonnet
Mailing List: http://eepurl.com/bol2p9

Made in the USA
Las Vegas, NV
28 May 2021